"Cassie, look at me."

I fought him, knowing from childhood that looking a vampire directly in the eyes made it easier for him to control you, but everyone ignored us, I guess under the assumption that I was just a lousy dancer.

Contrary to the legend, his body felt warm against mine and as smooth as muscled satin, but he may as well have been carved of steel for all the hope I had of breaking his hold. My pulse sped up and I thought I would faint when he bent his head and I felt lips trailing over my neck. I think my heart actually stopped as he delicately kissed the skin as if tasting the pulse under the surface. It felt like my blood could sense him, as if it moved slower and thicker in my veins, waiting for him to set it free. I broke into a sweat that had nothing to do with the heat of so many bodies crowded into a small place. Was he going to kill me right there, in front of a couple of hundred witnesses?

I should have known something like this was going to happen. Every time I trusted someone, he betrayed me; every time I loved someone, she died. Since he was already dead, I guessed the pattern held true.

Touch the Dark

KAREN CHANCE

A ROC BOOK

ROC

Published by New American Library, a division of
Penguin Group (USA) Inc., 375 Hudson Street,
New York, New York 10014, USA
Penguin Group (Canada), 90 Eglinton Avenue East, Suite 700, Toronto,
Ontario M4P 2Y3, Canada (a division of Pearson Penguin Canada Inc.)
Penguin Books Ltd., 80 Strand, London WC2R 0RL, England
Penguin Ireland, 25 St. Stephen's Green, Dublin 2,
Ireland (a division of Penguin Books Ltd.)
Penguin Group (Australia), 250 Camberwell Road, Camberwell, Victoria 3124,
Australia (a division of Pearson Australia Group Pty. Ltd.)
Penguin Books India Pvt. Ltd., 11 Community Centre, Panchsheel Park,
New Delhi - 110 017, India
Penguin Group (NZ), 67 Apollo Drive, Mairangi Bay,
Auckland 1311, New Zealand (a division of Pearson New Zealand Ltd.)
Penguin Books (South Africa) (Pty.) Ltd., 24 Sturdee Avenue,
Rosebank, Johannesburg 2196, South Africa

Penguin Books Ltd., Registered Offices:
80 Strand, London WC2R 0RL, England

First published by Roc, an imprint of New American Library,
a division of Penguin Group (USA) Inc.

First Printing, June 2006
10 9 8 7 6

Copyright © Karen Chance, 2006
All rights reserved

REGISTERED TRADEMARK—MARCA REGISTRADA

Printed in the United States of America

ACKNOWLEDGMENTS

I'd like to thank Mary for proofreading the first draft in all its typo-ridden horror, and Marlin for a place to crash while I polished it up. Thanks are also due to Anne Sowards, a great editor (any remaining mistakes are all mine), and to Louisa Edwards for thinking up the perfect title.

Chapter 1

I knew I was in trouble as soon as I saw the obituary. The fact that it had my name on it was sort of a clue. What I didn't know was how they'd found me, and who the guy was with the sense of humor. Antonio has never been much for comedy. I've never figured out if that has something to do with being dead, or if he's always been a morose son of a bitch.

The obit was on my office PC's screen in place of the usual travel agency logo. It looked like part of a newspaper page had been scanned and then set as the computer's wallpaper, and it hadn't been there when I'd gone to get a salad half an hour earlier. If I hadn't been so freaked out, I'd have been impressed. I didn't know that any of Tony's goons even knew what a computer was.

I scrambled around in a filing cabinet for my gun while I read the joker's description of my gruesome death later that evening. I had a better gun at my apartment, along with a few other surprises, but going back there probably wasn't my best move. And unless I was expecting enough trouble to make it worth the risk of carrying concealed, the only thing I kept in my purse was a small canister of mace for potential muggers. After more than three years of relative safety, I'd started to question the need for even that. I'd gotten careless and could only hope it wasn't about to get me killed.

Under my name was a paragraph-long description of an unfortunate incident involving me, an unknown rifleman and two bullets through the head. The paper had tomorrow's date, but the hit was to occur at 8:43 tonight on Peachtree Street. I glanced at my watch; it was twenty to eight, so I'd been given an hour's head start. That seemed too generous for Tony. My best guess for why I wasn't already dead was that killing me outright was too easy for a guy who had people killed all the time. In my case, he wanted something special.

I finally found my Smith & Wesson 3913 under a flyer for a cruise to Rio. I wondered if it was a sign. No way did I have the kind of cash to get out of the country, though, and a chubby-cheeked, blue-eyed blonde might look a little obvious next to all those sloe-eyed senhoritas. Plus, I didn't know if Tony had associates in Brazil, but I wouldn't put it past him. When you've been around long enough to remember drinking Michelangelo under the table, you make a few contacts.

I fished a pack of gum out of the gun compartment in my purse and shoved the Smith & Wesson in. It fit like it had been made for it, which it had. I'd bought the gun, my first, and three of the handbags almost four years ago on the recommendation of a Fed named Jerry Sydell. Like a lot of people, he'd thought I was a nut case, but since I'd helped to cripple one of the biggest crime families in Philly, he was willing to give me some free advice. He helped me pick out the 9-mm semiautomatic pistol, which combined a grip small enough for my hands with the power to discourage anything on two legs. "Except for the ghosts and ghoulies," he'd said with a grin. "You're on your own with them." He'd also taken me to a practice range every day for two weeks, and got me to the point that, even if I still couldn't hit the side of a barn, I didn't miss it by much. I'd kept up the practice sessions whenever I could afford them, so now I could definitely hit a barn—if it was a big one and I was standing within about ten feet of it. I was secretly hoping I'd never have to shoot anything besides a target. It wasn't my fault it didn't work out that way.

I think Jerry sort of liked me—I reminded him of his eldest kid—and he wanted to see me go straight. He thought I'd got in with the wrong crowd when too young to know better, which was truer than he knew, then wised up and decided to turn state's evidence. How he explained the fact that a twenty-year-old orphan knew all about the inner workings of a major crime family I'll never know, but it sure wasn't faith in "that witchcraft crap," as he put it. Jerry didn't believe in the supernatural—any of it. Since I didn't want him to lock me in a small padded cell somewhere, I didn't mention my visions, or how close he'd been with the ghosts and ghoulies comment.

I've always been kind of a ghost magnet. Maybe it's part of the whole clairvoyance thing; I don't know. Tony was always careful about what he let me study—I think he was afraid I'd figure out some way to use my abilities against him if I knew too much—so I'm not very knowledgeable about my talent. Of course, it might be that my attractiveness to the spirit world is simply because I can see them: it must be a downer haunting someone who doesn't even know you're there. Not that they haunt me, exactly, but they do like showing off when I'm around.

Sometimes that's not a bad thing, like with the old woman I met in an alley as a teenage runaway. I tend to see ghosts as solid much of the time, especially if they are new and powerful, so it took me a while to realize what she was. She was there to act as a sort of guardian angel over her grandson, whom she'd helped to raise. She died when he was ten, and her daughter's boyfriend started beating him as soon as he went to live with them. The boy ran away in less than a month. She told me that she hadn't spent a decade watching over him to abandon him now, and she was sure God wouldn't mind waiting on her a bit. At her request, I gave him enough money to get on a bus to her sister's place in San Diego before I moved on. Naturally, I didn't mention that sort of thing to Jerry. He didn't believe in anything he couldn't see, touch or put a bullet in, kind of limiting subjects for conversation. Needless to say, he also didn't believe in vampires, at least not until a couple of Tony's guys caught up with him one night and tore his throat out.

I knew what was about to happen to Jerry because I Saw his last few seconds as I was getting in the bath. As usual, I got a vivid, full-color, up-close-and-personal ticket to the carnage, which almost made me slip and break my neck on the slick bathroom floor. After I stopped shaking enough to hold a phone, I called the Witness Protection Program emergency number, but the agent who answered got suspicious when I wouldn't say how I knew what was about to happen. She said she'd get a message to Jerry but didn't sound too enthused about disturbing his weekend. So I called Tony's lead thug—a vamp named Alphonse—and reminded him that he was supposed to find out where the government had stashed me, not risk angering the Senate by killing humans who didn't even know anything. Jerry was useless to them because his information was about to be old news.

I'd never been very successful in altering my visions' outcomes, but I was hoping that use of the Senate's name would be enough to make Alphonse think twice. The Senate is a group of really old vamps who pass laws that the less powerful ones have to obey. While they don't think any more of humans than Tony does, they like the freedom of being only a myth and go to a lot of trouble not to draw mortal attention. Killing FBI agents is the sort of thing that tends to piss them off. But all Alphonse did was give me the usual runaround while his boys traced the call. In the end, the only thing I could do was make sure that by the time anybody got to my door, I was already on a bus out of town. I figured that since the government won't even admit that vampires exist, its chances of keeping me safe from them wasn't too good.

I thought my odds were better on my own, and for more than three years I'd been right. Until now.

I didn't bother to grab anything from the office except the gun: one thing about running for your life—it really narrows your priorities. Not that my 9 mm would do much to a vamp, but Tony often used human thugs for minor errands. I really hoped he hadn't thought me worth calling in actual talent. I wasn't thrilled about the idea of taking a few bullets to the brain, but I liked even less the prospect of ending up as one of his permanent acquisitions. He'd never let me be turned because he'd had a psychic once who became a vamp and was completely psi blind afterwards, and he thought my gift too useful to risk. Now I was worried that he'd take the gamble. If I lost my talent after the change, he could stake me and get payback for some of the hell I'd caused him. If not, he'd have an immortal adept with guaranteed loyalty, since it's really hard to go against the wishes of the vamp who made you. It was a win-win situation from his perspective, assuming he saw past his rage long enough to figure that out. I checked the gun and made sure it had a full clip. If they caught me, I wasn't going down without a fight, and if worse came to worst, I'd eat the last round before I called that bastard master.

Unlike last time, there was something I had to do before I caught a ride to yet another new life. I slipped out of the agency ASAP, just in case Tony's boys decided to fudge a little on the deadline, and avoided the front door by squirming through the bathroom window. It always seems so easy when people do that on TV. I ended up with a scraped thigh, torn hose and a bitten lip from trying not to swear. I finally managed it, ran down a dingy side street to a parking garage and cut across to a Waffle House. The trip was short but nerve-racking. Familiar alleys suddenly looked like perfect hiding places for Tony's thugs, and every noise sounded like a gun being cocked.

The Waffle House had bright halogen lights in the parking

lot, making me feel terribly exposed as I crossed it. Mercifully, the bank of phones was in shadow near one side of the
building. I parked myself in front of the one that worked and
dug some change out of my purse, but no one picked up at
the club. I let the phone ring twenty times while I bit my lip
and told myself it didn't mean anything. It was Friday
night—probably no one was able to hear a phone over the
din, or had time to answer if they did.

It took a while to get there on foot, since I was trying to
stay out of sight and to avoid breaking an ankle in my new,
over-the-knee, high-heeled boots. I'd bought them because
they matched the cute leather mini a salesgirl had talked me
into, and I'd planned to wow them at the club after work, but
they weren't exactly made for speed. I'm supposed to be this
powerful clairvoyant, but do you think anything popped into
my head earlier about maybe wearing tennis shoes, or at
least flats? Hell, no. Just like I never win the lottery. All I
See is the kind of stuff that nightmares and serious drinking
problems are made of.

It was one of those hot Georgia nights when the air feels
like a heavy blanket against your skin and the humidity is
off the charts. A thin mist showed up in the glow of the
lampposts, but most of the available light came from the
moon gleaming off rain-slick streets and turning puddles silver. The night had bleached the color from the buildings
downtown, fading them a soft gray that blended into the
shadows and hid the tops of the skyscrapers. The historic
district was like something out of time that night, especially
when I passed the Margaret Mitchell House on West Peachtree. It seemed perfectly natural when one of the horse-
drawn carriages that cater to the tourist trade came around
the corner—except that it was going at a full gallop and almost ran me over.

I had a second to see the frightened faces of the tourists
who were hanging on for dear life in the back seat, before
the carriage ricocheted off the sidewalk and careened down

the street out of sight. I dragged my mud-covered self out of the gutter and glared around suspiciously. Merry laughter from behind me explained how that fat old horse had been convinced to try for a new speed record. A trail of mist, almost indistinguishable from the light rain, drifted by. I grabbed it, metaphysically speaking.

"Portia! That wasn't funny!"

The laugh tinkled again and a pretty southern belle complete with swinging hoopskirts materialized in front of me. "Oh, yes, it was. Did you see their faces?" Mirth sparkled in what had once been eyes bluer than mine. Tonight they were the color of the churning clouds overhead.

I fished around in my purse for a tissue to wipe off my boots. "I thought you weren't going to do that anymore. If you scare off the tourists, who will you play with?" There aren't a lot of companies willing to pretend that Atlanta, like Savannah or Charleston, has enough of a historic district to make horse-drawn tours worthwhile. If Portia kept up her games, whatever southern charm had managed to survive the urban sprawl—which offered such time-honored favorites as the World of Coca-Cola, the CNN Center and the Underground Atlanta mall—was doomed.

Portia gave me a pout so attractive that she must have practiced it in front of a mirror when she was alive. "You're no fun, Cassie."

I shot her an unhappy look as I tried to clean the mud-splattered leather, but all I managed was to streak it. Never once had I made a run for it looking chic. "I'm plenty of fun, just not tonight." It had started to rain, and the droplets were falling through Portia to spatter on the concrete. I hate that; it's like looking at a TV through too much interference. "You haven't seen Billy Joe, have you?"

I call Billy Joe my guardian spirit, but that isn't entirely accurate. He's more of a pain in the ass who occasionally turns out to be useful, but right then I wasn't feeling picky. Billy is what remains of an Irish American gambler who failed to lose the right hand of cards in 1858. A couple of irate cowboys, who correctly assumed they'd been cheated, shoved him into a sack and tossed it in the Mississippi. Luckily for him, he'd recently relieved a visiting countess of a large, ugly necklace that served as a sort of supernatural battery, collecting magical energy from the natural world and storing it until needed. When his spirit left his body, it came to rest in the necklace, which he haunted the same way other ghosts did more conventional things, such as crypts. It gave him enough power to continue to exist, but it was my occasional donations of living energy that made him as mobile as he was. I had found the necklace in a junk shop when I was seventeen, and Billy and I had been a team ever since. Of course, he couldn't take a message to the club for me so I didn't have to go in person, but he could serve as lookout in case any bad guys got too close. Assuming I could find him, that was, something that required a little ghostly help.

There are a lot of ghosts in Atlanta, and most are your run-of-the-mill, let's-haunt-something-until-we-work-through-our-issues-or-fade-away types like Billy Joe. There are also a few guardian spirits and an occasional psychic imprint, not that the latter are technically ghosts. Imprints are like a supernatural theater that shows the same movie over and over until you want to scream. Since it's usually something traumatic, running into one isn't fun. I'd spent my free time for a couple of months after I moved in learning the streets in the area, and one of the main things I'd been looking for was imprint zones. I'd found about fifty dealing with the burning of the city during the Civil War, but most were too weak to cause me much more than a twinge. But there was a big one between my apartment and the agency where a slave had once been ripped apart by a pack of dogs. I started taking the long way around after I got caught in it one day. I have a lot of memories I'd just as soon forget; I don't need other people's nightmares.

Portia, however, isn't an imprint. Sometimes, I thought

she was worse. Portia is one of those ghosts who relive the tragic parts of their lives over and over, but not like a mindless movie. They're haunters with a fixation, similar to an obsessive human who wants to wash her hands fifty times a day. And they're mobile, so they can follow you around and run on about whatever is bothering them 24/7. I broke Billy Joe of that early—he's upset because he died young, but I can handle only so many choruses of "the life I should have had" before I start to get crabby.

Unfortunately, I'd caught Portia in a talkative mood, and it took more than ten minutes to find out—after a detailed description of the ivory buttons she'd sewn onto her never-used wedding gown—that she hadn't seen Billy Joe. Typical. I spend most of my time wishing he'd go away, but he never gets lost until I need him. My level of aggravation must have shown on my face, because Portia stopped in the middle of the story about a party where two officers had fought each other over the last place on her dance card. It was one of her favorites and she was clearly not pleased to see my attention wandering. "You aren't listening, Cassie. Is something wrong?" An angry snap of her little lace-edged fan said there had damn well better be.

"Tony's found me and I need to get out of town. But I have to go by the club first, and I need a lookout."

I knew as soon as I said it that I should have kept my mouth shut. Portia's eyes got even bigger, and she clapped her dainty gloved hands together delightedly. "Oh, what fun! I'll help!"

"Um, that's really generous of you, Portia, but I don't think . . . I mean, there's a lot of ways into the club, and you couldn't cover all of them." But Portia got a familiar, steely glint in her eyes and I immediately relented. Most of the time she was sugar sweet, but get her upset at you and things could get bad fast.

"I'll find help," she promised. "It'll be like a party!" She disappeared in a swirl of petticoats, and I sighed. Some of

Portia's friends were even more annoying than she was, but any lookouts were better than none. And I didn't have to worry about Tony's boys noticing them. Even if he'd sent vamps, they wouldn't see a thing.

As strange as it sounds, a lot of people in the supernatural community don't believe in ghosts. Oh, some will agree that there is the occasional troubled spirit who hangs around its grave for awhile before accepting the inevitable, but few would accept it if I told them just how many spirits stick around after death, how many different types there are, and how active some of them can be. Spirits like Portia and Billy Joe are, for the supernatural community, like vamps are to the human—old stories and legends that are dismissed without proof. What can I tell you? It's a weird world.

I arrived at the club a few minutes later, out of breath and with aching arches, but intact. Showing up was, of course, a really bad idea. Even if nobody had followed me, a dozen people at the agency and my apartment building knew I worked there part-time. It was also only a block from Peachtree, which was not a coincidence I liked. If it ended up getting me killed, I planned to come back and haunt Tony. But I couldn't leave without warning my roommate and making some kind of arrangement for him. I had enough guilt without adding another messed-up life to my total.

The club, with its high ceiling of exposed steel joints, graffiti-covered concrete walls and massive dance floor, was larger than most, but that night, there were enough gyrating figures under the hanging disco lights to make it almost claustrophobic. I was grateful for the crush, since it made it less likely that anyone would notice me. I slipped in the back way and didn't encounter any problems—at least, not of the gun-waving, homicidal variety.

One of the bartenders had called in sick, so they were shorthanded, and Mike tried to talk me into subbing as soon as he saw me. Normally I wouldn't have minded, since my usual job as one of his novelty acts didn't provide much in tips. I read tarot three nights a week, although I've never liked the cards. I used them because it's expected, but I don't need to squint at archaic images to know what's about to happen. My visions come in Technicolor and surround sound, and are a lot more complete. But most people would have preferred a standard reading to what I gave out. Like I said, I'm better at Seeing the bad stuff. Tonight, though, I declined the chance to make a few bucks. I didn't think bartending was the way I wanted to spend my last hour.

"What's the word?" Mike yelled at me cheerfully, doing a Tom Cruise with the liquor bottles to the rowdy appreciation of the crowd.

I sighed and dug in my purse. My fingers clenched around the greasy tarot deck that had been a tenth-birthday gift from my old governess, Eugenie. She'd had a charm put on the cards by some witch with a sense of humor, and I kept it with me because it was good for entertaining customers. But the predictions—which acted like a kind of karmic mood ring—had an eerie habit of being right on the money. I held it up and a card popped out. It wasn't one I wanted to see. "The Tower," a booming voice began, before I shoved it back in the pack and deep into my purse.

"Is that good?" Mike asked, before getting distracted by a pretty blonde's cleavage. I merely nodded and hurried off, losing myself in the crowd before he could hear anything else. The voice was only a muffled croak from my overcrowded bag, but I didn't need to hear it to know what it said. The Tower signifies a huge, cataclysmic change, the kind that leaves a life completely altered. I tried to tell myself that it could have been worse—it could have been Death—but it wasn't much comfort. The Tower is probably the most feared card in the deck. Death can have many meanings, most not the literal one, but the Tower always indicates trouble for anyone who wants a quiet life. I sighed—what else was new?

I finally located Tomas in the Dungeon—Mike's nick-

name for the basement room—wading through a sea of
black-clad bodies with a tray of used glasses. He looked ed-
ible, as usual, if your thing is slender muscles, skin like
honey over cream and sable hair that brushes his waist when
he doesn't keep it pulled back. His face should look too
rugged to be handsome, all high cheekbones and strong angles, but the delicacy of some of the features make up for it.
His hair was off his face in a thick braid, a sure sign he was
working, since he prefers it loose, but a few pieces had
worked free and billowed about his head in fine strands.
Mike had picked out the outfit: a black silk shirt knitted in a
cobweb design that revealed more than it covered, sleek
black jeans that fit him like a second skin and black leather
boots that climbed halfway up his thighs. He looked like he
ought to be headlining at a strip club instead of waiting ta-
bles, but the exotic, melt-in-your-mouth sex appeal pushed
a lot of buttons for the Goths. I didn't exactly find it hard on
the eyes, either.

Mike had decided about a year ago that Atlanta had
enough country-and-western bars, so he turned the family
drinking hole into a progressive haven upstairs and a Goth
dream in the basement. Some locals had grumbled, but the
younger crowd loved it. Tomas looked like he'd been designed for the place right along with the decor, and he
brought in a lot of business, but it worried me that he spent
half of every night fending off propositions. At least, I assumed he fended them off, since he never brought anyone
back to the apartment. But I sometimes wondered, given his
background, if getting him that particular job hadn't been
one of my dumber moves.

Tomas looked a lot better than when I first saw him,
hanging out at the local shelter with the kind of dead eyes
that I was familiar with from my own street days. Lisa
Porter, the manager and self-designated mother hen of the
place, introduced us when I stopped by for one of my erratic
volunteer sessions. We got to talking while sorting the

newest donated clothes into piles of the usable, the need-repair and the good-only-for-cleaning-rags. It says something about Tomas' personality that I mentioned him to Mike that very night, and that he was hired after a brief interview the next day. Mike said he was the smartest hire he'd ever made—never sick, never complained and looked like a dream. I wasn't so sure about that last part: the look was striking all right, but I personally thought he needed a pimple or a scar, some mark on all that pale gold skin to make him seem more real. He resembled the undead more than most vampires I knew, and had their unconscious poise and quiet assurance to boot. But he was alive, and as long as I got my seriously jinxed self away from him, he'd probably stay that way.

"Tomas, got a minute?"

I didn't think he heard me over the music, which the DJ kept painfully loud, but he nodded. I wasn't supposed to be there yet, so he knew something was up. We carved a path through the crowd, which earned me a dirty look from a woman with purple dreads and black lipstick for stealing off with the main attraction. Or maybe it was my happy-face T-shirt and earrings she didn't like. I usually did the Goth thing, or as close as I could get without looking truly awful—strawberry blondes don't wear black well—but that was when I was working. I found out pretty early that no one takes a fortune-teller seriously if she shows up in pastels. But on my days off I reserved the right not to look like I was going to a funeral. My life is depressing enough without help.

We ducked behind the bar to the back room. It was quieter there, which meant we could hear each other if we stood close and shouted, but the noise was less of a problem than looking into Tomas' face and figuring out what to say. Like me, he'd been on the street early. Unlike me, he'd had nothing to trade but himself. I didn't like the look that came into his eyes whenever I asked about his past, so I normally avoided it, but it was probably a variation on the usual theme. Most street kids have the same story to tell, revolving around being used, abused and thrown out with the trash. I'd thought I was doing him a favor, letting him stay in my spare room and getting him a real job for a change, but a share in Tony's wrath was a high price to pay for six months of stability.

Our relationship was not close enough to help me figure out how to keep Tomas safe without looking like I was bailing on him. Part of the problem was that neither of us liked opening up, and it didn't help that we'd gotten off to a rough start. I came out of the bathroom the night he moved in to find him lounging nude on my bed, his hair spread out like an ink blot against my white sheets. I'd stood there, clutching my Winnie the Pooh towel and gaping at him, while he stretched like a big cat on my feather comforter, all sleek muscles and boneless grace. He was completely unselfconscious and I could see why; he sure didn't look like a starved street kid. I'd never asked his age, but assumed he was younger than me. Which made him way too young to have that particular look in his eye.

I hadn't been able to keep from following the path of one long-fingered hand as he traced a line down the side of his body from nipples to groin. It was a blatant invitation, and it took me a second to stop drooling and realize what was going on. I finally figured out that he thought he was supposed to pay for his room in what he considered the usual way. On the streets, there's no such thing as free, so when I refused to take money, he assumed I wanted payment of another kind. I should have tried to explain, to tell him that my whole life had been about being used and that I sure as hell wasn't going to do it to someone else. Maybe if I had, we'd have started to talk and cleared up a few things. Unfortunately, what I did instead was to freak and toss him out of the bedroom, along with the blanket that I'd quickly thrown over him. I don't know what he thought about it all, since we never discussed that night. We eventually fell into a more or less relaxed routine, splitting the housework, cooking and shopping like any two roommates, but both of us guarded our secrets. I'd catch him watching me with a strange expression sometimes, and I figured he was waiting for me to abandon him like everyone else. I really hated it that I was about to do exactly that.

"Did you get off early?" He touched my cheek and I stepped back, wanting to be farther from those trusting eyes. There was no escaping what I had to do, but I wasn't looking forward to seeing his face shut down, and watching whatever faith he'd regained in people bleed away because of me.

"No." I shifted feet and tried to think how not to make this sound like a rejection. It wasn't his fault that my life was spiraling down the toilet. Again. "I have to tell you something important, and you need to listen and do what I ask, okay?"

"You're going." I don't know how he knew. Maybe I had that look. He'd probably seen it before.

"I don't have a choice." By mutual consent, we moved out the back door to the paved surface surrounding the stairs to street level. Not much of a view, but at least it was quieter. The air smelled of rain, but the downpour that had been building all afternoon was holding off. If I hurried, maybe I could make the bus station before getting soaked. "You know how I told you that I had some bad things happen a while ago?"

"Yes, but there is nothing to worry about now. I'm here." He smiled, and I didn't like the look in his eyes. I didn't want him fond of me, didn't want him to miss me. Damn, this wasn't going well. I decided to quit trying for subtlety; it wasn't my strong suit.

"There's some serious stuff going down soon, and I have to be gone before it hits the fan." It wasn't much of an explanation, but how do you tell someone that the vampire gangster who raised you and who you tried your best to destroy has put a price on your head? There was no way Tomas could understand the world I came from, not if I had all the time in the world to explain. "You can have the stuff in the apartment, but take my clothes to the shelter. Lisa will put them to good use." I had a momentary pang for my carefully assembled wardrobe, but it couldn't be helped.

"Cass . . ."

"I'll talk to Mike before I go. I'm sure he'll let you bunk here for a week or two, in case anyone drops by the apartment looking for me. It probably wouldn't be good for you to go back there for a while." There was a studio apartment at the top of the building left over from the era when owners sometimes lived over their businesses. Mike had used it fairly recently, so it should be in decent shape. And I would definitely feel better knowing Tomas was staying there. I didn't like the idea of a bunch of enraged vamps descending on our place looking for me and finding him instead.

"Cassie." Tomas took my hand gingerly, as if afraid I might snatch it away. He thought I was uptight about being touched since that initial misunderstanding. I'd never corrected him because I didn't want to give the wrong impression and, frankly, it was easier to behave myself if I kept a little distance between us. He didn't need to be hit on at home as well as at work. "I'm coming with you." He said it calmly, as if it was the most logical thing in the world.

I didn't want to hurt him, but I could not stand there and argue the point with an assassin after me. "You can't. I'm sorry, but two people are easier to find than one, and besides, if I'm caught . . ." I stopped because I couldn't think how to tell him how bad it would be and not sound like a raving lunatic. Of course, he'd probably seen enough weird things on the streets to make him more open-minded than the cops, who treated anyone who started talking about vampires as a druggie or a psychotic. But even if I could figure out a way to tell him, there wasn't time.

"I'm sorry; I have to go." That wasn't how I wanted to say good-bye. There were a lot of things I hadn't told Tomas because I was afraid it would sound like I was coming on to him. And now, when I could say whatever I wanted, I had to leave.

I started to pull away, but he held on to my hand and his grip was surprisingly strong. Before I could insist that he let me go, I had a very familiar, totally unwelcome feeling creep over me. The muggy night air was suddenly replaced by something colder, darker and far less friendly. I don't know what nonsensitives feel around vampires, but all my life I've been able to tell when they're near. It's like when people say that someone walks over their grave—kind of a shiver down the spine combined with a feeling of something being wrong. I never feel that way around ghosts like norms sometimes do, but it hits me with vamps every time. I looked up to see a dark shape silhouetted against the glare of the streetlights for an instant, before it melted into the night and was gone.

"Damn!" I drew my gun and pushed Tomas back into the storeroom. Not that it helped much; if Tony had sent vamps after me, we needed more protection than a simple door could give. I'd seen Tony rip a solid oak plank off its hinges in one movement of his delicate, ring-covered hands, just because he couldn't find his key and was in a mood.

"What is it?"

"Somebody I don't want to see." I looked at Tomas and got a vision of his face streaked with blood and his serene gaze empty with death. It wasn't a Seeing, just my brain coming up with its usual worst-case scenario, but it was enough to help me prioritize. The vamps wouldn't come in and slaughter half the club looking for me. Tony was too afraid of the Senate to okay mass murder, but he wouldn't think twice about removing some street kid who got in his way. It was the same attitude he'd demonstrated when he orphaned me at the age of four to ensure himself complete control over my abilities. My parents were an obstacle to his ambition, so they were removed. Simple. And the Senate wasn't likely to fuss over something that could be passed off as regular old gang activity. Priority number one, then, was to get Tomas out of the line of fire. "I have to get out of here or I'll endanger everybody. But now they might come after you since they saw us talking. They'll think you know where I'm going."

I dragged him back through the storeroom, trying to think. I'd been a fool to come here, to let them see Tomas and me together. Despite being told otherwise on a regular basis, half the people at the club assumed he was my lover. If Tony's thugs started asking about him and anyone told them that, they'd torture him to death trying to find me. I should have known better than to get involved, even platonically, with anyone. I was like some kind of poison—get anywhere near me, and you're lucky if you just die. Somehow, I had to get Tomas away as well as myself and, like me, he could never hope to return. Some life I'd helped him build.

There was also the problem that the vamp had let us go. I'd seen them look like they dissolved into the wind, they could move so quickly. He'd had more than enough time in those few seconds to strike, swift as a snake, or to shoot me from a nice, safe distance. Vamps didn't really need guns against mortals, but the Senate preferred hits to look as natural as possible, so most of Tony's guys carried them. He might have suspected I was armed, too, but I doubted he feared my gun even if he didn't know how bad a shot I was. The best I could hope for would be to slow him down. No, I was alive because whoever was out there had been ordered to play the game. The obit had said 8:43, and 8:43 it would be. I could hear Tony telling the family that he'd arranged a last little Seeing for his prophet, and this time, she didn't even have to do the work herself. I wondered if they planned to kill me here and carry me over to Peachtree, or if they'd simply overwhelm my mind and have me walk there like the proverbial sheep to slaughter. I wasn't real keen on either plan.

I licked suddenly dry lips. "Okay, here. Put this on and get your coat. Tuck your hair up." Mike had left one of his many baseball caps on a storage shelf and I grabbed it, but no way was all that hair going underneath it. "We need to find somebody who has a coat with a hood you can borrow. You're too easy to identify." Maybe one of the Goths would loan us a cape. If I could make Tomas look different enough, he might be able to sneak away while the vamps were concentrating on me.

"Cassie, listen. There is—" I never found out what Tomas had been about to say, because the door we'd just entered slammed open as if the lock wasn't even there, and five huge vampires rushed into the room. They looked like a bunch of linebackers who had joined a grunge band—all bulging muscles and shoulder-length, greasy hair.

For one frozen moment, we all stared at each other. Size is pretty much irrelevant when you're undead, but Tony likes them big, I guess for the intimidation factor. It worked—I was intimidated. The fact that they weren't bothering to hide their real faces under polite masks didn't help. I knew what a vampire looks like when hunting—I'd seen it enough times—but it was still the stuff of nightmares. I had time to wonder if I'd live long enough to need to worry about bad dreams before they moved in a blur of motion. I got a shot off into one in the general area of his heart, but it didn't stop him. I hadn't thought it would. Not that it mattered: I hadn't expected to rank five vamp assassins, and no way could I deal with those odds. Tony must be even more pissed than I'd thought.

Chapter 2

The gun was snatched from my hand and I was smashed into the mason-block wall, face first. In the same breath, my arm was wrenched up so far behind me that I was afraid it would break. I didn't see what happened then because I was too busy getting a concrete facial, but I heard what sounded like every metal shelving unit in the place being turned over. Someone gave a roar of rage, then a swell of power billowed through the room like a hot wind, crashing against my skin in a hail of sparks. If I'd had enough breath, I would have screamed, both at the sensation and at the sheer pettiness of the bastard who wouldn't allow me even a tiny chance of escape. Not only had Tony sent a whole squad of vamps after me, but at least one of them simply had to be a master. No one else could summon that kind of power, not even five ordinary vamps working together. And it wasn't just any old master, either.

Most vamps spend their immortal lives as little more than slaves, serving whoever made them without the ability to break away or to refuse an assignment. But some, usually those who were the strongest willed in life, over time gain power. When they reach master level, they can make other vampires to serve them, and are usually given some autonomy by their makers. Seventh level is the lowest master rank, and most never progress past it, but for those who do, each additional step up the ladder gains them new abilities and more freedom. I'd been around master vamps all my life, up to third-level ones like Tony, and I'd seen plenty of them lose their tempers. But it had never before felt like their power might actually burn holes in my skin. It seemed impossible that Tony had talked a senior vamp, second or first level, into taking on a sordid little assassination—offing me wasn't exactly a challenge—but there wasn't any other explanation.

I yelled for Tomas to run, even knowing it wouldn't do any good, and my vamp decided I must not be in enough pain if I could make all that noise. He lowered the hand holding the back of my head to my neck and squeezed. I remember thinking that, if I was lucky, he'd choke me to death before he remembered to bring me over. It didn't make for a great night for me, but it was better than looking at Tony's ugly face for eternity.

A second later, when I was beginning to see dots swirling around my vision and to hear a roaring in my ears, the vamp gave a high-pitched scream and the pressure suddenly let up. I gasped and fell to my knees, struggling to get a deep breath past my burning throat, while he flopped around in front of me, screeching as if he was literally being torn apart. It took me a few seconds to figure out what was wrong with him, since it wasn't an everyday occurrence. A big hint was the warm, almost liquid feeling tracing a lopsided pentagram on my back, as if someone had drizzled heated oil over my skin. Another clue was that the vamp's arm and part of his chest were covered in lines that glowed gold as they sizzled and popped, cooking the flesh between them and the bone. As I watched, one molten welt obscured the small indentation over his breast where my bullet had gone in and kept going. I stared at him in paralyzed shock. From the shape of the marks, it was pretty obvious that my ward had flared to life.

That was ironic, considering that Tony must have been the one to have it worked into my skin in the first place. I'd always thought he'd been gypped: its original pentagram shape had stretched as I grew older, and all I'd ended up with was an ugly tattoo that covered half my back and part of my left shoulder. But although it wasn't a very good-looking design anymore, it seemed to work pretty well. However, the vamp who attacked me wasn't a master—that surge of energy had come from somewhere behind us—and how my ward would fair against one of the big boys was an open question. I was pretty impressed that it had done this much; the only time it had flared up before, it hadn't put on nearly as much of a show. It had only burnt the would-be mugger's arm, singeing him enough that I was able to get away. Of course, then it had been a human trying to rip my head off. Maybe it became stronger depending on the strength of the one it was fighting? I had a bad feeling I was going to find out.

I know something about wards, since Tony always kept two wardsmiths on staff to maintain the fortress of magical protections around his home and businesses. I'd learned from them that there are three main categories: perimeter wards, energy wards and protection wards. Perimeter wards are what Tony uses as camouflage when he's up to something illegal—in other words, constantly. Energy wards are more complex: at their best, they are better than Prozac at relieving stress and helping people work through emotional problems. At their worst, which is the way Tony usually used them, they could allow him to influence important business negotiations. Everyone within the perimeter of the wards would start to feel very mellow and would suddenly decide that cutthroat tactics were too much trouble when they could simply do whatever Tony wanted. There are two types of protection wards: personal shields and guards. Eugenie instructed me in the first type when I was a kid. Without them, I could even sense the ghosts of ghosts—the thin energy trails stretching back in time like glowing lines on a map, telling me that once, maybe hundreds of years ago, a spirit had passed by. The older I got, the more distracted I became by the impressions, maybe because Tony's old mansion was sandwiched between an Indian burial ground and a colonial cemetery. Eugenie had finally tired of my mind wandering during lessons and gave me the tools to shield against them. She taught me to sense my energy field, what some people call an aura, then use my power to build a hedge around it for protection. Eventually, my shields became automatic, filtering out anything except active spirits in the here and now.

But shields are only as powerful as the person building them, since they usually draw on personal power, and most aren't enough to thwart a major spiritual or physical attack. That's where guards come in. Crafted by a group of magic users, they are designed to protect a person, object or location from harm. They can be set to fend off danger, usually by turning the evil intent back on its sender or, in cases like mine, ensuring that anyone touching me with harm in mind ends up screaming in agony.

These types of wards are big business in the supernatural community. Tony once paid a wardsmith a small fortune to craft a special perimeter-protection combo for a convoy of ships carrying some highly illegal substances. He was supposed to make them look like old garbage scowls to any observers—not the sort of thing the authorities enjoy searching too thoroughly. But the smith was young and careless, and the wards failed right as the ships were heading into port—almost in front of a Coast Guard patrol. Tony lost the cargo and the wardsmith lost his life. I had been too young when my ward was done to remember the experience, but whoever had crafted it knew what he or she was doing. Tony must have paid a pretty penny for it, although this was probably one instance when he wished he'd gone cut rate.

My eyes had begun to water from the stench of frying vampire flesh, not something you smell every day, and I gagged for a moment before suddenly realizing that I could move again. I looked around frantically for my weapon, before almost immediately giving up and scrambling around the edge of a shelving unit. There was no sign of my 9 mm, and no way was I going to make it to the door without it. And the few boxes on the unit that formed my sad excuse for a hiding spot were not going to fool anybody for long. No weapon, no way to hide and only a warped ward for protection. I decided on the better part of valor, also known as running and hiding, and started backing down the aisle.

If I could avoid the master vamp for a minute, maybe I could make it to the small door leading to the unfinished part of the basement. It had no doorway to the rest of the club but abutted the wall behind the far end of the bar. If I was out of sight, there was a tiny chance the vamp's senses might be confused and he'd assume I'd slipped into the bar again. That might buy me a few seconds to sneak out the back, if he didn't do the smart thing and leave one of his guys to watch it. Of course, even if he did, my ward might take out another low-level vamp. Then again, it might not.

I finally reached the half-sized door at the end of the last row of shelves, but hadn't even gotten it open before I heard a crash and an inhuman scream behind me. I looked over my shoulder, expecting to see one or more murderous vamps headed my way. It took my panicked brain a few seconds to realize that the person floating down the aisle was Portia, and that the sound of fighting was coming from several aisles over.

"I told you I would bring help, Cassie!" Her face was shining with excitement and the little rows of curls on either side of her head bobbed as she turned to gesture dramatically behind her. What looked like an entire Confederate brigade had muscled into the storeroom, even though there's no way it could have held anywhere near that many people. I'd seen that trick before—metaphysics tells regular old physics to go take a hike sometimes—but it was still impressive.

A dashing officer with a long mustache swept me a bow. "Captain Beauregard Lewis, at your service, ma'am." He looked kind of like Custer, an observation that probably wouldn't have gone down well if I'd been dumb enough to make it. But before I could say anything, a vamp reached through the shelving and the captain's insubstantial middle and grabbed me around the throat.

Beauregard unsheathed his sword and I had half a second to wonder what he thought he was going to do before it came down in a flashing arc that took off the vamp's arm at the elbow. He yelled and so did I, in my case because I'd been sprayed with a warm sheet of blood and because the severed arm was still tight around my throat, fingers digging for my windpipe. Vamp bodies don't die unless both head and heart are destroyed, so the arm was trying to complete the last order it had been given and choke me to death. Beauregard tried to pry it off, but his hand went right through me.

"I sure am sorry, ma'am," he said, while my vision threatened to go dark for the second time that night. "But I used most of my energy on that blow." He shook his head sadly. "Time has caused us to sadly diminish." He looked like he expected me to say something, but it's a little hard to sympathize when you can't draw a breath and fireworks are going off behind your eyelids.

The vamp made another lunge at me, but Portia managed to trip him with her parasol. "Get him!" she cried, and the battalion, which had been merely observing the scene until now, moved as one churning, massive river of gray. It was one of those moments when your eyes cross as the brain tells them they can't be seeing what they say they are. Several thousand troops converged on the same point, falling into it like water disappearing down a drain. Only the drain in question wasn't designed for that kind of thing and sure as hell didn't like it. The vamp started ricocheting off shelving units, his one arm flapping as if he could somehow beat off the invasion, while his skin turned a mottled shade of purple.

By the time I managed to pry the fingers around my neck loose and throw the arm on the floor, he had stopped moving, frozen like a statue at the end of the aisle. I tried to keep an eye on him but was distracted by the severed arm, which was trying to scrabble across the floor and grab me. I wasn't real clear on what was happening, but my best guess was that each ghost was freezing a tiny bit of the vamp, turning him into a big, ugly Popsicle. I had just begun to wonder what would happen when all those spirits tried to escape from his now unyielding flesh when the explosion came. I'd grabbed a wine bottle and started hitting the arm, so I missed the big event. All I know is that I ended up covered in icy bits of vampire flesh that hit me like tiny hailstones.

Portia drifted over, avoiding the repulsive floor by simply not touching it. She twirled her lacy parasol and beamed at me. "We must go, Cassie. That took a lot out of the boys and they need to rest. But we want you to know that we had a lovely time!" She took Beauregard's arm and curtsied while he made another bow; then they vanished along with the crowd that flowed out of the vamp's remains.

I sat in the middle of a patch of melting goo, too stunned for action, and rubbed my neck. My face stung from where the storm of vamp parts had hit me, but my throat was more of an issue. I couldn't seem to swallow, and it had me worried. I might have sat there quite a while, watching vamp bits melt and fall off the shelving, but Tomas appeared at the end of the aisle.

"Hurry!" He grabbed me by the wrist and hauled me into the main part of the room. I yelped in pain—he'd taken hold of the same wrist the vamp had almost twisted off—and in surprise at seeing him alive. I'd pretty much written us both off, but now it occurred to me to wonder who had been fighting with the vamps if Portia's group had been with me. His hand was dripping blood and for a second I thought it was his, but I couldn't see a wound. My yell must have startled him, because he abruptly let go and I slumped to the floor, wheezing and choking at the strain the scream had put on my abused throat. It was then, while cradling my wrist to my chest and trying not to be sick, that I noticed the bodies.

Other than my first attacker, who was now minus an arm and making gurgling sounds as the ward ate through his chest, the only one still moving was trapped under a shelving unit that looked like it had been torn from the wall and thrown on top of him. It had contained a bunch of metal sheets left over from the urban warehouse theme Mike had done on the club, which had been salvaged from a condemned factory. They weren't some designer's idea of stylish metal siding, but the real thing—thick, razor-edged pieces that Mike had had to be extra careful with when installing. They had apparently gotten up some momentum when the shelving was tossed around, turning them into lethal projectiles that had sliced up the vamp like a loaf of bread. He must have fed recently, because enough blood had poured from the multiple gashes to spread across the floor like a crimson blanket.

None of the strips had taken off his head or pierced his heart, however, so despite his gruesome injuries, he continued to live. He looked in my direction, and I saw him struggle to raise the gun he clutched in one hand. Tomas noticed and without hesitation walked over and pulled out the metal sheet embedded in the vamp's abdomen. He brought it down in a series of quick, meaty-sounding thuds while I stared at him in openmouthed disbelief. Within a few seconds, the thing on the floor resembled a pile of raw hamburger more than a person.

The vamp's eyes continued to glare at me in hatred, aware of what was happening even as he was butchered, and I couldn't scream, couldn't do anything. I'd been in some tight spots before, but the nerves forget what it is to remain bowstring tight every minute of every day when you don't have to live that way anymore. I watched Tomas sever the vamp's head from his body with a final jarring thud, and let out the breath I hadn't even known I was holding. We were alive. I couldn't believe it, and I sure as hell didn't understand it.

Growing up at Tony's had given me a fairly high tolerance for violence, so I was sort of holding things together until I noticed that the corpses of the fourth and fifth vamps had gaping, ragged holes where their hearts should have been. Staking is the traditional and still most popular way of dealing with a vamp, but I guess ripping the heart out manually works, too, although I'd never seen it done that way. I was thinking that I could live without ever seeing it again when I looked at Tomas and, suddenly, the room fell away.

Normally, I get some kind of warning when I'm about to have a vision. Not that I can stop them, but the thirty seconds or so of disorientation that precede them give me time to get out of other people's sight and let me mentally prepare. This time, I got nothing. It was as if the floor just gave way and I fell down a long, dark tunnel. When I landed, Tomas stood about six feet from me on a grassy plain that seemed to go on forever under a pale blue sky. His skin was burnished bronze instead of sun-kissed cream and he was dressed in a sleeveless, dirty, woolen tunic instead of Goth chic, but it was definitely him. His eyes were wild, glittering like two dark jewels in his face, and his expression was triumphant. A group of similarly dressed men surrounded him, all looking like their favorite team had just won the Super Bowl.

Waves crashed onto a rocky shore nearby, their color a green so deep it was almost black, and sent a cold breeze inland in icy gusts. It would have been a stark but beautiful scene if not for the couple of dozen bodies lying around. Most of them looked European, with the closest in an outfit that could have come out of an underfunded pirate movie: white cotton shirt with full sleeves, brown linen knee pants and soiled white hose. The man had lost his shoes and his hair was as wild as his expression.

As I watched in horrified fascination, Tomas thrust a crude bronze knife into the man's still-heaving chest and cut a deep gash that ripped it open from neck to belly. Heat from the wound mixed with the cold air to cause a cloud of steam to rise, but it wasn't thick enough to keep me from seeing him tear through the ribs like he was snapping twigs. Bright rivulets of blood bathed his hand as he brought out the trembling heart and held it aloft; then slowly, as if savoring the moment, he began to lower it to his mouth. His teeth sank into quivering flesh that was still trying to beat, then tore through a pulsing vein that sent a stream of blood gushing across his face and down his chin. The cascade pooled in the hollow in his throat, then sent red fingers down his chest into his tunic, leaving abstract designs behind so that he looked like he was wearing war paint. His throat convulsed and he swallowed, causing a cheer to go up from the watching warriors.

I must have made some type of noise, because he looked across at me and, flashing red-stained teeth in a horrible parody of a smile, held out the grisly mass of flesh as if to offer to share. He took a step forward and I realized I was rooted to the spot, unable to stop him, unable to get away, as that dripping hand with its gruesome offering came closer. My paralysis finally broke and I screamed.

It hurt my throat, but there was no way I could have held it back. The vision shattered and I was back in the gory storeroom, staring wildly at the new Tomas, who, for a split second, was superimposed on the old. His tongue slid out to lick up a tiny drop of red at the corner of his mouth, so small that it had been unnoticeable until he drew attention to it. I remember thinking that old habits die hard, right before I began shrieking at the top of my lungs.

He took a step towards me, hands held out in front of him as if to show how harmless he was, and I saw that they were almost clean again. As he came closer, a final stain on the pad of one palm dissolved, vanishing into his skin like a drop of water into desert sand. I realized that I was scuttling backwards like a crab, crying and swearing, but I didn't care. I slipped in blood and went down, and screamed harder when I saw that my legs were covered in red, like roses had bloomed on my hose and boots. Tomas came towards me slowly, speaking calmly, as if I were a skittish colt he was trying to tame. "Cassie, please listen. We've bought some time, but we must go. There will be others."

I slipped again and fell on my butt, bruising it on something hard. Some part of my brain that was still coherent recognized the shape of the object, and I snatched my gun from beneath me. "Don't come any closer or I'll kill you." I pointed it at Tomas and, despite the fact that it was shaking wildly in my less-than-steady grip, I could tell he knew I meant it. His eyes, usually soft and warm and open, were opaque black mirrors now. I couldn't see anything past them, and I didn't want to. God, I didn't want to.

"Cassie, you must listen to me." I looked into that handsome face, and some part of me detached itself to watch another illusion shatter and die. I thought I'd finally done something good, that I'd actually helped someone, saved somebody, instead of always watching every damn thing I did end in pain—either mine or someone else's. I should have known it was too good to be true, that he was too good. *Way out of your league, Cassie, my girl,* I thought as my back hit the door. *Maybe you should start smaller, adopt a kitten next time*—only I knew there was very little chance that there would be a next time.

I could hear the thud of music from the club through the door, some kind of chant mixed with techno, and it sounded like heaven. I wanted to lose myself in the crowd, make my way up to the street and run like hell. I was the hiding champ, and in the tourist district it would be easy to become an anonymous member of the happy, Friday-night throng. I had a separate bank account under yet another fake name and an emergency stash of nondescript clothes in a locker at the bus station, and I'd memorized every back alley in a fifteen-block radius. I'd get away all right, if only I could lose Tomas.

I slowly slid up the door, using it to steady myself and cursing my high heels. My skirt rode up but I didn't bother to straighten it; flashing Tomas was the least of my worries. I felt behind me with a hand slick with blood and finally found the doorknob. I fell through the opening on unsteady legs, slammed the door behind me and scrambled around the bar. I couldn't get a deep breath and my body convulsed like it wanted to be sick, but I held on. I didn't have time for that now.

The light show had started, and the bouncing, gyrating mass of dancers was slashed through by blinding blasts from the strobes. The pulsing rhythm and the noise of the crowd made me immediately deaf, but I didn't need to hear Tomas to know he was back there. The strobes leached the color from the blood on me, turning it alternately black and silver. The low lighting let me blend in without causing a stampede, although I doubted I looked normal. I slithered through every opening, trying to think as I ran, but my higher brain wasn't home, and all my instincts said was "Faster!" I tried, because there was nothing else to do but wait for him to catch me, but I already knew it wouldn't be enough.

I was halfway across the dance floor when Tomas grabbed me. He spun me around to face him, and I felt a hand slide through the burnt back of my T-shirt to meld our bodies together. It probably looked like we were dancing to everyone else; only I knew that I couldn't pull away. He had an iron grip on my gun hand, forcing the weapon down to my side and away from him. I wouldn't have tried to fire anyway. My palm was so sweaty that I was having trouble just holding on to the thing, and there were too many people around to risk a shot going wild. Besides, unless I missed my guess, a bullet wouldn't do much more than irritate him.

His fingers slid up my naked spine to the outline of my ward. He traced the edges almost reverently. "I heard stories of this but never believed them." His voice was full of something that sounded like awe. Somehow he made me hear him despite the deafening music, but I wasn't interested in conversation. I twisted, trying futilely to break his hold, and cursed the useless ward. It must have been exhausted by the previous fight or else it didn't work against those at his level, because it had no reaction to his touch.

"Cassie, look at me."

I fought him, knowing from childhood that looking a vampire directly in the eyes made it easier for him to control you. After the scene in the storeroom, there was no doubt in my mind what he was, and I desperately didn't want him in my head. Given that he'd gone right under my vamp radar and posed as human for months, there was no chance that I was dealing with less than a third-level master, and possibly higher. Make that probably, considering that, on rare occasions, I'd seen him walk around in full daylight, which even Tony couldn't do without risking a lot worse than a sunburn. Not that his level mattered; if he felt like it, any master could have me clucking like a chicken with little more than a glance.

Once, I'd had a level of protection from that sort of thing, but with my old defender the very one wanting me dead, I was fair game; no one would even avenge any harm that came to me. For all I knew, Tomas would get a bounty for bringing me in. Tony didn't mind paying for revenge, and considering how much I'd cost him, he'd probably pay up with a smile. Was that why Tomas had killed the other vamps, seeing them as rivals for his reward? How the hell much was Tony offering for me, anyway? And why had Tomas waited so long to cash in?

I struggled and fought but everyone ignored us, I guess

under the assumption that I was merely a lousy dancer. Tomas just clasped me tighter. Considering how seldom I touched him, it felt weird to be held so intimately now. It was hard to remember that this was Tomas. My brain had put him firmly in the friend category and was resisting moving him over to the file labeled psycho-assassin vampire. The way he was holding me wasn't helping the confusion—his hand felt a lot more than friendly as it slid up and down my almost bare back, pulling me into a dance far slower and more sensual than the music called for.

Contrary to legend, his body felt warm against mine and as smooth as muscled satin, but he may as well have been carved of steel for all the hope I had of breaking his hold. My pulse sped up and I thought I would faint when he bent his head and I felt lips trailing over my neck. I think my heart actually stopped as he delicately kissed the skin as if tasting the pulse under the surface. It felt like my blood could sense him, as if it moved slower and thicker in my veins, waiting for him to set it free. I broke out in a sweat that had nothing to do with the heat of so many bodies crowded into a small place. Was he going to kill me right there, in front of a couple of hundred witnesses? A chill ran through me when I realized that he could probably get away with it. He could definitely carry my body off and no one would think anything about it; all they'd see was Tomas taking care of his roommate, who'd fainted in the heat. What a gentleman.

I should have known something like this was going to happen. Every time I trusted someone, he betrayed me; every time I loved someone, she died. Since Tomas was already dead, I guessed the pattern held true.

"Please don't fight me." His breath over my clammy skin made me shiver. The suggestion ran like a drug through my veins, bathing me in a comfortable, rosy glow that took away some of the fear and most of the pain, but also made it harder to think. It wasn't as strong as if I'd made eye contact, but it still made me feel like I was surrounded by heavy water instead of air, with every tiny movement more of a struggle than it should have been. Not that it mattered: my efforts were doing nothing except sending dull pains through my sore wrist and exciting him. Nothing showed on his face, but his body was not as fully under control, and I could feel him stretched tight and firm against his jeans.

He brushed warm lips over mine. "I don't intend to hurt you," he whispered. If there had been any point, I'd have reminded him that whether he did the assassination himself or merely turned me over to Tony, the end result would be the same. But I didn't have time to say anything before his lips ghosted over mine again; then suddenly his control snapped and he covered my mouth in a bruising kiss that had none of the previous gentleness.

His arms tightened, pressing me against every inch of him, kissing me almost desperately, like a starving man at a feast. That strong hand slipped farther down my back until it found the edge of my short leather skirt and pushed it up. He suddenly lifted me completely off the floor and settled me against his waist, so that I had to twine my legs around him or fall, and the sensory overload was enough that it took me a minute to realize that he was dancing us back towards the storeroom. Apparently he preferred his kills to be private.

He was still kissing me when the first burst of energy radiated off him, sending a shudder down to my fingertips. Either something had broken his concentration or he wasn't bothering to shield anymore. And why should he? I was probably the only sensitive there, and I already knew what he was. He may have looked the same to everyone else, but to me, it was like his skin had been dipped in molten gold, causing him to shine like a miniature sun in the dark room. The amount of energy pouring off him raised little hairs all along my arms and at the back of my neck as it swirled and crackled around us. The very air seemed to gain weight, feeling like it does right before a storm breaks—everything was suddenly clearer, brighter, and more sharp edged. All that force soon found a focus. It hit me like high tide at the ocean, drenching me in wave after wave of his power, making it hard to remember why I was fighting, or much of anything else.

He broke off the kiss and I made a small, involuntary sound of protest before he slid his mouth down to my neck again. But this time I didn't mind; this time, it seemed a curiously tender gesture, although a small part of my brain noted that his hair fell across my ruined shirt, hiding it from the brighter lights near the bar. Lucille, who was filling an order a couple of yards away, gave me a surprised thumbs-up as we slipped behind the counter. I didn't try to call for help. I rationalized it by asking what Lucille could do against even a baby vamp, much less a master. The truth, though, was that I simply didn't care. But Tomas must have thought I was about to be foolish, or maybe he didn't want to take chances. He kissed me again, and whatever his motives, there was no doubt that he knew what he was doing. The silken feel of his lips on mine muddled my thoughts even more and, when we finally broke apart, I was too stunned to remember not to catch his gaze. My mind immediately froze, all thoughts except Tomas simply not there anymore, like a switch had been thrown in my brain. The light dimmed and the music receded until all I could see was his face and all I could hear was the pounding of my pulse in my ears.

Why had I never noticed the way his eyes tilted so enticingly upward? The lashes were a black silk fringe around the tiny flames the bar's lighting caused to dance in his pupils. Something in me reacted to the heat I saw in that stare, because my hands acquired a will of their own and began tracing the flat planes of his stomach through the insubstantial barrier of his shirt. All that seemed to matter was the feel of those hard muscles under that silky skin; all I wanted was to work my way up to his neck and bury my hands in that gleaming fall of midnight hair, to see whether it was as soft, thick and heavy as it looked. But then I was distracted by the sight of a dusky nipple bared by one of the many gaps in his shirt, the sort of thing that had driven me to distraction more times than I could count. I discovered that it tasted as good as it looked, as good as I'd always known it would, and it tightened nicely under the efforts of my lips and teeth as if it had been longing for my touch. All things considered, I barely noticed when Tomas carried me back into the store-room and shut the door with his foot.

He drew a deep, shuddering breath and slowly pulled away from me. After a moment he spoke in a hoarse voice completely unlike his usual tones. "Give me the gun, Cassie. Someone could get hurt if it accidentally goes off." The sound of his voice, harsh and curiously flat, cleared my head a little. Seeing my first attacker helped, too. He was lying in three pieces, having been eaten completely in half by the ward. Through the wreck of his body, I could see blackened splinters where part of a lopsided pentagram had been burnt into the wooden floor. I stared at the sight, feeling slightly dizzy and very odd. All of a sudden, I got the joke: *someone could get hurt.* Now, that was funny.

I clutched Tomas to keep from falling, my gun dangling uselessly against his back. He took it from my limp hand and tucked it away somewhere. I didn't see where he put it; it simply disappeared. He was looking at me with concern, and suddenly that was funny, too. I started to giggle. I hoped Tony paid him well—he was a riot.

"Cassie, I can carry you if you want, but we must go." He glanced at the clock on the wall. It said 8:37.

"Look, we have time to make our appointment." I was still giggling, and the voice didn't sound like mine. I vaguely realized that I was about to become hysterical, then Tomas moved. The next thing I knew, I was back in his arms and we were outside, running along a darkened road so quickly that the streetlights all blurred together in a long, silver line. A second later, two dark shapes joined us, one on either side.

"Sleep," Tomas commanded as the world raced past. I realized that I was terribly tired and sleep seemed a very good idea. I felt warm and comfortable, although my head was spinning so much that it looked like the night sky rushed down to meet us or that we were flying up to the stars. I remember thinking dreamily, right before I drifted off, that as deaths go, this one wasn't so bad.

Chapter 3

I woke tired, aching and seriously freaked out. My mood
wasn't improved by the fact that Tomas was looming over
me so that his blank, upside-down face was the first thing I
saw. "Get away from me!" I croaked as I struggled into a sitting position. I had to wait a few minutes for the room to
stop moving, and when it did, I was less than thrilled with
what I saw. Great. I'd been dumped in Hell's waiting room.
The small chamber was carved out of red sandstone and lit
by only a couple of scary-looking wall sconces. They were
made out of what appeared to be interlocking knives and
held actual, evil-smelling torches. That told me right away
that I was somewhere with a lot of powerful wards, which
would have interfered with electricity. Not good.

The place would have been perfect as a torture chamber,
except that instead of iron maidens and thumbscrews, it was
furnished only with the very uncomfortable black leather
sofa where I was lying and a small side table with a few
magazines. One was a copy of the *Oracle*, the equivalent of
Newsweek for the magical world, but like most waiting-
room reading matter, it was several months out of date. I'd
dropped by a certain coffeehouse in Atlanta on a weekly
basis to read it, in case anything happened in my other world
that might affect my new life. I doubted that the cover story
for this edition, on the effect of cheap Asian imports on the
magical medicines market, fell into that category, however,

and the other was just a scandal sheet. PYTHIA'S HEIR MISS-ING! the three-inch title on this week's *Crystal Gazing* screamed. TIME OUT OF WHACK! I rolled my eyes but stopped because it hurt. Guess the MARTIANS KIDNAP WITCHES story they'd been leading with had sort of run dry.

"*Mia stella*, the Senate assigned Tomas as your body-guard; he cannot leave you," a familiar voice reproached gently from beside the door. "Do not make things difficult."

"I'm not." After what I'd been through, I thought I was being reason personified. I felt seriously nauseous, so tired that I swayed when I forced myself to stand, and my eyes burned like I'd already had the good, hard cry I wanted. But I wasn't budging. "I don't want him anywhere near me."

I ignored Tomas and an unfamiliar guy wearing seventeenth-century court clothes and concentrated on the only friend I had in the room. I had no idea what Rafe was doing here. Not that I wasn't glad to have him—I could use all the friends I could get—but I didn't know where he fit in. Rafe was short for Raphael, the toast of Rome and the fa-vorite artist of the papacy until he'd made the mistake of turning down a commission from a wealthy Florentine mer-chant in 1520. Tony had been trying to compete artistically with the Medicis: they had Michelangelo, so he needed Raphael. Rafe told him he already had more commissions than he could handle, and that, anyway, he painted frescoes for the pope. He wasn't about to travel all the way to Flor-ence merely to paint a dining room. It hadn't been a good move. Ever since, Rafe had been painting whatever Tony wanted, including my bedroom when I was a child. He'd made my ceiling full of angels that looked so real, for years I thought they watched over me while I slept. He was one of the only people at Tony's whom I had ever regretted leaving, but I had snuck away without so much as a good-bye. I had no other choice: he belonged to Tony and, if asked a direct question by his master, had to tell him the truth. So if he was here now, it was because Tony wanted him here. It lessened my joy at the reunion somewhat.

Tomas said nothing, but he also didn't leave. I glared at him, but it didn't have any obvious effect. That was a problem since I needed to escape, and the more babysitters the bigger the challenge. There was also the fact that even looking at him made so many emotions surge through me that I was getting a headache. It wasn't the violence that bothered me so much. I'd seen enough growing up that I could shrug off the events at the club now that I was over the shock that Tomas was the one doing them. That I was no longer kneeling in a pool of blood helped, as did the fact that the vamps he'd killed had been trying to do the same to me. My attitude could be summed up pretty simply: I was alive, they were not, go me. Surviving at Tony's taught you to be practical about these things.

I also gave Tomas credit for saving my life, although I'd probably be far away from harm by now if I hadn't gone to warn him in the first place. I was even willing to overlook him carting me off without a word of explanation, considering that I hadn't been in any frame of mind for a calm discussion. All in all, I figured we were about even, except for the betrayal part. That was something else. That I wasn't likely to forgive anytime soon, if at all.

I had shared glimpses into my time on the streets with Tomas, things I never talked about with anyone, to encourage him to open up. I'd worried that he wasn't making friends despite all the attention at the club, and wondered if he had some of the same relationship phobias I did. I'd let myself get fond of him, damn it, and all the time, everything he'd told me had been a lie. Not to mention the fact that he'd deliberately stolen my will, causing me to make enough of a fool of myself that I was still fighting a blush. That sort of thing is considered serious stuff in vamp circles; had I been on Tony's good side, he would have pitched a fit about undue influence being exerted over his servant.

"Let me talk to her," Tomas told Rafe. Before I could protest, the others left the room to give us the illusion of privacy. It was all for show; with vamp hearing it didn't make any difference.

I didn't bother lowering my voice. "Let me make this simple," I said furiously. "You lied to me and you betrayed me. I don't want to see you, talk to you or even breathe the same air as you. Ever again. Got it?"

"Cassie, you must understand; I only did what I was forced to—"

I noticed that he had something in his hand. "And what are you doing with my purse?!" I should have known he'd go through it—Tony couldn't know what surprises I might have tucked away—but because it was Tomas, it felt like another betrayal. "Did you take anything?"

"No; it is as you left it. But Cassie—"

"Give it back!" I grabbed for it and almost fell down. "You had no right—"

"Tower! Tower! Tower!" My tarot deck fell onto the floor and appeared to be having a conniption. I felt tears in my eyes. It was just a stupid deck of cards, but it was the only thing I had that Eugenie had given me.

"You broke it!"

I scrambled to pick up the scattered cards, and Tomas knelt beside me. "It's the wards here," he said quietly. "There are too many—they interfere with the charm. It should be all right after we leave, or I can have it recast for you. It's a simple spell."

I slapped his hand away from my poor, confused cards. I knew how they felt. "Don't touch them!" I put them back clumsily, with shaking hands, while he sat back on his heels and watched me.

"I'm sorry, Cassie," he finally said. "I knew you would be upset—"

"*Upset*?!" I rounded on him, so angry I could hardly see. "You let me think you were some poor, abused kid who needed a friend, and stupid me, I fell for it! I trusted you, and you gave me up to—" I stopped and took a deep breath before I lost it. I wasn't going to give him the satisfaction of watching me cry. I wasn't. I shoved the cards back in my purse and checked on the rest of its contents to give myself time to get back in control. After a minute, I looked up. "Not everything that's broken can be fixed, Tomas."

"I didn't lie to you, Cassie; I swear it."

Looking into his so-sincere eyes, I almost believed him. Almost. "So you're, what, a poor, abused master vampire? Please."

"I did not lie," he repeated, more emphatically. "I was told to keep you safe. That is what I did. I had to win your trust for that, but I did not lie to do it. I never told you I was abused, although if I had, it would have been true enough. Any of Alejandro's servants could make that claim."

I couldn't believe he was doing this. I hadn't expected a heartfelt apology, but the fact that he wouldn't even admit what he'd done was too much. "You make me sick," I said, getting back to my feet. I walked to the door and stuck my head out. Rafe was in the corridor, trying to look like he hadn't heard every word. "He goes, or you get no cooperation from me."

The next second, Tomas' hands were around my upper arms, the grip just short of painful as he drew me back against him. "What do you know of abuse?" he demanded in a savage undertone. "Do you know how I became a vampire, Cassie? Would you like me better if I told you that they rounded me up with the rest of my village and took us to be hunted by Alejandro and his court? That the only reason I'm not dead is that one of his courtiers thought I was attractive enough to save for himself? That I had to watch people who had come through plague and conquest, who had fought at my side for years against overwhelming odds, be slaughtered by a madman for his sick amusement? Is that what you want to hear? If it isn't gruesome enough to win your forgiveness, believe me, I have many other stories. We could swap them, only I think you would run out before I do. You were on the streets for a handful of years; I was with Alejandro for three and a half centuries!"

"Tomas, please release Mademoiselle Palmer."

To my surprise, the oddly dressed man had intervened. I'd thought he looked like something out of Restoration England, but now realized his origins were on the other side of the Channel. His accent was faint but noticeably French. I'd almost forgotten he was there. Even weirder was that Tomas immediately did as he asked, stepping away like contact with me burned him, but those black eyes stayed on mine as if waiting for an answer. What was I supposed to say? You've had a tough time, so it's okay that you turned me over to people who may do even worse to me? Your life was messed up, so it's fine that you ruined mine? If so, he'd be waiting a long time.

"Perhaps you can trust me to guard her for a while?" It was phrased as a question, but the tall Frenchman ushered me down the corridor without waiting for an answer.

I soon got to see my old nemesis, but not in the circumstances I'd expected. Tony's fat face looked the same as always, which wasn't surprising since he hadn't changed since 1513 except for the clothes. He was wearing what I liked to think of as his goodfella suit—a pinstriped number that looked like something he'd stolen off a bouncer at a speakeasy, and maybe he had. He liked the suit because someone had told him once that vertical stripes made him look slimmer. They lied. Tony died at more than three hundred pounds, which on a five-foot-five frame meant he was approximately the shape of a soccer ball with legs. And no amount of diet and exercise was gonna change that now.

Even with the weight and the fashion sense from hell, Tony looked better than his chief enforcer, Alphonse, who stood, as always, behind his master's left shoulder. Although they were only reflections in a large mirror at the moment, I

could tell they were in the old stronghold in Philly. I was
surprised that even Tony would have that much nerve, to
move right back in, but I should have known; lack of balls
wasn't one of his failings. I knew where they were because
Tony was arrayed on his usual chair, a throne that had come
from a bishop's palace back when lots of carving and gilt
were the in thing. The back came to a point a good six feet
off the ground, but Alphonse didn't have to stretch to see
past it. His height didn't help his appearance, though. He
was built like someone who knew how a thug was supposed
to look had put him together, but he had one of the scariest
faces I've ever seen. I don't mean that in a sexy, Hollywood
villain kind of way—the guy was just plain ugly. I heard
once that he'd been one of Baby Face Nelson's hit men before he was turned, but it looked to me like he was the one
who'd been hit—repeatedly, with a baseball bat, in the face.
As a kid, I'd been fascinated with the fact that he had almost
no profile because his nose stood out no more than his Ne-
anderthal brow line.

I always crack up when movies depict vamps as gorgeous, sexy and with an endless closet of expensive clothes.
The fact is, when you're dead, you look pretty much the
same way you did when you were alive. Hundreds of years
can teach a person a few beauty tricks, I guess, but most
vamps don't bother. Some of the younger ones make an effort because it makes hunting easier, but most of the older
ones don't give a damn. When you can make someone believe you look like anything from Marilyn Monroe to Brad
Pitt with merely a suggestion, makeup starts to look like a
waste of money.

Despite both Tony's and his pet goon's presence via enchanted mirror, I was in a good mood. I looked a hell of a
lot more disreputable than either of them, with my pink bra
peeking out of my shredded shirt, my scraped face oozing
blood, and melted bits of vampire goo dripping down my
boots. But I was alive, still human, and Tony was looking

unhappy. It didn't get much better than that. Of course, Tony wasn't the only problem in sight, but I figured I stood a fighting chance since I'd made it this far. If the Senate wanted me dead, their spy could have taken me out any time in the past six months.

I glanced across the huge room to where Tomas had entered. He stood near the door, technically obeying my request to keep away, but it wasn't nearly far enough to suit me. He was talking to one of the chamber guards, a matched set of four six-foot blonds who looked like they'd walked out of a medieval tapestry, complete with battle-axes slung across their wide backs and helmets with little nose guards. I noticed that he'd thrown a black denim jacket over his club wear; it matched the jeans but made him look like a motorcycle badass. His face was in shadow so I couldn't see his expression, but it probably wouldn't have told me anything. At least, nothing I wanted to see.

It was creepy how I had to fight not to go to him, how I desperately wanted to see him light up for me the way he never did for other people, to hear him say that everything was going to be okay. I knew what he was, knew how he'd lied, yet part of me still wanted to trust him. I hoped it was only a lingering effect of the earlier mental invasion, and told myself to get over it. My eyes were going to have to get used to the fact that he might look like my Tomas, but he wasn't; the man I'd thought I knew had never existed outside my imagination.

I dragged my attention back to the main event, which shouldn't have been as hard as it was, considering the display. A thick mahogany slab had been carved into a massive rectangular table that, other than the row of seats along the far side, was the only furniture in the room. It looked like it weighed about a ton and was raised on an equally mammoth black marble platform reached by a set of gleaming steps. It lifted the Senate a good three feet above where lowly petitioners, or prisoners in my case, were allowed to stand. The rest of the room—or cavern, since I found out later it was several levels belowground—was carved out of red sandstone and painted with jumping flames by huge black iron chandeliers. The mirror propped up on the left of the table was a discordant, ugly note, but only because it currently reflected Tony's face. Other than that, the decorations consisted of the bright banners and coats of arms of the Senate members that hung behind each of their seats. Four of those shields were draped in black, and the heavy, brocaded chairs in front of them were turned to the wall. That didn't look good.

"I demand compensation!" I turned my attention back to Tony, who was repeating his demand for at least the fifth time. He belongs to the "reiterate your point until they give in" school of debate, mainly because he hasn't had a lot of practice. No one in his family ever does anything but bow and scrape and, after hundreds of years of that kind of thing, it dulls a person's edge. "I took her in, brought her up, treated her as one of our own, and she deceived me! I have every right to demand her heart!"

I could have pointed out that, since I wasn't a vamp, staking me was a little overkill, ha-ha, but preferred to concentrate on more important issues. Not that I thought the Senate would care about Tony's business arrangements, but it was a rare chance to tell off the slimeball and I wasn't about to miss it. "You had my parents killed so you could monopolize my talent. You told me my visions were helping you avoid the disasters I saw and were being passed on to warn others, while all the time you were profiting off them. You're mad that I cost you some money? If I ever get close enough, I'll cut off your head." I said it matter-of-factly since killing Tony was an old dream and not one I had much chance of fulfilling.

Tony didn't seem too upset about my outburst, which was what I'd expected. People had been threatening him for centuries, but he was still here. He'd told me once that survival was a more eloquent answer to his detractors than any other, and I suppose it still was. "She has no proof that I had anything to do with that unfortunate business. Am I to sit here and be insulted?"

"I Saw it!"

I turned to the Senate leader, officially called the Consul, intending to plead my case, but she was petting a cobra large enough to wrap twice around her body, which I found pretty distracting. It looked tame, but I kept an eye on it anyway. The vamps tend to forget that what would be annoying for them, like a bite from a poisonous snake, would be a bit more serious for the mortals who worked with them. Those of us who survived long enough learned to be real observant.

"The woman is delusional," Tony was protesting, spreading his chubby white hands innocently. "She has always been dangerously unstable."

"Then I am surprised you relied on her predictions."

The Consul's voice slithered around the room, almost a tangible presence against my skin. I shivered just from the overflow of her power, and was thankful it wasn't directed at me. At least not yet. She didn't dress in flowing white linen and gold headdresses anymore, but I guess when you're that strong, you don't need to show off. I wasn't disappointed, though, considering that her outfit consisted mostly of multicolored snakes slithering and twining over her so thickly that only occasionally a patch of bare skin showed. Their scales caught the torchlight and shimmered like she was clothed in living jewels: onyx, jade and emerald, with the occasional flash of ruby eyes. It was more than the outfit that commanded attention, though; the authority in her voice and the intelligence in those dark eyes showed that, in some ways, she was still a queen. I hadn't recognized her and no one had bothered to introduce themselves, but Rafe, at my back for moral support, I guess, had whispered a name in my ear as we approached the table. At my startled look, teeth had flashed in his dark beard as he gave me his usual rakish smile. "It wasn't an asp that bit her, *mia stella*."

"I did not rely on her," Tony was lying smoothly. "She was a convenience only."

Rafe's hand on my arm tightened, and I bit my lip. Repeated outbursts might annoy the Consul—not a smart move—but it was hard to stay silent. I had no idea how much money I'd made the little toad through the years, but it was a lot. I knew for a fact that he'd cleared at least ten million when he bought citrus futures right before a series of natural disasters wrecked the California orange crop and caused the price to skyrocket. That didn't happen every day, but it wasn't an isolated incident, either.

Tony's moneygrubbing had never been my main problem with him, though. The thing that caused me to snap, besides finding out about my parents, was his decision to let fire ravage a city block because he wanted to buy some real estate in the area cheap. I had told him about it a week in advance, plenty of time for him to have called in a warning, but of course he hadn't. I'd stared in horror at newspaper photos of charred children's bodies and had one of those lightbulb moments. Some checking had confirmed what I already suspected: he'd used my talent to help him plan assassinations, mastermind political coups and successfully run drugs and illegal weapons past the authorities. And those were just the things I knew about. The day I finally put all the pieces together, I'd promised myself that, somehow, I would make him pay. He had, too, but in my opinion, not nearly enough.

"Then she should be no great loss. You will be remunerated for your claim."

"Consul, with all due respect, the only thing I want is for her to be returned to me. I am her rightful master, as I am sure my own will agree."

"No." The dark gaze slid to me momentarily, and I suddenly knew what a rabbit feels when it looks up and sees a hawk. "We have plans for her."

Tony blustered on, and I began to notice that Alphonse wasn't making any effort to help his beleaguered employer. My estimation of his intelligence took a hike. If Tony argued himself into a belated grave—permanently this time—Alphonse would get a chance to seize control of the operation, and that worked for me. Alphonse and I weren't exactly friends, but as far as I knew, he had no reason to want me dead besides the fact that Tony had ordered it. I grinned; keep talking, Tony. Unfortunately, one of the two huge vamps in leopard-skin loincloths that framed the Consul's chair came forward and removed the mirror after a minute. Too bad; I'd started to enjoy myself.

Pressure from Rafe's hand warned me to keep a blank expression. Just as it wasn't a good idea to show fear or weakness in a court situation—and this was pretty much the court of courts—it also wasn't bright to show too much amusement. Somebody might take it as a challenge, and that would be very bad. I quickly readjusted my expression to the poker face I'd used growing up. It wasn't hard: the little joy I'd been able to summon would have died anyway when I turned back to the Senate. With no more Tony around to distract them, everyone's attention was suddenly on me, and it was unnerving, even to someone who had regularly attended family meetings. Tony had insisted, after his resident telepath was turned and lost her powers, that I be there, especially if rival families were going to send reps. I don't know why. I can't read minds and the odds of my Seeing something about anyone present were slim. I'd told him a hundred times, I can't switch on the gift like turning on a TV, and when it does come, I don't get to choose the channel. He'd ignored me, maybe because he liked the prestige of having his personal clairvoyant at his side like a trained dog. Anyway, after the number of very frightening people

Karen Chance

I'd seen, I had thought nothing could impress me. I'd been wrong.

Besides the Consul's, there were twelve places at the table. More than half were empty, but the ones that were filled made up for it. A dark-haired woman sat nearest to me, dressed in a long velvet gown. A little cap decorated with pearls as big as my thumb framed her face, and heavy gold embroidery traced its way up her burgundy skirts. Her skin had the opalescent sheen of naturally pale skin that hasn't seen the sun in centuries, and was marred only by a ridge of scar tissue around her throat that a silk ribbon didn't quite conceal. Someone had gotten close enough to this beauty to take her head but hadn't heard that this alone won't kill a vamp. If the heart is intact, the body will mend, although I winced at the amount of effort it must have taken to heal a wound like that.

Next to her sat the only person at the table I recognized. I could hardly fail to do so since Tony boasted about his connection to the famous Dracula line at every opportunity, and had portraits of all three brothers on the wall of his throne room. He had been made not by Vlad III Tepes, the Dracula of legend, but by the great man's elder brother, Mircea. We'd entertained him in Philly when I was eleven. Like many children, I loved a good story, which was lucky since there was little Mircea liked better than to go on about the bad old days. He'd told me how, when his younger brothers Vlad and Radu were in Adrianople as hostages—the Ottoman sultan didn't trust their father to honor a treaty otherwise—Mircea encountered a vengeful gypsy. She hated his father for seducing and then throwing aside her sister, who'd been Dracula's mother, so she cursed Mircea with vampirism. I think the idea was to end the family line, since a vampire can't father children and everybody had assumed that the hostages weren't coming back. But, as Mircea pointed out, she actually did him a favor. Shortly thereafter, Hungarian assassins working with some local nobles captured, tortured and buried him alive, something that might have been a real downer if he hadn't already been dead. Under the circumstances, it was more an inconvenience than anything else.

I'd been too young when I met him to realize that the handsome young man who told me Romanian folk tales was actually older than Tony by about a century. He sent me an encouraging smile now out of a face that had looked thirty for five hundred years. I smiled back in spite of myself; I'd had my first crush on those brown velvet eyes, and I'd forgotten how attractive he was. Those same features had won his longer-lived brother Radu the title of "the Handsome" back in the sixteenth century. Mircea paused to brush a speck of lint off his snazzy black suit. Other than Rafe, who preferred more casual chic, Mircea was the only vamp I knew who cared much about modern fashion. Maybe that was why I'd never seen him wearing the court regalia of old Wallachia, or possibly the clothes then had just sucked. In any case, he looked completely up-to-date now, except for the long, black ponytail. I was glad to see him, but even assuming he remembered me fondly, I doubted one vote would do me much good.

Speaking of a need to update a wardrobe, the vamp next to Mircea—the same one who had been loitering around the waiting room—looked like a *GQ* ad, if the magazine had been printed in the seventeenth century. Considering that I'd spent a lot of time in a Goth club, I didn't object to the embroidered frock coat, frothy shirt and knee britches he was wearing. I'd seen weirder getups, and at least this one was flattering—silk hose shows off legs better than most modern styles, and his were worth playing up. The sticking point was that the whole deal was in buttercup yellow satin. I'm sorry, but a vamp in yellow is just wrong, especially when you throw in bright blue eyes and glossy auburn curls cascading halfway down his back. He was very handsome, with one of those open, honest faces you automatically trust. It really irritated me that it belonged to a vamp. I gave him a tentative smile anyway on the theory that it couldn't hurt, and thought maybe I'd get a brownie point for being the only other one in yellow in the room. Of course, my happy-face T wasn't looking its best at the moment, which maybe explains why he didn't smile back. He was watching me almost hungrily, the weight of his gaze so intense that I spared a thought to hope he'd already eaten. I needed to get this blood off me before I started looking to someone like a walking hors d'oeuvre.

The remaining vamps, two on the far side of the Consul, were so alike that I assumed they had to be related. I found out later that it was a coincidence. The man was almost as old as the Consul, having started life as one of Nero's body-guards even though his mother had been a slave captured somewhere much farther north than Italy. He'd been one of the emperor's favorites for having even more sadistic tastes than his master: want to guess who really burned Rome? The woman, who looked so much like Portia that I did a double take, had been born in the antebellum South. She was said to have killed more Union soldiers in the twenty miles or so around her family home than the Confederate military did, and to have mourned the end of the war and the easy hunting that had gone with it. So, different eras, countries and backgrounds, but they looked like twins with their milky complexions and wavy dark hair. They even had similar eye color, a light brownish gold, like the light through autumn leaves, and were dressed in complementary outfits of white and silver. Admittedly, his was a toga while she looked like she was on her way to a Savannah ball, but they looked good together.

The Consul gave me time to size everyone up before she spoke, but when she did, I had no desire to look anywhere else. Wherever her kohl-rimmed gaze landed, it felt like tiny pinpricks along my skin. The sensation was not quite painful, but I had the impression that the pins could become

swords very easily. "You see how many of our seats are
empty, how many voices silenced." I blinked in surprise. I'd
assumed there was a problem, but not that—four ancient
vampires aren't exactly easy to kill. But she confirmed it.
"We are greatly weakened. The loss of some of the greatest
among us is felt keenly by all in this room, but if it contin-
ues, it will echo around the world."

She stopped, and at first I thought it was for a dramatic
pause, but then she zoned out on me. Some of the really old
ones do that sometimes, drawing into themselves for a
minute or an hour or a day, and forgetting that anyone else
exists. I'd gotten used to little time-outs with Tony, so I
didn't let it bother me. I noticed that Tomas had been joined
at the door by yet another guy I didn't know. What looked
like a life-sized statue stood near him, a rather crude one
with no paint to cover its clay exterior and poorly defined
features. Tomas and the new guy seemed to be arguing about
something, but their voices were too low to hear. I had a
brief moment of nostalgia for Tony's audience hall, where
most of those present were murderous scumbags, but at least
I knew their names. I was jumpy enough standing in blood-
soaked clothing in front of a group of vamps powerful
enough to kill me with little more than a thought, without
also having to work in the dark. Rafe was a comfort at my
back, but I'd have preferred someone whose specialty was
more in the guns-and-knives line.

"We are missing six of our number," the Consul abruptly
continued. "Four are irrecoverable, and two others hover on
the edge of the abyss. If any power known to us can restore
them, it will be done. But it may well be that we strive in
vain, for our enemy has lately obtained a new weapon,
which can undo us at our very conception." I resisted the
urge to glance back at Rafe, whom I hoped was following
this better than I was. Maybe he could fill me in later if the
Consul never got around to making sense.

"Tomas, attend us." She had barely finished speaking

before Tomas appeared beside me. "Can she be of use?" He was resolutely not looking at me. I wanted to yell at him, to ask what kind of coward couldn't even hold my gaze while he betrayed me, but Rafe's fingers tightened almost painfully and I regained control.

"I believe so. She occasionally speaks when there seems to be no one there, and tonight . . . I cannot explain what happened to one of the assassins. There were five. I killed three, and her ward dealt with another; but as for the last . . ."

"Tomas, don't." I definitely did not want him to finish that sentence. It would not be good if the Senate decided I was a threat, and if they found out about the exploding vamp, they might feel a tad on edge. How can even an ancient master fight against something she can't see or feel? Of course, Portia's intervention had been a fluke—I don't go around with an army of ghosts and I sure as hell can't command any that I meet up with to fight for me—but there was no way the Senate could know that. I somehow doubted they'd take my word. Most ghosts are too weak to do what Portia's friends had managed; she must have called every active spirit in the cemetery and, even working together, they had barely had enough power. It wasn't something I could duplicate, but if the Senate didn't believe that, it could get me killed.

Tomas' jaw tightened, but he didn't look at me. Big surprise. "I am not sure how the last assassin died. Cassandra must have killed it, but I did not see how." That was true, but he had definitely seen frozen vamp parts all over the aisle, and there weren't a lot of ways they could have gotten there. I was surprised he'd hedged his reply for me, but it didn't matter. One glance at the Consul was enough to show that she wasn't fooled.

Before she could call him on it, the short blond who'd been eavesdropping from the doorway suddenly darted around the guards and ran towards us. I wasn't worried; it was easy to see by the way he moved and the suntan on his cheeks that this was no vampire. Two of the guards followed, so quickly that they were just smears of color against the red sandstone walls, then overtook him. They reached us first and put themselves between Rafe and me and the newcomer, although they didn't try to restrain him. In fact, they seemed more interested in keeping an eye on me.

"I will speak, Consul, and you had best instruct your servants not to lay hands on me unless you wish to escalate this to war!" The blond's booming voice was well-educated British, but his outfit didn't match it. His hair was the only normal thing about him—close cropped and without noticeable style. But his T-shirt was crossed with enough ammunition to take out a platoon, and he had a tool belt slung low on his hips that, along with a strap across his back, looked like it carried one of every type of handheld weapon on the market. I recognized a machete, two knives, a sawed-off shotgun, a crossbow, two handguns—one strapped to his thigh—and a couple of honest-to-God grenades. There were other things I couldn't identify, including a row of cork-topped bottles along the front of the belt. The getup, sort of mad scientist meets Rambo, would have made me smile, except that I believe in showing respect for someone carrying that much hardware.

"You are here on sufferance, Pritkin. Do not forget that." The Consul sounded bored, but several of her snakes hissed in the guy's direction.

The man sneered, and his bright green eyes were scornful. I wondered if he had a death wish, and pressed back against Rafe. His arms slid around my waist and I felt a little better. "She is not vampire—you have no right to speak for her!"

"That can easily be remedied." I jumped as a low, sibilant voice spoke in my ear. I twisted in Rafe's grip to see a tall, cadaverous vamp with greasy black hair and glittering beetle eyes bending towards me. I'd met him only once before, and we hadn't gotten along. I somehow didn't think this time would be any different.

Jack, still sometimes called by his famous nickname, had had an abrupt end to his early career in the streets of London when he met Senate member Augusta, one of those missing at the moment, while she was on a European vacation. She showed him what a truly ripping good time was before bringing him over. He had been promoted to the Senate only recently, but had served as their unofficial torturer almost since she made him. He'd come to Philly to do some free-lance work once and hadn't liked that Tony refused to throw me in as a bonus for a job well done. I'd been relieved not to see him in the Senate chamber when I arrived, and there was no entrance on that side of the room. But figuring out where he'd come from was not as big a priority as wonder-ing why his lips were curled back and his long, dingy fangs fully extended.

Rafe jerked me away and Tomas shifted to be able to watch both new arrivals. Before things got more interesting, the Consul intervened. "Sit down, Jack. She belongs to Lord Mircea, as you know." Mircea smiled at me, apparently un-fazed. Either he trusted Jack a lot more than I did, or the fact that he was Tony's master, and by vampire law mine as well, didn't mean much to him. I was betting on the latter, know-ing my luck.

Jack backed away, but he didn't like it. He gave a whine like a child deprived of a treat as he assumed his seat. "She looks like a slut."

"Better than like an undertaker." It was true—his heavy Victorian clothes would have looked perfectly at home in a funeral parlor—but that wasn't why I said it. I'd learned early that fear was power, and I was deathly afraid of Jack. Even in life he'd been a monster; now he was the sort that even vamps gave a wide berth. But I wasn't going to give him the advantage of knowing how he affected me. Not to mention that terror was an aphrodisiac to him—Tony had said that he actually preferred his victims' fright to their pain—and I wouldn't give him the pleasure. He bared his fangs at me again in response. It could have been a smile, but I doubted it.

"The mages do not have a monopoly on honor, Pritkin," the Consul continued, ignoring Jack and me like we were two naughty children acting up in front of a guest. "We will keep our agreement with them if they keep theirs with us."

I started, and gave the man—no, the mage—another look. I'd met mages before, but only renegades who occasionally did jobs for Tony. They had never impressed me much. Most of them had serious addictions to one illegal substance or another—a by-product of living constantly under a death threat—and their habit had Tony's blessing since it kept them eager for work. But I'd never before seen one in good standing, especially not a Circle member, if that's what he was. Tony feared both the Silver Circle and the Black, so I'd always been curious about them. The rumors that circulated about the Silver Circle, whose members supposedly practiced only white magic, were scary, but the Black wasn't talked about at all. When even vamps find a group too daunting to gossip about, it's probably best to avoid it. I wondered which type he was, but there was no sign or insignia that I could see anywhere on that weird getup.

He gestured at me. "She is human and a magic user; that makes her fate ours to decide." He flexed his hands as if he'd like to grab something, maybe a weapon, maybe me, maybe both. "Give her to me and I swear you will never have reason to regret it."

Mircea was regarding him the way a good housewife looks at a bug crawling across her newly cleaned kitchen floor. "But Cassie might, would she not?" he asked in his usual mild voice. I'd never heard him raise it, although he'd stayed with Tony for almost a year.

The Consul looked as cool as a bronze statue, but a wave

of power fluttered by me, like a warm summer breeze with tiny drops of acid in it. I flinched and resisted the urge to wipe at my skin. If the mage noticed it, he gave no sign. "We have yet to determine who has the better claim, Pritkin."

"There is nothing to discuss. The Pythia wants the rogue returned to her. I have been sent to fetch her, and by our treaty you have no right to interfere. She belongs with her people."

I had no idea what he was talking about but thought it strange that he seemed so concerned with my future. I'd never met him before in my life and it didn't help my confusion that none of the mages who came to Tony's had ever given me a second glance. As merely the vampire's pet clairvoyant, I'd been beneath contempt. It had annoyed me that outcasts with no more status in the magical community than I had treated me like a charlatan at a carnival. But at the moment I'd gladly take a little scornful indifference. The whole session was beginning to feel like a bunch of dogs fighting over a bone, with me as the bone. I didn't like it, but there wasn't a lot I could do about it.

"She belongs with those who can best defend her and her gift." The Consul did serene well. I wondered if it was natural talent or if her two-thousand-odd years of life had helped teach her composure. Maybe both. "I find it interesting, Pritkin, that your Circle now speaks of protecting her. Not so long ago you asked our help in finding her, dead or alive, with the implication being that the former was preferable."

The blond's eyes flashed dangerously. "Do not presume to put words in the mouth of the Circle! You don't understand the danger. Only the Circle can protect her, and protect others from her." For the first time he looked directly at me, and the snarl on his face would have bared fangs if he'd been a vamp. As it was, it told me I had another enemy to worry about. His gaze flicked over me like a whip, and he didn't seem to like what he saw. "She has been allowed to mature unschooled, cut off from everyone who could have taught her control. It is a recipe for disaster."

I met those narrowed green eyes and something that looked almost like fear crossed over them for a second. His hand moved to the knife in a sheath on his wrist, and for a moment, I actually thought he was going to throw it at me. Rafe must have thought so, too, for he tensed, but the Consul's voice cut in before anyone could move. "The Silver Circle was once great, Pritkin. Do you tell us that you cannot protect one of your own merely because she roams beyond the fold? Have you become so weak?"

His face darkened with anger and his hand continued to fondle the knife, although it stayed in its little leather holder. I looked into those crystalline green eyes and suddenly the picture came together. I knew who, or at least what, he was. The Silver Circle was said to have a group of mages who were trained in combat techniques, both human and magical, who enforced their will. The mages at Tony's had been scared to death of them because they were authorized to kill rogue magic users on sight. Mages who pissed off the Circle weren't allowed ever to use magic again; if they did and were discovered, it was a death sentence. But why had the Silver Circle sent a freaking war mage after me? Most people even in the magical community treat clairvoyants like shysters with no more ability than a Halloween witch; we don't even register on the radar for them. But the fact that there are a lot of con artists doesn't mean that some of us aren't real. I wondered if the Circle had finally come to that conclusion, too, and decided to start eliminating rivals to their power, beginning with me. It sounded like my kind of luck.

If the mage attacked me while I was under the Senate's protection, I was pretty sure they could kill him and get away with it. Even the Silver Circle couldn't protest the death of one of their members if he'd brought it on himself. The odds were good, then, that he wouldn't kill me, but I still sent Tomas a glare. He could have given back my gun once we'd arrived. It wasn't like I could hurt any of the Senate with it, even if I was crazy enough to try, and it would have been a comfort. Especially if he'd planned on letting war mages come in armed to the teeth.

"She already bears our greatest ward. She drew strength from all of us tonight; it was not only your vampire who saved her!"

"No, it was a joint effort, as this entire enterprise must be," GQ cut in smoothly. I was surprised that anyone dared to speak for the Consul, but no one challenged him or even seemed to find it odd. Maybe the Senate was a democratic bunch, but if so, they'd be the first vamps I knew who fit that category. The hierarchy at Tony's was based on strength, with "might makes right" pretty much the only rule. The other families were the same, as far as I knew. The Senate ruled because they were strong enough to scare even vamps like Tony, which meant the redhead couldn't be as harmless as he looked, or they'd have eaten him alive years ago.

To my surprise, GQ acknowledged that I was in the room instead of simply talking about me like I was a stick of furniture. "Allow me to introduce myself. I am Louis-César," he said and executed a damn good bow. *"A votre service, mademoiselle."* His eyes were intent as he looked at me, but he'd toned it down some. I no longer had the impression that I might be on the menu.

Unlike most twenty-first-century females, I know the proper response to a formal bow. Both the governess and chief tutor Tony assigned me had been born in the Victorian era, so I can curtsy with the best of them. I thought I'd forgotten most of that early training, but something about Louis-César made it come flooding back. He missed the no doubt amusing sight of me trying to live up to nanny's standards in blood-spattered four-inch go-go boots and a micro-mini because he was looking at the Consul again.

I was so focused on the scene at the high table that I completely failed to notice the second attempt on my life that night. My first clue was when a wave of power hit me like a sandstorm had blown up out of nowhere. Hot, stinging flecks scoured my cheeks for a second, before Tomas shoved Rafe aside and tackled me, hard enough to knock the breath out of my lungs when we slammed into the floor. I was faceup, which allowed me to see two of the chamber guards standing immobile in the middle of the room, their flesh slowly evaporating from their bones like it was being eaten off by invisible insects. A second later, the bare skeletons crashed to the floor, hearts and brains having disappeared along with the rest of their soft tissue.

I barely saw what happened next because none of it was at normal human speed, and Pritkin was in my way. He was beside me in a crouch with a wicked-looking knife in one hand and a gun in the other. Another knife and a couple of small vials hovered in the air beside his head, as if held by invisible strings. For a second, I thought he'd decided to take me out with the whole Senate watching, but he wasn't looking at me. The statue I'd seen by the door earlier was suddenly beside us. Despite the fact that it had only vague indentations for eyes, it seemed to be looking at Pritkin as if awaiting orders. I recognized what it was now that I saw it move, although I'd never seen one before. Golems had been feared by the wizards Tony employed only slightly less than the war mages. They were clay figures brought to life by ancient Hebrew Kabbalah magic. Originally, they ran errands for rabbis strong enough to create them. Maybe some still did, but these days most served the knights, as the war mages were properly called.

Pritkin pointed to me and the golem turned its blank stare in my direction. "Protect her!" The golem took his place, its empty eyes fixed on me, while its master joined the fight. I looked away from the creature, which was creeping me out more than the assassins, to see Jack rounding off against one of the remaining guards. The guard was growling, low in his throat like an animal, but Jack looked like a kid on Christmas morning, all flushed cheeks and bright eyes. He waved Pritkin off with an impatient gesture that clearly said, *This one's mine.*

The other guard was out of the picture, clawing at his chest where blood was welling up around the rapier that had been thrust completely through him, as if his heavy chain mail wasn't even there. Its blade stuck almost a foot out of his back, glinting a dull red in the flickering light of the chandeliers. I'd always thought rapiers were dainty, almost effeminate things when I'd seen them in the movies, but apparently I'd been wrong. This one had a wicked blade, as if a double-edged dagger had been stretched out to an inch wide and three feet long. As I fought to get a breath, Louis-César pulled it out of the vamp's chest and, in the same, flowing motion, decapitated him. It was done with a liquid speed that fooled my eyes for a moment into believing he'd missed. Then the head fell off the neck and bounced across the floor.

The vamp's eyelids were fluttering and his fangs were bared when his head rolled to a halt not a foot away from me, its helmet miraculously still on. I swear the mouth moved, snapping on empty air as if trying to reach my neck, even as his life's blood spread around him in a widening stain. I must have been making some type of strangled noise, or else the golem perceived the head as a threat, because it quickly kicked it away. That would have been nice, except that it overestimated the weight and sent it sailing across the Senate table to thud wetly against the wall behind the belle's careful coiffure.

A trail of blood marred the shining tabletop in front of her and a spray of droplets descended on her hair, where they sparkled like tiny rubies. She fished the head out from under the table and politely offered it to her companion, who equally politely declined. He was busy cleaning up the table by holding his hand over the spilled blood. Droplets flew up to meet his palm like they were iron and he was a magnet. As with Tomas earlier, they disappeared into his skin like lotion. "This sort of thing is getting tiresome," he said conversationally, and the belle nodded in between licks of the glistening spine that peeped out of the ruined neck of her prize.

I had to close my eyes for a moment and fight to keep my stomach in place, but at least I wasn't screaming. First, it wouldn't have looked strong in front of the Senate, and that would be bad. Second, my throat was still raw from almost getting strangled earlier. Third, I couldn't get enough air, thanks to Tomas' weight. I tried to shift him to one side, but it was like trying to move a marble statue. He only pressed down harder until I cried out in pain; then his body softened, melting against me like a warm satin comforter. It might have been soothing except that I couldn't breathe deeply or move, and Jack and the other guard had danced dangerously close.

I didn't understand why no one had killed the guard, especially since he had drawn his huge battle-axe and was looking at me with the single-minded concentration most guys reserve for the Playboy channel. If the Senate wanted me dead, wouldn't it have been easier to let Tony do it for them? And if they didn't, why wasn't Louis-César doing an encore of his previous performance instead of simply standing there? Maybe he figured the guard would never get past Pritkin, Rafe and Tomas, but I wasn't so sure. The axe blade looked awfully sharp to me, and I knew how fast vamps could move. All the guard needed was a split second and I would be the main course for Miss Georgia 1860 whenever she finished her appetizer. But no one did anything except for Tomas, and he merely crawled higher up my body, to the point that he would have been able to give a detailed report on the lace pattern in my bra if he'd been asked. He looked calm, but I could feel his heart jumping against my skin. It wasn't comforting to know that he was worried, too.

I looked past his dark head to where flames from the candles were dancing along the axe's huge blade, which was all of about four yards away. As I stared, the guard lunged towards me, gnashing his teeth like a cornered tiger, and it was all over as suddenly as it had started. Jack was a streak of ugly, dark green fabric and a flash of pale hands. I blinked, and the guard was on the ground, his limbs pinned down by four large knives buried through his flesh in the underlying stone. Two of them were substantial things with old wood handles, like they might once have been kitchen implements. The others were the shiny silver pieces belonging to the mage, who called them back to him with a gesture once Jack was in control of the captive. They tore out of the vamp with an audible ripping sound and flew to him, one settling into the wrist sheath and the other disappearing down his boot. He hadn't even bothered to use the ones at his waist. He and the golem moved off to allow Tomas to haul me to my feet. Although he'd just helped save my life, his eyes were cold when he looked at me, like chips of green ice.

The Consul appeared unruffled by the disturbance, but a tiny frown marred her otherwise perfect face. "Be careful, Jack. I want answers, not a corpse."

Jack smiled beatifically up at her. "You'll have both," he promised and bent towards the body. I quickly looked away but heard the sounds of ripping flesh and popping bones. I guessed that he'd retrieved his knives, breaking the limbs of his victim in the process. I swallowed hard several times. I'd forgotten how interesting court life could be.

"As I was saying, madame, *la mademoiselle* is obviously unwell. Perhaps we could explain things to her after she has had a chance to rest?" Louis-César spoke as casually as if the events of the last few minutes had never happened. Meanwhile Jack had taken a set of gleaming surgical tools from a case he'd pulled out of a pocket. He lined them up slowly by the side of his struggling victim, giving a soft, hissing laugh as he did so. Great; at least someone was having fun.

"We do not have the time to waste, Louis-César, as you know."

"*Ma chère madame*, we have all the time in the world . . . now." They exchanged a look, but I couldn't interpret it. "If I may suggest, I could explain to Mademoiselle Palmer our dilemma and report back before dawn. That would give you time to complete the . . . interrogation." He gave me a glance, and my panic at the thought of being alone with a guy who'd just shish-kebabed a powerful vamp must have shown. He quickly added, "Raphael may accompany us, of course."

I didn't like the fact that he could read me so easily, but knowing I'd have a friend along did make me feel better. At least until I saw Jack start to pull a long, gleaming cord of intestines out of the vamp's now open gut, draping them like a string of sausages over his arm. He paused to lick his fingers like a kid with ice cream, then glanced up and gave me a wink. The skin between my shoulders crawled like it would like to creep off somewhere else. I decided I wasn't going to enjoy this conversation no matter who was involved.

Chapter 4

It was finally decided that Louis-César, Rafe and Mircea would accompany me to my room and fill me in. Pritkin didn't like it, but he wasn't prepared to challenge the Consul's decision. Considering that it would have meant facing her in a duel, I was relieved to hear it. I'd had about all the fighting I could stand for one night; besides, I didn't know what would happen if a war mage of the Silver Circle went up against a two-thousand-year-old vampire, but it wasn't a show I wanted to see.

I was thankful that two out of three of my companions were friends or at least friendly neutrals, but it made me anxious, too. The Senate was acting suspiciously nice, defending me against would-be assassins, not handing me over to Tony or the Circle, clucking over my health and making sure that my companions were ones I would like. It made me wonder what they wanted, and how much I wasn't going to enjoy giving it to them.

Barely a minute later, I wasn't so sure giving up my bodyguard had been a good idea after all. We were about halfway up a second flight of stairs when we met a werewolf on the way down. He was a huge gray and black specimen with the characteristic long muzzle and mouth full of razor-sharp teeth. Chartreuse eyes locked with mine for a second, and I froze, one foot halfway to the next step. I'd seen only one werewolf before, and never this close, but I knew instinctively what he was. It was more than his size; there was intelligence in those eyes that no animal would have had. What I couldn't figure out was what he was doing there.

To say that vamps and weres don't get along is a laughable understatement. Maybe it has something to do with them both being predators, or maybe Tony was right when he insisted that weres envy the vamps their immortality. Whatever the cause, they're like oil and water. Or more often, blood and fur, both of which go flying when they meet up. I expected a reaction, probably a severe one, from one or more of my escorts, but the only thing I noticed was Rafe's hand tightening slightly on my wrist. Louis-César nodded a greeting at the were as if he regularly met giant wolves in the stairway. "Sebastian, good to see you." The were didn't respond, of course, since he was in animal form, but he slipped by us without offering challenge. It was a seriously surreal experience. It also told me I wasn't in Kansas anymore, or Atlanta, either, for that matter.

As we emerged from the stairs to the aboveground areas, I finally got a glimpse out a window and confirmed that, wherever I was, it wasn't north Georgia. The view also explained why the Consul was worried about time. I must have lost more hours than I'd thought after Tomas bespelled me, enough for me to be moved, and not merely across the state. The colors outside the window were a different palette than you could see anywhere in Georgia: the dappled greens and grays of the deep South had been replaced by midnight blue skies and indigo clouds. A black, star-studded canopy stretched overhead, but the line of deep violet along the horizon showed that the desert was beginning to remember the day.

"It will be dawn soon."

Louis-César followed my gaze as he threw open a door. "Not for some time yet," he replied easily. I narrowed my eyes at the offhand tone. Even Rafe, old as he was, became uptight as dawn approached, with a tendency to talk too

much and to drop things. The younger the vamp, the earlier
it started. It was sort of a built-in security net to make sure
no one ended up getting fried, and I had never seen anyone
left completely unaffected. Yet the Frenchman seemed perfectly at ease. He was either a lot more powerful than the
vamps I knew or a great actor; either way, it didn't make me
feel better.

I walked past him and found myself standing in the living area of a suite decorated to match what I imagined the
daytime view out the windows would be. Pale turquoise
walls were clothed in Native American blankets in burnt
umber, turquoise and Navajo red, a matching rug had been
flung over the rough wood floor and terracotta tile outlined
the fireplace. The leather sofa, chair and ottoman were a
complimentary shade of deep red, with enough wear on
them to look comfortable. It was an oddly cheerful room;
apparently, the Senate didn't share Tony's love of the
Gothic.

"Please, *mademoiselle, asseyez-vous.*" Louis-César moved
to stand beside the overstuffed armchair near the fireplace. I
glanced at Rafe, but he stood resolutely looking out over the
view, what there was of it. His hands were clasped together
tightly behind his back and his shoulders were tense. Yep,
right on schedule: dawn was coming. What I wanted was to
drag him off and get some straight answers, but even assuming he was in the mood for it, I wasn't given the chance.

Mircea put a light hand under my elbow, just enough of
a touch to guide me into the chair. "Louis-César will not sit
when a lady is standing, *dulceață.*" My dear one: his pet
term for me when I'd sat on his knee and listened to his stories. I hoped he meant it; if Rafe was my only friend in the
room, I was in trouble.

I plopped down and the Frenchman knelt in front of me.
He smiled reassuringly. I blinked. The man—no, the master
vampire—had dimples. Big ones. "I wish to attend to your
wound. If you permit?"

I nodded cautiously, not convinced that a vamp was the best person to clean off blood, especially one who had looked pretty hungry earlier. But the dried variety doesn't appeal to them and besides, it wasn't like I had a choice. He was being polite, asking my permission as if it mattered what I said, but I knew better. There were two Senate members in the room; they could play gentlemen as long as it amused them, but when it came down to it, I would do what they wanted. They knew it, and so did I.

Louis-César smiled approvingly and I suddenly realized why he was making me jumpy. This close, I could tell that he was one of the most human-looking vamps I'd ever seen. Barring Tomas, who'd had a reason to look as human as possible, most vamps forget little things like breathing, making their hearts beat and turning their skin a more believable color than new-fallen snow. Even Rafe, who was fairly convincing, usually remembered to blink only a few times an hour. But I could have passed this one on the street and mistaken for him for human, assuming he got a wardrobe change. I found myself counting the seconds between breaths to see if he missed any. He didn't.

Growing up I'd seen thousands of vamps from all over the world, some as flamboyant and otherworldly as the Consul and some as normal-looking as Rafe. Before today I would have sworn that I'd know one anywhere, but Tomas had fooled me at close quarters for months, and Louis-César could have done the same if he'd wanted. I didn't like that—it made me feel like a nonsensitive, like one of the millions with no protection from the supernatural world because they can't even sense that it's there. I'd grown up around vamps, but the power the Senate members radiated was like nothing I'd ever experienced. It had me wondering what else I was overlooking, and the thought made me cold.

Louis-César was examining my face slowly, I think more to give me a chance to get used to him than out of any real need. It didn't work. When a glossy brown curl, which had come loose from the cluster at his neck, brushed against my shoulder, I jumped as if he'd slapped me. His hand, which had been reaching for my hair, immediately stilled. "*Mille pardons, mademoiselle.* But perhaps you will pull your hair back for me? It would help to see the extent of the injury."

He handed me a golden clip that he'd pulled from his own hair. I took it, careful not to brush his fingers with mine. My hair was barely shoulder length, but I got most of it into a messy ponytail as he watched. I tried to talk myself out of the near panic attack I was having, but it didn't work. Some instinct older than reason, older than polite phrases spoken in well-lit rooms, wanted me to run and hide. Of course, that could have been a reaction to the night I was having, but part of me definitely didn't like him so close. I forced myself to sit still as he finished his examination, to pretend that my arms hadn't broken out in goose bumps and that my pulse wasn't racing through my veins like I was already fleeing for my life. I didn't understand my reaction, but harsh experience had taught me to trust my instincts, and every one I had was loudly begging me to get away. "*Ah, bon. Ce n'est pas très grave*," he murmured. Seeing my expression, he smiled, and it lit even his eyes. "It is not serious," he translated. I fought not to scream.

Louis-César rose and walked to a nearby table, and suddenly I could breathe again. I tried to figure out what there was about him that so alarmed me, but there was nothing tangible. His face, which was set in pleasant, friendly lines, looked to be that of a man maybe five or six years older than me, although if his clothes were anything to go by, he'd been around for centuries. His eyes were mild—a calm blue with flecks of gray that held no discernable attempt to influence me—and his movements, while graceful, were nothing a mere mortal couldn't have imitated. Admittedly, my nerves weren't in great shape—even I wasn't used to almost getting killed twice in the same night—but that didn't explain

why, out of all the possible candidates, it was Louis-César
who was freaking me out.

He returned, and my panic rose with every step he took.
I watched him the way a small animal does a predator, staying quiet, barely breathing, in hope that the big, bad thing
won't pounce. He knelt again in a puddle of gleaming satin
and lace, and the overhead lights glinted on a few strands of
auburn threaded through his hair. He'd brought back a first
aid kit, and he lined up an antiseptic, several gauze pads and
a packet of baby wipes on the tiles in front of the fireplace.
"I will clean the wound, *mademoiselle*, and bandage it for
you. A nurse will come tomorrow and improve on my
clumsy efforts." He was relaxed, even cheerful, but it took
every bit of self-control I had not to run for the door.

A pale, slender hand framed in cascading white lace en-
gulfed my filthy, blood-stained one. His fingers were cool
and his grip light, as if he thought his touch would give re-
assurance. It didn't. No matter how careful he was, I knew
that hold could tighten in an instant, trapping me as securely
as a steel handcuff. I felt the fingers of his other hand moving deftly over my scraped skin, then the barest brush of the
cloth as he began cleaning it. Although the antiseptic stung
only lightly, I shuddered and closed my eyes. I had a very
bad feeling that I knew what was coming.

"*Mademoiselle*, are you ill?" His voice came from a distance and echoed hollowly in my ears. I felt a familiar sense
of disorientation wash over me, and I fought it with everything I had. I struggled harder than ever before, trying to
push it back inside whatever part of me usually held it, begging it to go back to sleep. Whatever it wanted to show me,
I was absolutely certain I didn't want to See it. But, as ever,
the gift was stronger than I was; it always had been. I gave
in to the inevitable when I felt a cold chill settle on my face.
It wasn't cold in the sitting room, but part of me was no
longer there. I took a deep breath and opened my eyes.

The chill came from a window partially open to the night.

The breeze was nipping at my bare skin, raising goose bumps all along my exposed flesh. The window looked sort of like stained glass, except that there was no color and no pattern, other than small diamond shapes where its many panes had been joined together. The glass was thick and wavy, like in some of the historic houses in Philly, and it gave back only an indistinct reflection. But it was enough to make me begin to breathe faster.

I looked around in panic and my eyes lit on a mirror across the room. The image it returned was also dim, but more because of the faint light, which came from a few candles and a low-burning fire, than because of poor construction. In fact, it was a masterpiece of a mirror, huge, with a massive gilt frame, opulent like the rest of the heavy, carved-wood furniture. The room had a feeling of luxury about it: the dark cherry of the great four-poster bed gleamed with reflected flames from the marble fireplace, and echoed the color of the heavy velvet drapes of the canopy. The walls were stone, but hung with tapestries, their colors as bright and vibrant as if they had been completed only that day. A bouquet of deep-red roses sat on a nearby table in a painted porcelain bowl. I was in no mood to appreciate the scene, though, being far too distracted by the reflection in the mirror.

A man knelt on a bed approximately where I should have been. I couldn't tell who it was because a black velvet mask covered most of his face except for cutouts for the eyes. It looked comical, like part of a bad Halloween costume, but I didn't feel like laughing. Maybe because it was the only thing he wore. Long auburn curls hung below the velvet, sticking to his upper body, and in the candlelight they gleamed with strands of bronze and hints of gold. The warm, faintly golden light of the room drenched him, dripping down his skin from the muscular chest to the flat planes of his stomach and the slight indentation of his navel. It glistened on the tiny beads of sweat dewing his torso that the chill from the window had yet to dry, so he looked like he was wearing a transparent shirt strung with tiny diamonds. He was a gilt statue come to life, except that statues aren't generally rampantly erect. I swallowed and so did he, and the blue eyes in the mirror widened as realization hit.

But that was crazy, not to mention impossible. I didn't star in my visions. I was a watcher, off to the sidelines, as unseen and uninvolved as a ghost. Or, at least, I had been until tonight. Before I could even start to think what to do, I felt a warm hand close over me in a very personal place, and looked down in shock to find a brunette young woman lying beneath me, almost buried in the heap of blankets on the bed. The room smelled of sex, musty and heavy, and now I knew why.

A dainty little hand played over my—his—flesh with a sure touch. She stroked me again, harder this time, and I watched with something close to horror as an anatomical part I'd never possessed grew even longer under her hand. A flood of familiar sensations came from that very unfamiliar equipment, along with thoughts I was absolutely sure weren't mine. She flicked a fingernail over the rosy tip that had curved towards her and I almost screamed. Arousal had never felt like this. Of course, my experience wasn't exactly extensive, and it came from the other side of the coin, but this was almost unbearable. I was used to a languid heat that built slowly and spread from my core outwards along my veins, not this desperate need to thrust into her white body as deeply as I could.

She writhed in the blankets that lay thick and soft against our naked skin. "What is wrong, handsome one? Don't tell me you've lost interest already!" She sped up her pace and I suddenly found it hard to breathe. "You can manage a third; I know it."

My almost-trance broke when she moved closer, wetting her lips, and I flung myself back. I yelped in pain, both because she hesitated for a second before letting go, and from

my borrowed body's demand for release. It was so stimu-
lated it was painful, but I was in no way interested in what
was on offer. I honestly thought I was going to be sick as I
stared from her bemused expression to the undeniably male
form I was wearing. There are no words for what I was feeling—utter confusion and disbelief miss it by a hell of a lot.

My hands scrambled for the edge of the mask and yanked
it up. Staring at me from the mirror was Louis-César's face,
white with shock. I wanted to scream at him to make this
stop, to get out of me, but I knew it was the other way
around. Somehow, I had invaded him, and I had no idea how
I'd done it or how to undo it. The woman let out a shriek and
grabbed for the mask, tugging it out of my hand and trying
to put it back in place.

"Don't take risks, *monsieur*! You know how literal your
keepers can be—never take it off." She smiled up at me
wickedly. "Besides, I like it when you wear it while we
make love." She wrapped her arms around my neck and
tried to draw me down to her. "I'm cold without your heat.
Kiss me."

I jerked away from her and scrambled to the end of the
bed, wondering what would happen if I gave in to the black
fog at the edge of my vision and fainted. Would I wake up
back where I belonged, or was I stuck here? I decided to not
even think about that last possibility. After a moment, the
woman sighed and lay back on the bed, caressing her small
breasts lightly. Her nipples were very brown against the
white of her skin, and she watched me with a knowing
smile. "Are you tired, my love?" Her hand trailed lower, tangling in the dark hair of her groin, and she smirked. "I'll
wager I can revive you."

Before I could even try to persuade my overloaded brain
to think up an answer, the heavy oak door opened and a
middle-aged woman entered, flanked by four guards. Her
expression told me she hadn't come to join in, thank God.
"Get him up." Two of the guards dragged me out of the bed,

and the woman I'd recently gotten to know far too well shrieked and pulled the covers up to her chin.

"Marie! What are you doing? Get out this minute! Get out, get out!"

The older woman ignored her and looked at me, the scorn on her already unattractive face not improving her looks. Her eyes ran over me contemptuously. "Always ready, I see. You get that from your father." She glanced at the guards. "Bring him."

I was forced out of the room with no chance to get dressed. The brunette tossed me a heavy brocaded robe, which I slipped over the embarrassing evidence of my condition, but there was no time to get shoes or even trousers. The girl in the bed screeched strange obscenities after us, most directed at the older woman. It dawned on me that she was not speaking English, although I could understand her perfectly. Or maybe this body could, and was somehow translating for me. I had no time to wonder about it, since I was manhandled down a long stone corridor to a set of stairs. They had deep hollows in the center of each step, where thousands of feet had walked over hundreds of years. It was dark down there and the air coming up was freezing, to the point that I was surprised that I couldn't see my breath in front of my face.

The woman paused at the top of the stairs and turned to me. She didn't look scornful now; the emotion in her dark eyes was closer to fear. "I will go no farther. I have already seen what waits for you, and have no wish to do so again." Her expression changed to something like pity. "All your life, you have experienced the rewards that come from silence. Tonight you will learn the punishment for breaking it."

She turned away without another word and the guards started to muscle me towards that black hole. I was stronger in this body, but nowhere near enough to allow me to take on those guys. I looked wildly back at the woman, but she was already walking away, spine stiff and straight under her mulberry-colored dress. "Please! *Madame*! Why are you doing this? I have said nothing, I swear it!" The words weren't mine—they popped to my lips uninvited—and they didn't stop her.

"If you want to know who to credit with this night's work, ask your brother," she flung over her shoulder before disappearing into a room and shutting the door firmly behind her. It was a very final sound.

The stairs were too narrow for my captors to keep hold of my arms, but since they were behind me and there was nowhere to go but down, it didn't really matter. There was almost no light; only a few thin slivers of moonlight filtered in through ridiculously narrow windows as we descended. The steps were slick with damp, and the depression in the middle made it almost impossible to keep my footing, especially without shoes. I was also uncomfortably cold despite the robe, although at least that seemed to have gotten rid of any lingering arousal. But a very unfamiliar weight hung slack between my legs, an unwelcome and alien sensation that was doing more than anything else to make me want to start yelling and just not stop. I stubbed my toe about halfway down but was almost grateful for the pain; I was very close to losing it entirely, and the throbbing in my foot gave me something else to think about.

Torchlight flickered on the stairs as we finally came to the bottom, making shadows dance over everything and gleaming off the trails of liquid that seeped down the walls. Suddenly it was not chilly anymore; it was cold, intensely so, as if my blood had turned to ice in my veins. I was surprised not to see frost hugging the walls, but the damp trickles ran freely.

Far worse than the burning cold or the surroundings were the piteous wails that came from behind an iron-banded door a few yards ahead. They were soft, muffled by the thick wood, but they nonetheless hurt the mind. It was painful to hear voices so raw, so full of despair, and so sure that the

help they called for would never come. I instinctively tried
to back away, moving into a puddle of light cast by a nearby
sconce, when a rough hand shoved me forward. I stumbled,
striking my knees on the uneven stone of the floor.

"In there."

I was slow obeying the command, but a kick to my ribs
winded me and a rough hand pulled me upright. I looked
down and saw a man, balding, overweight, wearing a blood-
stained apron and rough, dirty wool trousers. At five foot
four, I'm not used to looking down at many men, and I
blinked at him in pain and confusion. Fleshy lips split into a
grin, showing a mouth full of gray teeth, and I flinched back.
That seemed to please him. "Good. Be afraid, *M'sieur le
Tour*. Remember, you're no prince tonight." He looked me
up and down. "Soon we'll see if you live up to your name.
Tonight, you're mine!"

A huge iron key was fitted into the lock, and the door
swung open. I had a brief glimpse of a large, square room
with thick stone walls and high ceilings before I was pushed
through. I fell again, this time onto filthy straw that stank of
urine and worse, and did little to soften the hard floor. Some
part of me was outraged at the way this crude man was treat-
ing me, but a moment later, all feelings besides horror
melted. I met the eyes of the emaciated, naked woman
stretched impossibly tight on a rack and I was unable to look
away. Blood had run in rivulets from her tortured body and
dried in thick, viscous rivers on her skin, and brown stains
covered the floor below her. There was so much blood, I
couldn't believe one body had held it all.

Men in chains along the walls were crying, begging me
to save them, but I barely noticed. All my attention was on
the woman, although she made no sound. The torchlight reflected in her open eyes, and I couldn't tell if it was a trick
of the light or if some life still burned in there. For her sake,
I hoped not. The man saw the direction of my stare and
walked over to her. "Yes, your friend won't be fun much

longer." He tested one of the ropes binding her hands, and I saw that her nails were missing. The ends of her fingers looked as if they had been shredded, or eaten away by some animal, and the knuckles were swollen so large that there was no way she could have closed her hands, even if she'd been free to do so.

I'd seen a lot at Tony's through the years, but the violence had usually been fast and unexpected, like what I'd been through tonight. By the time I had a chance to react, it was normally all over. Tony used torture at times, but I hadn't seen it. Eugenie had been very strict on that point, and I was beginning to see why. This was worse than the ferocity I knew: it was too casual, too matter-of-fact, too studied. There was no anger behind it, nothing personal to mitigate it or at least make it understandable. Her pain was just part of the job.

"She'll do for a demonstration, though," the man continued. He motioned to one of the pair of men working the rack and he brought forward a grimy wine bottle. "This is what happens to all who anger the king. Watch and remember, bastard."

As I stood frozen, saying nothing, the man poured the wine over the woman's head, face and neck. It soaked her hair until it dripped onto the stone floor below her in a thin red puddle. I snapped out of my shock when I realized what was coming.

His hand reached for a candle stub and I moved. "No! You can't! Please, *m'sieur*, I beg you . . ." I could already tell from the delight flooding his face that I'd given him exactly the reaction he'd wanted, and that he had no intention of stopping. He watched my face with something like glee as he held the candle to a nearby torch. It had almost guttered, but a tiny flame caught on the candlewick nonetheless. I didn't try to argue with him again, but launched myself forwards, grabbing for the burning candle. I wrestled it from his grip, but the two torturers grabbed my arms and dragged me off him. The man, who I assumed was the head jailer, turned eyes on me that had little humanity left in them; then he smiled. He bent and, very slowly, picked up the candle stub and relit it.

I looked at the woman as he approached; I couldn't help myself. There was a sheen of tears in her light brown eyes, and she blinked once, drops of wine falling from her lashes, before his body obscured my view. Part of my mind said that he would stop short, that he would not, could not, do this. A voice spoke in my head, saying that he wanted to terrorize me, that this scene had been staged to make me more pliable later, and that may have been true. But it didn't save her.

The scene before me wavered, and thoughts that I didn't recognize began to flood my mind. Scenes flashed before my eyes of other places, other people, like a film was being projected onto a transparent veil in front of me. Through it all, I could still see the woman and the torturer, frozen a second before the impossible occurred.

That voice in my head piped up again, gibbering about being brought up in captivity but never knowing true cruelty. I dressed in fine linen and handmade lace, it insisted; I had my books, my guitar and my paints with which to amuse myself; my jailors bowed low when they entered my room and did not sit in my presence unless I gave them permission. Royal blood flowed in my veins, and no one ever forgot that. Never had I seen brutality like this; never had I known such fear. And following quickly behind it was a red rush of pure rage. This was not justice, was not necessary to preserve peace or the stability of the land, or whatever high-sounding phrases they were currently using. It was the actions of a sadistic coward who kept his hands lily white at court, while such things were done behind closed doors in his name. And they called me the abomination.

I shook my head and tried to get the voice to shut up and to clear the cobwebs off my vision; after a second, it worked. But then I was back in the nightmare, with a clear view of that candle inching towards its destination. I watched in stunned incredulity as the torturer held the tiny flame to a few strands of the woman's wine-soaked hair. It caught with an audible whoosh and the blaze spread eagerly to the rest of her head and shoulders. Within seconds, the top part of her body was only a dark outline in a dancing curtain of fire. I screamed, since I couldn't do anything else. The other prisoners took up the cry until the room was filled with shrieks and the sound of chains beating uselessly against unyielding stone. We could do nothing else for her, so we made our cries almost shake the walls, but the woman herself made no sound as she burned.

"Mademoiselle Palmer, what is it? What is wrong?" Louis-César's face appeared in front of my eyes and I vaguely felt someone shaking me. The high-pitched, hopeless cry of the cell filled the room, and it took a minute to realize that it was coming from me.

"*Mia stella*, be calm, be calm!" Rafe pushed the Frenchman away and drew me against his chest. I ran my hands under the cashmere of his sweater, pulling him as close as I could, and buried my face in the soft silk of his shirt. I breathed deeply of the familiar scent of Rafe's cologne, but it didn't drive out the smell of the urine-soaked prison and the cooking flesh of what had once been a woman little older than me.

After a minute, I looked up and met Louis-César's eyes. "Tell me she was already dead, that she didn't know!" My voice was desperate, and my face in the mirror over the fireplace had wide, haunted eyes. They looked like the woman's, only hers had seen far worse things than had mine.

"*Mademoiselle*, I assure you; I am willing to do all in my power to assist you, but I do not understand what it is you ask."

Rafe was stroking my hair and rubbing soothing circles on my back. "It was a vision, *mia stella*, only a vision," he whispered. "You have had them before; you know that the images, they will fade in time."

I shook my head and shivered in his arms until he drew me closer. I hugged him so tightly that, if he'd been human, he would have been in pain. "Not like this. Never like this. They tortured her and then they burned her alive, and I couldn't . . . I just stood there . . ." My teeth wanted to chatter, but I bit down on my lip and wouldn't let them. It would make me remember the terrible cold of that place, and then I might think of the only source of heat. I wouldn't think of it; I wouldn't, and it would go away. But even as I echoed Rafe's words, I knew I lied.

I had had thousands of visions in my life, some of the past, some of the future, and none very pleasant. I'd Seen all kinds of terrible things, but nothing had ever affected me like this. With time and practice, I'd learned to let go of what I Saw, to treat it the way other people do disturbing news reports on television—as distant and not quite real. But then, I'd never before been part of the action, smelled the smells and tasted the fear of someone who had lived the events. It was the difference between driving by a brutal car accident and being in one. I didn't think I would forget that woman's stare anytime soon.

"*Mon Dieu*, you saw Françoise?" Louis-César stepped towards us, looking stricken, and I cringed away.

"Don't touch me!" Before he had smelled vaguely like some expensive cologne, but now he seemed to reek of the woman's cooking flesh. Not only did I not want him to touch me; I didn't even want him in the same room.

He backed off and his frown deepened. "My sincere apologies, *mademoiselle*. I would not have wished you to witness that, not for any cause."

Rafe looked at him over my head. "Are you satisfied, *signore*? I told you we should not use the Tears yet, that when she is already upset or ill, the visions, they are not pleasant. But no one listens. Maybe now you understand." He paused when Mircea appeared at my elbow and handed him a short crystal glass.

"Let her drink this," he commanded, and Rafe immediately obeyed.

"But I did not," Louis-César protested. "I do not even have them with me."

Rafe ignored him. "Drink it, *mia stella*; it will do you good." He settled alongside me in the large armchair, and I sipped the whiskey for a few minutes until my breathing returned to normal. It was so strong that it felt like it etched my throat on the way down, but the sensation was welcome. Anything that pushed away the memories would have been. I realized that I had knotted a fist in Rafe's once pristine cashmere sweater, reducing it to a sodden, wadded mess. I let go and he smiled. "I have others, Cassie. You are well and I am here. Think on that, not whatever it was you Saw."

It was good advice, but I was having trouble following it. Every time I glanced at Louis-César, the images threatened to overcome me again. Why had the Senate wanted me to See something tonight, especially something like that? What had he done to me, to make the vision so different?

"I need a bath," I announced abruptly. It was mainly a way to get away from Louis-César, but there was no doubt I could use one.

Mircea took my hand and walked me to a door opposite the entryway. "There is a bathroom in there, and it should have a robe. I will have food brought while you bathe, and we will talk when you are ready. If you require anything, do not hesitate to ask." I nodded, gave the almost-empty glass back to him, and escaped into the cool, blue-tiled oasis of the bathroom.

The tub was large enough to count as a sauna, and I climbed in gratefully after peeling away my ruined outfit. I turned the water up as hot as it would go and leaned back, so tired that I simply stared at the soap for a minute, vaguely wishing for someone to wash my back. My emotions, thankfully, had fled somewhere, leaving me feeling blank. I had been exhausted physically and now my mental state wasn't much better.

I finally got down to the process of cleaning the dried blood off my body and out of my hair. I told myself that what I Saw had nothing to do with the modern world, that that poor woman had suffered and died centuries before I was even born. As horrible as it had been, it wasn't a warning of an impending disaster or anything else I could do something about. I tried to believe that it was only a more intense version of one of the psychic hiccups I sometimes got when touching very old things that had been in traumatic circumstances, but it hadn't felt like that.

I'd learned early to be careful of negative psychic vibrations. Alphonse collected old weapons of all kinds, and once as a child I accidentally brushed against a tommy gun he had recently acquired and was in the process of cleaning. I immediately flashed on the mob slaying in which it had been used, and what I Saw gave me nightmares for weeks. Usually I could tell if an item was likely to cause trouble before I touched it, almost as if it gave off a warning I could feel if I was paying attention. But few people triggered the reaction—even ones centuries old, like Louis-César, who had undoubtedly seen their share of tragedy. Still, I'd made it a habit to avoid shaking hands with strangers so I wouldn't accidentally learn who was cheating on his wife or was about to commit a crime. And I never, ever touched Tony, not even in passing. I decided that a new name had just made the avoid-at-all-costs list.

I rinsed off, let out the bloody bathwater, and started over. I wanted to feel clean, and something told me that that was going to take a very long time. I put in enough bubble bath that the foam puffed over the sides of the tub and ran onto the floor. I didn't care. My only thought was to wonder whether I could hang out in the bath until daybreak and postpone hearing whatever the Senate had planned for me. I

was grateful they were protecting me but doubted the help
would come without a heavy price tag. Not that it mattered.
I didn't know where I was and, even if I escaped, I'd just be
running straight back into the mess with Tony. Whatever the
Senate wanted, I'd probably have to pay up.

The problem was that I'd promised myself, other than
where Tony and his goons were concerned, never to let my
abilities be used to hurt anyone again. I had no idea—a fact
for which I was really grateful—how many people I'd indirectly harmed or killed while working for the slime king, but
I knew it wasn't a small number. I hadn't known at the time
what some of my visions were being used for, but that didn't
make me feel a hell of a lot better. The people who make nu-
clear bombs don't set the policies that decide when to use
them, but I wonder if that helps them sleep at night. I hadn't
been sleeping well for a long time. If what the Senate
wanted would result in harm to others, which seemed a safe
bet, I was about to find out exactly what my principles were
worth to me.

Chapter 5

I decided that my left wrist was sprained but not broken, and that the scrape on my cheek was not as bad as I'd initially thought, although my butt hadn't fared as well. Falling on top of my gun back in the storeroom had left me with a bruise the size of my palm, and it had turned an unappealing purple. Great. It matched the finger marks around my neck, so at least I was coordinated.

I'd just finished the inspection when Billy Joe drifted in the window. I glanced at the door, really wanting to tell him off but not liking the idea of an audience. Billy was my ace in the hole and best chance of getting out of here. I didn't want anybody to know he was around.

He saw my expression and grinned. "Don't worry. Somebody put one doozy of a silencing spell on these rooms. Whatever they're planning, they're serious about not being overheard."

"Well, in that case: where the hell have you been?" My emotions came flooding back at the sight of him trying to look casual, as if he hadn't left me out to dry earlier.

Billy Joe, a hard-drinking, cigar-smoking card shark in life, was one of my only friends now that he was many years dead. But he'd screwed up on this one and he knew it. The big, tough gambler fiddled with his little string tie and looked embarrassed. I knew his reaction was the real deal and not another of his put-ons because he hadn't yet made a lecherous comment about my lack of clothing.

"I ran into Portia and she told me what happened. I went to the club looking for you, but you'd left already." He pushed up his Stetson with a nearly transparent finger, then solidified a bit more. "Did you do all that? The back room was a mess, and there were police crawling all over the place."

"Yeah, I'm in the habit of knocking off five vamps, then leaving the bodies for the police to have a fit over." Standard policy among the supernatural community was to clean up your own mess. In some circumstances, you could get in more trouble for leaving bodies lying around that might give a pathologist heart palpitations than for the actual killings. That didn't used to be the case, which was how a lot of those old legends got started, I imagine, but the more the human population expanded, the more the policy became vital. The Senate didn't care for the idea of seeing vamps chopped up in laboratories while some human scientist tried to figure out the secret to eternal life, or having freaked-out governments start a modern version of the Inquisition.

"What bodies?" Billy Joe solidified to the point that I could see a hint of red in his fashionable ruffled shirt—fashionable for 1858 anyway, the year the cowboys had given him an up-close-and-personal tour of the bottom of the Mississippi. "Blood was everywhere and it looked like a cyclone blew through, but there weren't any bodies."

I shrugged. I wasn't real interested in knowing that Tomas had a partner who'd called in a cleanup crew. If any of the other people I'd trusted had been lying to me, I didn't want to know about it. "Great, so make up for letting me almost get killed. What do you know about my problem here?"

Billy Joe spat a wad of ghostly chewing tobacco against the bathroom wall. It left a slimy trail of ectoplasm as it slid down, and I frowned at him. "Don't do that."

"Hey, are you nekkid under there?" He sat on the side of the tub and batted ineffectually at my bubbles. If he concentrated, he could move things, but he was only playing, so his hand passed through. I made him turn around while I got out and dried off. I know it's stupid, but Billy Joe hasn't been with a woman in 150 years and sometimes he gets distracted. It's best not to let his mind wander.

"Talk to me. What do you know?"

"Not a lot. I had trouble finding you. Do you know you're in Nevada?"

"How could I . . . wait a minute. Why did you have trouble finding me?" Most ghosts are tied to a single location—usually a house or a crypt—but Billy Joe haunts the necklace I bought at a junk store when I was seventeen, so he's more mobile. I'd purchased it because I thought it was only a piece of Victorian pastiche that might work for Eugenie's birthday. If I had known what came with it, I'm not sure I wouldn't have left it in the case. Since I hadn't, though, and since I was wearing it as usual, he shouldn't have had any problem locating me. As for travel time, well, let's just say he takes a more direct route than most.

"What have you been doing instead of checking things out around here?" Billy Joe looked guilty, a fact that did not keep him from trying to look down my towel. "Stop that." I had an epiphany. "Hang on. We're somewhere near Vegas, aren't we?"

"Yeah, about thirty miles out. This place looks like a ranch, 'cept there're no horses, no tourists and the ranch hands dress a little funny. 'Course, it don't matter, since all any humans ever see is a big, bare canyon with a lot of keep-out signs."

"Thirty miles?" Billy could draw energy from the stored reserves in his necklace for up to fifty. "Don't tell me that while I've been bespelled, moved halfway across the country, threatened and imprisoned, you've been at the casinos!"

"Now, Cassie darlin' . . ."

"I can't believe this!" I don't get angry with him often, since it's mostly a waste of time—he is the definition of incorrigible—but this was the last straw. "I was almost killed! Twice! If you don't care about that, think about what happens to your precious necklace if somebody guns me down or rips my throat open. Let me spell it out for you: it ends up in some old lady's jewelry box in Podunk, USA, a hundred miles from nowhere!"

Billy Joe looked chastened, but I doubted it was guilt over what might have happened to me. He is unable to stay away from his home base for too long or his power runs dry—which was why I knew he'd be along sooner or later. The farther from the source he gets, the faster his strength bottoms out. His nightmare is getting stuck in a rural, one-horse town with no honky-tonks, strip clubs or gambling dens within reach. For him, it would be the equivalent of Hell. With me he had a guaranteed urban environment, since it's hard to hide in a small town. He also had something even more important.

Over time, we'd developed a sort of symbiotic relationship. Billy Joe is one of those spirits who can absorb energy from a living donor, rather like a vamp. Vamps take life energy through blood, which in magical terms is the repository for the life force of a person. When they feed, they receive part of the donor's life, which substitutes for the one they lost when they crossed over, at least for a while. Some ghosts can do the same thing, and like vamps, they don't always ask first. But Billy Joe vastly prefers a willing donor, not to mention that he says the "hit" is much longer lasting from me for some reason. In return for my agreeing to give him additional energy from time to time, he had agreed to keep watch for signs of Tony's impending return. Right then, I felt cheated.

"If you aren't going to be any use, I should sell this ugly thing." I rubbed some steam off the mirror and took a look at the monstrosity around my neck. It was hand-wrought gold, heavy and intricate, with a mass of squirming vines and flowers around a central cabochon ruby. The junk dealer had assumed it was glass, since he wasn't used to seeing nonfaceted jewels and it had been encrusted with years of accumulated dirt. Even all cleaned up, it was, without doubt, one of the ugliest necklaces I'd ever seen. I usually wore it inside my clothes.

"I'll have you know, I won that off a countess!"

"And judging by all the pawn marks, it was real important to you, wasn't it?"

"I always redeemed it, didn't I?" Billy Joe was starting to sulk, so I decided to lay off. I needed him cooperative if I was going to find out anything.

"I don't want a fight. I'm not up for it tonight. I just need to know some stuff, like why the Senate grabbed me and . . ."

Billy Joe held up a hand. "Please, I know my job." He settled back on the tub and talked while I examined my knees. Raw-looking scrapes and bruises had flowered on both of them despite the height of my boots, promising stiffness by tomorrow. I knew I should feel lucky that I was alive to be an aching mess, but somehow that thought failed to cheer me up. Maybe because I didn't think I'd stay that way for long. "That vamp outside, Louis-César, is on loan from Europe. He's some kind of dueling champion. It's said that he's never lost a fight, and from what I hear he's been in hundreds."

"He can add another to the total after tonight." Not that it had looked like the guard was much of a challenge, but I guess it counted since he had decapitated the guy. "Did you know Tony bribed some lunatics to kill me right in front of the Senate?"

"That's nuts. Mircea'd kill him."

I brightened slightly. I hadn't thought of it that way. If Tony had been behind the second attempt on my life, he'd just made Mircea look bad, since nothing lowered your rep

quicker in vamp circles than not to be able to control an un-
derling. Even though I usually liked him, I'd always gotten
the impression that Mircea would be a bad person to cross.

"We can only hope so."

"Yeah, well, it don't sound like Tony's style to me." I
shrugged. In my opinion, Tony didn't have any style. "Anyway, when I learned Louis-César is second in the European
Senate, I did some digging for you."

"Great. So tell me something I care about."

Billy Joe gave a long-suffering sigh. "All right. You're in
the main headquarters of MAGIC, the Metaphysical Alliance for Greater Interspecies Cooperation, better known as
party central for things that go bump in the night."

"I know that." Actually, I think I had figured it out, at
least subconsciously. I'd never been there before, but where
else could a mage bust in on a Senate meeting and a vamp
greet a were like an old buddy? I just hadn't had time to
think about it, and it wasn't like I knew a lot about what
passed for the supernatural UN. Tony wasn't interested in
talking through problems. He was more the stake-'em-and-
forget-'em type, a practice that worked on much more than
vamps. It's one of the similarities among species that
MAGIC hasn't chosen to highlight: nothing lives too well
with a big piece of wood stuck through its heart.

"Well, maybe here's something you don't know. The
Senate is leading on this one because it's a vamp who's
causing the trouble, but everybody's upset. You know that
Russian master Tony used to do business with, the guy running half the rackets in Moscow?"

"Rasputin?" The old adviser to Nicholas II, the last tsar
of all the Russias, had been poisoned, shot, stabbed and
drowned by some prince who thought he had too much influence over the royal family. He was right: the tsarina loved
the unkempt, self-proclaimed monk because her son was a
hemophiliac, and only Rasputin's hypnotic stare was able to
heal him. In return, Rasputin got power, and a lot of his

friends were appointed to important government jobs. The prince and the group of nobles he'd talked into helping him remove the new power in town had been real surprised that poison, stabbing and gunshot wounds hadn't seemed to faze Rasputin. It wasn't until he fell off a bridge and they hauled his apparently lifeless corpse out of the freezing water that they were satisfied. Historians had been arguing ever since about why it took him so long to die. The Russian mafia could have told them: it's hard to kill somebody who's already dead.

"Yeah, that's the one. Rasputin got annoyed 'cause the Senate seat he wanted went to Mei Ling. He doesn't stand a chance of getting onto the European Senate—most of those crazy sons of bitches make even him look soft—but he thought he was a shoo-in over here. Word is, he didn't take the rejection well. He disappeared for a while, then about six months ago showed up again and began attacking Senate members. He's killed four and wounded two others so bad, no one knows if they'll pull through, and now he's challenged the Consul to a duel to try and take over the whole shebang. She called in a favor from the Consul in Europe and brought this Louis-César over as her champion. But, of course, that didn't make Mei Ling happy."

"I bet." I'd met the Consul's second, a tiny Chinese American beauty who was all of four foot ten and weighed maybe eighty-five pounds, when I was seven. She'd left quite an impression. The second's position isn't like that of an American vice president. He or she isn't there to take over if the Consul is killed—the remaining Senate members will vote on a replacement unless a duel decides it, in which case it's winner take all. The title also doesn't imply that the holder is the second most powerful member on the Senate—it's possible, but it isn't a job requirement. Each Senate member has a specific function for that body, sort of like the presidential cabinet. Seconds are appointed for one reason and one only: they're intimidating. Whoever holds the office is also known as "the Enforcer," because he or she enforces the decrees of the Senate by whatever means are necessary. Those can include everything from diplomacy to violence, but Mei Ling was known to prefer the latter.

She'd made that clear the day she'd visited Tony's audience hall to drag off one of his vamps for questioning. Whatever the guy had done, he definitely didn't want to talk to the Senate about it. In fact, he was so opposed to the idea that he issued a challenge. Mei Ling was new to the position and didn't have much of a reputation; she was also only about 120 years old and looked like a China doll, so I guess he thought he could take her.

It amazes me how even old vamps sometimes forget that it isn't size but power that matters, and while that often correlates to age, it doesn't always. Some vamps many centuries older than Mei Ling will never have her strength, and I've seen hulking bruisers forced to their knees by the glance of a child. The transition to vampire doesn't make you gorgeous if you were plain, intelligent if you were stupid or powerful if you were weak: a loser in life is a loser vamp, spending his or her immortality serving someone else. It's one of the major drawbacks to the condition, something the movies never seem to highlight. But occasionally it does give someone who was overlooked as a mortal a chance to shine. That day I saw a tiny, fragile-looking flower literally rip a vamp into bloody shreds. I also saw how much pleasure she took in it, how her dark eyes glowed with a fierce joy at the fact that she could do this, that once again a man had underestimated her, and this time he would pay for it.

She never did kill him that I saw. His head was intact and screaming when she ordered the pieces packed into baskets to be carted off to the Senate. I never saw him afterwards, and nobody present that day, to my knowledge, ever again challenged Mei Ling.

"Why did the Consul bring in a ringer? I'd think she or Mei Ling could deal with a simple challenge."

"The Consul's powerful, but she ain't a duelist. And Mei Ling don't have Rasputin's experience. He was already old when he tried to take over in Russia; rumor is that he's never been defeated in a fight, and that he don't much care how he wins. No one saw the fights with the dead senators, but the first two to be attacked are still alive—so to speak. And Marlowe stayed conscious long enough after they found him to say that Rasputin somehow turned three of his own vamps against him, and one of them had been with him over two hundred years."

A few scattered puzzle pieces started to come together. I filled Billy Joe in on my most recent escape, and he looked thoughtful. "Yeah, that would make sense. I don't know how the Senate guards are chosen, but it's almost sure to be from the stable of one of the members, since who'd ever think any of them would turn?"

"But why would Rasputin want me dead?" I shivered, and it wasn't from cold. I was used to the idea that Tony wanted to kill me, but there were suddenly a whole bunch of newcomers trying to jump on the bandwagon. And any one of them would be enough to give a sane person a serious case of paranoia.

"Beats me." Billy Joe looked way too cheerful and I glared at him. He enjoys recounting a good fight almost as much as being in one, but I wasn't his entertainment. He hurried on. "But you haven't heard the best yet. Marlowe took out a couple of his attackers before passing out, and the bodies were left behind when his reserves showed up. But nobody can ID the dead vamps. It's like they came outta nowhere."

"That's impossible."

I didn't doubt the part about Chris Marlowe being tough to kill. Before he crossed over, he'd been the bad boy of Elizabethan England and had been in a few hundred bar fights in between writing some of the best plays of the era. The only ones anybody thought rivaled them were by a guy named Shakespeare, who conveniently showed up a few years after Marlowe transitioned and had a real similar writing style. Eventually, when the two-bit actor he'd set up as a front died, Marlowe turned to his other hobby for kicks. He'd done some spying for the queen's government in life, and he added to his bag of tricks afterwards. He was now the Senate's chief of intelligence, using his family of vamps as spies on the supernatural community in general and the other senates in particular. He helped ensure the peace by taking out anybody likely to disturb it, which might explain why Tony had been more worried about Marlowe than about Mei Ling. The only time I'd ever seen him, when he dropped in to talk to Mircea one night during his visit, I'd thought he looked rather nice with his laughing dark eyes, messy curls and a goatee he kept getting in the wine. But, of course, I hadn't been planning to take out the Consul. If I had, I might have hit him first, too.

The part of Billy Joe's story I found hard to credit was the two unidentified vamps. That was literally impossible. All vampires are under the control of a master, either the one who made them or the one who bought them from their maker or won them in a duel. The only way not to have a master is to reach first-level master power yourself. Anything else, including killing off your own master, won't do any good; someone else will simply bind you to them. Since there are fewer than one hundred first-degree masters in the world, and they mostly hold seats on one of the six vamp senates, this makes for a nice hierarchal structure and keeps everyone organized. Most masters give their more powerful followers some freedom, although a certain amount of their revenues are sent as yearly "presents," and any servants they make are subject to their masters' whims. The masters also check on them from time to time, like Mircea with Tony, because they are always responsible for them. If Tony had ordered an attack on me after he knew I was under Senate protection, it would be Mircea who would be expected to deal with him.

It's a fairly uncomplicated system, at least for a government, because there aren't that many vampires powerful enough to have stables of followers. Unlike Hollywood seems to believe, not every vamp can make new ones. I remember watching an old Dracula movie once with Alphonse and having him laugh himself sick at the sight of a vamp only a few days out of the grave supposedly raising another one. He'd been impossible for weeks afterwards, mercilessly teasing all the weaker vamps in court about the three-day-old baby that was more powerful than them. But for all who do reach master level and create new vamps, it is a requirement that they record them with their respective Senate. As a result, there simply aren't any unknown vampires running around.

"Were they babies?" It was the only thing I could think of, although that didn't make sense, either. What good would a couple of newly made, and therefore weak, vamps do against any Senate member, much less Marlowe? It would be like sending children off to fight an armored tank. And what master would risk his head and heart by failing to report any new vamps he'd made? All the senates were strict on the rules, since anything else raised the specter of a master secretly assembling an army, and brought back memories of the bad old days when there had been almost constant war. As it was, the number of vamps anyone could have under his or her control at one time was strictly regulated to maintain a balance of power.

"Nope. It's kinda hard to tell with only the bodies to work with, but based on how much damage they did, the rumor is that they were masters." At my expression, he put up placating hands. "Hey, you asked me what I heard, and I'm tellin' ya."

"Where'd you get the info?"

"A couple of vamps in Mircea's entourage." Billy Joe didn't mean that he'd asked them. He has the ability to drift through people and eavesdrop on them mentally, picking up whatever they're thinking at the time. It isn't as good as real telepathy, since he can't go digging for information, but it comes in handy surprisingly often. "It wasn't hard to get. It's the main topic of conversation these days."

I shook my head, puzzled. "I don't get it. If Rasputin has been messing with the rules and ambushing people, why is the Consul preparing to fight him? He lost that right when he ignored the rules, didn't he?" It seemed to me that Rasputin was in deep shit, a thought that made me feel much better. If he got himself killed, it was one less bad guy for me to worry about.

The problem wasn't the attacks on senators—that was perfectly legal—but rather the way he'd gone about them. During the Reformation, the six senates had collectively banned open warfare as a way to solve problems. After the religious divide, both the Catholic and Protestant clergy had been supersensitive, warning their flocks to be watchful for evildoers who could rob them of God's favor. Religion had also been a big political issue, with Catholic powers trying to assassinate Protestant leaders and vice versa, a Catholic armada trying to invade Protestant England and a major holy war going on in Germany. Everybody was spying on everybody, and as a result, more people were beginning to notice supernatural activity. Even though most of the accused were as human as their accusers—and usually more innocent—the authorities occasionally got lucky and staked a real vamp or burned a real witch. Open warfare between senates or even feuds between prominent houses were only going to draw more notice to the supernatural community. So dueling became the new, approved way of solving disputes.

Of course, Tony wasn't about to risk his fat little neck in open combat, and there were plenty of others whose skills didn't run to battle who also didn't like the new system. So the practice evolved into choosing champions to fight for you if you didn't want to do it yourself. Once the two duelists were agreed on, though, the rules were very strict about what was and was not allowed. Ambushes were definite no-nos, and what Rasputin had done would earn him an automatic staking anywhere in the world. The North American Senate would never stop hunting him, and the others would lend a hand to discourage this type of thing in their own areas. I decided that he was either crazy or really, really stupid.

"I guess she figures it's better than letting him pick off people one by one. Besides, unless Marlowe or Ismitta pulls through enough to testify, there's no actual proof he cheated. Right now he can say he challenged them and they lost, fair and square."

"But if he has to meet the Consul in front of the entire MAGIC council, he can't cheat."

"Bingo. Besides, she don't got a lot of choices. Ol' Ras has left the Senate with a diplomatic nightmare on its hands 'cause of his rampage. The Fey are livid and say if the vamps can't deal with this they'll do it themselves. They lost one of their nobles in the crossfire, and you know how they are about that kind of thing." Actually, I didn't. I'd never even seen an elf or talked to anyone who had. Some of the vamps at Tony's didn't even believe they existed. The rumor was that they were some elaborate prank the mages had been playing for centuries, to try to convince the vamps that they had powerful allies. "The mage's circle is pissed, too, though I don't know why, and are calling for Rasputin's head on a platter. The Consul has to deal with this soon or people will start thinking she's weak. Mei Ling's good, but she can't fight all the challengers who're going to climb out of the woodwork if this ain't stopped."

"But she isn't fighting Rasputin."

"No, and like I said, she ain't happy about that. Word is,

that's why she ain't here—she's off hunting him. She's almost outta time, though. The duel is set for tomorrow at midnight. I think she plans to bring back his head on a pike before then."

"Okay, I wish her luck. But you still haven't told me what all this has to do with me."

"'Cause I don't know, honey chile." I hate it when Billy Joe gets southern. It means he's either joking or about to turn sarcastic, and I didn't want to deal with either. His usual accent is a Mississippi drawl combined with bits of Irish brogue left over from a childhood starving on the Emerald Isle. He'd immigrated, changed his name, and made a new life in the New World, but he'd never completely lost the accent. I glared at him. No way was I putting up with attitude now. He'd done pretty well, but I was pissed that he'd totally missed Tony's return. That was, after all, his main job.

"What else do you know? Is that everything?" I had learned a long time ago that Billy Joe is a damned good spy, but he can't be trusted. Oh, he's never lied to me—that I know of—but if he can get away with leaving something out that might cause him trouble, he'll do it.

"I wasn't sure whether to tell you, after that whole thing with Tomas. You probably don't need to hear about another bottom-feeder right now."

"Tell me what?" I ignored the dig at Tomas, whom Billy Joe had never liked, mainly because I agreed with it. I started checking out my sorry pile of once-expensive club wear and decided that the boots and skirt, both leather, could be salvaged. But the shirt was wrecked and the bra was partially burnt, although my back felt fine. It was one of the few parts of my body that didn't hurt. The shirt was no big loss except that I didn't have anything to replace it with, and would prefer not to go back into the living room in nothing but a robe. I actually didn't want to go back in there at all but couldn't think of a good excuse to avoid it.

"Jimmy the Rat is in town."

I stopped trying to scrub the dried blood off my skirt and slowly looked up. See why I've put up with Billy for almost seven years? Every once in a while, he earns his keep. "Where?"

"Now, Cassie, love, don't go doing something crazy."

"I'm not." Jimmy was Tony's favorite hit man. It had been his hand that planted the bomb in my parents' car, thereby ending any chance I had for a normal life. I'd been looking for him even before I broke with Tony, but he'd proven surprisingly elusive. I did not intend for him to slip past me again. "Where did you see him?"

Billy Joe ran a hand through what had once been chestnut curls and sighed deeply. That's not an automatic thing for a ghost; he does it on purpose. "He's at Dante's on the strip, one of Tony's new places. He manages a bar there. But I don't think surprising him is a good idea. The place is probably crawling with Tony's thugs. Las Vegas is second only to Philly in his operation."

"Don't lecture me about the business I grew up with." I stopped before I went on a rant about Billy perusing the sights of Sin City instead of checking out the place properly, so I'd know exactly what I was facing. I'd forgive a lot if his addiction to gambling resulted in me being able to get my hands around Jimmy's neck. "I need a shirt and a way into town, plus Tomas took my gun. I want it back."

"Um, you might want to rethink that." Billy looked shifty and I groaned.

"What? There's more? Out with it!"

He glanced about, but there was no help in sight. "You don't have to worry about Jimmy anymore. He did something to upset Tony, and when I left, he was being taken to the basement."

"Meaning what?"

"Meaning, he's probably out of the picture already, or

will be soon, so there's no reason to run off. At least not in that direction. I was thinking maybe Reno . . ."

"You don't know that he's dead. He could be down there rigging slot machines or something." The basement had been a euphemism for Tony's underground torture chambers in Philly, but here it might mean exactly what it said. "Besides, nobody gets to kill him but me."

In reality, although he certainly deserved it, I had serious doubts that I could kill anybody, even Jimmy. But that didn't mean I had no reason to want to see him. Tony had done his best to make sure that I never learned anything about my parents: I had no photos, no letters, no high school yearbooks. Hell, it had taken me years to even find out their names, from old newspaper accounts of their deaths, which I'd had to sneak around my bodyguards to read. Eugenie and my tutors had all been people whom Tony acquired from other masters shortly after my arrival at court and didn't know anything about the operation before then. Those vamps who had been with Tony for years and might know something were so closemouthed that I knew without asking that they'd been warned not to talk to me. I wasn't stupid enough to believe that he'd gone to that much trouble simply to focus my affection on him, especially since he rarely made any efforts to win me over. No, there was something about my parents Tony didn't want me to know, and if he and Jimmy had actually fallen out, I might finally have someone willing to tell me about it.

Billy Joe bitched, of course, but I was too busy trying to make the salvageable part of my outfit presentable to care. He finally gave up. "Fine, but I'll need an energy draw if you expect me to play fetch. It's been a tough night, and I don't got the juice to spare."

I wasn't pleased. I felt like crap and had to go off someone in Vegas; I didn't need this. But I could hardly go scouting around MAGIC headquarters myself, so I motioned him over without the usual fuss. Billy Joe put a hand on his chest. "Be still my heart."

"Just do it."

I swear he felt me up as we merged, assuming that a cloud of mist can feel. Knowing him, I'm pretty sure it can. He blew against me and, as always, the feel of him was soothing to my frazzled nerves. I've heard that norms find the company of ghosts terrifying or, at best, chilling; to me, they've always been like a cool breeze on a hot day. Under the circumstances, I didn't just open up and welcome him; whatever part of me convened with ghosts pulled him inside like a frightened child gripping a teddy bear.

For an instant I had flashes of his life: our ship pulled away from a distant shore and we watched the gray, windswept coast recede through a haze of tears; a pretty girl, maybe fifteen, wearing too much makeup and a dance-hall costume, gave us a knowing smile; a young, would-be hustler tried to cheat us, and we laughed as we pulled the ace out of his boot, then had to dodge the knife his accomplice threw. It was often like this, and through the years I'd Seen enough mini newsreels to be amazed that Billy had survived as long as he had.

Finally, he got comfortable and started the draw. It was usually not an unpleasant experience, just tiring, but this time pain flared through my body as soon as he began. It wasn't overwhelming, more like a burst of static electricity on a doorknob, but it sizzled along my veins until silver sparkles flickered behind my eyelids. I tried to order him out, to say that something was wrong, but all that left my mouth was a startled wheeze. A second later, the sensation flashed bright enough to leave negative imprints on my vision. Then, as quickly as it had come, it was gone. A warm wind swept across me, so thick it felt like liquid; then Billy Joe erupted out of me and zoomed around the ceiling a few times.

"Woo-hoo! Now *that's* what I call a meal!" His eyes were sparkling and his color was bright, more so than it should have been.

I straightened up and, for the first time in a while, didn't feel like collapsing. Instead of being tired and a little cranky—my usual reaction to Billy Joe's snack sessions—I felt wonderful, rejuvenated. It was like having a full night's sleep compressed into a few minutes, and it was definitely not normal. "Not that I'm complaining, but what just happened here?"

Billy Joe grinned. "Some vamp has been leeching your strength, darlin', probably to keep you from trying to escape. He drained a lot of your energy into a sort of metaphysical holding pot, and warded it with some of his own so you couldn't access it until he released you. I accidentally broke through the wards when I tried to draw from you, and got one hell of a rush." He waggled his eyebrows at me, and they were almost as brown and solid as they must have been in life. "Damn, let's party!"

"Party later. Right now I need my stuff."

Billy Joe saluted smartly and streamed out of the window like a glittering comet. I sat on the side of the tub and wondered who it was who had done the hocus-pocus. Not that it mattered; it just gave me yet another reason not to trust anyone. Not that I'd been planning on it.

I'd finished the cleanup by the time Billy Joe got back. He floated through the window, scowling, and his hands were empty. "I left everything outside. That thing's gonna be a problem."

"What thing?" I grabbed a towel to keep from standing around in only my panties and walked over to the window. I saw what he meant as soon as my hand reached for the latch and it tried to scream. I stuffed the end of my towel into its newly acquired mouth and stared at it in annoyance. Wasn't it enough that they'd put wards on my energy, parked a bunch of master-level vamps outside my door and stranded me somewhere in the middle of the desert? Did they really need a charm on the window, too? Apparently, someone thought they did.

"Somebody cast a Marley on it," Billy said.

"You think?" I asked sarcastically, squatting to examine it more closely. The old-fashioned, bulbous latch had suddenly grown a pair of beady little eyes and a big, fat mouth. It was trying to spit out my towel so it could yell a warning, one that would no doubt slice right through the silencing spell and alert everyone in the outer room. When I tried to grab it to hold it in place, it started sliding back and forth along the length of the window, avoiding my hands. Looking at its expression, I think it would have bitten me if it could have. I narrowed my eyes at it. "Get me some toilet paper," I told Billy. "A lot of it."

A few minutes and a lot of silent swearing later, the little Marley sat immobilized, with a full roll of toilet paper stuffed in its mouth and the cords from the window blinds tied around it about nine times. "That won't hold it for long," Billy said dubiously, as the tiny alarm vibrated with indignation. A few wisps of paper drifted out of its mouth and floated to the floor as we watched.

"It doesn't have to." I lifted the sash and jammed it open with the plunger Billy found under the sink. "They'll know we've escaped soon enough anyway—this place is warded all to hell."

I began quickly sorting through the pile he dragged in the window and decided that, overall, he'd done a good job. My gun was back and I even had an extra clip he'd rounded up somewhere, plus he'd dropped a set of car keys on top of the shirts. On the down side, the tops were not exactly what I would have chosen. I should have specified no hooker wear, but a gal can't think of everything. My boots and mini looked cute and sassy when I was adequately covered up on top; spilling out from the most conservative of Billy Joe's finds, I looked like I ought to be charging by the hour. I pulled my hair into a ponytail using Louis-César's clip, but although it was neater, it didn't make me look much more innocent. I took one last look at my appearance in the mirror, sighed and pocketed the keys. As soon as I managed to find the garage, I'd take out the stress of the day on a certain old acquaintance and probably feel much better.

Chapter 6

Tony is a scumbag, but I can't fault his business sense. Dante's, on a prime stretch of land near the Luxor, had a crowd even at four thirty in the morning. I wasn't surprised: it's perfect for Las Vegas. Modeled on the *Divine Comedy*, it has nine different areas, each with a theme corresponding to one of Dante Aligheri's nine circles of Hell. Visitors enter through a set of huge wrought-iron gates decorated with basalt statues writhing in agony and the famous phrase ABANDON HOPE, ALL YE WHO ENTER HERE. They are then rowed across a shallow river by one of several gray-robed Charons and deposited in the cavelike vestibule, where a red and gold layout of the place is painted mural-sized on the wall.

A guy dressed like King Minos—with a convenient name tag explaining that he was the guy who assigned sinners to their punishments—was handing out paper copies of the map when I arrived, but I didn't need one. The layout was kind of logical: the buffet, for example, was in the third circle, where the sin of gluttony is punished. It wasn't difficult to figure out where to look for Jimmy; where else but circle two, where all those guilty of the sin of lust are chastised, to find a real, live satyr?

Sure enough, Pan's Flute was the watering hole for the second circle. In case you somehow missed the Hell and damnation theme the lobby had going, the bar was a bit more blatant. I didn't so much as flinch on entering, since I'd seen similar rooms before. For someone a little more sensitive, however, it must have been a shock to enter a room that was decorated almost entirely with dismembered skeletons. Renaissance Italy, where Tony had been born, experienced regular outbreaks of plague. Seeing their friends and family die and hearing of whole villages being wiped out made people somewhat morbid. Ossuaries, chapels built entirely out of the bones of the deceased, were the era at its most extreme, and Tony's homage was no exception. Elaborate chandeliers made of what looked like—and, knowing Tony, possibly were—human bones swung from the ceiling, interspersed with garlands of skulls. More death's-heads were used for candle holders, and drinks were served in skull-shaped goblets. They were fakes, with tacky glass "rubies" for eyes, but I wasn't so sure about some of the others. The napkins showed the *Dance of Death* in black on a red background, with a grinning skeleton leading a parade of sinners off to perdition. After guests adjusted to all that, I guess the waiters weren't as big a surprise.

I had expected humans in togas and furry trousers, but the creature who greeted me at the entrance was the real deal. How the hell they convinced people that their waiters were only wearing elaborate costumes I'll never know. The rudimentary horns that poked out of the satyr's nest of mahogany curls could have been as fake as the ring of acanthus leaves he was wearing, but his costume—consisting solely of an overstrained leather G-string—did nothing to conceal his obviously real fur-covered haunches and glossy black hooves. It also showed without a doubt that he approved of the plunging neckline of my purloined black spandex top. Since satyrs generally approve of anyone female and breathing, I didn't take it as a compliment.

"I'm here to see Jimmy."

The satyr's big brown eyes, which had been sparkling with pleasure, clouded over slightly. He took my arm in an attempt to draw me against him, but I stepped back. Of course he followed. He was young and handsome, if the whole half-goat thing didn't make you want to run screaming. Satyrs tend to be well endowed by human standards, and he was gifted even for one of them. Since sexual prowess is the defining element in satyr society, he was probably accustomed to getting a lot of attention. He didn't do much for me, but I didn't want to appear rude. Satyrs, even the old, bald ones, think they're God's gift to women, and messing with their happy fantasy tends to have bad results. Not that they turn violent—they're more likely to run than fight—but a depressed satyr is a miserable sight. They get drunk, play sad songs and loudly complain about the duplicity of women. Once they get started, they don't stop until they pass out, and I wanted information.

I let him tell me how beautiful I was for a few minutes. It seemed to make him happy, and he finally agreed to go see whether Jimmy was available after I swore that the boss and I were only friends. I really hoped Billy had been wrong for once about Jimmy's predicament. Running around the lower levels of Tony's version of Hell didn't appeal.

I had thought of a plan on the way over that might get me the information I wanted, assuming Jimmy was still alive to give it to me. Since I'd seen him outside more than once in daylight, I was pretty sure he wasn't a vamp. Most magical creatures can't be turned—not to mention that I've had vamps tell me they taste really foul—but I wasn't so sure about Jimmy. I knew he wasn't a full satyr, since he had human legs and his horns were noticeable only if he got a really close haircut. There were many things that other half could be, but I'd never seen him demonstrate any impressive powers or start turning purple or something, so I was pretty sure he was half human. That would be in keeping with Tony's habit of keeping a few nonvamps around to manage business when his regular muscle was asleep. I wasn't completely certain that a human-satyr hybrid couldn't be turned, and some of the most powerful vamps can stand daylight in small doses if they're willing to expend a lot of energy for the privilege. But I really doubted that a first- or second-level master would be running errands for Tony. Besides, I'd never gotten that good old vampy feeling around Jimmy. So, unless Jimmy was warded nine ways to Sunday, Billy Joe ought to be able to manage a brief possession.

Billy hadn't liked the idea when I'd explained what I wanted in the car. This was the most powerful he'd felt in a long time, and if he was going to waste it on a possession, he stated plainly that Jimmy would not be his first choice. But, like I told him, all I needed was time enough for the loser to tell me what I wanted to know, and then confess his sins to the Vegas PD. Even if he denied it all later, if he had provided enough particulars on a bunch of unsolved cases, he would have trouble eluding justice. And, if plan A didn't work, I could always shoot him. I was already on the run from Tony, his allied families, the Silver Circle and the vampire Senate; after that, the cops didn't scare me much.

Billy Joe and I sat at the end of the bar. I hadn't seen him this juiced up in a while—those wards he ate really must have been something. He looked almost completely solid, to the point that I could tell he hadn't shaved for a day or two before his death. But no one else seemed to notice him, although no one tried to sit on his stool, either. If they had, and they were norms, they'd have felt like a bucket of ice water had been dumped over their heads. Which was why we took seats far away from everyone else.

"You going to tell me why we're here?"

I glanced about, but there was no one close enough to notice if I started talking to myself. Most of the bar, which seemed to have an exclusively female clientele, was busy ogling the waiters, who happily ogled right back. A handsome black-haired satyr nearby was encouraging one of the patrons to see whether she could figure out where his "costume" began. She had the glassy-eyed look of someone who'd been drinking for a while, but the hands she was running over his sleek black flanks were remarkably steady. I frowned; if I'd still been with Tony, I'd have reported him. He was practically asking for someone to figure things out and run screaming to the cops.

"You know why. He killed my parents. He must know something about them."

"You're risking us getting caught by the Senate, who are not going to underestimate you again, I might add, to ask a couple questions about people you don't even remember? You're not planning on blowing this guy away, are you? A little payback for messing with you? Not that I mind, but it might draw attention."

I ignored the question and ate some peanuts out of a little bloodred serving bowl. Wasting Jimmy wouldn't be as satisfying as taking out Tony, but at least it would be something. A sign to the universe that I'd had enough of people screwing up my life; I was perfectly capable of doing that all by myself. The only problem was the actual killing part of that scenario, which frankly made me nauseous to even think about. "You'll see what he did in a minute if the possession goes okay."

"That's a big if. Demons are the possession experts; I'm only a lowly ghost."

"You never have trouble with me." Billy Joe had been heavily into wine, women and song in life, with a strong emphasis on the first two. I can't help him much with the second need, and I hate his taste in music, which runs to Elvis and Hank Williams. But I occasionally reward him with a drink if he's been exceptionally good, and, of course, that means a little more than buying him a six-pack. Those instances aren't a real possession, though. Although I let him in to use my taste buds, I remain in full control. He plays nice during these infrequent events because he knows that if he doesn't, when his power runs out I'll bury his necklace in the middle of nowhere and leave it to rot. But as long as he keeps to the rules, I let him in on special occasions so he can eat, drink and be merry right along with me. Since I'm not in the habit of getting plastered and trashing bars, it's never quite wild enough for his tastes, but it's better than nothing.

"You're an unusual case. It's a lot harder with other people. Anyway, humor me and answer the question."

I toyed with a tiny death's-head swizzle stick and wondered why I hesitated. My parents' deaths weren't that hard to talk about. I had memories from my street years that I would never willingly revisit, but as Billy Joe had pointed out, I'd been only four when Tony ordered the hit. My memories before that are hazy: Mom is actually more a smell than anything else—the rose talcum powder she must have liked—and Dad is a sensation. I remember strong hands throwing me into the air and spinning me around when they caught me; I know his laugh, too, a deep, rich chuckle that warmed me down to my toes and made me feel protected. Safe isn't something I feel very often, so maybe that's why the memory is so sharp. Other than that, all I know about them came from the vision I had at age fourteen.

Along with puberty, my cosmic birthday present that year was to see my parents' car explode in an orange and black fireball that left nothing but twisted metal and burning leather seats behind. I'd watched it from Jimmy's car while he made a phone call to the boss. He lit a cigarette and calmly let him know that the hit had gone as planned and that he should pick up the kid from the babysitter before the cops started looking for me. Then it faded, and I was alone in my bedroom at Tony's country estate, shivering with reaction. Childhood pretty much ended for me that night. I'd run away an hour later, as soon as dawn came and all good little vampires were in their safe rooms. I'd been gone three years.

Not having bothered to plan out my escape in advance, I didn't have any of the perks the Feds had thoughtfully provided the second time around to cushion the experience.

There was no fake social security card or birth certificate, no guaranteed employment and no one to go to if things went wrong. I'd also had no real idea how the world worked outside Tony's court, where people might be tortured to death from time to time, but nobody ever dressed poorly or went hungry. If I hadn't had help from an unlikely source, I'd never have made it.

My best friend as a child was Laura, the spirit of the youngest girl in a family Tony had murdered around the turn of the last century. Her family home was an old German-built farmhouse that sat on sixty pretty acres outside Philadelphia. It had some enormous trees that were probably already old when Ben Franklin lived in the area and a stone bridge over a small stream, not that its beauty was the main attraction for Tony. He liked it for the privacy and the fact that it was only an hour's commute to the city, and he didn't take the family's refusal to sell very well. Of course, he could have simply bought another house in the area, but I doubt that even crossed his mind. I guess losing our families to Tony's ambition gave Laura and me a bond. Whatever the reason, she had refused to stay in her grave under the old barn out back and roamed the estate at will.

That was lucky for me, since the only other little girl around Tony's was Christina, a 180-year-old vampire whose idea of playtime wasn't the same as mine, or any other sane person's. Laura was probably close to a century old herself, but she always looked and acted about six. That made her a wise older sibling when I first came to Tony's, who taught me the joys of mud pies and playing practical jokes. Years later, she showed me where to find her dad's hidden safe— with more than ten thousand dollars in it that Tony had missed—and acted as a lookout when I ran away the first time. She made a nearly impossible task feasible, but I never had a chance to thank her. By the time I returned, she had gone. I guess she'd done her job and moved on.

The ten thousand bucks—along with the paranoia I'd

learned at Tony's—had allowed me to survive on the streets, but it was still a time I tried to avoid thinking about. The lack of material comforts and occasional danger weren't what convinced me to go back, however. I'd made that decision based on the realization that I'd never be able to get revenge from outside the organization. If I wanted Tony to suffer for what he'd done, I would have to return.

It easily ranked as the hardest thing I've ever done, not only because I hate Tony so much, but also because I didn't know whether his greed would override his anger. Yes, I made him a lot of money and was a useful weapon he could hold over the heads of his competitors. They never knew what I might tell him about them and, while it didn't keep them completely honest, it did cut down on the more blatant cheating. But that didn't reassure me much. Tony isn't always predictable: he's smart, and he usually makes decisions for financially sound reasons, but there are times when his temper gets away from him.

He once took on another master over a minor territorial dispute that could have been solved with negotiators from either side sitting down together for a few hours. Instead, we went to war, always a dangerous business (if the Senate finds out about it, you're dead whether you lose or not), and lost more than thirty vamps. Some of them were among the first Tony ever made. I saw him crying over the bodies after the cleanup crew brought them back to us, but knew it wouldn't make any difference the next time. Nothing ever did. So all things considered, I hadn't known whether to expect open arms or a session in the basement. It had been the former, but I'd always had the feeling that this was as much because I caught Tony on a good day as because I was useful to him.

It took three very long years to amass enough proof to destroy Tony's operation through the human justice system. I couldn't go to the Senate, since nothing Tony had done actually violated vamp laws. Killing my parents was perfectly okay, since neither had the support of another master, and the hit had been made to look like something human criminals had done. As for misuse of my powers, they'd probably have applauded his business acumen. Assuming I even got in to see them, they would have merely returned me to my master for appropriate punishment. But no human DA was going to listen to anything I had to say if I started talking about vampires, much less some of the stuff that went down at Tony's on a regular basis.

In the end, I'd had to set him up the same way the Feds got Capone. We nailed him on enough racketeering and tax-evasion charges to put him away for a hundred years. That isn't all that long to an immortal, but I was hoping the Senate would stake him for drawing too much attention to himself long before he had to worry about whether his cell had a window or not.

But when the sting went down, Tony was nowhere to be found. The Feds managed to round up and indict some of his human servants, but of the fat man himself there was no sign. Both his warehouses in Philly and his mansion in the country were empty, and my old nurse was dead in pieces in the basement. Tony had left me a letter explaining how his instincts had warned him that something was wrong, so he'd had Jimmy torture Eugenie to find out what I was doing. Vamps can take a lot of abuse, and Genie loved me; it took a long time to break her, but, as Tony said, he's the patient type. He wrote that he'd left me the body so I could dispose of it properly, since he knew how much she had meant to me. And so I'd know what I had to look forward to one of these days.

"I don't know what I'm going to do," I admitted to Billy. "But my parents weren't the only ones he killed who were important to me."

"I'm sorry." To his credit, Billy Joe knew when to stop pushing, and we sat in silence until the waiter returned with effusive apologies. The boss was unavailable for the evening. Apparently, Jimmy had gone home with a headache.

I flirted with the satyr for a few seconds before sending him off for another drink. As he left, Billy emerged from his head, looking surly. "And I thought I had a dirty mind! You don't even want to know what he was thinking about you."

"Got that right. So where's Jimmy?"

"In the basement, like I told you. They posted a loss last quarter, so Jimmy's being sent to the ring."

Talk about childish. The Senate wouldn't let Tony kill me, so he was taking it out on someone else. I stood up and headed for the exit. There were a few things I wanted to ask Jimmy before he made his contribution to the evening's entertainment. But I knew I'd better hurry. The ring was Tony's favorite spectator sport, but it tended to have a detrimental effect on the participants. He had decided a century ago that it was a shame to simply kill anybody who displeased him, and had set up a boxing ring to decide things instead. But it wasn't used for boxing, and only one fighter walked out alive after each anything-goes match. It beat the usual Vegas fights all to hell, and like them, was usually rigged so the right person lost. "How do I get down there?"

Billy located a service stairway by the ladies' room for me, while he disappeared through the floor to do some advance scouting. He reappeared about the time I hit the lower levels, with less than happy news. "Jimmy's scheduled to be up next, and they got him matched against a werewolf. I think it's one of that pack Tony took on a few years ago."

I winced. Great. Tony had ordered their alpha killed to encourage them to move out of his territory, and Jimmy had done the deed. So any member of that pack was required to kill him on sight or die trying. If he got in the ring, he was not walking out again.

I reached for the service door only to find Billy barring the way. "Move. You know I don't like walking through you." I'd fed him once tonight, and that was enough.

"You aren't going in there. I'm serious; don't even think about it."

"The only person who might tell me about my parents is about to be eaten. Get out of the way!"

"Why, so you can join him?" Billy pointed a very substantial-looking finger. "Through that door is a hallway. At the end of it are two armed guards. They're human, but if by some miracle you get past 'em, there's a whole roomful of vamps on the other side. You go in there and you're dead, and without you I'll soon fade too far to do any damage. End result—Tony wins. Is that what you want?"

I glared at him. I hate it when he's right. "Then what do you suggest? I'm not leaving until I see him."

Billy grimaced. "Then come this way, fast."

We fled down the corridor in the opposite direction, and I was soon glad that Billy was there to provide directions. The place was a rabbit warren of tunnels, all painted the same industrial gray. In minutes I had no idea where I was. We stopped several times to duck into rooms, most of which were filled with cleaning supplies, broken gambling machines and, in one case, wall after wall of computers. The one thing they didn't have was people—I guess everyone who was off duty was at the fights.

I thought we were avoiding being seen again when Billy disappeared into another wall, so I didn't waste any time flinging open the door. This time, I was met with a large room stuffed to the ceiling with what looked to be extra props and decorations. A collection of African masks and spears sat beside a suit of armor that was missing the bottom half of one leg. A rather ratty-looking stuffed lion's head leaned against a mummy case, which had been modified to house a poster board advertising a magic show. It was watched over by a huge statue of Anubis, the jackal-headed Egyptian god, who seemed to be glaring at something in the far corner. I followed the line of its glassy, fixed stare and found Jimmy's ugly face peering out of a heavy-duty reinforced cage. The pointed features, slicked-back black hair and shifty eyes were those I remembered, but he must have been doing pretty well recently, because his usual baggy suit had been replaced with a sleek tan number that looked like it had been made for him.

It took him a few seconds to place me. When he'd known me, my hair had reached the small of my back and I dressed in Eugenie's version of appropriate attire for young ladies, which meant long skirts and high-necked blouses. The hair had been sacrificed to a more practical, and far less memorable, bob as soon as I went with the Witness Protection people. It had grown out some since then, but not enough to make much difference. And Jimmy had never seen me in anything like the leather number. After a confused few seconds, though, it clicked. So much for my great disguise.

"Cassandra! Goddamn, it's good to see you! I always knew you'd be back someday. Let me outta here, would you? There's been a big misunderstanding!"

"Misunderstanding?" I found it hard to believe that he really thought I'd just walked back into the organization. Tony might forgive a fourteen-year-old who had run off in what he assumed was a fit of adolescent angst, but an adult who had conspired to destroy him was another matter. I debated leaving Jimmy where he was, but although I liked having him securely behind bars, I preferred to talk somewhere less likely to be interrupted by Tony's thugs.

"Yeah. One of my assistants is trying to get ahead the easy way, and lied about me to the boss. I can straighten things out, but I gotta talk to Tony—"

"You certainly took your time." I looked around at the sound of a tiny voice but didn't see anything. "I found the witches, but one of the vamps caught me. Get me out!"

I glanced at Billy. "Who said that?"

"I'm over here! Are you blind?" I followed the squeak to a small birdcage that was almost hidden behind a peacock-feather fan. Inside was a woman about eight inches high and mad as a hornet. Flaming red hair framed a perfect Barbie-doll face and a pair of pissed-off lavender eyes. I blinked. What the hell was the bar putting in the drinks?

"It's a pixie, Cass," Billy said, looking unhappy. He drifted in front of her cage, and she scowled at him.

Tiny fists grabbed the bars of her cage and rattled them angrily. "Are you deaf, woman?! I said, get me out! And keep that thing away from me!"

"You know her?" I asked Billy, surprised. Apparently, he'd had a more interesting social life than I'd thought.

He shook his head. "Not that one, but I've met others. Don't listen to her, Cass. None of the Fey are anything but trouble."

"She's probably headed for the ring," I protested, trying to deal with the fact that Tony had found a way into Faerie, which wasn't a myth after all.

"These bars are *iron*, human! I feel sick already. Release me right *now*!" I blinked, surprised that a tiny voice could echo like that.

"Don't do it, Cass," Billy warned. "Doing the Fey favors is never a good idea. It comes back on you, and not in a good way." Her teeny face flushed an ugly red and she let out a string of imprecations in a language that I didn't know, but he obviously did. "Nasty, vile creature!" he spluttered. "Let her go to the ring, and good riddance!"

I sighed. Whatever or whoever she was, I wasn't leaving anybody to be entertainment for the bastard or his boys. "If I let you out, you have to promise not to interfere with anything I'm doing," I told her severely. "No blowing the whistle on us, okay?"

"You've lost your mind," she said flatly. "And when did you change clothes? What is going on around here?"

That's what I wanted to know. "Do I know you?"

Tiny green and lavender wings ruffled agitatedly on her back. "I can't believe this," she said in disgust. "I'm on a mission with an idiot." Her eyes narrowed as she scanned me. "Oh, no. You aren't my Cassandra, are you?" She threw up minuscule hands. "I knew it! I should have listened to Granddam: never, ever work with humans!"

"Hey, a little help here," Jimmy called from behind me.

"Just go," the pixie told me. "And take the ghost and the rat with you. I'll deal with this myself."

I had the feeling I needed to know what was going on, but staying around for a prolonged conversation probably wasn't smart. I pulled the latch on her cage, ignoring Billy's comments, and ran back to Jimmy. Unfortunately, his pen had a lock on it that required a key to open. "How do I get you out of there?"

"Here," Jimmy slid up next to the bars. "They forgot to frisk me. The key's in my coat. Hurry up; they'll be back anytime!"

I reached for his jacket, but my hand stopped a foot away from the bars and simply refused to go any closer. It felt like an invisible wall of thick, sticky molasses had closed around it, one that didn't want to turn loose. The pixie buzzed over while I was struggling to pull my hand back. "I'll free the witches," she said, "but I need you to open a door for me."

"I can't even open this one," I told her, using my left hand to try to pull the right free. That backfired, leaving me with two hands that wouldn't go forwards or pull back. I was well and truly stuck.

"It's a tar-baby spell," Billy said, hovering about anxiously. "We need the release."

"It's a what?"

"That's slang for a really strong variation of a *prehendo*. I'm guessing that anything that gets within a certain perimeter of the cage is gonna get caught like a bug on flypaper, and the more you struggle, the tighter you're gonna be trapped. Try not to move."

"Now you tell me." His warning came about a second after I'd panicked and kicked out with my foot, only to have it get caught, too. Sometimes I really *hated* magic. "Billy! What do I do?"

"Stay still! I'll look around. It's gotta be here somewhere."

"Come back!" I yelled after him as he streamed off towards the suit of armor. "Get me out!"

Jimmy swore. "It has to be that thing." he said, pointing upwards. I now noticed what looked like a week-old baked apple hanging from a chain above the door. A second later I recognized it as one of those ugly, shrunken-head key chains they had in the lobby gift shop, along with skeleton tie tacks and "I did it at Dante's" T-shirts. Tony has no shame when it comes to making a buck. "It's the only thing that shouldn't be here."

The pixie flew up to examine it and almost bumped heads with Billy Joe, who'd come back to have a look. "Stay out of my way, remnant," she ordered. Billy was about to say something—probably fairly profane—but someone beat him to it. A shriveled, raisinlike eye popped open on the head and regarded the pixie with annoyance. "Call me that again, Tinkerbell, and you'll never get this door open."

I just stood there, not able to believe I was watching a pixie have a conversation with a shrunken head. I think that was about the time I gave up on logic and just decided to go with the flow. If I was lucky, someone had spiked my drink and I was hallucinating. No one said anything, so I figured it was up to me. "Can you please open the door?" I asked calmly.

The eye—there seemed to be only one working—swiveled to me. "That depends. What can you do for me?"

I stared at it. It was a shrunken head. The options were pretty limited. "What?"

"Hey, you look familiar. You ever come by the voodoo bar? It's in the Seventh Circle, upstairs. I was the star attraction, you know, a lot more popular than those lousy floor shows this loser booked. People would tell me their orders and I'd shout them out to the bartenders. It went over great. Everyone thought I was this sophisticated audio-animatronics thingy. Sometimes I told jokes, too. Like, what would they call Bugsy Seigel if he became a vamp? A fangster!" The little thing cackled maniacally. "I crack myself up, you know that?"

"It is evil," the pixie stated flatly. I nodded in agreement. Extensive warding was impossible in a place that ran off electricity, but was this really the best solution Tony had been able to find?

"Oh, we got a heckler, huh? Okay, how about this one? A guy walks into a bar in Hell and asks for a beer. The bartender says, sorry, but we only serve spirits here!"

"She's right; it is evil," Billy Joe said.

The pixie conked the head with the flat of a tiny sword she pulled off her belt. "Release her, or I will chop you into bits!"

The eye managed to look surprised. "Hey! You're not supposed to be able to do that! Why aren't you stuck like her?"

"Because I'm not human," the pixie said through gritted teeth. "Now, do as I say and stop stalling!"

"I would, honest, but I can't without authorization. I messed up once and look where that got me. All I wanted was a fast car and some faster women to put in it. Now I'd settle for my body back. Only, it's scattered around all over the place since that voodoo bitch carved me up. Give me a break. I got a little behind in my payments, sure, but come on."

"You owed Tony money," I guessed.

"I had what you might call a run of bad luck with the cards," it said with dignity.

"So Tony sold you to a voodoo priestess?" It didn't surprise me. Tony gave a new meaning to the phrase "pound of flesh."

"And then made me work in his stupid casino," the head

ranted. "Then a few months ago, they got worried cause one of the regulars began to suspect that I wasn't just a pretty face, and I got stuck down here. No more parties, no more pretty girls, nada. It's been damn depressing. But hey, maybe they'll shrink you and we can hang out together. Literally. What do you—"

The pixie stopped the tirade by making good on her promise and hacking the head clean in two. I stared as the two halves swung free for a few seconds, each on one end of the thin chain; then they knitted themselves back together in front of my eyes. "Hello, already dead, remember?" the head said testily. "You may be able to hurt me, Tink, but it won't be in time to help your friends, here. For that, we hafta cut a deal."

"What do you want?" I asked quickly.

"My body, of course. Get those witches in there to reverse the bokor's mojo and put me back."

I stared at the crazed little thing. "That's insane. No one can reverse something like that. Even if we somehow looked up this voodoo woman, even she couldn't—"

"I'll promise," the pixie said impatiently. "Now, release her."

The head turned back to her so fast it would have had whiplash if it still had a neck. "Say that again."

To my surprise, she looked perfectly serious. "I will take you into Faerie. I don't make any promises about what you will look like, but you may acquire a body. Some spirits manifest there in a physical form."

"They do?" Billy asked with more interest than I liked. The pixie ignored him.

The head paused. "I gotta think about this," it said and suddenly stopped moving.

"Why does this thing say 'Made in Taiwan' on the bottom?" Billy asked, peering at it from about an inch away.

We exchanged looks, and Billy didn't need any prompting. He passed into the head and reappeared a few seconds later, looking pissed. "There's no consciousness in there, Cass, not to mention that it's plastic! Someone enchanted it to wake up if anyone got stuck in the tar baby. I'm guessing it set off an alarm and was trying to delay us long enough for someone to get here."

"Then why did it suddenly shut up?"

"As a guess, we made an offer it didn't know how to answer."

I closed my eyes and forced myself to calm down before I had a heart attack and saved Tony some reward bucks. "So, what are we supposed to do? We already tried attacking it!"

"We need the password, Cass—the release. Sometimes it's an object that you have to touch, or it can be a password. But this place is full of stuff! It'll take me some time to work through it all."

"What's going on? Who're you talking to?" Jimmy demanded.

"There's supposed to be a trigger around here, or a word that can force that thing to release me," I explained briefly. "It isn't real; it was triggered by the spell."

Jimmy looked surprised. "You mean that ain't Danny?"

"And Danny would be?"

"That shrunken head Tony made outta what was left of some guy back in the forties. We made it the model for our key rings." He looked annoyed. "You mean they put one of those novelty heads down here? What, I don't even rate the real thing?"

It was just as well I was stuck, or I'd have been tempted to thump him. "Do you know what the release is or not?"

He shrugged, still scowling. "Try 'banjo.'" As soon as he said it, the stuff holding me in place was simply not there anymore. I'd been pulling away, useless though it was, and the momentum landed me on the floor on my already bruised backside. Jimmy grabbed me through the bars and hauled me to my feet. "You're wasting time!"

"Banjo?"

"We have passwords for restricted areas that are changed every few weeks. I approved the new list a couple days ago, and that was the first word on it." He saw my expression. "The boys are hired for brawn, not brain."

"But why 'banjo'?"

"Why not? Look, I have to come up with a couple hundred of these a year, okay? I ran out of abracadabras a long time ago. Besides, you wouldn't have guessed it, right?"

"I still need you to open the door," the pixie reminded me as I finally found a leather key chain in Jimmy's suit coat. My hands were shaking, but it was obvious he couldn't let himself out. Somebody had run out of handcuffs, or maybe they didn't like him any better than I did. Both his hands had been smashed, and they weren't merely broken, but ruined to the point that not a finger or joint appeared to be working. I was betting that, even if he got out of this, he'd made his last hit.

"I'm trying!"

"Not that one," she said impatiently. "The one by the cage where they put me." She whirled around my head like a tiny cyclone. "Against the far wall. My hands aren't big enough to turn that oversized knob."

"Give me a minute," I told her as the stubborn lock finally sprang open. Jimmy shot out of there at a dead run, heading for the hall. I glanced from him to the demanding pixie. "Follow him," I told Billy. "I'll be right there."

"Cass—"

"Just do it!"

Billy went off in a huff and I rushed to open the door the tiny virago indicated. I was about to turn and follow Billy when I found out what Tony's latest business venture was. Three brunette women, all about my age, sat back-to-back on the floor inside a rust-colored circle. Their hands and feet were bound, and makeshift gags had been stuffed in their mouths. I stared. "My God. He's slaving now?" Even for Tony, that was low.

"As good as," the pixie replied, flying over to the women. She grimaced and looked back at me. "This is worse than I thought. I can deal with the circle, but I can't get them loose."

I ran forward, wondering if one of the other keys on Jimmy's ring would work, and hit what felt like a solid wall. It didn't look like there was anything there, but my bruised nose said otherwise, and my ward flared, spilling golden light around the room. The pixie began chattering agitatedly. "Stupid witch! It's a circle of power! I'll destroy it, *then* you free the women!"

I moved backwards and my ward calmed down, although I could still feel it warm against my back. "I'm not a witch," I said resentfully, wondering if my nose was broken.

The pixie had dropped to the floor and started rubbing at the circle. It was made of a dried substance that flaked off slowly. "Okay. The Pythia's not a witch. Got it."

"Can't you hurry?" I asked after a minute, wondering how far Jimmy had gotten in his condition. "And my name is Cassie."

Sharp lavender eyes gave an exaggerated roll. "I used to think it was the position that made you so annoying, but you were born this way, weren't you? And I'm doing the best I can! The blood has dried and it's not coming off easily."

"Blood?"

"How do you think dark mages perform a spell? It takes a death, stupid." She started mumbling in that other language, while I hugged myself and tried not to think about what Tony was doing with a member of the Fey, some slaves and a circle of blood. He'd been on the wrong side of human law as long as I'd known him, but this contravened both mage and vampire rules as well. I didn't know when he'd turned suicidal, but I suddenly wanted out of the casino in the worst way.

Finally, my small accomplice finished cleaning a narrow

line through the circle, and I heard a small pop. "Is that it?" I asked her. It seemed kind of anticlimactic.

She sat on the floor and panted. "Well, try it!"

I walked forward, tentatively this time, but nothing blocked me. I knelt quickly by the nearest woman and started trying keys. Thankfully, the third one worked. I pulled the gag out of her mouth, and she started screaming. I started to stuff it back in, before she alerted the whole casino, but she caught my hand. She began a rapid string of French in between kissing my wrist and whatever else she could reach. I didn't understand much of what she was saying—my only other modern language is Italian, and there aren't a lot of crossovers between the two—but the light brown eyes that were looking at me almost worshipfully rang a bell.

I got a weird feeling in my stomach. I knew this woman. She was plumper and looked far less haggard, but otherwise, little had changed since I'd seen her stretched on a rack enveloped in flames. I did a double take, but there was no denying it. That face was seared into my memory, and a glance at her fingertips showed them to be heavily scarred. As impossible as it was, a seventeenth-century witch was sitting in a casino in modern-day Vegas. Presumably a dead witch, since no one could have survived what I'd seen her put through. Any other day, I would have seriously considered passing out; as it was, I just pressed the key into her hand and scrambled back out of reach.

"I have to go," I said shortly and fled. My plan was simple: find Jimmy, question him, turn him over to the cops, then run like hell. Other complications I could do without.

I didn't need Billy to figure out that going back the way we'd come wasn't a great idea. If anyone was coming for Jimmy, that's the route they'd take, and my one gun wouldn't help much against the kind of hardware Tony's thugs carried. Not that I had seen any employees, muscle or otherwise, since hitting the lower levels, a fact that was beginning to worry me. It was early morning, sure, but a place like this never slept. There should be people around, especially if the ring was on tonight, but the hallways echoed emptily. I followed the corridor until I came to where it diverged. I paused, confused, until Billy floated through a wall and beckoned to me. "In here."

I entered through a nearby door to find myself in an empty employee break room. Jimmy was half-hidden behind a soda machine. "There's a doorknob," he said when he saw me, and pointed at the wall with his elbow, "right about there. But I can't do anything with these." He held up his mutilated hands and I hurried forward. Behind the machine was what looked like an expanse of the same off-white, slightly stained drywall that made up the rest of the room. But it rippled around the edges, although I wouldn't have noticed if I hadn't been expecting it. The perimeter ward was getting old. I slid my hands along the wall until I grasped what felt like a knob, and pushed.

A door opened onto a narrow corridor that, judging by the dust on the floor, didn't get a lot of use. It wasn't a surprise. Tony always had multiple exits, half of them hidden, in his businesses. He told me once that it was a leftover from his youth, when armies went marching through Rome on a regular basis. He'd almost burnt to death when some Spanish soldiers in Charles V's army sacked his villa in the 1530s, and ever since he'd been paranoid. For once, I was grateful for it.

We ran down the hidden hallway, then climbed up a ladder at the end. Or, rather, I climbed and shoved Jimmy up in front of me. His hands were a major handicap, but he used his elbows, I pushed from below and somehow we made it. We burst out of a trapdoor into a locker room. A human wearing a sequined devil costume blinked at us blearily but didn't ask questions. He worked for Tony, so he was probably used to assorted oddities.

Jimmy scrambled to his feet and ran for the door, puffing

like a freight train, and I wasn't much better off. I definitely needed to add gym visits to my to-do list, right after running for my life and killing Tony. The locker room exited onto another of those plain gray hallways, but mercifully, it was a short one. A few seconds later, we were standing near a forest of faux stalagmites overlooking the river. A Charon was rowing a few weary gamblers back towards the entrance a few yards away.

"Hey, where do you think you're going?!" Jimmy had started off without a word and didn't so much as flinch at my shout. Wrestling him to the ground wasn't an option, but fortunately, I knew something that was. "Billy, get him!"

I took off after Jimmy and felt Billy Joe flow past me like a warm breeze. He was usually cold or at least chilly, but he was hopped up on some vamp's wards and had energy to burn. But Jimmy reached the vestibule in record time and was heading for the gates when he suddenly stopped and stumbled backwards. I realized why when I saw Pritkin, Tomas and Louis-César coming in the main entrance. I didn't worry about how they'd found me or what they had planned. I grabbed a handful of Jimmy's elegant suit coat and dragged him back into the hallway.

"You aren't going anywhere until we talk about my parents," I informed him. Some of the larger stalagmites were between us and the trio from MAGIC, and I briefly thought we'd gotten away without being seen. Then I heard Tomas call my name. Damn, I was busted.

Chapter 7

My predicament wasn't a complete shock. The Senate has plenty of money to hire wardsmiths to run screens across every window and door in MAGIC, and probably to ward their vehicles as well. I'd initially been impressed that Billy Joe had gotten me car keys so quickly, but when I reached the garage, I'd seen a whole tag board of them hanging just inside the door. That, and the fact that nobody was guarding the cars, had told me something about the quality of the wards. I'd probably broken through more than one, what with crawling out the bathroom window, passing through the garage door and stealing a nice black Mercedes for my ride into town, but it still should have taken them longer than this to track me.

Good wards are better than a security alarm because they tell you basic facts about who it was who broke in—human or not, aural imprint—and, if you get a good enough one, what they did while in your place. But they don't tell you where the intruder went after he or she left, unless you get one of the really intricate, expensive über-wards specially crafted by a wardmaster. Since the members of the Silver Circle are the ones who license wardsmiths, it wouldn't be hard for them to get the best in the business to design their defenses, and they use MAGIC's premises as much as anyone. But even the best wards available don't tell you exactly where a person can be found, only if you're hot or cold on

the trail. Otherwise, I'd never have been able to elude
Tony's goons long enough for his spells to wear off. So the
vamps would know I was in Vegas, but it should have taken
them hours to narrow down the precise spot. Someone who
knew me well and who knew Jimmy was here must have
told them where to look for me. Otherwise they'd be staking
out the airport and wandering around the strip. I was going
to have a less than friendly talk with Rafe if I ever saw him
again.

Jimmy got his head together, shook off my hold and
bolted down the hall. A silver cloud descended from the ceiling and started after him just as the EMPLOYEES ONLY door
behind us was kicked in from the outside. So much for not
alarming the humans. I didn't even turn around, but ran
down the corridor after my fleeing captive. No way was I
letting him slip away while I tried to reason with the Senate's stooges.

I heard Pritkin swear, but by then I had reached the door
to the locker room and I slammed it shut after me. Since the
door would hold them for all of about a second, I needed to
find Jimmy fast. I ignored a question from a half-dressed
man in a demon suit and dodged past benches and open
lockers to the exit. A gust of warm desert air ruffled my hair
as I emerged, and I looked up to see that I'd exited the building. I was along one side, in a spot where the elaborate dec-
oration of the front gave way to a plain asphalt lot bounded
by a chain-link fence. It was probably where the employees
parked. I cursed, thinking it would be hard to find Jimmy
among the rows and rows of vehicles, but then I saw him
darting towards the back of the lot. Billy's sparkling cloud
was trailing after him like a misplaced halo.

I drew my gun and continued my pursuit. I was a still
shaky on whether I could actually kill anyone, even someone who deserved it as much as Jimmy, but I could definitely wound him. And that would give Billy Joe time to try
out his possession skills. I took off through a row of cars at

a dead run after checking that my safety was still on. It wouldn't be funny if I saved everyone the trouble and shot myself.

I hadn't gotten halfway down the row before I heard the door behind me burst open with enough force to wrench it off its hinges. Strangely enough, instead of picking up speed, Jimmy skidded to a stop at the same moment, only a few yards ahead of me. I thought he'd reached his car and was trying to figure out how to use his keys with mangled hands, but a minute later I realized that what he'd actually found was backup. A couple dozen ugly guys rose out of the lot like scarecrows popping out of a wheat field. I didn't take time to count, but at least five or six were vamps. How the hell had Jimmy managed to fix up an ambush?

I skidded to a stop at the same time that a familiar iron grip caught me around the waist. It was sort of ironic, really. I'd spent more time than I wanted to admit fantasizing about being in Tomas' arms, but now that I'd spent much of a night there, it was getting old. Pritkin moved into view as Tomas dragged me backwards. He had his shotgun out and was glaring at me with something close to hatred in those clear eyes.

It rattled me until I realized that he was actually looking over my shoulder. A loud creaking and popping sound came from where Jimmy was standing, as if a forest of trees had all decided to fall at once, and I glanced up. "You have got to be kidding," was as much as I got out before Tomas threw himself on top of me and we went down in a pile. I scraped my hands against the asphalt, losing a bit more skin, but keeping hold of the gun through some miracle. Yep, definitely getting old.

I managed to get a partial glimpse of the sight in front of us through a curtain of Tomas' hair. Most of the mob at Tony's had nicknames. I think it's some kind of unwritten gangster rule, because virtually everyone had one tied to either their favorite weapon or most prominent physical feature. Alphonse was "Baseball" because of what he could do with a bat, and they weren't talking about on a diamond. I'd always assumed that Jimmy's nickname came from his looks, which were rather ratlike, or his personality. I'd been wrong. It seemed that Jimmy the half satyr was also Jimmy the wererat. Or something. Weres weren't my specialty, but I'd never seen anything quite like that. I squinted. I'd never even heard of anything like that. Probably for good reason, since anybody who saw one was going to want to forget it as soon as possible.

Whatever it was had a giant, furry body that looked like it was molting in patches. Its narrow head had goat horns growing out of it, its big, chipped teeth were the color of a rusty sink and its pink tail was as thick around as my calf. It had goat hooves on its hind legs and stunk to high heaven. And, whatever Jimmy had morphed into, some serious nepotism had been going on at Dante's, because a tribe of his relations surrounded him.

My brain kept telling my eyes that they were seeing things. Number one, satyrs are already magical creatures, and as such are supposed to be immune from were bites, so what I was seeing was technically impossible. Number two, why would a whole group of were-anythings be working for Tony? That sort of cooperation just didn't happen; everyone knew that. But then, it was hard to argue with the evidence twitching wiry black whiskers a few feet away.

"Rats." It took me a second to realize that Pritkin was commenting on the type of shape-shifters we were dealing with instead of expressing mild irritation.

Okay, I'd been right. Point for me. I'd gotten confused because the were-DNA seemed to have gotten mixed up with the satyr genes for a really unappealing mess. Jimmy— I assumed it was him because he was wearing the remains of his once stylish suit—was a gray and white tower of fur with three-inch claws dangling from arms ropy with muscle. The change seemed to have helped with his hands. They were still bloody but looked like they might be functional. Something else had changed, too. He'd never been all that menacing in his usual form—it was one of the reasons he'd made a good hit man, since people tended to underestimate him—but he was doing pretty well at the moment. I was armed, but Tomas had trapped both my arm and my gun underneath me. Jimmy stood right in front of me, and I couldn't do more than glare into his beady eyes.

I wasn't happy, but neither was anyone else. Pritkin hadn't bothered to worry about firearm regulations, having simply thrown a leather trench coat over his collection. He had the shotgun in one hand and a pistol in the other, and was pointing them both at Jimmy. Louis-César had his rapier out, which looked really weird considering that he'd changed into more normal-looking clothes for the trip outside MAGIC. He was wearing a tight-fitting T-shirt and a pair of jeans faded almost white. They molded to his lower body so tightly that they might as well have been painted on, and I decided that I'd been wrong before; modern clothes showed off his physique just fine. He was looking the weres over as if trying to decide which to carve up first. They must have thought the same thing, because the attention of most of the rats was focused on him instead of me.

"Tomas, take Mademoiselle Palmer back to her suite and see that she is comfortable. We'll be along presently." Louis-César sounded as calm as if all he and Pritkin planned was to have a couple of drinks and maybe play some blackjack.

I was getting really tired of people ordering me around. "No! There is no freaking way I'm leaving until—"

"I will take her." Pritkin spoke at the same time I did and moved towards me in a sort of sideways shuffle to let him keep his weapons leveled on the rat pack and their vamp outriders. I was about to tell him to go to hell—I wasn't going anywhere with him and his arsenal—when Tomas picked me up and started backing away.

"Tomas, put me down! You don't understand—I've been
looking for him for years!" I may as well not have bothered
talking for all the attention he paid me, and struggling would
only be a waste of time. I gave up and raised my gun, hoping that the close quarters would compensate for the lousy
angle and let me get at least a couple shots into Jimmy. I
doubted that I'd do much damage, both because of my lack
of skill and because weres are notoriously resilient, but all I
needed was to slow him down enough for Billy to do his
thing. He could find out what I wanted to know and fill me
in later. But before I could fire, Tomas shifted me into one
arm and snatched the gun away with the other. I was beginning to be very tired of his doing that, but, armed or not, I
wasn't giving in. This might be my only chance to deal with
Genie's killer, and I wasn't about to miss it. "Billy Joe—
what the hell are you waiting for? Do it already!"

The hovering cloud gathered itself and dropped onto
Jimmy like a stone. Tomas tried to pull me away but I fought
him. He didn't want to hurt me and it slowed him down a
fraction. A second passed, no more than that; then Billy Joe
burst out of Jimmy as if he'd been fired from a cannon and
slammed straight into me. I didn't resist him, thinking that
he might not have had enough energy left for the possession
and needed a draw to complete the process. But the force
kept pushing on me until I thought I would suffocate, as if
there was more of him than usual and there wasn't room inside my skin for both of us.

I had no time to think, much less react, before a tremendous explosion rocked me from the inside out, like an air-
liner losing cabin pressure. I felt something tearing and
thought it was my blouse, what little there was of it. I instinctively clutched at it since I'd had to leave the ruined bra
behind, but my hand didn't encounter my familiar curves
under spandex. Instead, my fingers slid over well-worn
denim. I looked down to see the top of my head. I blinked,
but the view didn't change: I was still clutching myself to

my chest. I had a complete sense of disorientation, but no time to deal with it because Jimmy decided to rush me and all hell broke loose.

Jimmy tore into me, literally, latching on to my arm with those knifelike teeth. I screamed and dropped the body I was carrying onto the ground. I had time to see a pair of huge blue eyes looking up at me in amazement before Jimmy started to shake his head, trying to rip my arm off. I reacted without thinking, pulling away from the piercing pain, and stared in shock as his body went sailing past me and crashed into a nearby car. Throwing him had been unbelievably easy, like he weighed no more than a doll.

I looked around and it seemed as if everyone was moving in slow motion. I watched Pritkin blow a basketball-sized hole through the unfortunate car Jimmy had been standing in front of before I sent him sailing. I could see the explosion as it blasted out of the muzzle of the gun, and the glass that burst out from the windshield seemed to float to the ground as slowly as leaves falling from a tree. Pritkin turned equally slowly to meet the tide of furry bodies coming towards him at a gentle lope instead of an all-out charge.

The only person moving at normal speed was Louis-César, who skewered a rat through the heart and, as I watched, pulled out his blade to turn it on another. "Did you not hear me? Get her out of here!" He was looking at me, and I blinked at him, wondering what he was talking about. Then he whipped out a short throwing knife, which he sent into the throat of a rat that had somehow snuck up on the body lying at my feet. The knife caught it in the back of the neck and it squealed, pawing at the knife with claws extended so that it cut its own flesh. It rolled away from the person it had been about to attack, and I stared down at the sight of myself lying on the asphalt.

I finally noticed that the bloody arm Jimmy had been gnawing on wasn't mine. I felt the pain, saw the blood, but the flesh underneath the gore was a light, even honey tone, a color I couldn't get unless I had it sprayed on. The hand was long fingered, the arm was muscular and the chest supporting this new arm of mine was as flat as a man's. It took me a few seconds to realize that it was a man's, and that it was wearing Tomas' cobweb shirt and denim jacket. I staggered against a nearby Volkswagen and the body at my feet sat up.

"Cassie, where are you?" My blue eyes shone with anger and what looked like fear. It was hard to tell; I wasn't used to reading my own expression. "Answer me, damn it!"

I knelt beside what had been my body and looked into those familiar eyes. The face looked wrong for a second, until I realized that I was seeing myself the way everyone else did, instead of the usual mirror view. There was no way to deny it: somehow, I had ended up in Tomas' body. Which left the question, who the hell was in mine?

"Who are you?" I grabbed my arm, trying not to notice that Jack had had a point about my wardrobe lately, and my body let out a shriek.

"Cut that out, goddamnit!" If blue eyes could let off sparks, mine were doing a pretty good job.

"Who are you? Who's in there?" Before I could get an answer, Jimmy shook off the blow I'd dealt him and came at us again. I had plenty of time to grab my gun from Tomas' waistband and shoot him. I saw a crimson flower bloom on his chest, slightly below the heart, if a rat's heart is in the same place as a human's, but he kept coming. I shot him again, in the arm this time. It was a mistake—I was aiming for his head—but it turned out to be a good thing because he had been in the process of raising a gun. He dropped it and scrabbled at his chest, while I knelt there wondering where he'd hidden a weapon in the few remaining pieces of his suit. He paused a few feet away, giving me plenty of time to finish the job, but he wasn't looking at me.

"Call off your pet gorilla or you'll never find your dad." The voice was unmistakably Jimmy's, so I learned another new thing—weres could talk in their altered forms, or at least half satyrs could.

"What?" I eased my finger off the trigger, and Jimmy threw me a dirty glance.

"I wasn't talking to you." He looked down at whoever was in my body and grimaced. "We can make a deal; don't be stupid—call him off. Tony ain't gonna tell you what you want to know. He likes Rog too much where he is."

"My father is dead." I couldn't understand what Jimmy thought he was playing at, but it wasn't going to work.

He looked pissed, although that could have been because of the blood seeping out from between his fingers and splattering the asphalt. "Damn it, I'm not talking to you!"

An explosion caused me to look up, and I saw that Pritkin and Louis-César had been busy. Six furry bodies littered the lot, sprawled over cars and slumped on the ground, about the same number that were still active. Louis-César was methodically butchering two of the remaining ones while dodging the flying talons that were trying to decapitate him. Pritkin, though, was really tearing loose, and by the expression on his face loving every minute of it. He blew up another car, shooting through a large wererat who looked down at his missing middle in surprise before keeling over. Then he stopped another that had leapt at him from the roof of a minivan by yelling something that caused the were to burst into flames in midair. Blazing pieces rained down on Pritkin's shields—I could see them spark in electric blue wherever one hit—but none got through.

I couldn't believe that no one from the bar was concerned about the noise. Shotgun blasts are not exactly quiet, and neither were the grunting, squealing and scuffling that accompanied them. It was also strange that the vamps weren't attacking but hadn't left, either. Five of them stood around, watching the action as if waiting for something.

"Tomas, behind you!" Louis-César jumped over the body of the huge rat in front of him and started towards me. His expression, and a curse in my own voice from behind me, told me that had I picked a really bad time to be distracted. I whirled around to see that Jimmy had grabbed my body by the hair and had one of those three-inch claws pressed to my throat. "I told you to get her out of here!" Louis-César was looking at Jimmy, but he was talking to me. Or, rather, to Tomas, only he didn't appear to be home. I wasn't too worried about the enraged vampire at my side, though; the claw, which had cut a fine line across my throat, was holding all my attention.

A stream of very inventive curses poured out of my body's mouth, some of which sounded real familiar. Well, at least I knew who was keeping house. "Shut up, Billy. Don't make this worse."

The blue eyes widened and focused on me. "Wait a minute, you're in *there*? Good God, I thought you were dead! I thought . . ."

"I said, shut up." I wasn't in the mood for one of Billy's harangues, and I needed to think. Okay, one problem at a time. It wouldn't do me much good to figure out how to get my body back if its throat had been cut in the meantime, so deal with Jimmy now and freak out later.

"What do you want, Jimmy?"

"Be silent, Tomas! You have done enough damage tonight. I will deal with this." Louis-César seemed behind on the action, but I wasn't about to take the time to get him up to speed.

"Shut up," I told him, and the expression of incredulity that passed over his face would have been funny in other circumstances. "Come on, Jimmy, what do you want to let . . . her . . . go? You wanted a deal, remember?" It was surreal, standing there in someone else's body and arguing with a giant rat, but all I could see was my body with Billy Joe's frightened expression. I couldn't rely on him to get us out of this: he'd never even made it to thirty before he ended up drowned like an unwanted kitten.

"I want out of here alive; what you think?" Jimmy glanced, not at the vamps at my side, but at the ones lounging around the fight. Okay, maybe they weren't his buddies after all. "And cutie here is going with me. Tony will forget about our little problem if I bring him Cassie, and that's exactly what's gonna happen."

"No way." I was not going to stand there and let Jimmy cart me off. None of my fantasies about Tomas' body had included taking up permanent residence. "Try again."

"Okay, fine. How about I slit her throat? Like that any better? Tony'd prefer her alive, but I'm betting even a corpse would get me outta the doghouse."

"If you harm her, I swear it will take you days to die, and you will beg for death before it comes." Louis-César sounded utterly convincing, but killing Jimmy, however slowly, wasn't going to bring me back to life.

"He's got a point, Jimmy. The only thing keeping you alive right now is Cassie. If you kill her, we'll deal with you before Tony gets the chance."

"So, what? I let her go, then you kill me anyway? I don't think so."

"You should recall that there are many ways to die," Louis-César put in, and I could have kicked him.

"How many times do I have to tell you to shut the hell up?" I heard the edge of panic in my voice and forced myself to calm down. If I lost it now, no way were Pretty Boy and Rambo going to talk us out of this. Especially since Pritkin seemed to have disappeared, off chasing wererats probably.

"We will talk when this is done," Louis-César said quietly. "I do not know what is wrong with you . . ."

"Exactly. You don't. You really, really don't."

I smiled at Jimmy, but it only seemed to unnerve him. I figured out why a second later when I nicked my lip on a fang. Tomas' were fully extended, but I didn't know how to retract them. Great, bargaining for my life with a lisp—

exactly my luck. "Okay, how about this, Jimmy? You give us Cassie, and we give you a head start. Say, two hours? I'll even promise to distract the vamps over there long enough for you to make a run for it. They're Tony's boys, aren't they? They'll stand there and watch us kill you, or finish the job if you get past us. But we can keep them busy and off your back for a while. Now, that's fair, isn't it?"

Jimmy licked his muzzle with a long, pale tongue, and his little rat ears twitched. "You'd say anything to get her back, then kill me or let them do it. Besides, if I don't take her to Tony, I'm dead anyway."

I sneered. "Since when do weres take orders from vamps? I can't believe you toadied to him all these years!"

Jimmy squealed; I guess I hit a nerve. "There's a new order coming, vampire, and a lotta things are about to change. You may be taking orders from us soon!"

I backpedaled. I wanted to hit his pride, not goad him into doing something stupid. "Maybe, but it won't do you much good if you don't live to see it, right? You don't know me, so you won't take my word. But what about Cassie's? How about if she promises to guarantee our good behavior?" Jimmy looked torn, like he really wanted to believe me, and I knew why. The bullet wound in his arm didn't look too bad, but the injury to his torso was another thing. The long white strip of fur down his front had a widening red stain, and his breath sounded labored and a little bubbly. Ten to one I'd hit a lung, and even a shape-shifter was going to have trouble healing that.

"Come on, Jimmy. It's the best offer you're going to get."

"Tell your muscle to back off if you want a deal, or she dies." He spat on the ground at my feet to underline the threat, and there was blood in it. Jimmy was running out of time and, as soon as he figured that out, so was I. His whiskers twitched, and I realized with surprise that I could actually smell his fear. It was a tangible thing, to the point that I felt like I could roll it around on my tongue like wine.

It was musky with a sweet undertaste, although the latter
might have been from his blood. Now that I had noticed the
heightened senses of this new body, they were proving very
distracting.

I suddenly understood that Louis-César was not angry;
he was furious: a simmering, peppery scent radiated off him
in waves, and I had the feeling that as much of it was directed at me—or rather at Tomas—as at Jimmy. It was
mixed up with the myriad scents suddenly hammering me
from all around: the faint, far-off whiff of the sewers running beneath the earth, diesel fumes and cigarette butts from
the parking lot and the reek of sauerkraut from a day-old
reuben in a Dumpster. My body, on the other hand, smelled
good, really good, and at first I thought it was because it was
familiar. Then I realized with a shock that it actually smelled
like a favorite meal, hot and fresh and ready to eat. I had
never thought of blood smelling sweet, like warm apple pie
or steaming cider on a cold day, but now it did. I could almost taste the blood running under the warmth of that skin,
and feel how rich it would be sliding down my throat. The
idea that I smelled like food to Tomas staggered me to the
point that I didn't see what happened in front of me until it
was half over.

A suffocating cloud of bluish gas billowed around us, ob-
scuring the parking lot and causing my eyes to burn. Several
shots went off, and I heard Louis-César shout for Pritkin to
stand down. I think he was afraid that the maniac, who had
circled around to come at the fight from a new angle, was
going to hit me instead of Jimmy. Since I shared that opinion, I didn't interfere. I was about to go wading into the blue,
trying to find me before I ended up dead, when my body
came crawling out of the noxious cloud, crying and gasping
for breath. I didn't understand what was wrong with it—I
wasn't having any trouble breathing—until I remembered
that Tomas didn't have to breathe and that I hadn't been
doing so the whole time I'd been inside him. That made me

start gasping like a fish, while my body crawled up and grabbed me around the ankles. "Help!"

"Am I okay?" I dropped to my knees, almost bowling us both over in the process, and began scrambling around in my clothes. "Tell me you didn't let me get cut up!" I could barely speak past the pulse in my throat, but other than for the thin-edged wound on my abused neck and the dazed, watering eyes, I seemed intact. "Stay here," I told a very confused Billy Joe. "I'm going after Jimmy." My head nodded and a hand flapped at me. I paused to hike up Billy's blouse before anything tumbled out, then crawled into the fray.

Pritkin was yelling something, but although I could hear him, I could also hear everything else, and I do mean everything. Conversations in the locker room were as clear as if they weren't happening half a parking lot away. Music, the ring of slot machines and an argument between a waiter and one of the chefs in the kitchen were all clear as a bell. The heartbeats of the few surviving weres, some of which I could hear trying to crawl away underneath the cars, the breathing of everyone around me and the sound of a small piece of paper being blown across the lot turned the quiet night into rush hour at Grand Central Station. Maybe vamps learned how to be selective and to differentiate between trivial stuff and more important things. I guess they have to or go insane. But I didn't know how, and although I could see Pritkin's grim face, I couldn't make out what he was angry about.

Once in the heart of the swirling blue miasma, I found that Tomas' eyes could see outlines, but no distinct features. Still, it wasn't too hard to make out the fallen body of a giant rat. Damn. I knew they'd screw it up. I wasn't likely to waste any tears on Jimmy, but I'd wanted to know what he'd promised to tell me about my father. Besides, we'd made a deal, and I didn't like that my so-called allies had taken it on themselves to alter it without so much as a word in my direction.

"He better not be dead," I began, as Louis-César's flushed face appeared in front of me. I got no further because his hand reached out and caught me in a stranglehold that would have crushed a human's throat. He was saying something in a harsh tone that didn't sound much like his usual voice, but I couldn't understand him. I had a second to think, *Oh, crap*, before the familiar disorientation flooded over me and the blue faded away. I closed my eyes, not wanting to believe this was real, that I was going to have a vision *now* of all times, but there was no way to deny it. I was suddenly back in that same unwelcoming, cold, stone corridor, hearing voices filled with unimaginable despair.

I fell to my knees in shock, not at the surroundings, although they were far from welcome, but at the voices. I'd thought before that it was the people inside the torture room making the high-pitched keening, but now I knew it wasn't. The men chained to the wall had started crying out only when they saw me, and their tones, although desperate, hadn't sounded like this. This was a chorus of hundreds, thousands maybe, and they weren't alive, at least not anymore.

I realized that the icy cold of the corridor was less from the weather than from the positive miasma of spirits crowded into it. Never had I felt so many ghosts in one place at one time, like a spiritual mist permeating the walls and filling the air to the point of suffocation. It was despair made tangible, like a film of freezing grease on my face that ran down my throat until I thought I would choke on it. This time I was alone and, without the bully of a jailer to distract me, I could concentrate on the voices. Slowly they became a little clearer. I quickly wished they hadn't.

There was a definite feeling of intelligence, of many minds here, and none of them were happy. I thought at first that they might be demonic, there was that much—for lack of a stronger word—rage floating around. But they didn't feel like the few demons I'd met; they felt like ghosts. After a few minutes' soaking up their fury, I finally figured it out. Haunters are usually dealing with one of three main issues: they died before their time, they died unjustly—usually, but not always, murdered—or they died with something vital unfinished. Sometimes there are other contributing factors—ghosts, like people, can have many issues bugging them at the same time—but normally one of the big three is there. What I was sensing was thousands of ghosts who had all three of the big ones and a whole galaxy of contributing issues as well. If they'd still been alive, they could have kept every shrink in the United States working around the clock for the next century trying to sort them out. But they don't have psychiatrists in the ghost world. What they have is revenge.

A ghost created by vengeance issues either gets some satisfaction, gets some payback, or hangs around lusting for it until its energy runs out. Most ghosts don't have regular energy donors like I am for Billy Joe, so they fade over time, getting less and less powerful until only their voices remain, and then finally passing on to wherever it is ghosts go. I sensed that some in this throng were about to run out of juice, while others were as powerful as if they'd died yesterday, which maybe they had. The implication was staggering: wherever I was, it had been used for torture for decades at least, and probably for centuries, racking up enough spiritual dark energy to be felt even by nonsensitives. I doubted there was anyone, no matter how obtuse to the psychic world, who could walk into this chamber of horrors and not get a serious case of the creeps.

I looked around, but it was still just me and the chorus line. I didn't know what to do. I was used to my visions behaving in a predictable way: they came; they hit me like a freight train; they left; I cried; I got over it. But lately, my psychic abilities were branching out into new and uncomfortable areas, and I was feeling resentful that the universe had suddenly decided to change the rules. Especially since, if I had to get stranded anywhere, I sure wouldn't have picked this place. A cold wind slapped my face—they were getting impatient.

"What do you want?" I barely whispered it, but you'd have thought I'd taken a stick and stirred a hornet's nest. So many spirits descended on me at once that I got only flashes of color, flickers of images and a roaring in my ears like a hurricane had decided to blow through the hall. "Stop! Stop it! I can't understand you!"

I backed against the wall and realized only when I fell through it that I didn't have a body, at least not a corporeal one. After a stunned instant I recognized the torture room I'd visited before, but this time only the victims were there. I got up and took a few tentative steps forward. I felt very solid. My feet didn't disappear into the stone as I'd half expected, and I could see my arm. Thankfully it was mine instead of Tomas'; at least my spirit knew which body was mine. I felt the arm and it was solid, too. I could take my pulse. I was breathing. And yet none of the prisoners seemed to notice me.

The woman I'd freed at the casino was lying right in front of me, back on the rack as I remembered, except she wasn't burnt. She didn't look good, but I could see a faint rise and fall of her chest and an occasional flutter of her lashes, so I knew she lived. I heard a noise behind me and looked back over my shoulder to see a couple of thousand people, all standing quietly, watching me. The room couldn't possibly hold that many, but they were there anyway. And, unlike my experience with Portia's brigade, that didn't seem to be playing havoc with my senses. I could see them without my eyes crossing or trying to crawl out of my head; maybe I was getting used to it. "I don't know what to do," I said, but no one gave me any hints.

I turned back to the woman and saw with surprise that she was looking straight at me. She tried to say something, but nothing came out of her cracked lips except a thin croak. Someone handed me a dipper of water. It was slimy and vaguely green, and I looked at it dubiously. "This stuff is gross."

"I know, but there doesn't appear to be anything else." It shows you how out of it I was that it took me at least five seconds to connect the voice to the person.

I looked up slowly, then jumped back, sending the slimy water sloshing across the room in a wide arc. "Shit! Tomas!" I swallowed my heart back down to where it belonged. "What are you doing here?" He was holding a bucket with more of the disgusting water in it. He looked solid, but that didn't mean anything. So did I, and I'd just fallen through a wall.

"I don't know." I was inclined to believe him since he looked as shaken as I felt. I suppose even for a vampire this counted as strange. The water in the bucket was trembling in a grip that wasn't entirely steady, and neither was his voice when he spoke. "I remember you taking control of my body, and being unable to speak or react. Then, suddenly, we were here." He looked around in amazement. "Where is this place?"

"I'm not sure."

"Is this where you went before?" Something that looked like eagerness came over his features. "Is that Françoise?" He saw my surprise. "Raphael told me about the vision that upset you. Is this the woman you saw?"

"I guess." I was still staring at the bucket he was holding, because it had occurred to me that he shouldn't have had it. If he'd somehow piggybacked onto my vision, we should both be bound by the usual rules. We weren't actually here; this was a record, an image of something that had happened long ago. We should be nothing more to it than the viewers of a movie are to what happens onscreen. But there he stood, holding a heavy wooden bucket like it was no big deal. "Where did you get that?"

He looked bemused. "It was in the corner." He gestured with his free hand to a spot where the condition of the straw made it obvious that it doubled as a latrine. Of course, the whole room smelled like a cross between an open sewer and a butcher shop, one where the meat wasn't too fresh and unused bits were allowed to rot in the corners. I thought irrelevantly that it was unfair that I had to smell this when I didn't even have a body. My old visions had never come complete with scents and sensations, and I vastly preferred it that way.

"I can't give her that." Screw the metaphysics; I'd figure them out later. If Tomas could hold a bucket, obviously we could interact with this place, at least a little. And if that was true, maybe we could change a few things that had gone—or were about to go—seriously wrong. My first priority was to get the woman out of here, but she wasn't going to last long without something to drink, and she kept sending longing glances toward the filthy bucket. I wondered how thirsty you had to be before something like that looked good.

Tomas smelled it and dipped his finger in for a taste. I remembered how acute his senses were when he made a sound of distaste and spat it back out. "You're right. It is about a third salt. It is merely another form of torture." He threw it down and the noxious stuff soaked into the dry straw. "I will try to find something else."

"No! You need to stay here."

"Why? Am I not merely a spirit here? What could happen?"

I looked nervously at the thousands of ghosts quietly observing us and wondered whether I should tell him. Normally, spirits don't frighten me. There are rare examples who, like Billy, can feed off the energy of humans to a limited degree, but I have always been able to repel them at will. Besides, most find that it requires more energy to attack a human than they get from the process, so they usually don't bother unless you irritate them. But things had

changed. Here, I didn't have the protection of a body and all
the defenses that went along with it. I was a foreign spirit on
their turf, and if they decided to be annoyed about it, I might
be in big trouble. Billy had told me that ghosts can canni-
balize one another for energy—apparently it's a lot easier
than using human donors. He'd been mugged more than
once, and one time it had been so bad that I'd had to donate
some power quickly or he might have faded too far to come
back. Now here I was, facing several thousand hungry
ghosts who had every reason to be steamed that I was in-
truding on their territory. So far they hadn't made a move,
but they might not like us roaming around their castle. I
didn't intend to find out.

"You don't want to know," I told him shortly.

He didn't argue, but his brows drew together as he sur-
veyed the woman. He appeared genuinely concerned about
her, which thawed my attitude towards him a little. It also
made me wonder whether he was in equal danger himself.
Billy Joe was back in our time, babysitting my body, but
Tomas currently had no spirit in residence—which was another way of saying he was dead. Of course, he died every
day when the sun came up, but this wasn't the usual way. I
hoped we weren't going to find a permanent corpse when
we got back.

"Let's get her loose," I said, to distract myself as much as
him. We began trying to pry the woman off the rack, but it
was harder than it sounds. Although I tried not to hurt her, I
did some damage. The ropes had eaten into her flesh, and
blood had dried around them almost like glue; when I pulled
them away from her wrists and ankles, bits of gory tissue
came off, too.

I glanced around the room, hoping to see another source
of water, but there was nothing except the men chained to
the walls. One was hanging from a lip of stone about nine
feet off the ground. His arms were bound behind him, pulled
up at a terrible angle, and weights had been attached to his

feet. He wasn't moving but swung there like a limp doll. Another was lying in the straw below, moaning softly. I did a double take; he actually looked like he'd been boiled. His skin was a horrible mottled red and was peeling away in strips. The other emaciated men showed signs that the torturers had already had some time with them. Backs were beaten raw, hands and feet were missing here and there, and pieces of flesh had been gouged out. I turned away before I was sick.

Something nudged my elbow and I looked down to see a flask floating in the air beside me. I took hold of it gingerly, eyeing the watching crowd with some suspicion. But none of them made any threatening moves, and the container smelled like whiskey. I'd have preferred water, but the alcohol might dull her pain. "Here, drink this." I knelt by the woman's head and held the flask to her lips. She swallowed a little of the contents, then mercifully passed out.

I left Tomas tending to her and went to try to free the men, but it soon became obvious that it wasn't going to happen. The woman had been tied with ropes, I guess because chains don't stretch well, but the men were in iron. I glanced at Tomas. I didn't want to talk to him, much less ask for help, but there was no way I could get them free on my own. "Can you break these?" I finally asked.

"I can try." He came over and we both gave it our best, but nothing happened. It was all we could do to lift the heavy chains, much less manage anything as strenuous as breaking them. We seemed to have lost a lot of strength in the transition. Just pulling the woman loose had felt like I'd spent three hours on a treadmill set on high.

Overall, I decided, things weren't looking good. I didn't know where I was, how I was going to get back or when the torturers were likely to show up. A rat in the corner twitched tiny whiskers at me and I kicked the ladle at it. Oh, yeah, and if I did get back where I belonged, I'd be in the middle of a fight that I wasn't completely sure we were winning. Even for me this counted as a really bad day.

"This is useless, Cassie," Tomas said after a few minutes. "I am as weak as a human here, and my strength is fading quickly. We should help the woman while we can. There is nothing to be done for the rest."

I reluctantly agreed. It seemed to be my night for rescues. I eyed the ghostly army that was staring at me patiently. "Um, does anybody know how to get out of here?"

The ghosts looked at me, then at each other. Some shuffling was done until one was pushed out of the throng. It was a young man, maybe eighteen, dressed in an outfit that looked like a poor relation's version of Louis-César's. It was blue wool and he had a brown hat in his hand with a jaunty yellow feather sticking out of the broad brim. I guessed he'd been a dandy in life, since his cravat was very frothy, his wig was long and curled to within an inch of its life and his buff leather shoes had comical, big yellow bows on them. Pretty colorful for a ghost; based on experience, I guessed he'd been dead a year or less.

He gave a bow, and although it wasn't as courtly as Louis-César's, he used the same phrase. *"A votre service, mademoiselle."*

Great, just great. I looked at Tomas, who was kneeling by the woman, checking her pulse. "I don't suppose you speak French?"

He shook his head. "A few phrases, but nothing that would help here." He looked bitter. "I am rarely allowed at Senate headquarters."

"Since when do they speak French in Vegas?"

He looked at me impatiently. "The European Senate is based in Paris, Cassie."

"I didn't know you were with them."

"There are a great many things you don't know."

I didn't have time to figure out what he was talking about. I regarded the young ghost with some annoyance. As grateful as I was not to be back in Louis-César's body, I missed having access to his knowledge. "We don't speak French," I told him.

The young man looked confused, and some more shuffling was done. Another man, older this time and dressed more plainly in simple fawn-colored knee pants and a navy blue coat, was pushed forward. He hadn't bothered to cover his bald head with a wig, and he looked like the no-nonsense type. "I was a wine trader in life, *mademoiselle*. I often had reason to visit Angleterre; perhaps I may be of service?"

"Look, I don't know what I'm doing here. Or where this is. Or what you want. Some information would help."

He looked puzzled. "Your pardon, *mademoiselle*, but we also are at something of a loss. You are spirits, but not like us. Are you angels, sent at last in answer to our prayers?"

I snorted. I'd been compared to a lot of things in life, but never that. And Tomas sure as hell didn't qualify, unless fallen angels counted. "Um, no. Not really." The younger man said something and the older one looked shocked. "What'd he say?"

The man seemed embarrassed. "He fears for his lover's life, that she will die as he did, as we all did, in this place of everlasting suffering. He said that he would not care if you were from *le diable*, from Satan himself, if you come bearing hope of vengeance. But he did not mean it."

Looking at the anger on the young man's face, I doubted that. "We're not demons. We're . . . it's complicated. I just want to get her out of here before the jailer gets back. Can you tell me where I am?"

"You are in Carcassonne, *mademoiselle*, the very gate of Hell."

"And that's where? I mean, is this France?" The man looked at me as if I'd asked him what year it was, which had actually been my next question. Screw it. I didn't have time to explain to a ghost that, no, I wasn't actually crazy. At least, I didn't think so. "Never mind. Just tell me where to take her. They're going to kill her—she's got to escape."

"No one escapes." He looked let down. "Are you not here to avenge Françoise's death?"

I was getting a little peeved. I don't have a lot of patience anyway, and what I'd had was pretty much gone. "I'd rather she didn't die in the first place. Are you going to help me or not?"

Something I said got through to the young man, because he began to speak rapidly to his companion. The woman came around while they were arguing back and forth, and I patted her arm, since there was nowhere below her wrists that I could touch without hurting her. She looked at me with wide eyes but didn't say anything. That was just as well; neither of us was in any shape for twenty questions.

The older man turned to me, looking disapproving. "Even if we help you, she may die as others have done. Would you forgo vengeance because she lives a few days?"

I lost it. It had been a long day and I was absolutely not standing there getting lectured by a pain-in-the-ass ghost. I already had Billy Joe for that. "I am not the freaking angel of death, all right? I'm not here to get revenge for you. If you want it, go get it yourselves. That's what ghosts do. Now either help me or get the hell out of my way."

The older man drew himself up indignantly. "We cannot avenge ourselves, or we would already have done so! This castle has been used for torture for centuries, and something has been done to it, some spell laid, making it impossible for us to interfere. Do you really believe we could have stood by, letting such atrocities happen, if we had a choice? If you are not a spirit, then you must be a powerful sorceress. Help us! Help us, and we will be your slaves." He got down on one knee, and suddenly, the whole group was kneeling. This was completely unfair.

"Um, what's your name?"

"Pierre, *mademoiselle*."

"Okay, Pierre. I'm not a witch; I'm a clairvoyant. You probably know more magic than I do. I can't undo a spell for you, any spell. All I know is that woman is going to die very soon if we don't get her out of here." He didn't look satisfied, but the young man beside him had had enough. He darted forward and started pulling on my hand and babbling so fast that, even if I'd known French, I probably wouldn't have understood him.

Pierre regarded me unfavorably, but he did agree to translate after some prompting by the younger ghost. "There is an underground passage, *mademoiselle*, from the foot of one of the towers to the river Aude. It has long been an escape route in times of trouble. Etienne can show you."

I looked dubiously at Tomas. "Can you carry her?" He nodded and moved to pick her up. His eyes widened slightly and he stumbled before getting to his feet. "What is it?"

"She weighs more than I expected." He frowned. "We must hurry, Cassie, or my strength may fail entirely."

I agreed and tugged at the door handle. It finally opened after a few false starts—I kept putting my hand through it. I could solidify enough to manipulate things, but Tomas was right—it was getting harder. I was panting by the time we made it to the corridor, but there was nobody to hear. Guess all the torturers were on a coffee break. Unlike at Dante's, though, I knew for a fact that people were around, and that they were coming soon.

The young ghost faded in and out as we started down a different flight of stairs from the one I'd used last time. This one wasn't any brighter, but the yellow feather in his hat had that good old ghostly luminescence and we followed it as if it was a candle. I didn't stub a toe this time, although I was soon wishing I hadn't skipped my jogging session so often. Simply walking down the stairs was starting to feel like running a marathon. I began to have sympathy for Billy Joe's bitch sessions every time I asked him to bring me something.

By the time we got to the bottom of the staircase, I was whipped. I started to lean against the wall but stopped when I almost fell through it. "How much farther?" The young man didn't reply, only motioned me forward desperately. I looked around, but the chorus hadn't come along. I wasn't upset. They seemed more interested in hurting somebody than in saving a life, something that didn't endear them to me.

We stumbled into a passage so dark that the only light came from the bobbing feather on our guide's hat. It became steadily more damp as we continued, to the point that we were soon sloshing through puddles we couldn't see, which I hoped meant we were getting close to the river. The damned tunnel seemed endless, and decades' worth of cobwebs caught in the woman's hair, but I didn't have the energy to brush them off. Finally we emerged on the other side, but only a tiny crescent moon and the spreading Milky Way arching over us gave the scene any light. Night without modern electricity is damn dark, but it seemed almost bright to me after the tunnel.

Tomas' strength gave out a short time later and I had to help him. We put the woman between us and all but dragged her along narrow cobblestone paths. I didn't want to risk hurting her, but sticking around wasn't a good idea, either. I knew what that psycho jailor had planned. Even if she died in the escape, it beat the hell out of burning to death.

The city that surrounded the castle was seriously creepy at night, with the rows of houses leaning so far over the road in places that neighbors on opposite sides of the street could have shaken hands. We jumped whenever an owl hooted or a dog barked, but we kept going. I tried not to look back at the hulking outline of the castle, with its conical roofs making ominous black shadows against the dark sky. I hoped whatever destination Feather had in mind was close. It took a lifetime, it took forever, to the point that all I could do was concentrate on putting one foot in front of the other and not falling over. Finally, when I was about to have to call a halt or collapse anyway, I saw a tiny light in the distance, so dim that I thought I'd imagined it at first. It slowly grew brighter and coalesced into a candle sitting in the window of a small house. Feather didn't materialize, maybe because he was as worn out as I was, but I summoned enough energy to knock on the door instead of putting my fist through it. Finally, it opened and light spilled out, looking unbearably bright after the darkness. I scrunched up my eyes and, when I opened them, I was looking into Louis-César's worried face.

Chapter 8

I was lying on the ground. It took me a second to realize that I was both back in my correct time and back in my own body. I would have cried with relief if I'd had the strength.

Billy Joe coalesced over me and he looked pissed. "Why didn't you tell me you could do that? I got trapped in there! I could have died!"

I didn't try to sit up, since the asphalt seemed to be doing a pretty violent version of the hula beneath me. "Don't be a drama queen. You're already dead."

"That was completely uncalled for."

"Cry me a river." Billy Joe was about to say something else but had to move because Louis-César bent over me and he wasn't about to get caught in any more bodies.

"Mademoiselle Palmer, are you all right? Can you hear me?"

"Don't touch me." I decided I wanted to sit up after all, mainly because my skirt had ridden up to the point that my pink lace undies were showing, but no way did I want him near me. Every time we touched, I ended up thrown through time. My senses had been trying to warn me earlier, but it had been impossible to tell the difference between the fear caused by his nearness and the general terror of being captured by the Senate. In any case, I'd had all the out-of-body experiences I needed for a very long time. "Where's

Tomas?" I was still unhappy with him, but the thought that I might have accidentally killed him wasn't pleasant.

"He is here." Louis-César moved away about a foot, and I could see Tomas standing behind him. He was looking at the Frenchman with a weird expression, sort of stunned, almost like he didn't recognize him.

"Are you ok?" I asked him in concern. I hoped somebody was home, since I had no idea how to go about finding some wandering spirit. After a long moment, Tomas nodded, but he didn't speak. I decided that wasn't good. "How many fingers am I holding up?"

"Oh, for God's sake!" Billy Joe pushed in between us, careful not to touch anybody, and glared at me. "He's fine. He came around a few minutes ago when you decided to rejoin us." He scowled. "What's the idea of going on vacation when there's a crisis on?"

I ignored him. "Give me a hand up." Tomas thought I was talking to him and bent over, forcing Billy Joe to dodge out of the way. I sat and looked about. There were eleven dead wererats, including Jimmy. His glassy rat eyes stared at me accusingly through the dissipating smoke, and I swore. "Damn it! I wanted to talk to him!" I rounded on Pritkin, who was standing with his arms raised theatrically, almost like he was pushing on something, only there was nothing there but air. "You killed him before I could ask about my father!"

Pritkin wasn't paying me any attention. His eyes were focused outside our circle and he didn't look good. His face was red, his eyes were glazed and the cords on the sides of his neck were bulging. When he spoke, it was in a strangled whisper. "I can't hold much longer." That didn't make sense until I noticed a faint blue tinge to the air around us and realized that we were standing inside the mage's shields. He'd created a defensive bubble around us by expanding his own protection, but it looked thin and weak, not like his old shields at all. Perhaps he'd stretched it too far; personal shields were designed for one person only. He was right; it wasn't going to last.

"We have to get Cassie out of here," Tomas said, and I noticed that his face also looked strained. Not as if he were bench-pressing a few hundred pounds like Pritkin, but as if he was terrified. He wasn't watching the mage, though, or anything beyond him. He was looking at me.

Louis-César was the only one who seemed normal, with no visible signs of strain on that pleasant face. "*Mademoiselle*, if you have recovered sufficiently, may I suggest that you return to MAGIC? Tomas will take you."

Pritkin mumbled something and a glowing symbol wrote itself in the air for an instant, so close I could have reached out and touched it, before dissolving into the shields. I knew what he was doing since one of the mages at Tony's had set up a perimeter ward on his vault using words of power. I had been intrigued that he could build a protective spell on something as intangible as a spoken word, but he'd explained that he was using it as a focus for his own energy.

Magic comes from many sources. The Fey and, to a much lesser degree, lycanthropes are said to get theirs from nature, drawing on the massive energy of the planet as it moves at terrifying speeds through space. Gravity, sunlight, the pull of the moon, can all be converted to energy if you know how. I've even heard speculation that the Earth generates a magical field the same way it does a gravitational one, and that someday, someone will figure out how to tap it. That is the holy grail of modern magical theory, though, and no one has managed to do it so far—although countless hours have been lost trying. Until the mystery is solved, human magic users can borrow only a tiny amount from nature; most of their power has to come from themselves. Except for dark-magic users, who can borrow tremendous magical energy by stealing the lives of others or from the netherworld, but they pay a huge price for it.

Some mages are inherently stronger than others, but most

use some kind of cheat to enhance their abilities. Most have talismans to gather natural energy like batteries over long periods, to be disbursed at the mage's command, like Billy's necklace. Some form links with other magic users that allow them to borrow power in time of need, like the Silver Circle. Others enlist as allies magical creatures who can absorb natural energy better than they. I didn't know what Pritkin might be using besides his own power, but it didn't appear to be working too well. His shields glowed a bit brighter after the symbol touched them but almost immediately dulled again. Something was sapping their strength, and at a very fast rate.

I looked around but couldn't find the source of the threat. The parking lot looked quiet if not exactly peaceful—the burning hulk of a couple of nearby cars showed dimly through the dispersing blue smoke. I narrowed my eyes at Louis-César but doubted he'd tell me much. Luckily, I didn't need him. "Billy? What's going on?"

"To whom are you speaking?" Louis-César began to look less than calm for the first time. "She may have a concussion," he told Tomas. "Be careful with her."

I ignored him because Billy was floating near Pritkin and he'd started gesturing wildly at him, then all around, then out at the night. "Billy! What in the world are you doing? It's not like anyone else can hear you—spit it out!"

"Your familiar cannot help you, sybil." The voice came out of the dark, and I noticed that the five vamps lounging around the outer edges of the lot had been joined by a friend. He was hard to see in the predawn light, but the feeling emanating off him wasn't nice. It made me glad I couldn't see his face. "I have warded against him. No one can help you, but then, you do not need it. You are in no danger, sybil. Come with me and I guarantee that no one will harm you. We value your gifts and want to help you develop them, not to keep you hiding and afraid all your life. Come to me, and I will let your friends, if they are friends, go in peace."

"My name's Cassie. You've got the wrong girl." I wasn't interested in a conversation, but Billy Joe was trying to tell me something and I had to give him time to play charades.

"I used your proper title, Miss Palmer, although your name is interesting, too. Did anyone ever tell you its significance?" He laughed. "Don't tell me they have allowed you to grow up completely in ignorance? How lacking in foresight. We will not make the same mistake."

"Cassandra was a seer in Greek mythology. The lover of Apollo." Eugenie had made sure we did myths of the Greeks and Romans as part of my schoolwork—apparently it was an important part of a young lady's education back in her day—and I hadn't complained because I thought it was kind of fun. I'd forgotten most of it but remembered my namesake. I'd thought Cassandra a good name for a clairvoyant, until now.

"Not quite, my dear." The voice was full and rich and might have been attractive if it hadn't been accompanied by that vague, underlying something that reminded me of rotten fruit: overripe and mealy. "Apollo, the god of all seers, loved the beautiful human Cassandra, but she did not return his affections. She pretended to love, long enough to gain the gift of foreknowledge; then she ran away. He finally found her, of course—like you, she could not hide forever—and exacted his revenge. She could keep the gift, he said, but she would see only tragic events, and no one would believe her when she prophesied until it was too late."

I shivered; I couldn't help it. His words cut a little too close to the bone. He somehow seemed to know he'd made a hit, and laughed again. "Don't worry, lovely Cassandra. I will teach you that there can be beauty in the dark."

"What is going on?" I hissed at Billy, more to block out that seductive, awful voice than because I expected an answer.

The dark mage responded, even though he shouldn't have been able to hear a whisper that far away. "The white knight's wards are failing, sybil. We will talk face-to-face soon."

I decided that was not a talk I'd enjoy. I glanced at Billy Joe. "Do you remember those three days after I left Philly the last time?" He stared at me blankly for a second, then violently shook his head and started making wild gestures. Yep, he remembered all right.

I knew only one power word. It wasn't a weapon but was designed to add stamina in times of emergency by drawing on the body's reserves—all its reserves. It was dangerous to use, since if the power it gave ran out before the threat was over, you'd be as weak as a kitten when the bad guys caught you, but it packed a hell of a punch while it lasted. I'd used it to stay awake for more than three days straight after fleeing from Tony the second time. I'd researched it and practiced with one of the rogue mages at court, since I'd known from experience that it would take seventy-two hours for the trace charms on Tony's wards to wear off. I'd gotten lucky the first time I left—I fell asleep on a bus, and my pursuers hadn't been able to tell which of the half dozen vehicles that had just left the crowded station was mine. By the time they picked up the trail, I'd woken up, panicked and switched buses. I managed to stay ahead of them for the required three days, but I'd had several close calls and hadn't wanted to try that trick twice. Tony's guys had gotten a lot of practice tracking me during my first disappearance, and this time I wouldn't have the value of surprise.

My plan had worked, but the price was high: when the jolt finally wore off, I slept for a week and lost ten pounds. I'd have probably lost a lot more—like my life—except that Billy Joe and I had figured out that the energy exchange between us worked both ways. He could give me juice as well as take it, and right now he was tanked.

Billy drifted lower, increasing the arm waving and scowling. He was obviously trying to tell me that he didn't want to talk out loud, and there was only one alternative. I sighed.

"Come on in." A warm wash settled over me, and Billy flowed inside, giving me a replay of him digging his mother's grave in Ireland as he settled down.

"Have you lost your mind?!"

"Just tell me if it will work—can we reinforce the shields?"

"What do you mean, 'we'?"

I sighed. "Don't bitch; you know you can spare it! Can we do it?"

"Shit if I know!" Billy was at his acidic best. "I don't go playing around with words of power! If this thing backfires, it could be bad—real bad."

"It worked last time."

"You almost died last time!"

"Why, Billy, I didn't know you cared. Now, answer the question."

"I don't know," he repeated stubbornly. "In theory, I should be able to redirect the power outward instead of inward, but—"

"Great." I focused on the shimmering shields, ignoring the fact that Louis-César and Tomas were having some sort of argument. It had been a long time since I tried this, and if I screwed it up, I might not get another chance. Pritkin was almost purple, and only the whites of his eyes were showing.

"Wait! I need to think a minute! Hold your horses—" Billy kept talking, but I tuned him out. We didn't have time for a prolonged discussion. I couldn't extend my ward like Pritkin had done; if his shields disappeared altogether before I could strengthen them, we were toast. I concentrated and spoke the only power word I knew.

Energy flowed through me to the point that I thought I was going to levitate right off the asphalt. A second later Billy carved a glowing gold rune in the air that hovered in front of my face for a minute, shiny and bright and perfect. But I didn't have much time to admire it, since I was knocked flat on my ass a second later when the energy left me in the same bone-jarring rush in which it had come. I suddenly, vividly recalled why I didn't do this kind of thing often.

I rolled onto my side and groaned, trying to keep from throwing up. I had the definite feeling I wasn't going to make it. Then Billy started to feed me some of his stolen power. I hadn't expected to feel anything—when he'd helped me out before, I hadn't known about it until after the fact—but this I felt. Sparkling, warm, wonderful energy coursed through me, and I sat up abruptly. Damn! I could get addicted to this. Billy's laughter echoed in my head and I grinned. No wonder he'd been zooming around like a comet earlier.

"What did you do?" Pritkin was also sitting up, looking bewildered. He focused on me. "*You* reinforced my shields?" He stared in incredulity while I admired my and Billy's handiwork. Pretty blue walls, so opaque they could probably have been seen by norms and so thick I could have driven a car around inside their ring, glimmered under the halogen lights. Pritkin must ward with water, because there were ripples like gentle waves spreading through them.

"We do good work," I congratulated my helper. "And I don't even feel like puking anymore."

"What did you do?!" Pritkin grabbed me by the arms and my ward sizzled slightly. He let go, glowering and rubbing his hands. "You cannot have that much power—no human can!"

"Maybe I borrowed it."

His eyes narrowed. "From whom, or what?"

I didn't feel like trying to explain. "Would someone please tell me what's going on?" Before anyone could answer, the shields began to spit and hiss. What looked like a black cloud had begun nibbling at them, swallowing that beautiful power in tiny bites, like a swarm of locusts descending on a prairie. Okay, maybe we weren't out of the woods yet.

I decided to get some answers from the one person here who would tell me the truth. I went inside and found Billy. "Spill it."

"I can't *believe* you did that! Do you have any idea what would have happened if I hadn't been able to channel that much power all at once? It could have ricocheted off the inside of the shield and fried all of us!"

I interrupted. "Yell at me later. Just tell me what's going on, fast."

"Mages from the two circles are fighting, and we're stuck in the middle. How's that for brief?"

"Okay, now the version that makes sense."

I heard something odd and realized it sounded like grinding teeth. I hadn't known he could do that. "I drifted through the dark mage after you came back to your body, but he caught on and warded against me. I don't think I can do it again. But before he kicked me out, I learned that the Black Circle is allied with Rasputin, along with a lot of other groups who're not happy with the status quo. They seem to think he's got a real chance to take it all, and they don't wanna miss out on the spoils. And, even more fun, it seems like Tony's also buddy-buddy with them. He's been selling magic users to the light elves, and he knows that if anyone finds out at MAGIC, he'll be lucky if all they do is stake him."

"What? You aren't making sense." I'd only just found out Faerie wasn't a myth. I certainly didn't understand enough about it to follow Billy's ramblings.

"It's a long story. All you need to know is that Tony wants protection. The dark elves have traced the problem to him, and they aren't happy. They can't afford for the light Fey to outbreed them, but with fertile magic users to help with the population shortage, that's what's going to happen fairly soon. And then the light will rule all of Faerie."

"But that's good, right?" I didn't know how many of my nursery school stories were based on fact, but if the dark Fey really were composed of trolls, banshees, goblins and the like, wouldn't it be better for the light to win?

Billy sighed. "You and I gotta have a long talk sometime. No, it would not be good. I don't trust any of the Fey, but at least the dark have rules. The light have been getting more and more anarchic lately—in the past few centuries, I mean—and there's no telling what they'll do if there is nothing to balance them. That's why that demented pixie was here. She couldn't give a damn about enslaved humans normally, but if the trade is going to benefit the light, she wants to stop it. Anyway, the point for us is that Rasputin has promised to protect Tony in return for him killing you. It wasn't a hard sell."

"I bet." So I had yet another enemy. I was going to have to start keeping a list. "Why does Rasputin want to kill me?"

"He sees you as a threat, but I don't know why. The mage may know, but I didn't get it. But I did find out that Rasputin called Tony's boys about half an hour ago and said you were on your way here. That's probably why Jimmy was still alive. They were too busy deploying every spare thug around the casino to catch you to bother killing him. Only nobody expected you to just waltz in the front entrance. They were watching the side and back entries, so you threw them a little." Well, at least that explained why I'd been able to stroll around deserted hallways.

Something occurred to me. "I didn't even know I was coming until right before I left. How did Rasputin figure it out?"

"Good question."

I decided to leave it for the moment. "But why would Tony defy Mircea and the Circle by something as risky as slaving?" Dealing in magic users was not unknown, but most people had decided that the huge profits to be made by selling powerful telepaths or wardsmiths wasn't worth the penalties imposed if the Circle caught up with you. I'd heard Tony himself say it was a game for fools. So what had happened to change his mind? "Mircea will kill him."

"Not if Rasputin kills Mircea and the rest of the Senate first. In that case, Tony gets a Senate seat, out from under the control of his master, and no more dues to pay. Power and wealth, the usual suspects."

"Tony isn't strong enough to stand on his own, even without Mircea. He's third level at best; you know that."

"Maybe he thinks Ras'll help him. Or maybe he's been holding out. He's old enough to have advanced to second level if he's ever gonna do it. Maybe he didn't tell anybody, 'cause that would have made Mircea watch him a whole lot closer. He could've been waiting for a chance to break with him but didn't dare move without a big-time ally."

"Which he now has."

"Looks that way. So, partner, whaddya wanna do?"

"What exactly are we up against?"

Billy Joe sighed theatrically. It was the sound he makes when he knows I'm not going to like what he has to say. "Two dark mages, five vamps here and fifteen others spread around the area, and at least six are master level. Oh, and eight norms armed to the teeth."

"What?!"

"Well, whaddya expect? Vegas is one of Tony's strongholds. And more will be coming—I saw another half dozen norms and eight or nine vamps in the basement. As soon as they figure out that you've been sighted, they'll be along. This place is about to get very busy."

I sat there, stunned. "We're screwed."

"That's the consensus. The plan right now is to have Tomas grab you and fly outta here, while Louis-César and the mage stay behind and try to slow everybody down long enough for you to get away."

"That's suicide!"

"Yeah, and the worst part is, it probably won't even

work. We're surrounded, darlin'. Ain't no way Tomas is gonna make it past all of them."

"Shit." I thought for a second. "What about reinforcements?"

I was interrupted by Louis-César yelling in my ear. "*Mademoiselle*, can you hear me?"

I jerked away before he could touch me. "What do you want? I'm kind of busy."

He looked at me oddly, but he moderated his voice. "You have to go now, *mademoiselle*. I am sorry, but we cannot give you more time to recover."

"I'm not going anywhere. Tomas will never get past a gauntlet like that and you know it. Two black knights, six masters and at least fourteen other vamps? Come on."

I found out what Louis-César looked like when someone had rattled his cool. "How can you possibly know what we are facing?"

"Her ghost servant told her," Pritkin said, and I noticed that he was back on his knees, concentrating on the rapidly evaporating shields.

"You can see Billy?" I was surprised. Very few people could.

"No," Pritkin said through clenched teeth. His jaw was tight enough that the small muscle on the side stood out. "But I was told what you can do. At least, some of it." Sweat ran in rivers down his face, soaking his shirt, and he looked at me desperately. "If you have any more tricks, I suggest you use them. I can only slow the process; I can't stop it."

I sighed. Why did I think I was going to regret this? "Give me a minute."

I went back inside to find out if Billy Joe had any bright ideas. He did, but I didn't like it. "I can't possess the mage 'cause he's warded against me. But you're far stronger in spirit form than I am, 'cause you're alive. If we could duplicate what happened—"

"No! No way am I possessing anybody else! What if I

can't get back? What if I get stuck? Come up with some-thing else." I hadn't enjoyed being Louis-César and I defi-nitely didn't want to find out what the inside of a dark-magic user felt like.

"I don't think you'll get stuck. He's a mage. Once you get in, you ain't gonna have much time before he forces you out. But you won't need that long. If you can distract him for a couple minutes, I'm betting our three heroes can deal with the vamps."

"Three against twenty? Don't you think that's being a lit-tle optimistic?"

"You just don't wanna do this."

"Damn straight."

"You got a better idea?"

I swallowed thickly. There had to be an alternative. The Senate had sent three powerful operatives merely to drag me back from Dante's, so they wanted me pretty badly. When we didn't come back and nobody reported in, they were sure to send reinforcements, but there was no way to tell how long that would take. "How far away is sunrise? Maybe we can hold Tony's guys off until they have to duck for cover. Louis-César should be able to handle a little sun, and I know Tomas can."

Billy Joe laughed, but it didn't sound happy. "Sure, and you think our mage is gonna last that long?"

I glanced at Pritkin and couldn't argue the point. His eyes were bulging and several blood vessels must have popped, because it looked like he was crying red tears. But I was in no position to help him. I'd seen a lot of magic worked through the years, but I'd just performed the only bit I knew, and Billy Joe couldn't replace that kind of energy loss twice. But if I didn't do something soon, my trip to get revenge on Jimmy might end up costing three lives.

"Okay." I gulped some air. "Do it."

I couldn't see Billy Joe when he was inside me, but I could feel his emotions better than I could read his face, and he was skeptical. "You sure? 'Cause I don't wanna have to hear about this for eternity if you end up a spirit permanently. I know you. You'd haunt me."

"I thought you said that won't happen!"

"I said it probably won't. I'm new at this."

"Like you asked me, have you got another plan? Because if not—" That was as far as I got before Billy Joe crashed into me like a linebacker tackling a quarterback. He kept pushing until I would have called the whole thing off, done anything, said anything, to stop that awful pressure, except I couldn't move. It was like getting trapped between a steamroller and the side of a mountain; there was nowhere to go. A second after I decided I was going to die if the pressure didn't stop, I was suddenly flying free. It was a major relief, but the nice, floaty feeling lasted only about a second before I slammed into something that felt like a brick wall. It hurt so badly that I would have thought every bone in my body was broken, except that it suddenly dawned on me that I didn't have a body.

I heard a laugh echo around me. "Oh, no, little ghost. I already told you. You won't trick me again so easily. Go home to your mistress before I send you somewhere you won't like."

I realized what the wall was; it represented the mage's wards, and they were a lot more formidable than I'd expected. But I couldn't follow his advice. I didn't know how to get back without Billy Joe's help, so I had to go forward. Getting through those wards was matter of life and death, literally.

You can shield with anything as long as it has meaning for you: rock, metal, water, even air. It's simply a way of visualizing and manipulating your power. Eugenie had shielded with mist, which I'd thought was weird, but it seemed to work for her. The mage's wards were strong, but of a fairly normal type: like me, he imagined a wall, only his was wood and mine has always been fire. When I concentrated, I was able to see a fortress of huge trees, like California redwoods, stretching up so high that their tops were lost to sight. In reality, of course, they didn't have "tops"; I knew that wherever I went along his ward line, I would see this same, impenetrable wall.

I looked back to where I had "landed" and saw that an imprint of my body had been burned into the logs, splintering the wood all around it from the impact. That must have been how he had felt me, and it gave me an idea. I hadn't ever heard of anyone doing this before, but then, that went for most of the stuff that had happened to me today. I concentrated, not on his wards, but on mine.

I don't usually feel my wards. The technique is so ingrained that it's like walking upright: it's hard when you're nine months old, but by the time you're an adult, you don't have to think to cross a room. But now I took a few seconds to concentrate, and the familiar curtain of flame rose up around me, a comforting warmth instead of a searing heat. I focused and, slowly, a tiny tendril of fire, shaped like a child's hand, reached out from my ward to touch the nearest log. It caught like dry tinder touched by summer lightning, and soon a whole section of the wall was ablaze. I vaguely heard the mage cursing me, making threats and swearing to bind me to the lowest hall of Hell for eternity. I ignored him. It was taking everything I had to keep the fire blazing and refuse to allow new wood to knit up around the old. I didn't have the strength for smart comebacks.

Finally, after what felt like a week, a tiny hole appeared in the wood. I didn't wait for it to get bigger, but squeezed through. It was a tight fit, and it felt like my sides were being scraped into bloody lines by splinters, even though I knew that was impossible. All of a sudden, the smoke and fire of the burning forest melted away and I could see. The dark parking lot spread around me and a breeze blew across my face. Pritkin, Tomas and Louis-César were across the lot, and my body was looking at me with wide eyes.

I yelled at Billy Joe. "It's okay! I'm in control!"

"Then drop the damned attack! Pritkin's about to have a stroke!"

I looked around in confusion, then peered inside. "I'm not doing anything!" It was true, as far as I could tell. I'd assumed that taking over would break the mage's concentration and solve the problem. But I could see that Pritkin's shields had shrunk to the point where they barely covered the three men and would likely fail any second. "What now?"

I saw my body bend over and whisper to Pritkin. He looked across at me and I waved. His eyes got big. He said something, but I couldn't make it out. "What?"

"The bracelet!" My voice bellowed across the parking lot as Billy Joe yelled at the top of my lungs. "He said to destroy it!"

A dark shape started running at me from across the lot. It had the same deeply unhealthy feeling I'd received from the mage, so I didn't need introductions. Somehow, the other dark knight had figured out what was going on, and he didn't like it.

I looked down and found a bracelet on the mage's left wrist. It was silver and formed of what looked like tiny, interlocking daggers. I couldn't find a clasp; it seemed to have been soldered onto his arm. I looked across at Pritkin and saw desperation on his face. Damn it, this thing had to go now. When tugging didn't work, I bit it, tearing at it with his teeth, concentrating on the bit where two of the daggers came together. Finally, after his fingers were a bloody mess, it came loose.

I didn't have to ask whether I'd gotten it right, because Pritkin slumped to the ground, panting in relief, and the vamps around him sprang into action. Louis-César sent a knife flying into the vamp at my side, which would have taken off the head except that it collided with the oversized steel choker he was wearing. It didn't buy him much time, though. Tomas held out a hand and I finally got to see what had happened back in the storeroom. The vamp dropped to his knees and gave a choked gurgle, and his heart literally leapt out of his chest. It went sailing across to Tomas, who caught it like it was a slightly oversized baseball.

The other dark knight was less than two car lengths away from me. He stopped and raised a hand, and suddenly I couldn't move. But before I could panic, the three witches I'd helped free from the casino stepped out from behind a parked van and formed a circle around him. I was about to yell at them to run for it, when the mage suddenly collapsed, screaming, and the pressure on me let up.

It was a relief, but I didn't feel better for long. What felt like an icy stream of water began lapping at my feet. I couldn't see anything, but my wards started to sizzle out around the bottoms. If I concentrated, I could see a stream rising up from the ground to flow around me. Clever mage; he could shield with more than one element. And my fire didn't seem to be doing so hot against his water. As the flames went out, tiny tendrils of wood, some bearing twigs with leaves, began to wind up my metaphysical legs. Great. The dark mage was going to be seriously pissed off when he got back in charge, which at the rate he was going would take all of about two minutes.

"What's wrong with you?" A vampire ran up to me. I recognized him vaguely from Tony's court, a big, shaggy blond whom I'd always thought needed a tan—his surfer looks didn't go well with dead white skin. "You said you could neutralize him! He'll wipe the floor with us!" I followed his gesture to where the fight had resumed big-time. I wondered which "he" the guy meant, because all three looked pretty deadly to me.

Pritkin might be a hostile son of a bitch, but he was a damn good guy to have in a fight. He was on the ground, but his amazing hovering knives were back. In fact, it looked like his whole arsenal was on the move. As I watched, he blew apart a vamp with a shotgun blast while five knives went hurtling into another, one almost severing his head. The vamp must have been a master, because he didn't go down, but the animated knives followed him about, sticking in and pulling out like a swarm of especially lethal bees. He swatted at them as blood started to pour out of a couple dozen deep cuts, but they kept coming back. He roared in rage but preferred getting sliced to ribbons to running. But a couple of other vamps, who were being pursued by grenades, chose not to follow his example. I decided if that's what Pritkin fought like when half dead, I really didn't want to see him at full strength.

Tomas was doing okay, too, tying up two vamps in a knife fight that was so fast and furious I couldn't see any of it, except for an occasional blade flashing in the parking lot lights. Several others lay around him with the now familiar gaping holes in their chests. Louis-César, meanwhile, had decided to take the attack on the offensive all by himself. While Pritkin and Tomas kept the attackers busy, he charged the cluster of vamps around me. The beach bum must not have heard of the Frenchman's reputation, because he leapt for him and lasted all of about a second. That wicked-looking rapier was back in action, and skewering him didn't cause Louis-César even to break his stride. He threw a knife at the second dark mage, but it bounced off him like he was wearing body armor. But whatever the three witches were doing was having more of an effect. The mage was on the ground, scrambling for purchase as ineffectively as a beetle turned upside down, as they began closing in, chanting something in unison.

I was initially pleased to see the Frenchman, since it took only one look at him for the remaining vamps around me to take off, but I quickly changed my mind. I blinked, and Louis-César's bloody blade was somehow under my chin. The look in his eyes made it very clear that he had no idea who I was. "Your Circle made a mistake challenging us," he told me calmly, as if we were chatting at a party. "Fortunately, *monsieur*, I do not need you alive to send a declaration of war. It should be sufficient that I have your body left somewhere your people frequent."

"Louis-César, no!" I couldn't speak for fear of jamming his rapier farther into my throat, but the voice coming from behind him was mine anyway, as was the hand clutching his sword arm. It looked like Billy Joe had decided to earn his keep.

"*Mademoiselle*, please go back to Tomas. This will not be pleasant."

"Tomas is kinda busy right now," Billy replied, "and anyway, I'm not Cassie. She's in there." He pointed at me. "And I don't know what'll happen if you kill the body while she's in it. Maybe she'll come back here, but maybe not."

Louis-César's voice softened slightly. "You are delusional, *mademoiselle*. You may have a concussion and must not exert yourself. Give me a moment and I will escort you from here myself."

I swallowed. I knew that with his strength he could run the rapier through me even with Billy Joe hanging off his arm. I could feel the mage panic, too, and his fear fuelled the battle of wills we were having. The tide of what felt like chilly water was up to my knees.

"Billy! How do I get out of here?" The movement of my mouth pushed the edge of the rapier into the mage's skin, and I could feel a warm stream of blood begin to trickle down his neck. Someone screamed in my head, but I ignored it.

"I don't know." Billy Joe was gripping Louis-César's arm with both hands and practically hanging off it. Sweat was pouring down my face, but it didn't look like he was making any difference at all. "I'm stuck in here until you get back. Your body knows it'll die without a spirit, so it's got a death grip on me. There's no way for me to help you."

"I can't believe you talked me into this!"

"How the hell do you think I feel? I don't want to end up inside a woman!" He paused. "Well, at least not that way."

Louis-César was losing patience. In a swift movement that didn't cause the rapier to waver even slightly, he pulled Billy Joe against him. "You may wish to close your eyes *mademoiselle*. I do not wish to cause you further distress."

"I think it's safe to say that killin' her counts as distressing," Billy Joe choked out, but Louis-César wasn't paying him any attention. He'd written me off as a hysterical female, and that was that. If I ever got out of this mess alive, I'd show him hysterical.

I only had one idea, and it was a long shot. "Don't kill me! I know about Françoise!" It was all I could think of, the only fact about Louis-César that I knew that the mage probably didn't, but it didn't seem to make much of an impression.

"You will not save yourself with feeble lies, Jonathan. I know your tricks from of old."

"What about Carcassonne? Huh? What about that damn torture room? I—you—saw her burn! We were talking about it a few hours ago!"

"Enough! You die." Billy Joe kicked upwards at the last second and hit the blade so that it went through the mage's shoulder instead of his heart, but it hurt like a bitch. I yelled and wrenched back, but the blade was so long that I was still trapped on it like a butterfly on a pin.

I finally got some help when a small vial flew into my hand. Apparently Mr. Mage had decided we had a common cause. It looked like one of the row of small containers Pritkin had strapped to his belt, but this had leapt out of some inner pocket. The cool water was up to my waist, and I didn't know what would happen if it overwhelmed me, but at the moment I was more concerned with Louis-César. I didn't try to resist the impulses that ran through my brain, but thrust the vial at him.

"I will gut you before you can say the incantation," he

promised, but I noticed that he eyed the tiny vial with a certain amount of respect.

"I don't need the incantation at this range. Kill me, and you die, too. So does she." The words appeared in my brain, but they weren't mine. I said them anyway. They seemed to have an effect, for Louis-César hesitated.

The mage must have been waiting for that reaction, because he took the opportunity to step up the inner fight. I was suddenly up to my neck in icy water. "Billy! He's winning, what do I do?"

"I'm thinking . . . let him?" Billy Joe didn't sound very sure of himself, but he'd done this a lot more than me.

"What?"

If he answered, I didn't hear, because the water closed over my head. But, instead of drowning as I'd half expected, I was abruptly flying again. I landed hard, and the disorientation I'd felt when Tomas and I returned was nothing to what hit me a second later. It was like there were two of me, each going in a different direction, tearing me apart in the process. I screamed and someone tightened their hold around my waist. My blood was pounding in my veins as if it was about to burst out of the top of my head, and the pain was awful. It felt like every migraine I'd ever had all rolled into one. I wanted to pass out, but no such luck. I stayed conscious as the world rocked wildly around me like a carnival ride gone crazy, until I threw up on the asphalt.

"Cassie, Cassie!" Billy Joe appeared before me, his eyes so wide that I could see a strip of white all around the pupil. It took me a second to realize that they were his eyes, and that he was in his usual gambler–cowboy–ladies' man getup instead of my skin. His ruffled shirt was bright red, his hazel eyes as clear and sharp as if he hadn't been dead for a century and a half. At that moment, I really believed I could reach out and touch him and he'd be solid. Then it occurred to me that it was my energy making his eyes shine like that and flushing his cheeks. Bastard. I would have told him off for draining me almost dry in my hour of need, but I was way too sick. It felt like someone had reached inside and turned my stomach inside out. I wanted to throw up again but didn't have the energy.

Louis-César picked me up as if I weighed as much as a rag doll, and I looked around, bewildered. How could he pick me up with only one arm? Didn't he need the other one to hold the rapier on the mage? Only there was no mage and no body. It was just me, a master vampire and a really tanked-up ghost; nothing to worry about.

We rejoined Pritkin and Tomas, me being carried because I was in no shape to walk. I was having trouble figuring out which way was up, since it seemed to be changing on a regular basis. I did notice that Tomas was busy bespelling a rather large group of people, including several police officers, who had come by to see what all the commotion was about. I hadn't known he could trick multiple norms at once. Come to think of it, I hadn't known anyone could. Just another clue that I wasn't dealing with a run-of-the-mill vamp. No, those types were scattered about all over the landscape, interspersed with the dead weres. The hearts and heads were several feet away from the bodies, but at least they all appeared to be there.

Pritkin was stowing away his arsenal, which hovered in front of him in an obedient little line, each weapon waiting its turn. He looked at me with narrowed eyes as he wiped off and tucked away his bloody knives. "You possessed a member of the Black Circle," he said, as if this was news, "and have powerful witches in your service. Who were they?"

I glanced back to where the women had been, but only the second dark knight was there, lying at an unnatural angle, his bone white face turned up to the first rays of the sun. His eyes were open, but I doubted he saw anything. I realized that they must have killed him, but at the moment it didn't matter much to me.

"I don't know." My voice came out all croaky, which

considering the amount of abuse my vocal cords had taken lately, shouldn't have been a surprise. But it was.

"You are not human." It wasn't a question, and Pritkin looked like he expected me to sprout another head at any moment.

"Sorry to disappoint you, but I'm not a demon," I told him. I seemed to be having to say that a lot lately. Probably not a good sign.

"Then what are you?"

Billy Joe floated by and gave me a thumbs-up and a cheeky grin. "I'm gonna check out some stuff. See you later."

I sighed. It was barely sunrise, hardly the best time to get into trouble even in Vegas. So why was I absolutely certain Billy Joe would manage? "I'm your friendly neighborhood clairvoyant," I told Pritkin wearily. "Cross my palm with silver, meester, and I'll tell you your fortune. Only"—I was interrupted by a huge yawn—"you probably won't like it." I snuggled closer into the wall of warm cotton behind me and drifted off.

Chapter 9

I woke because little fingers of sunshine were getting in my eyes. They were coming from a large window over the queen-sized bed somebody had put me on. I yawned and grimaced. My mouth was all cottony and tasted awful, and my eyes were so gummy I had to pry them apart to see. When I could, I blinked in confusion. It did not look like vamps had furnished the place, unless it was Louis-César's room. It was yellow from the painted stucco walls to the patchwork quilt and shams. Only a few washed-out pastels in the braided rug and a couple of Native American–inspired prints fought with the yellow tide, but it looked like they were losing.

I sat up and quickly decided that hadn't been a good idea. My stomach tried to heave something up, but there wasn't anything there. I felt as weak as if I'd had the flu for a week, and I desperately wanted to brush my teeth. After the room stopped spinning, I staggered to my feet and went exploring. Poking my head out the bedroom door, I learned two things: I was back in my rooms at MAGIC and I had guests. The short hall outside my room ended in the living area where I'd been taken before my side trip to Dante's. Several very familiar heads swiveled towards me and I scowled at them until I spotted the entrance to a blue-tiled sanctuary a few yards away. Someone, and I really hoped it had been Rafe, had peeled off my battered clothes and wrapped me in a terrycloth robe. It was okay except that it was about three sizes too big and tended to trip me up at odd moments. But I made it to the bathroom without falling, and shut the door in Tomas' face.

For the hell of it, I checked the window. No angry little face greeted me this time. Instead of the Marley, the wards had been strengthened to the point that I didn't even have to concentrate to see the glittering silver web that blocked my only way out. It was a little much, considering that an armed human guard was also right outside. You'd think they had something really scary in here, instead of a beat-up clairvoyant with what felt like the mother of all hangovers. I pulled the curtains closed and shrugged. I hadn't really expected to get away with that twice.

No one interrupted even though I took a long bath. It didn't help much. My list of injuries had lengthened and I was exhausted despite having had, at a guess, six hours' sleep. I'd also received a gift. Someone had put the dark mage's bracelet firmly around my wrist. Someone had also repaired it, because a perfect circle of tiny daggers ran under my fingers, like beads on a rosary. Great; exactly what I needed: another piece of tacky jewelry. I tried to get it off, but it wouldn't fit over my hand, and I didn't feel like trying to bite it. The last time had been with the mage's teeth; this time it would be with mine.

I got stiffly out of the bath, feeling about a hundred, and peered in the mirror. I've never been particularly vain, but it was a shock to see myself looking so haggard. My hair stood up in little clumps and had almost come out of the gold slide. I fixed it as well as I could with only my hands to work with, but there was nothing I could do about my dead white complexion or the dark circles that rimmed my eyes like a professional football player's. I guess almost getting killed about a dozen times takes it out of you.

I turned away from the mirror and searched for some sign of my clothes. I found only the boots, which had been cleaned and polished and tucked behind the door. I didn't

think they went with terrycloth, and left them where they
were. I'd have given a lot to at least have had some clean
underwear, but I couldn't find any. I finally shrugged back
into the robe and decided to go bare underneath rather than
put back on the tattered, bloodstained remnants of what had
once been a nice set of lingerie. I was grateful for the robe's
bulkiness, since at least everything was covered. It made me
look about twelve, but maybe the Senate would spring for
something else if I asked. They'd been in a good mood earlier. Of course, that was before I ran off and almost got three
people killed, four if you counted me. I took a deep breath
and went to face the music.

There were six people in the outer room, if you included
the golem in the corner. It took me a second to notice him
because the blackout curtains had been drawn over the windows, blocking the sunlight. Electric lights were on and
sputtering a little because of the wards, but the room was
dim.

Louis-César, still in the tight jeans outfit, was leaning on
the mantel, looking stressed for once. Tomas was in the red
leather chair by the fire. He and Rafe were in almost identi-
cal black dress slacks and long-sleeved silk shirts, except
that Tomas' was as black as his hair and Rafe's was a dull
crimson. Rafe was on the couch with Mircea, who alone
among the group appeared the same as the night before.
Looking at him, relaxed and elegant, I could almost believe
that I'd accidentally fallen asleep in the bath and that none
of the stuff at Dante's had ever happened. That happy
thought was crushed by the sight of Pritkin, in khaki everything like some big-game hunter, standing by the door. He
didn't take his eyes off me, as if he'd like to see my head
mounted on his wall over a sign reading PROBLEM SOLVED.
Oh, yeah, this was gonna be loads of fun.

Rafe moved as soon as he saw me. "*Mia stella!* You are
feeling better, yes? We were so worried!" He hugged me
tightly. "Lord Mircea and I went to Antonio's headquarters

in the city, but you were not there. If Louis-César and Tomas had not found you—"

"But they did, so everything's fine, Rafe." He nodded and tried to guide me toward the sofa, but I didn't want to be wedged in there. It wasn't like I could escape, no matter where I sat, but I didn't like the idea of being confined. Besides, the only people in the room I could sort of trust were Rafe and maybe Mircea, and I preferred to be where I could see their faces. I sat on the ottoman near Tomas' feet and concentrated on keeping my robe together. "I am sorry, but your clothes were unsalvageable," Rafe said apologetically. "Others are being arranged for you."

"Okay." I didn't attempt to make small talk. I was about to learn what the Senate wanted, and since I was absolutely sure I wasn't going to like it, I didn't feel like helping things along.

"*Mia stella.*" Rafe glanced at Mircea, who cocked an eyebrow at him unhelpfully. Poor Rafe; he always got the crappy jobs. "Could you tell us, who is Françoise?"

I stared at him. Of all the things I'd thought he might say, that would have been near the bottom. In fact, it wasn't even on the list. "What?"

"You mentioned her to me," Louis-César said, moving to crouch in front of me. I shrank back, even though he'd carried me around the parking lot and nothing had happened. I didn't feel like taking chances. "At the casino."

"Don't you want to talk about Tony? He's selling slaves to the Fey."

"We know," Mircea answered. "One of the witches you assisted came to the Circle to describe her captivity. I was allowed to sit in on the questioning, since Antonio is my responsibility. The mages are . . . quite concerned, as you can imagine."

I was confused. "Maybe I'm being slow here, but why witches? Wouldn't humans be easier targets?" The women

I'd freed had certainly been no welterweights, as one dead mage proved.

"For centuries, after their own bloodlines began to die out, that was their strategy. Have you not heard the stories about human infants being spirited away by the Fey?" Mircea asked. I nodded—it was standard fairy tale stuff. "Such children were brought up in Faerie and married into some of their great houses. It did improve their fertility, but they soon noticed that the magical ability in the children of such unions was considerably less than their own."

"So they started stealing witches."

"Yes, but an agreement was worked out between the Fey and the Silver Circle in 1624, stating that no more abductions were to take place."

"I guess it's sort of void now."

Mircea smiled. "On the contrary. The light elves swear they know nothing of this practice, and that it is solely the dark who are involved." I frowned. From what Billy had said, it sounded like the opposite was true. "The dark, of course, claim the reverse," Mircea said, noticing my expression, "but in any case, it is not our concern. We will not be drawn into Fey politics because of one person's greed, as we made clear to their ambassadors a few hours ago. Antonio will be dealt with, but that ends our involvement."

I wasn't surprised. Despite their presence at MAGIC, the vamps had never been all that interested in other species' affairs. They cooperated as far as they did only to guard their own interests. "Just the one witch came forward? What happened to the other two?"

"They must have been dark," Pritkin said, watching me narrowly, "under interdict by the Circle for their crimes. Otherwise they would not have been so quick to flee. Our witch learned little about them because they were gagged much of the time. But she said that one of them recognized you and insisted that they help you against the dark mage. Yet you said you did not know them."

"I don't." I couldn't tell him about Françoise—it would sound crazy and I didn't understand it myself. Magic users tend to live longer than most humans, but witch or no, if it had really been her in that French castle, she should be long dead of old age. Not to mention that it took some memory to immediately recall the face of a person seen for a few minutes hundreds of years ago. I'd recognized her because, for me, our meeting had just happened. But how she had known me was an open question.

"And I suppose you also do not know the pixie who aided you in freeing your servants? She is a well-known operative of the Dark Fey."

Pritkin was getting on my nerves. "No, I don't. And they weren't my servants."

"You told me you watched Françoise burn to death." Louis-César was apparently a single-minded kind of guy.

I decided to go with his comment, since Pritkin didn't believe anything I said anyway. "What happened to the mage? Did you kill him?"

"You see; she doesn't even try to deny it!" Pritkin came striding across the room. I'd have figured out he was pissed off even if I hadn't been able to see him, since my new toy jumped against my wrist with an almost electric tickle. I managed not to yelp, but I stuffed my hand farther into the pocket of the robe so the bracelet didn't show. Something told me Pritkin wouldn't be happy to see it.

Tomas had moved to stand between us. It unnerved me that I hadn't seen him do it, but I was grateful to have a barrier between me and the mage. The guys at Tony's had always believed that war mages were dangerous, bloodthirsty and crazy. Considering that the people saying this were multiple murderers who worked for a homicidal vampire, I tended to take their opinion seriously.

"Why would I deny it? Possessing him saved your life." I hadn't expected a thank-you, but it would've been nice if he'd stopped glaring at me.

"I would prefer to die than be saved by the dark arts!"

"We'll keep that in mind next time," Tomas said. I giggled. I wasn't trying to antagonize anyone, but I was dizzy from hunger and exhausted. At the moment, it really was funny. Only Pritkin didn't seem to think so.

Mircea stood up as someone rapped on the door. "Ah, breakfast. Tempers will doubtless be better after we have dined." A young man wheeled in a cart that had me salivating from the smell alone.

A few minutes later, I was halfway through a tray of pancakes, sausage, hash browns and fresh fruit. It had been served on a nice silver platter with real china dishes, linen napkins and genuine maple syrup, mellowing my mood towards the Senate considerably. I'd just poured myself more tea when Pritkin made a sound of disgust. I couldn't imagine what his problem was; he had a tray, too.

"It doesn't bother you at all, does it?" he demanded. I noticed that not only was he not eating, but he was staring at me the way I had probably looked at the wererats at the casino. Like I was something he couldn't quite figure out but knew he didn't like. My mouth was full so I raised an eyebrow at him. He gestured wildly. "Look at them!"

I forked up some sausage and glanced around. The vampires were feeding, but they weren't having pancakes. They can eat solid food, as Tony proved often enough, but they can't obtain nourishment from it. There's only one thing that will give them that, and they were taking full advantage. Louis-César had apparently already eaten, or maybe it was true about what they said of the Senate, that its members were so powerful that they had to feed only about once a week. Rafe, Mircea and Tomas had joined me for breakfast, however, and they were, of course, dining on the satyr-were hybrids from Dante's.

I'd seen similar scenes so often growing up that it had hardly registered. Any prisoners taken alive were always used for food. One of the few things considered truly depraved in vamp circles is to waste blood, even that of shape-shifters. Blood is precious; blood is life. I had grown up with that mantra; apparently, Pritkin had not.

The only thing that sort of threw me was the sight of Tomas feeding from the neck of a handsome young were who looked vaguely familiar. He had chocolate brown eyes that matched the dark fur that started halfway down his hips and framed his heavy sex. He'd been stripped and bound hand and foot with thick silver chains. That was standard operating procedure since humiliation was part of the punishment, but I thought it might be less than effective in this case. I didn't know how he felt about the chains—weres aren't fond of silver—but satyrs actually prefer to be nude. They believe wearing clothing suggests they have something to hide, that some part of their bodies isn't perfect. This one didn't have anything to be ashamed of, and his body was reacting to the feeding in the usual manner, making him even more impressive. It must have been an involuntary response, though; his face was so distorted with fear that it took me a minute to identify him as the waiter who had greeted me at the satyr bar.

The scene bothered me, and it wasn't because I had met the were or because he was obviously terrified. Better that he learn his lesson now and avoid trying the Senate's patience in future; they weren't known for giving third chances. I finally decided that my brain was objecting to the sight of fangs extending from Tomas' lips, and to seeing him swallow the satyr's blood like it was his favorite vintage. It seemed I was still having trouble putting "Tomas" and "vampire" in the same category.

Despite my unease, I didn't look away. It was considered a sign of weakness to show emotion when witnessing a punishment, and rude to ignore it since the whole point of having it in public is for it to be seen. I did, however, refocus my attention on Mircea. Watching him enjoy his meal bothered me less than watching Tomas, and he was in my line of sight anyway.

"I thought you didn't like were blood," I said, trying for what passed for normal conversation at the courts. Mircea had been present when Tony had the alpha executed, but had declined the honor of draining him. "You told me once that they're bitter."

"It is an acquired taste," Mircea responded, letting the black were draped over his knees fall to the floor. "But I cannot be choosy. I will need my strength tonight."

I poured more tea and eyed Pritkin's untouched plate lustfully. "Are you going to eat that?" I couldn't help it; I was starving for some reason, probably thanks to Billy Joe. The mage ignored me, staring at the unconscious were in horror. Mircea slid the mage's plate across to me and I dug in gratefully.

"Did Antonio have any more trouble with that pack, after their leader was killed?" he asked, as if he knew what I'd been thinking.

I poured syrup over the mage's untouched hotcakes and slathered on some butter. "I don't think so. At least, I never heard of any more problems. Tony didn't always tell me everything, though."

Mircea gave me a sardonic look. "That makes two of us, *dulceață. Bogăția strică pe om.*"

"You know I don't understand Romanian, Mircea."

"Prosperity, like want, ruins many."

I shook my head. No way would Tony risk angering the Senate and the Circle for profit alone. "I'm thinking it's more power Tony wants. He has money."

"You are wise beyond your years. Do your ghosts teach you such things?"

I almost blew hot tea all over Tomas. "Ha! Not likely." The only things Billy had ever taught me were some illegal card tricks and a few dirty limericks.

"Do you hear yourself?" Pritkin was looking at me with

revulsion. "That thing just committed murder and you didn't even blink! Are you enslaving the spirits of the dead, as you did your ghost servant and the dark witches? Is that why you sit there and say nothing?"

I almost decided it wasn't worth the trouble. But I was feeling much better since polishing off the pancakes, and Pritkin really needed a reality check. "First of all, the were isn't dead; he only passed out. Second, I don't 'enslave' spirits; as far as I know, that isn't even possible. And third, weres don't leave ghosts. Neither do vamps. I don't know why, but they don't."

"Because their souls have already gone to Hell?" he asked, with apparent unconcern for the looks Mircea and Rafe sent him. The others didn't react; Tomas because he was eating, and Louis-César because he was apparently suffering from a severe migraine.

"When I saw how you acted in the Senate, I wondered if you have a death wish. I'm beginning to think you really do."

"Then you admit they would as soon kill me as not."

I glanced at Mircea, who was looking like he was contemplating having dessert. "Sooner, at the rate you're going." I figured I'd better explain before the mage had a conniption. "This guy was part of a group that tried to kill us a few hours ago. But the vamps aren't going to kill him, at least not this time. A warning is given for the first offense, along with an object lesson to make it memorable. If the lesson is impressive enough, most people don't have to be told twice."

Pritkin looked disgusted. "So they're not monsters and murderous beasts, only misunderstood; is that it?"

Mircea was trying not to laugh. He wasn't trying very hard. I felt my own lips quirk as I caught his eye. "Are you a murderous beast, Mircea?"

"Of a certainty, *dulceaţă*," he replied cheerfully.

Mircea winked at me before trading his cowed victim for another that had just been brought in. This one was human, part of Tony's daytime muscle, I assumed. He must have been one of those hired for brawn instead of brains, because his hazel eyes were bright with outrage he didn't bother to hide. Apparently he'd already mouthed off to someone, since in addition to the chains he wore on his ankles and wrists, he had a gag stuffed in his mouth. I glanced at Pritkin and saw his jaw tighten. If he objected to weres being given the usual punishment for defiance, what was he going to think about a human undergoing it?

Maybe because the young man looked so rebellious, Mircea passed over the neck, the usual feeding point, with nothing more than a contemplative glance. The man was physically close to perfect, with tousled copper curls, classic features and well-defined muscles. But there was a small scar just below his left nipple that drew Mircea's attention. The vampire's long, white fingers ran across the slight blemish as if he was memorizing it—or, knowing Mircea, thinking of adding a matching one on the other side. The breast is another popular feeding point, and the man stiffened as if he knew that. I saw sweat bloom on his upper lip and he swallowed nervously. The nub hidden in the man's thick ginger body hair drew up temptingly under Mircea's touch, and his nerve broke. He jerked away, eyes wide, but got all of about a foot before a nod from Mircea caused Rafe to return him to the sofa.

Their captive tensed from the feel of Rafe's body pressed up behind him, one arm circling his waist like a vise. He seemed more worried about him than about the way Mircea was eyeing his pulse points as if trying to decide between favorite items on a menu. The man looked up and met my eyes and his own widened in surprise, as if that was the first time he'd noticed that the room held other people. The flush that already colored his cheeks quickly ran halfway down his chest. It made me wonder how long he'd been with Tony's outfit; most of them hadn't blushed even when they were alive. But he forgot about me when Mircea's deceptively slender hands suddenly forced him to his knees. He hadn't realized that struggling only made it more fun for the vamps, and the muscles of his calves and upper legs bulged as he resisted. I saw the direction of Mircea's gaze and knew what was coming.

The man was dragged onto the sofa and his knees pried apart. He seemed more concerned about being exposed in front of a group of strangers than about his imminent danger, but when a set of perfect, gleaming fangs appeared on Mircea's handsome face, he forgot to be embarrassed. He tried to roll off the couch, but his shackled ankles and arms allowed him little purchase. Mircea hauled him back to his knees to get a better angle but did not take him immediately. He drew it out, letting the man's panic rise as he discovered exactly how strong a vampire can be. He bucked uselessly against Mircea's hold, small whimpers escaping from behind the gag. Even I could see the femoral artery, bulging noticeably in his straining thigh.

When his struggles finally lessened, either because of fatigue or because nothing else had happened, Mircea struck, sinking those fangs into the silky skin at the junction of the man's hip. A muffled scream came from behind the gag when the artery was pierced, and his eyes bulged when Mircea's lips sealed over the bite and he began to suck. The struggles renewed, but Rafe moved up to ensure that his master could feed without having to bother to restrain his meal.

Pritkin flinched noticeably when Rafe suddenly bit into the straining jugular, but he was smart enough not to interfere. The vamps were well within their rights as long as the feeding stopped short of death. Looking at their captive's expression, I wondered whether anyone had told him that. Somehow I doubted it. But although it wasn't a pretty scene, I didn't like the revulsion on the mage's face. The man was an attempted murderer who was getting off pretty damned lightly. And Pritkin certainly had no room to talk. "How many did you kill tonight, Pritkin? Half a dozen? More? I didn't keep count."

The mage bristled. "That was in self-defense, and to protect you from the results of your folly." He looked at the man, who had started to sob like a baby, with growing anger. He flushed and his hands clenched at his sides as the captive contorted his body wildly in an effort to get away from the burning pain every pull of their lips caused. "This is grotesque."

I would have considered it far more grotesque if I'd been the one who ended up writhing in agony so the guy could bag a reward from Tony. But then, I'm practical like that. "They have to feed. Would you prefer it if they hunted at large like in the bad old days?"

"Everyone knows they feed from anyone who can't defend themselves! The Circle was created to give humans a fighting chance against such things, and yet you, supposedly a human, sit there defending them! You disgust me more than they do." Pritkin wanted a fight. It was in the set of his jaw and his wide-legged stance. He wanted to hit someone but didn't dare, so verbal assault it would be. Too bad I wasn't feeling very diplomatic.

"I'm as human as you are, and I saw you tonight, Pritkin. Until the Black Circle got involved, you were having a good time and you know it. Don't give me that self-defense crap. You're a predator. I grew up around enough to know."

I broke off because the man on the sofa chose that moment to put on a show. The vamps must have felt it coming, because they sat back to watch as their victim was gripped by a fine shiver that spread along the length of him like tremors from an earthquake. A few seconds later, he arched his back at what seemed an impossible angle, so that only his bound hands and the back of his thighs were still in contact with the sofa. Then he climaxed powerfully, spasming helplessly again and again. His head was thrown back and his eyes wanted to close, but Rafe caught his gaze and held it, refusing his prisoner the slightest chance of distancing himself from what was happening. The man stared at him, wide-eyed and shaking, as he spilled over his own tanned skin and the polished wood of the floor.

It seemed to go on forever, as if his body couldn't calm itself and he would keep erupting until his heart gave out. But finally he finished, slumping bonelessly forward so that his hair covered his flushed face. The vamps gave a slight shove, and his body fell heavily onto the floor between the sofa and coffee table. I realized that they'd been waiting for the sexual side effect of the feeding to hit him before they stopped, banking on the triple whammy of humiliation, pain and fear being enough to ensure that they never had to deal with him again. Judging by the shattered look on his face as he lay there, trembling, I was betting they had succeeded.

The mage was resolutely not looking at the pathetic heap on the floor. I felt slightly guilty that I wasn't more upset about the man myself. I wasn't sure that I ought to be, but looking at Pritkin's set face made me wonder. It also made me defensive, although what I told him was the truth. "Vamps don't go around killing humans unless they try to kill them first. The Senate doesn't like it—too many chances someone will see and start dangerous rumors, or that a new vamp will fail to dispose of a body and cause an investigation. Unrestricted hunting hasn't been legal since 1583, when the European Senate made a deal with your Circle. Even Tony's guys don't do it."

"I am relieved to hear it," Mircea commented, taking out a monogrammed handkerchief to wipe his mouth. Other than his lips, he didn't have a speck on him—practice, I supposed. Since he hadn't bothered to just absorb the excess blood, I figured he was pretty sated. The guy must have held on longer than he'd expected.

"I know what their laws say." Pritkin looked around the room with a sneer: I was beginning to wonder if he had another expression. "But there are thousands of vampires spread all over the world. Most of them feed at least every other day. That is a lot of enemies. Or are you going to tell me that they live off the blood of animals? I know that's a lie!"

"Don't put words in my mouth." I noticed that none of the vamps were bothering to defend themselves. Maybe they were tired of it, or didn't think Pritkin worth the trouble. Or maybe they doubted that he'd believe anything they had to say. They were probably right, but I didn't feel like giving him the last word. "Vamps don't waste blood, ever, so any living enemies are dealt with like this. But they are allowed a second chance, which from what I hear is more than your Circle gives rogue magic users. Only vamps get an automatic death sentence for defiance."

Pritkin watched helplessly as the human tried to crawl away on his bound limbs, his eyes still wide with shock, but he was hobbled by his exhaustion and the tight restraints. Lack of blood made him clumsy, and he slipped twice on the sticky floor. He finally made it to the door by using an undulating wiggle, but it did him little good since he couldn't get the latch open. He tried using his mouth, but failed, and had to turn and face the room again to give his bound hands access to the door. I finally felt a twinge of pity for him, despite the fact that he'd probably have put a bullet in my brain earlier without a second thought. It was hard to think of him as a cold-blooded killer, with his flaccid sex drooping between his sticky thighs, and his neck and groin oozing thin lines of blood that he couldn't wipe away. I was really glad that he didn't meet anyone's eyes this time.

Pritkin's face was angry when he turned to me. "You're telling me they punish their own people more than outsiders? You lie. Monsters understand nothing of mercy!"

I shrugged. "Believe what you want, but it's true. You don't see any vamps here, do you? If any were taken prisoner, they'll have been staked by now." Assuming they responded well to questioning. If not, Jack was probably having a field day.

"It isn't a matter of mercy, Mage Pritkin, I assure you," Rafe put in, his eyes on the man who was now all but clawing at the door with his bound hands. "We simply do not feel that your people are much of a threat." Pritkin made a sound of disgust and marched over to swing open the door. The man fell backwards into the hall, and several servants looked at him in surprise before hauling him away for his lecture. I doubted he needed it.

"So how do they usually feed? Do you expect me to believe they won't finish what they started later, when there are no witnesses?" Pritkin obviously wasn't going to let it go. I couldn't believe he didn't know. I had never seen a mage show surprise at Tony's during a feeding. Maybe they had simply learned to school their faces, but my impression had been that it wasn't a big secret. Yet Pritkin seemed genuinely confused. What the hell do they teach war mages, anyway?

I looked at Mircea. "You want to show him?"

Mircea laughed delightedly. "I would love to, *dulceață*, but I don't trust myself. The temptation to rid us of his annoying presence would be too great, and the Consul said most specifically that he was not to be harmed unless he gave cause." He slid his eyes in Pritkin's direction. "And alas, so far he has behaved himself."

"I meant with me."

"No." Tomas spoke up, causing me to jump slightly in surprise. He'd been so quiet that I'd almost forgotten he was there. "She is not to be harmed."

"I think, Tomas, that is the point our dear Cassandra is trying to make," Mircea replied. "That, done properly, it is not harmful." He looked at me. "You must have been a frequent donor at court, yes? You understand the procedure?"

I nodded. "Yep, not to mention feeding a ravenous ghost on occasion." Having done both, I knew that what the vamps did was little different than Billy Joe's feedings, except that he could absorb life energy directly and they had to get it through blood. Billy was able to skip that step, a good thing since his body was somewhere at the bottom of the Mississippi. He'd have trouble metabolizing even a liquid diet.

Mircea glided over with that peculiar grace of his. All the undead have it, but he made even most vamps look clumsy. He was an old hand at this; I knew he wouldn't hurt me and he was too full to take much. It was Billy Joe I would have liked to throttle—if the coward hadn't run off somewhere. Billy's feedings normally didn't bother me, since I could replenish the energy he took with food and rest. But he knew the rules about how much I was willing to donate at once, and tonight he'd broken them all to hell.

"What are you going to do?" Pritkin started forward, but Tomas would not let him by. Neither looked happy.

"Make sure he has a good view, Tomas," Mircea said, looking down at me thoughtfully. "I will do this only once. Cassandra is already tired, and we have much to talk about. I do not wish to put her to sleep." He smiled and cupped my chin in his hand. He felt warm, but then, he always did. The old ones don't have temperature fluctuations based on whether they have eaten recently or not. "I will not hurt you," he promised.

I was remembering why I'd always liked Mircea. The deep brown eyes and graceful physique had certainly played a part, adolescent hormones being what they are, but his appearance had been less important to me than his honesty. I had never once caught him in a lie. I was sure he was a capable enough liar when he wanted to be—it would be pretty much impossible to function at court otherwise—but he had always been frank with me. It might sound like a little thing, but in a system run by deception and evasion, sincerity was priceless. I smiled up at him, only half for Pritkin's sake. "I know."

Pritkin couldn't get to me, but he could still yell. "This is insane! You're going to let him feed off you? Willingly? You'll end up like one of them!"

Mircea answered for me, his dark eyes steady on mine. They were not a true brown, I realized, but a combination of many colors: cappuccino, cinnamon, gold and a few flecks of deep green. They were beautiful. "If we fed on the population at large as you seem to think, Mage Pritkin, how could we avoid making thousands, even millions of new vampires? It only takes three bites over consecutive days from a seventh-level master or higher. Can you believe that, with no restrictions, it would not happen time and again? Either by accident or intentionally? Soon, we would be no longer merely a myth, and would again be hunted."

He stopped, but he didn't need to go on. I couldn't believe that even Pritkin was unaware of what had happened to Dracula, and Mircea himself had been almost caught and killed many times in the early years. Radu, his younger brother, had not been so lucky. He had been taken by a mob in Paris and delivered to the Inquisition. They had tortured him for well over a century, until, when Mircea finally found and freed him, he was dangerously mad. Radu had been locked away ever since.

"It was constant war once," Mircea continued, as if he knew what I had been thinking. "Between us and the humans, between families of vampyre, between us and the mages, and on and on. Until the senates rose, until they said enough, or we will destroy ourselves in the end. No one wants to return to that, especially the conflict with the humans. Even if we won against the billions who would oppose us, we would lose, for who would feed us if they were gone?" He looked at Pritkin. "We do not wish for huge numbers of us, running wild, with no supervision and no hope of secrecy, any more than you do. We bite to drain a subject in an execution, or to frighten as with the captives today. But for a normal feeding," he said, returning his attention to me, "we prefer a gentler method." He smiled, and it was like the sun broke through the clouds after days of rain. It was breathtaking.

"What are you doing to her?" Pritkin looked around Tomas' shoulders. "You're not doing anything." He sounded almost disappointed.

Tomas reached out and removed Mircea's hand from my face. "Leave her alone."

Mircea regarded him with amusement. "She offered, Tomas; you heard her. What is the trouble? I have promised to be gentle." Tomas' eyes flashed and his jaw clenched. He did not look appeased. Mircea's eyes widened slightly, then sparkled wickedly. "Forgive me; I did not understand. But surely you cannot begrudge me one small taste?" He stroked my face, a lazy caress, but his eyes were on Tomas. "Is she as sweet as she looks?" Tomas actually growled at him, and this time he flung Mircea's hand away.

I wished Mircea would get on with it. I wanted to question Pritkin, and I couldn't while he was on his vampire fixation. "Can we just do this?"

"I will do it, if it must be done," Tomas said and bent his head towards me.

I immediately pulled away. "Uh-uh. I never agreed to that." I owed Tomas a few things all right, but a feeding wasn't one of them.

Mircea laughed again, a rich, mellow sound. "Tomas! You did not tell her?"

"Tell me what?" My mood was not improving.

The glint in Mircea's eyes was pure mischief. "Only that he has been feeding from you for months, *dulceață*, and, as often happens in such cases, he has become . . . territorial."

I looked at Tomas in shock. "Tell me he's kidding."

The answer was on his face before he spoke, and I felt the world tilt. In vamp circles, feeding has strict rules. Even the same norm can't be fed from regularly, as it creates a feeling of possession in the vamp involved and can lead to all sorts of problems because of jealousy. But taking blood without permission from someone connected with our world is considered even more of a violation. That's not only because of the often sexual by-product of the feeding process, but also because anyone recognized as part of the supernatural community has special rights. Tomas had just broken a whole group of laws, not to mention betraying me yet again. So everything about him had been one vampire trick or another, from the way he looked to the way I'd felt. I might have eventually been able to forgive him the deception, but not this. I couldn't believe he'd done it, but looking at him, I knew he had.

Tomas licked his lips. "It was not frequent, Cassie. I had to know where you were at all times, and regular feedings create a bond. They helped me keep you safe."

"How very generous of you." I could barely get the words out; it felt like someone had hit me.

I started to rise—I'm not sure why—when Mircea put a restraining hand on my shoulder. His expression was suddenly serious, as if he realized something of how much the news had affected me. "You have every right to be annoyed with Tomas, *dulceață*, but now is not the time. It is my fault; I shouldn't have teased him. I will refrain, if you will please let it go for the moment. Otherwise we will waste the day in arguments."

"I don't want to argue," I said, and it was true. I wanted to throw something at Tomas' head, preferably something heavy. But that wouldn't get me answers, and right then, I needed information more than revenge. "Fine. Just get him away from me."

"Done. Tomas, if you please?" Tomas looked like he was going to argue, but after a noticeable pause he moved off about two feet. Then he stopped, looking mulish. I would have pushed the issue, but he would only have said that he needed to be close to watch Pritkin. Since I tended to agree with that, I kept quiet.

Mircea sighed and cupped my face again. He didn't prolong it this time. His fingers gently stroked down my chin to
my neck, and I could feel his power calling to me. His caress was delicate, barely a touch at all, but I shivered as a
warm surge of pleasure danced through my body, driving
away some of the shock I felt at Tomas' actions. My skin tin-
gled and a mist of sparkling, delicious energy rose between
us. I suddenly knew whose wards Billy Joe had broken earlier, whose power we had borrowed to fight off the attack at
Dante's. This was the same giddy, bubbling, champagne-on-
ice sensation I'd felt at the casino, a heady mix of desire and
laughter and warmth that was almost instantly addictive. I
knew I should be aggravated about the wards he'd put on my
power, but no one could have bathed in that feeling and
stayed angry. It was simply impossible. It poured over me
like sunlight given form, and I laughed in wonder.

Mircea started when our energies mingled, then went
very still. I barely noticed. I was happily drowning in a glorious, golden glow. It felt as though he was touching something far more intimate than my neck and, for a second, I
actually thought that my robe had disappeared and a warm
hand was caressing all the way down my body. I tried to
swallow, but my mouth had gone dry and a pulse began to
throb insistently in tender places. I flashed on a long-ago
evening, Mircea and I curled up together on the divan in
Tony's study, him stroking my hair as he told me a story. I'd
spent more time with him on that visit than Tony had, half
of it snuggled in his lap, but I'd never reacted this way. Of
course, I'd been eleven. Sitting on his lap now took on a
completely new connotation.

Mircea was wearing an odd expression, almost confused,
as if he'd never seen me before. He searched my face for a
moment, then took my hand and bowed over it. I felt a brief
touch of lips, then he released me and stepped back. The
whole thing had taken maybe ten seconds, but it left me
breathless, flushed and momentarily heartbroken, like the

most precious thing in my life had been snatched away. I almost reached for him but managed to stop before I humiliated myself. I sat there, trying to lower my pulse back to something approaching normal, and stared at him.

I'd forgotten how much more personal vamp feedings were than what Billy did. I hadn't thought about that aspect with Mircea, a fact that amazed me now. He had the charisma for which his family was famous, his power was great enough for him to win and hold a Senate seat and there was no denying his masculine beauty. I had, of course, never met Dracula, who died long before I was born, or the unfortunate Radu, but looking at Mircea, I could understand why the family had become legendary. If you met one of them, you weren't likely to forget it, no matter what tricks were used to fog the memory.

I looked up to see Tomas scowling, his eyes moving back and forth between Mircea and me. What was his problem now? It was over. Then I glanced at my reflection and saw that my eyes had lost focus, I was rosy and my lips were half parted. I looked like I'd just had really good sex, which was not far from the truth. I quickly rearranged my face to look less like afterglow.

Pritkin appeared let down, as if he'd have liked to see something that caused pain, not pleasure. "I don't believe you fed. You didn't take blood; you never even broke the skin."

"On the contrary," Mircea adjusted his collar in an almost nervous gesture. "That was a feeding, if a very mild one." He glanced at Tomas as if he was going to say something, then decided against it. He suddenly turned a wolfish smile on Pritkin. "Raphael will demonstrate it for you, if you like."

Rafe had crossed the room and wrapped his fingers around Pritkin's wrist before I could blink. Power surged out from the mage in a panicked wash, and I felt my bracelet shiver against my wrist. "I'm not going to hurt you," Rafe told him, contemptuously. "I won't do anything other than what was done to Cassie. Are you less brave than she?"

Pritkin wasn't hearing him. His expression would have sent me scurrying for cover, but Rafe held his ground. He couldn't do otherwise, having been given a direct order by his master's master. "Let go, vampire, or by the Circle you will regret it!"

Abruptly, Pritkin's elements were all around me. He warded with both earth and water, and they flowed out from him at the same time so that I felt like I was simultaneously being buried and drowned. My bracelet leapt like I'd captured a small wild animal that desperately wanted to get away. I fought to draw a breath and couldn't. I tore at the neck of the robe, but it was no help; it wasn't the material that was threatening to choke me. I gasped for air, but it was like my lungs were solid, heavy lumps in my chest that had forgotten how to breathe. I slowly slid down in the chair, my vision going dark. My only thought was that, in a room full of vampires, it would be my luck to get killed by the only other human.

Chapter 10

A warm hand slipped under my collar to rest lightly on the skin of my collarbone, and a brief tingle ran up my arm. All of a sudden the suffocating sensation let up a little. The air was heavy and hard to breathe, but I could manage it.

"Release him, Raphael," Mircea barked, and I looked up to see that it was his touch that had broken through the mage's power. Rafe immediately complied, wiping his hand on his thigh as if he hadn't enjoyed touching Pritkin any more than vice versa. The mage shook with the effort of reining in his power. It continued to surge, but it was less violent, like waves lapping at the edge of a lake instead of crashing onto the shore.

Mircea nodded at Rafe, who went to the door and gave one of the servants an order. A few seconds later, another of the satyr-weres was brought in. He was a young blond male who, like the others, had reverted to his more nonthreatening form. His fur was a tawny gold color that complemented his hair and the faded denim of his eyes. He was easily six feet tall and as well built as most young satyrs are. If they aren't born that way, they work at it—nothing is worse in their view than being considered unattractive, unless it's impotence. Not that he had any problems either way. The uncertainty of the holding cell had wilted him, but he perked back up immediately at the sight of me. I forgave him; they literally couldn't help themselves.

"Watch and learn, mage." Raphael took out a knife and, with no warning, drew a shallow cut across the satyr's chest. The creature didn't moan, and I wasn't surprised. They weren't usually brave, but they'd never willingly show fear in front of a half-dressed female.

Rafe held his hand about a foot away from the satyr's torso, and slowly, as if pulled by invisible strings, drops of blood began to leap across the air between them to splash against his palm. As soon as they landed, they were absorbed.

"We can do it without the cut, without any wound at all," Mircea said softly. "Anytime, to anyone, anywhere. A brush against you in the subway, a handshake"—his gaze slid down to me—"or more pleasurable things; all will suffice."

I held Mircea's dark eyes and for a second I couldn't breathe again, although this time it was my own body I was fighting rather than someone else's power. No one's eyes should be able to look like that, as if they held the secret to every dream you've ever had, every wish come spectacularly true. The hand he kept on my naked flesh was suddenly stimulating rather than comforting. His expression changed, and I couldn't even begin to name it, but my body interpreted it as erotic. I had to actually clutch at the chair arms to keep from throwing myself into his arms. Damn, this was unexpected.

Mircea stepped away after a moment, and some of the river of heat flowing through me dissipated, but the longing remained. The problem, other than the fact that he might have to kill me on the Consul's orders, was that I couldn't be sure how much of what I was feeling was real, and how much was simply what Mircea wanted me to feel. I thought about that first night with Tomas, and his attempted seduction. I found it hard to believe that he'd been so overcome by lust at the sight of me in my big, cartoon-covered towel that he couldn't help himself. Had Tomas acted on the Senate's orders? Was Mircea doing the same thing now?

I knew Tomas hadn't needed to touch me to feed. Mircea hadn't told Pritkin, but a master doesn't need tactile contact. Any of them could have drained me from across the room, pulling my life from me in invisible, microscopic particles that wouldn't be seen or noticed by anyone else. And if they were as good as Mircea, there wouldn't even be a bruise or other telltale mark to show that blood had been stolen. I didn't think Pritkin would react too well to that tidbit of information, especially not with the hunted, half-panicked expression he still wore. He looked like a man who'd awakened from a dream to find himself surrounded by monsters.

I could have reassured him, if he'd have believed anything I had to say. Most vamps wouldn't be able to feed from him easily, if at all. His wards were almost certainly too strong—he would have had to drop them for Rafe to complete the demonstration—and his training would probably tell him that some form of threat was being made. But a norm wouldn't notice a thing, except perhaps for a slight feeling of lethargy. Vamps only left a fang-marked body behind in the movies, or if they were making a point. Tony would no doubt be receiving some shortly.

Louis-César took that minute to decide that Mircea had had enough fun for one day. "If you are so interested in our habits, Mage Pritkin, I can recommend several excellent treatises for you to study. This, however, is not the time." He looked at his colleague. "The day is passing, and the night will be full. May we proceed?"

Mircea inclined his head and sprawled elegantly back onto the couch, pausing to remove his suit jacket and toss it over the coffee table. He also loosened the top fastening of his high-collared shirt, as if the room had suddenly grown too warm. The shirt was a thick eggshell silk made in a Chinese pattern, with little toggles holding it together instead of buttons. The material had a lustrous sheen, the kind that made you want to run your hands over it to see if it felt as

buttery soft as it looked, but no design. His suit was also
plain, unrelieved black, but on him the understated look
worked. It was like a simple frame around a fine painting:
all you saw was the total effect, and it was stunning. I shifted
in my thick robe. I agreed with him—the room was way too
warm.

Pritkin's skin had turned the color of old mushrooms. I
think some of the implications had started to dawn on him.
He turned on Mircea. "Can you make more vampires in such
ways? Can you call your victims?" I bit my lip.

Pritkin had definitely been out to lunch when Vampire
101 was in session. His ignorance made it seem odd that the
Silver Circle would have sent him as their liaison to the Senate. From things the mages at Tony's had said, I'd gotten the
idea that the war mages had different branches, each of
which concentrated on a different major category of nonhumans—vamps, weres, demons, Fey, and magical creatures like dragons. It made me wonder what his specialty
was.

Louis-César frowned at him, maybe thinking the same
thing, and Mircea held out a hand to me theatrically. "Come
to me, Cassandra," he thundered. "I command you!" His
usual slight accent had thickened to the point that he
sounded like Bela Lugosi. I smiled in spite of myself.
Mircea's sense of humor was notoriously horrible, but it did
help to break the tension.

I snuggled closer against the softness of the overstuffed
armchair. "Thanks for the offer, but I'm quite comfortable
where I am." In fact, the couch looked far more attractive at
the moment, which made staying where I was a very good
idea. I knew perfectly well that part of my trouble was the
aftereffects of the feeding, but Mircea would have tempted
a saint all on his own. I didn't need any more complications,
especially with a Senate member. He might genuinely like
me, but in the end, he'd do whatever the Consul wanted.
They all would.

Mircea was taunting Pritkin. "You see, my friend? Nothing. She spurns me. My allure must not be as strong as I thought."

"Only a bite can allow us to call one of you," Tomas told him shortly. He glanced at me, and his eyes were black with some emotion I couldn't read.

I kept my mouth shut, not wanting to start a debate. But the truth was that, even if Mircea had bitten me, it probably wouldn't have made a difference. Vampires could control most norms through their bite: one was usually enough, two always were, and after three, the victim became a vamp bound to his or her master, so it was a moot point. But Tony had bitten me twice to ensure loyalty, once when I was a child and then again after my return to him as a teenager. Yet, if he'd been trying to summon me—a safe bet—it had failed.

My theory was that my constant association with ghosts had interrupted the signal. Billy Joe was almost always with me and I constantly wore his necklace, which bound us together even when we were apart. And vamps can't read ghosts. One of the points Billy had used to make our deal was that, with luck, he'd run a kind of spiritual interference. Maybe it had worked, or maybe I was one of the few who had natural resistance to the call. I doubted that, since it was usually only the case with particularly powerful magic users, but weirder things had happened. Hell, weirder things happened to me all the time.

Mircea was looking at me with exaggerated longing, and I smiled. "You could always join me." The minute I said it, I wanted to take it back. A clear head was impossible around him, and I wanted whatever abilities I had to be sharp. But I needn't have worried. Mircea looked for a moment like he was considering it, then smiled and shook his head.

"You are kind to offer, *dulceață*, but I am also quite comfortable here." He glanced at Tomas. "Perhaps later."

Louis-César planted himself in front of me while Tomas

walked Pritkin back to his place by the door. The Frenchman appeared slightly stressed. From what little I'd observed of him, that was probably the equivalent of anyone else throwing a fit. "*Mademoiselle*, I need your attention for a moment, if you please. I know that you are tired and that this experience has been difficult, but please try to concentrate." I felt like pointing out that I hadn't been the one getting us off topic, but thought better of it. "Do you recall the name Françoise?"

I looked at him warily. So we were back to that again. "Yes."

"Please explain why you thought that name would convince me to spare you."

I looked at Tomas. He nodded curtly. "I have told them what I know, but I did not understand much of what we did. I only know that—"

"Be silent!" Louis-César ordered him sharply. "We cannot afford to have anything you say influence her." He turned back to me, and his eyes were a dark blue-gray like gathering storm clouds over the ocean. "Please tell me."

"Fine, but then I want to ask a few questions, okay?"

He nodded, so I went through it all, how he'd touched me and I'd somehow ended up in the castle, skipping over exactly where I was and what we were doing when I first arrived. "They burned her to death, but there was nothing I—we—could do. We had to stand there and watch it happen. Then I came back and you said something about wishing I hadn't had to see that, and you called her Françoise. Don't you remember?"

Louis-César looked faintly green. "No, *mademoiselle*, that is not how I remember our short time in this room. Neither does Mircea, nor Raphael. You fainted while I was attending your cheek, and when you awoke, you were upset and disoriented for a time. We attributed it to your recent experiences. You did not mention anything about a woman named Françoise. I was given a tour of the dungeons of Carcassonne once, it is true, but as far as I am aware, no one died that night." He closed his eyes for a moment. "It was quite horrible enough without that."

"I didn't dream it!" I was getting more confused by the minute. "You're saying you never knew anyone by that name?"

"One." Louis-César's voice was quiet, but his eyes could have ignited a match. "A young gypsy, the daughter of one of the guards at the castle. She worked as a servant, I believe in order to save for her wedding to some young man."

"What happened to her?"

He looked sick. "I never knew. I assumed her father thought we were becoming . . . too close, and had her sent away. I had something of a reputation in those days, and Françoise was one of the servants who regularly attended me. But I never touched her. I do not want a woman in my bed who is not there willingly. And a servant would have had little choice if I had . . . made advances. I would not have put her in such a position."

"Then why did someone want to kill her?"

He sat down on the edge of the sofa as if I'd punched him. "Because I was fond of her. I gave her a necklace—a mere trifle—because she had no jewelry and such beauty should be adorned. And twice I gave her money—again, trivial sums only, as my own resources were not great in those days. I thought only to help with her wedding expenses, and to repay her for her kindness. She must have told someone, or else they saw her wear the necklace and guessed . . ." He said the last as if talking to himself.

This wasn't helping. "Why would someone kill her just because you liked her? Who hated you that much?"

He leaned over, elbows on his knees, and his hair hid his face. "My brother." The voice was chokingly bitter. "He did worse to frighten me into submission through the years."

"Can you tell us anything else about that vision, Cassie?" Mircea's face was very serious. "Any detail could be vital."

"I don't think so." I thought about it—I hadn't been in the best mental state for making observations at the time—but I'd covered pretty much everything. "Except that the jailer used a weird name for me—us, I mean. *M'sieur le Tour*, or something like that."

Louis-César jerked as though I'd struck him. "Is that significant?" Mircea asked him.

He shook his head. "No. It is only—I have not heard that name in a great many years. I was called that once, although not usually to my face. It translates as 'the man in the tower'; I was often imprisoned in one. It had other meanings, too, at times," he added softly.

I glanced at Mircea, who looked grave but didn't comment. "Tell us about the second vision, *dulceață*."

I nodded, trying to ignore the fact that my little tarot cards had been even more on the ball than usual. I decided not to mention it. Louis-César had said the name wasn't important, and I didn't want them taken away. "Fine, but I don't understand it, either. Normally I See what once happened or what's about to happen, but it's like watching TV. I observe, and that's it."

"But not lately."

I shifted uncomfortably. I hadn't had time to process what had been happening yet myself, so how could I explain it to someone else? "It's been . . . different in the last day or so. I don't know why. Maybe because I was in someone else's body when I shifted the second time. That's never happened before."

"You never possessed anyone before tonight?" It was Pritkin's voice, and it was laced with skepticism. I wanted to ignore him, but I also wanted to know what was going on.

"No. I don't know how I did it, but when Billy Joe slammed into me . . . "

"Billy Joe is your familiar's name?"

"I don't have a familiar," I snapped. "Once and for all, I'm not a witch, okay? I am not a demon; I am not the freaking bogeyman! I'm a clairvoyant. Do you know what that is?!"

Maybe it was because I lost my temper, or maybe the bracelet remembered him and held a grudge. But without warning, twin knives, looking as gaseous and insubstantial as Billy after a wild night out, appeared in front of me and flew straight at him. They didn't look real—it was more like light had been carved into shapes—but they worked well enough. I didn't mean to hurt him, but the bracelet apparently thought otherwise, for the daggers plunged deeply into his chest. He screamed and I instinctively shrank back. The daggers came with me, flying back across the room to disappear into the bracelet.

"I'm sorry!" I watched, appalled, as two bright red wounds bloomed on his chest. "I didn't know it would do that!" I looked at the thing on my wrist in shock. It shouldn't have been able to harm a mage, but it had sliced through his shields like they weren't there.

"Where did you get it?" Mircea looked at my bracelet with interest.

"I, uh, sort of found it, recently."

"It deserted the dark mage for her!" Pritkin's voice had roughened with pain, and he was looking at me with hate. I really couldn't blame him this time. "Dark weapons are fickle; they always go to the greatest source of power, in order to increase their own." He grimaced and dropped to his knees. "She is dangerous, evil!"

Pritkin's chest, as messed up as if he'd been hit with real weapons, was gushing blood. I stared at him in horror, not quite believing what I'd done. I didn't like him, but killing him had definitely not been any part of my plan. He tore open his shirt and dragged in a lungful of air. He let it out slowly, muttering something. Within a few seconds, the gashes in his chest began to close over. So much for being all for the humans—he healed as fast as a vamp.

His lip curled. "So, sybil, you say you are human. Yet

you wield a dark weapon, one that steals power from its opponents and turns it against them. Dark witches fight for you, and this night I saw you do something even a dark mage could not have done. The Black Circle itself does not have the power to steal someone's body, much less that of a mage who was warded against such things!" He grabbed the door latch and hauled himself to his feet.

"I didn't steal—"

He cut me off with a savage gesture. "But I have seen something similar before, a creature who takes others' lives and uses them for its own." He tried to push past Tomas but didn't get anywhere. That seemed to piss him off, and he shouted at me over Tomas' shoulder. "It is the darkest of magic, only available to the vilest of demons! The Circle was right to send me to you. They knew I would realize what you really are. How many lives have you stolen, sibyl?! How many murders has it taken to sustain your miserable existence?"

I stood up, and Louis-César didn't try to stop me. "My name is Cassie Palmer! I have a birth certificate to prove it. I don't go around stealing bodies. I am not a freaking demon!" I looked at Mircea, who was watching the whole scene like most people would a particularly entertaining movie. "Why do I have to keep saying that?"

He shrugged. "I have been saying it for years, *dulceață*, and no one believes me."

Pritkin took advantage of my momentary distraction to have a fit. Out of nowhere, his bevy of magical knives came streaming right at me. I wasn't expecting the attack and stood there like an idiot, with my mouth hanging open. Tomas moved like lightning but caught only two of the weapons. Two more dodged around his flailing arms to zero in on me. I didn't have time to think, much less do anything to protect myself. I felt my ward flare but didn't know if it could deal with enchanted weapons. A second later, I still didn't, because the knives were sticking out of the golem's torso, vibrating with the impact. I stared at it in incomprehension, until it dawned on me that Pritkin must have forgotten to withdraw his order for it to protect me. He bellowed for it to move out of the way, but by then Tomas had grabbed him.

I don't know if Tomas hadn't dealt with war mages before, but he underestimated this one. One of Pritkin's tiny vials flew at Tomas' head, splashing him with a red substance that looked like blood but burned like acid. Tomas didn't release him, but the stuff had gotten into his eyes and he was momentarily blind. Pritkin made an odd gesture, like jerking on an invisible rope, and the two knives sticking out of the golem came flying back to him. One hit Tomas in the leg and the other almost severed his left wrist. He went to one knee and Pritkin managed to break away. He dodged a knife thrown by Louis-César, leapt out of the way of Tomas' thrashing limbs, and pointed both his guns at me.

I didn't think; I reacted, which is probably what saved me. My hand jerked up and two gaseous knives flew at Pritkin, knocking the guns out of his hands as he fired. He got several bullets off anyway, but they disappeared harmlessly into the golem's clay. I glanced at it in surprise. It looked so awkward; it was hard to believe how fast it could move. At a word from its enraged master it was suddenly gone, and a second later was across the room battling with Louis-César. The Frenchman plunged his rapier into it again and again, but it had no vital organs to hit. He dodged its blows, despite the fact that they were so fast I could barely see them, but it was slowly driving him back towards the far wall and away from the fight.

Pritkin yelled something and threw himself at me, a grenade in his palm. Tomas, who launched himself at him like he'd been fired from a cannon, froze in midair and crashed to the ground where he lay, unmoving. A split second later I understood why, when what felt like a giant, invisible hand grabbed me, holding me and my bracelet motionless. It was similar to the trick the dark mage had used, only there was no one to counter it this time. Pritkin vaulted over Tomas and dodged around Rafe, who had also been caught in the spell. The whole room was a frozen tableau, and I saw a grim smile flash across the mage's face. His eyes met mine, and I knew the crazy man was actually going to kill me, even if he died for it.

But Pritkin and I had both forgotten Mircea. He came out of nowhere, a dark blur across my vision, grabbed the mage, broke his wrist, and threw the grenade out the window. While I was still blinking in surprise, Mircea grabbed Pritkin around the throat and lifted him off the ground. Louis-César vaulted over the sofa a second later, the golem in pieces behind him, but I saw the realization cross his face that he would have been too late.

I still couldn't move, but Raphael had managed to throw off the spell and was batting at a couple of little vials that had homed in on him, using Mircea's discarded coat so that he didn't have to touch them. Then the grenade's explosion rocked the room, sending plaster raining down from the ceiling and shards of glass flying past the heavy curtain to scatter across the floor. The invisible hand finally released me and I coughed, falling back into the chair, choking on plaster dust and almost deaf from the loud ringing in my ears.

I shot a wild glance at Pritkin, but he was well and truly immobilized. His arsenal was another thing, but Louis-César had started chanting something under his breath that made the flying pieces sluggish. Rafe grabbed two vials that were hovering in front of his face and stuffed them in the fireplace basket after dumping a dried flower arrangement all over the tiles. He shut the wicker lid and then gathered up the other bits and pieces of the flying arsenal and added them to his collection. I could see the lid bump slightly up and down as his captives struggled to get free. One of the ones he missed tried to sneak up on me, moving slowly across the floor unnoticed by everyone else. I stared at it, wondering what defense wouldn't shatter the glass and end up dousing me with the contents after all, but my bracelet knew how to fight better than I did. It pulled my arm up and sent a knife to shatter against the vial. The tiny container evaporated with a pop, leaving only an odd, musty smell behind.

Mircea's voice was calm but utterly convincing. "Call them off, mage, or I will happily demonstrate an old-style feeding for you."

I believed him, but Pritkin was more stubborn, or more stupid. The shotgun rose off the ground on its own, pointing at me. "Go ahead, but I will take your demon whore with me!"

Louis-César leapt for the gun and jerked it up just as it went off. It blew a hole in the fireplace behind me. An inch to the left, and I would have been in more pieces than the golem. A hail of brick and mortar joined the dust cloud, and several flying bits nicked my skin. I cried out, and the next second it was like a hurricane had blown into the room. Through the storm of dust and debris that whirled around us, I could see that Mircea's jovial mask had peeled away and something feral looked out of his face. I'd seen other vampires without the human gloss, but they hadn't looked like this. He was terrible and beautiful at the same time, with glowing, alabaster skin, inch-long fangs and eyes of flaming, molten lava.

The wind blew Pritkin against the wall, and the force beating against him caused his face to distort wildly. His vision was unimpeded, though, and the expression in his eyes made it clear that he hadn't guessed what lay under the perfect facade. What had he thought, that the Senate members earned their spots through charity work? I was amazed the man had lasted this long.

"Cassandra is mine," Mircea told him in a voice that could have melted glass. "Touch her again and, Circle or no,

I will bring you over and ensure that you spend the rest of
eternity begging for death."

"Mircea!" Louis-César did not attempt to touch him, but
his voice cut through the storm like boiling water through a
snow drift. "Please; you know the situation. There are other
ways to deal with him."

The wind slowly subsided and I found myself shaking
from an excess of adrenaline. I got my trembling legs under
me and walked to where Pritkin was still held against the
wall by Mircea's power, although he no longer looked in
danger of being forced through it. Several trickles of blood
ran down my face into the collar of the robe, but I ignored
them. Compared to Tomas, I had gotten off amazingly
lightly. A very battered version of my former roommate was
searching Pritkin for weapons. Tomas' wrist had already
started to knit back together, tendons and ligaments reform-
ing before my eyes, but his face was a mass of scalded flesh
and only one eye appeared to be working. I shuddered at his
expression, which clearly said that the only reason the mage
wasn't already dead was because Tomas hadn't figured out
which execution method would hurt the most.

I glanced at Mircea, and his face was no more comforting. The man I knew had always been an even-tempered, almost gentle presence, who told convoluted stories and awful
jokes, liked dressing up and didn't mind playing endless
games of checkers with an infatuated eleven-year-old. I
wasn't as naive as Pritkin—I had known the truth was far
more complex. Mircea had grown up in a court where assassination and cruelty were the order of the day, where his
own father had traded two of his sons for a treaty he had no
intention of keeping and where he had been tortured to what
would have been a horrible death if the gypsy hadn't gotten
to him first. That sort of thing didn't allow for much com-
passion. Still, a softer side was there, wasn't it? I honestly
didn't know anymore.

I had never felt any kind of threat from him as a child. He

had been serene, kind Mircea with laughing brown eyes that crinkled a bit at the corners. It was hard to reconcile that person with what I saw now. Was that terrifying aspect always there, simmering below the surface, and I had simply been too blind to see it? I saw it now, and it created a problem. As much as I disliked Pritkin, I didn't want him dead. He might be—make that probably was—crazy, but I needed him to explain what was happening to me, or to contact someone who could. It wasn't like I knew anyone else to ask. "Don't kill him, Mircea."

"We have no intention of killing him, *mademoiselle*," Louis-César answered, although he kept a wary eye on his colleague. Tomas had finished stripping off the mage's weapons, at least the ones we could see. I had a feeling that a lot were still available to him, and my bracelet seemed to agree. It glowed warm against my wrist, feeling heavier than it had a few minutes ago. I would have liked to get it off—it was starting to creep me out—but this wasn't a good time. "As of this night, we are already at war with the Dark Circle; we have no wish to also fight the Light."

"Be careful," Rafe said from beside me. "Make sure he's completely unarmed."

"He's a war mage," Mircea said flatly. "He's never unarmed."

"Until he's dead," Tomas added, and I noticed that he still gripped a struggling knife in his good hand. He moved like lightning—I guess he liked the irony of killing Pritkin with his own weapon—but Louis-César was a fraction faster. His hand caught Tomas' wrist a hairsbreadth from Pritkin's chest.

"Tomas! I will not have you start a war!"

"If you harbor that thing"—Pritkin all but spat at me—"you'll be at war with us whether you will it or not. I was sent here to find out what she was and to deal with her if she posed a threat. I expected to find merely a cassandra, a fallen sybil, but this is far worse than I anticipated. And what I know, the Circle knows. If I fail to kill her, expect a dozen, a hundred others, to come in my place." He looked at me, and if looks could kill, he'd have just saved his Circle the trouble. "I've fought one of these things before. I know what they can do and I won't leave it alive."

He lunged for me again, but all it accomplished was to almost choke him, since Mircea's invisible grip had all the give of a steel glove. It was weird, because Mircea's face was back to its usual placid expression. The eyes were no more than vaguely interested, the cheeks were their normal color and a slight smile curved his lips. The incandescent anger was nowhere to be seen. I shivered. Acting skills like those worried me. I turned my attention back to the mage, and it dawned on me that the only person who I was sure wasn't deceiving me was the man who'd just tried to kill me. Nice.

"I'm not an *it*," I told him, staying well out of reach. "I don't know what you think is happening here, but I'm not a threat to you."

He laughed, a rather strangled sound under the circumstances. "Of course not. I'm too old for a lamia to take an interest. I tracked the one I killed over the bodies of twenty children it used to sustain its abomination of a life. I won't let that happen again."

I fought down anger and turned to the window, parting the blackout curtain to see a flat, reddish-tan landscape and pale blue sky. Quite a group had gathered around the hole left by the grenade, but no one bothered us. I guess they figured we could take care of ourselves. I turned back to that hate-filled face. "What if you're wrong and I'm not some evil thing? Wouldn't you rather know for sure before killing me?"

"I already know. No human can do what you did. It isn't possible."

"A few days ago, I would have agreed with you. Now I know different." I found it hard to meet his eyes. I'd never had anyone look at me with that level of hatred. Tony wanted to kill me, but I was willing to bet that if he ever caught up with me his eyes wouldn't look like that. He viewed me as a royal pain and a way to seal a bargain, not as the incarnation of evil. Even though I knew Pritkin was wrong, I felt guilty, and that made me mad in a way his physical attack hadn't. I wasn't the homicidal lunatic here.

"You said you've hunted these things before. Isn't there some kind of test you use, to make sure you're right? Or do you kill anyone you suspect on sight?"

"There are tests," Pritkin said through clenched teeth, as if even talking to me was torture. "But your vampire allies wouldn't like them. They involve holy water and crosses."

I looked at Mircea in astonishment, and he rolled his eyes. What the hell kind of stuff was Pritkin reading? Bram freaking Stoker? Demons might be afraid of holy items, but vamps certainly weren't. Mircea's family crest showed a dragon, the symbol of courage, embracing a cross, a sign of the family's Catholicism. It decorated the wall behind his seat in the Senate, but I guess Pritkin had been too busy glaring at me to notice. I thought about giving him the lecture on vampirism being sort of like lycanthropy, in that it was a metaphysical disease. But I doubted he'd believe that the legends claiming that a demon came to roost in every new vampire had been caused by the hysteria of the Middle Ages. Pritkin seemed to see demons everywhere, whether any were there or not. In fact, the only ones of Hollywood's arsenal of weapons that actually worked on vamps were sunlight—for the younger ones, anyway—stakes and garlic, and the latter only if employed as part of a protection ward. Simply hanging the stuff over a door would have no effect at all—hell, Tony loved it on bruschetta with a little olive oil.

Mircea was no help; he only grinned at me. "And to think, I always believed that my least favorite things were bad wine and poor fashion." He smiled tolerantly at my expression. "Very well, *dulceață*. I think we can find a few crosses somewhere. And unless I mistake it, Rafe is keeping several vials of holy water imprisoned as we speak."

Rafe came forward with his box. It sounded like a bunch of Mexican jumping beans were inside, urgently trying to get out, and all of us looked at it doubtfully. "I don't agree with this," Tomas spoke up. "I was charged by the Consul to keep Cassie safe. What if he lies, and those things contain acid or explosives? You know we cannot trust him."

"Never trust a mage," Rafe agreed, as if quoting something.

"I will test them," Louis-César said and extracted a vial so quickly that I didn't have a chance to stop him. He didn't pour it over his own flesh as I'd half feared, but held the stoppered vial under Pritkin's nose. "I am about to spill this over your arm. If it is not safe to do so, it would be well if you told me now."

Pritkin ignored him, his glare still on me, as if he was more worried about what I might do than a roomful of master vamps. He obviously hadn't been around them long enough to understand nuances. Louis-César had said only that they wouldn't kill him—that still left a lot of possibilities wide open. I'd have been worried, but Pritkin was so busy giving me the glower of death that he barely noticed when a few drops of colorless liquid were drizzled over his skin. We all watched as if expecting his arm to start to melt, but nothing happened. Louis-César reached for me, but Tomas grabbed his wrist.

The Frenchman's eyes flashed silver. "Be careful, Tomas," he said softly. "You are not possessed this time."

Tomas ignored the warning. "That could be poison—he could have taken the antidote, or be willing to die with her. I will not have her harmed."

"I will take responsibility before the Consul if anything occurs."

"I don't care about the Consul."

"Then you had best care about me."

Two tides of shimmering energy began to build, enough to raise goose bumps on my arms and to set my bracelet dancing against my skin. "Enough!" Mircea waved a hand and the power in the room faded considerably. He plucked the vial from the Frenchman's hand and sniffed it delicately. "Water, Tomas—it is only water and nothing more." He handed it to me and I took it before Tomas could argue.

I trusted Mircea, and besides, neither the bracelet nor my ward reacted to it. "It's okay."

"No!" Tomas reached for the bottle, but Louis-César knocked his hand away.

I looked at Pritkin, who was watching me avidly. "Bottoms up." I swallowed the whole thing. Just as Mircea had said, it was only water, if a bit stale. Pritkin stared at me, as if expecting wisps of steam to start coming out of my ears or something. "Satisfied? Or do you want to hang a few crosses around my neck?"

"What are you?" he whispered.

I went back to my chair, but it was covered in brick dust so I opted for the couch instead. The window had shattered when Mircea tossed the grenade through it, so I had to brush shards of glass onto the floor first. Pritkin had better have some answers, because he was really getting on my nerves. "Tired, stiff and sick to death of you," I told him honestly.

Mircea laughed. "You haven't changed, *dulceață*."

Pritkin stared at me, and some of that terrible anger faded from his face. "I don't understand. You cannot have drunk holy water and shown no reaction if you are demon kind. But you cannot be human and do what I have seen you do."

Mircea settled himself on the sofa after carefully dusting it off with his handkerchief. He picked up one of my bare feet and stroked it idly. I suddenly felt a lot better. "I have learned, Mage Pritkin, never to say never to the universe." He glanced at me, and his expression was wry. "It delights in giving us that which we declare most emphatically can-not be."

Louis-César looked expectantly at me, and I nodded. "Yeah, I know. If people will stop trying to kill me for a minute, I'll tell you about Françoise, at least as much as I can." I quickly explained about my second trip, in as much detail as I could remember without mentioning that a seventeenth-century witch appeared to be wandering around Vegas. I didn't want my cell, if I ended up in one, to have padded walls.

"That is approximately what Tomas said," Louis-César commented when I was done. "But that is not as I remember it."

"Which leaves us with three possibilities." Mircea ticked them off on his fingers. "That both Tomas and Cassandra are lying for no obvious reason, that they hallucinated the same thing at the same time, or that they are telling the truth. I do not smell a lie on either of them." He looked at Louis-César, who nodded. "And must I point out the absurdity of a dual hallucination of that degree of detail, about events neither could have known had they not been there?"

"Which leaves us with the truth." Louis-César gave a sigh that sounded like relief. "And that means . . ."

Mircea finished for him. "That they changed history."

Chapter 11

"That's not possible." I felt that I was on pretty solid ground. "I see the past; I don't change it."

"The Pythia's power is passing," Pritkin murmured, as if he hadn't heard me. "But no. It's impossible." He suddenly looked like a confused little boy. "The Pythia cannot possess anyone. She can't have given you that ability; she doesn't have it."

"Leave that aside," Louis-César said almost breathlessly. He stared at Pritkin, his face eager. "Could the Pythia's power allow Cassandra to travel metaphysically to other places, other times?"

Pritkin looked even more unsure. "I need to consult my Circle," he said, his voice slightly unsteady. "I was not prepared for this. They told me she was only a suspected rogue. The Pythia has an heir. Her powers should not come to this . . . person."

"What powers?" I decided to press my advantage now that I was back to person status, however tentatively. Better to find out what he knew before he decided I was some other weird kind of demon.

"No." Pritkin shook his head adamantly. "I cannot speak for the Circle."

"You've been trying to speak for them all evening," Tomas said, grabbing the mage's shoulder hard enough that he would have stumbled if Mircea's power hadn't still held him. "But now that you can help us by doing so, you refuse?" Tomas' wrist had healed except for an ugly red scar; but his face was no better. His temper didn't seem to have improved, either.

"I . . . these are dangerous matters. I cannot speak of them without authorization."

"You said they know what you know," Tomas growled. "Contact them; get permission."

Pritkin looked about wildly, as if searching for help. He didn't find any. "I will try, but I know they will want to meet to discuss this. And they will want her brought before them. It will not be decided quickly."

"How long?" Louis-César had joined Tomas, and together they did intimidating really well. Hell, they did okay separately.

Pritkin made the mistake of trying to cover his nervousness with rudeness. He was far too offhand to deal with a senator. "I don't know. Perhaps days."

Louis-César's blue eyes abruptly flashed to a shimmering gray, like mercury, and his pupils almost completely disappeared. I held my breath, and I wasn't alone. The only sound in the room was Pritkin's harsh breathing, and it echoed loudly like someone had slipped a microphone on him. Mircea abruptly released him and he would have slumped to the floor if Louis-César hadn't grabbed his shirt and slammed him back into the wall.

Seeing Louis-César in action at the casino hadn't convinced me that here was a predator's predator. He fought well, but I'd seen a lot of good fighters through the years, and I wasn't sold on the idea that a rapier, however long and sharp, was a substitute for a decent firearm. I'd spent too much time at Tony's, better known as Guns R Us, for that. I understood why he scared the crap out of me—he was my portal to the land of crazed ghosts and filthy dungeons—but other people didn't have that problem, so I hadn't understood why they seemed so afraid of him. Most of the time, he looked almost sweet, with his big blue eyes and his dimples. But I finally got the message. He was still handsome, but it was the splendor of a tornado right before it rips through a city. In that second, I believed that he could have made that crazy plan at Dante's work, that he really could have held off twenty vamps while Tomas got me to safety. "We don't have days," he hissed, and the blood drained the rest of the way from Pritkin's face.

Mircea spoke, and his voice was like a calm stream of water flowing about the room, quieting tempers and cooling cheeks. I felt my heartbeat slow down and I was finally able to get a deep breath. "Perhaps Mage Pritkin would like to contact his Circle elsewhere? I think he has told us what we needed to know, by implication, if nothing else." He smiled at Pritkin. "You might think to ask them why they sent you, their best-known demon hunter, after Cassie. You have something of a reputation for being—how shall I put it?— extremely single-minded? If I were the suspicious type, I might almost believe that they wanted you to mistake what she was, and remove a possible rival from contention." Pritkin stared at him, and his face slowly flushed an angry brick red. I hoped his heart wasn't getting as much of a workout as his complexion. I had the feeling that if he didn't give himself a heart attack, someone in the Circle was about to have some explaining to do.

"He isn't leaving!" Louis-César and I spoke at the same time. He deferred to me with a graceful gesture, and I watched him nervously as I scrambled up to face Pritkin. The vamp's eyes were still silver, and I didn't want to find out what happened when he really lost his temper.

"You aren't going anywhere until I get some answers. Who is the Pythia, why do you keep calling me sybil and what powers are you talking about?"

Pritkin complied without even an argument. The fight seemed to have gone out of him for the moment, and his voice was slightly hoarse. "The Pythia was the name of the ancient seer of Delphi, Apollo's greatest temple. For two thousand years, the women selected for the position were considered the oracle of the world, with kings and emperors deciding policy based on their advice. The position lapsed with the decline of Greece, but the term is still used out of respect. It is the title of the world's chief seer, a strong ally of the Circle. She is one of our chief assets, since nonhumans do not have the gift."

"What does this have to do with me?"

"Every time a new Pythia is chosen, a sybil—our name for a true clairvoyant—is selected as her heir. She is carefully trained from childhood to understand the burden and how to bear it. The Pythia is old and her control of the power is failing. It should pass to her heir, but she was kidnapped by Rasputin and the Dark Circle more than six months ago." His eyes looked haunted. "The Pythia's power has passed in an unbroken tradition for thousands of years. But now, I fear for the succession. The heir must be dead. Why else would the power come to you, even in part? A rogue with no training, no understanding of what the position entails?"

Two words of that speech echoed in my brain. I stared at him in horror. "In part?! What the hell does that mean?" My voice had gotten shrill and I paused to calm down a little. "No way. Tell your Circle that I don't want the job."

"It is not a job. It is a calling. And the heir has no choice."

"Like hell I don't! You need to find this sybil person and get her back." I looked at Tomas, and it was almost painful to do so. "And what did you use on his face? It isn't healing."

Rafe answered. "It was dragon's blood, *mia stella.* Don't worry, it will heal with time." Tomas sent me a surprised look, as if he hadn't expected me to care what happened to him, and I looked away. I noticed Mircea regarding me thoughtfully, and I put on as neutral a face as possible. Let them think whatever they liked. I would have been as concerned about anyone who got hurt trying to help me.

Pritkin spoke in a tired voice. "We have searched for her. For the last six months, we have done little else. The Pythia is very old and has had to carry the power far longer than she should have done. Her health is failing, and her control along with it. We understand the necessity for speed better than you, but our search has been in vain."

I didn't see the problem here. "Then appoint someone else heir."

"I told you; it is not an appointed position. The power goes where it will, to whoever is most worthy, the ancient texts say. There should have been no contest. You are young and untrained, whereas our sybil has studied for years for the position. She was selected late, but she was trained well. We did not think you would be a rival . . ."

He stopped, too late, and I pounced. "You knew about me? How?"

The arrogance began to bleed back into his face. "Your entire line is tainted. Your mother was the same; you even look like her."

"Wait a minute. You knew my mother? How?" He looked about thirty-five, maybe younger. So he wasn't aging at normal speed, either, unless the Circle admitted its members at fifteen.

"She was the heir," Pritkin told me, his lips thin with rage. "She had to be pure, untouched, as she knew very well. But she had an affair with your father, a vampire's servant! And worse, she hid it from the Circle until she became pregnant with you and ran away with him. Who knows what would have happened to the power, had we let it fill an unclean vessel?"

"Unclean?" Okay, now I was pissed. "She was my mother!"

"She was unfit to be the heir! I can only be grateful we discovered her in time."

"So, if someone's not a virgin, they can't be heir?"

"Exactly." He smiled nastily at me. "Yet another reason you are disqualified."

I didn't bother to correct him. I was willing to bet that my sexual experience gave their pure-as-the-driven-snow sybil a run for her money, although not for the same reasons. Eugenie had guarded me like a hawk, and when I wasn't with her, I was running for my life. I'd never trusted anyone enough to get that close. It also helped that most of the vamps at Tony's had rivaled Alphonse in the looks department, and that they'd been warned off me anyway. The most temptation I'd experienced had been with Tomas, the Senate's spy who had been feeding off me without permission, and Mircea, who was probably plotting some nefarious scheme. I have no taste in men.

"Let me get this straight. First you decide I'm a demon because of a power I didn't ask for and don't even understand. Then, when that falls through, you label me a fallen sybil and a ho. Am I missing something, or do you just not like me?"

Mircea laughed, and even Louis-César's lips twitched. Tomas either didn't get the joke or wasn't in a laughing mood. Pritkin, of course, was annoyed. "Everything you say only confirms my initial impression. You would be a disaster as Pythia."

"The power doesn't seem to care."

"That is why the Circle exists, to intervene in these cases!" He glared at me, so fiercely that I flinched back before I could stop myself. "Haven't you ever wondered why your mother named you Cassandra? It is our term for a fallen sybil, one who uses her power for ill instead of good. One allied with the Black Circle. One who might be able to summon ghosts and dark witches to fight for her, to possess humans like a demon, and to command a dark weapon so easily. The power will not be allowed to pass to someone like you!"

"And if it does?"

"It won't." It was emphatic enough that I mentally added

another group to the long list of people who wanted me dead.

"The Senate will protect you," Louis-César assured me.

I turned jaded eyes on him. "Sure it will. As long as I do whatever it wants."

Mircea smirked at Louis-César's expression. "She grew up at one of our courts. Did you really think she would not grasp the situation? Now remove the mage," he ordered Raphael. "We will talk business with our Cassandra in private." Pritkin was wrestled from the room, and I for one was glad to see him go. If I never met another war mage in my life, I'd count myself lucky. I waited to see what the Senate's continued help was going to cost me.

"We will not turn you over to the Circle, *mademoiselle*." Louis-César's eyes, which were back to blue, shone with sincerity. I stared at him. Was he really that naive, or was it all part of the honorable-little-boy routine?

"But we may not be able to protect you if their ally wins the duel tonight," Mircea added. "Rasputin would decide things then, and I would not like to see you in his power. The Silver Circle might kill you if you fall into their hands, but I do not wish to speculate about what the Black will do. It is to your advantage that we win, Cassandra."

We looked at each other and had one of those moments of perfect understanding. Ah, enlightened self-interest: the coin of my old world. It felt good to get back on familiar ground. No talk of honor with Mircea; just plain business. "Did you train Tony or what?"

Mircea laughed delightedly. Louis-César shot him an unhappy look before turning his eyes back to me. "*Mademoiselle*, until tonight, I did not truly believe that anyone could do what you can. But now that I know, I have hope again. The Pythia is the final arbiter of disagreements within the magical community, our Supreme Court, if you like. Without a strong Pythia, with the power to enforce her rulings, the problem between the light Fey and the Silver Circle may escalate to war, as ours with the Black already has. The structure of our world is fracturing."

He glanced at the door and Mircea cocked his head slightly. "The spell is active. Even with enhanced hearing, Pritkin cannot eavesdrop. Tell her."

Louis-César looked at me and I got that feeling again of power sliding along my skin. His control was slipping. I thrust my bracelet into my pocket so it wouldn't go nuts. I didn't want to find out what would happen if it attacked him. "We believe that a challenger to the Consul, Lord Rasputin, is using the missing sybil in his bid for power. For months, Senate members have been attacked by their own retainers. In some cases those who have served them for centuries, who were thought completely loyal, have turned on them without warning. The guards in the Senate chamber who attacked you were some of these. Sworn to the Consul's own power, still they turned. Now we may understand why."

Maybe I was missing something. I wasn't exactly at my best. "Okay, why?"

Rafe came forward and knelt at my feet. I petted his messy curls and felt a little better. He couldn't do a damn thing for me, but it was nice having him around. "Don't you see, *mia stella*? The sybil must have traveled in time as you did, and somehow she interfered with the bonding between servants and masters. It has long been thought that the Pythia experiences all times at once, instead of traveling only in one direction as we do. It may be that the missing sybil is gaining power as you have recently done. Only she has used the power for harm."

"Wait a minute." My head hurt. "There are so many problems with that statement, I don't know where to start. How do you interfere with a bond that close? And how about the fact that I'm not the heir? Pritkin made that pretty clear."

"No," Louis-César said, "he made it clear that he did not wish the power to come to you. But obviously he fears that it has, at least in part, or he would not have tried to kill you.

I apologize for that. If we had truly believed him that hostile, we would not have allowed him to stay. But we hoped he would confirm our suspicions."

"Which he did, after a fashion," Mircea commented. "He may not have said as much, but his reactions make it clear that part of the power the Pythia holds has leaked to Cassie, and therefore in all likelihood to the other heir as well."

I shook my head. "But Pritkin said the Pythia can't possess people, so her heir wouldn't be able to either, right? And if that's true, it would really limit what she could do. Energy reserves are used up fast in other times, real fast. Especially if you do anything more than stand around. When I was, um, in Louis-César, I didn't have that problem, but if she can't latch on to a human energy source, she won't last long enough to do very much."

"She might not need long," Mircea said thoughtfully. "The act of creating a new vampire is a delicate process. Any deviation can have very unfortunate results."

I'd heard a few horror stories. Best-case scenario, the new vamp simply never rose. He or she stayed dead after three days, and you knew there had been a problem. Worst-case scenario, they rose without any higher brain functions, a horrible mess called a revenant. They were like animals who lived only to hunt. And because they couldn't reason, they didn't acknowledge the mastery of the one who made them. The only thing to do was to hunt them down before they went crazy on a group of humans.

"What could someone with no more power than a new ghost do in, what, about an hour?" I looked at Tomas. "Is that right? How long were we there?"

"It could not have been much longer, but we were exerting ourselves heavily. We might have been able to prolong our stay otherwise."

"Yeah, but I wouldn't know how to interfere with a vamp making a new servant, and even as a spirit, I wouldn't like to try. How would she do it?"

"The sybil has Rasputin to tell her what to do," Louis-César reminded me. "She would go with detailed instructions, and possibly others to aid her."

"It would not be so difficult," Mircea added. "The individual in question has to be pure, with no bites from another vampire in the last few years. They have to be willing and at peace when they are made, and healthy, or at least not seriously ill. If someone tampered with any of these conditions, centuries later, a powerful master such as Rasputin might be able to override the weakened bond." He thought about it for a minute. "Interference in the first condition seems to me unlikely. That would result in the subjects failing to rise, which would not help Rasputin's cause; the master would have simply selected other servants. It is also likely that a master would detect another's bite and pass them by."

"What would she have to do?"

He shrugged. "There are many possibilities. Poison them with a slow-acting toxin, for instance. They would die before it became obvious that they were seriously weakened, and the poison would not harm them once they rose. Yet it would severely diminish their attachment to their master. Or they could be given a stimulant powerful enough that they remained aware and afraid through the transition, instead of peaceful and euphoric."

"But you can't take stuff with you in spirit form," I pointed out. "Where would she get the poison?"

"She likely retrieved whatever medium she used from where her allies had placed it. The Black Circle has existed almost as long as the Silver—it dates to the middle of the third millennium B.C.E.—and poison has always been a favorite weapon of its members. They could easily have provided what was needed."

"But why would the old Black Circle trust Rasputin?" If he was strong enough to cause this much hell, I doubted the guy had actually been born a Russian peasant in the latter nineteenth century. It was probably a name he'd adopted, possibly after killing the owner or by making it up and using mental tricks to make people believe his story. But it didn't seem likely that he'd been around long enough to have been at Carcassonne when I was there. The Senate would not have so badly underestimated a vamp that old.

"He is allied with their modern counterparts, who could tell him what to say," Mircea explained. "The sybil could have taken a message to the dark mages, asking for aid. The Silver Circle is allied with us, and it is an old alliance. Disrupting it would be a coup for the dark."

My head was swimming. I had a hard time believing that the Black Circle in any era would exert themselves for future gain that none of them would live to see. But it wasn't my problem. "What do you expect me to do? Go back and arm wrestle her or something? Shouldn't you be more worried about the duel?"

"We are." Louis-César was grim. "In less than twelve hours, I am scheduled to duel Rasputin to the death. I will defeat him, if I am still here."

"You planning on going somewhere?"

I meant it as a joke, but he didn't look like he found it funny. "Possibly. Rasputin agreed to the duel believing that he would face Mei Ling. It was thought that, when I was named champion instead, he would withdraw. But he did not, even though he must know that he cannot defeat me."

I decided not to point out how conceited that sounded. "But he can't interfere with you. You're a first-level master; he isn't strong enough to influence you. Even if he weakened your bond with your old master, at your level, it doesn't matter anymore. The tactics he's used on the other vamps won't work."

"No, but he could prevent me from being made at all."

I debated whether to point out the obvious. I decided to risk it. "No offense—I'm sure you deserve your rep—but there's got to be other champions the Consul could choose.

She's been around two thousand years; she has to know people."

"True." Louis-César didn't look insulted, to my relief. "She had other names in mind if I declined."

"Then what's the problem, other than for you personally?"

"The problem, *dulceață*," Mircea said, "is that Rasputin has also never lost a duel. There were other names on the Consul's list, but none that we are confident can manage victory no matter the trickery used against him. Louis-César has fought more duels than the rest of the Consul's choices combined. He must be our champion, for our champion must win."

"And that has to do with me how?" I was getting a very bad feeling.

"We need to ensure that he does not alter time again, *dulceață*. We need you to go back and stop him from interfering with the birth of our champion."

"How would she do that?" Tomas asked before I could. "How can she guard him from a curse?"

Louis-César was looking at Tomas as if he'd lost his mind. "What curse?"

"Is that not how you were made?"

"You know perfectly well it was not!"

Billy Joe streamed in the window, a dove gray cloud. "Did I miss anything?"

"You are completely out of your mind," I informed them. Too bad for their plans, but I wasn't about to die for the Consul, or for anybody else if I could help it. "Do you get the implications here? I took Tomas back with me. Okay, it was by mistake, but if they've been doing this as long as you say, they've almost certainly figured out how to do it, too." Someone had brought the gypsy into this century, and it hadn't been me. "I could be facing Rasputin himself, and I'm not a duelist!"

"I missed something, didn't I?" Billy Joe drifted around, but I ignored him.

"You took Tomas with you when you were inhabiting his body. The sybil can't do that; Pritkin told us as much, *dulceață*."

"Pritkin's an idiot," I reminded Mircea. "We don't know that's why Tomas was able to hitch a ride. Maybe all I have to do is touch someone. Maybe she can do it, too."

Billy drifted in front of my vision, making the whole room look like I was seeing it through a glittery gray scarf. "We need to talk, Cass. You won't believe what I found out at Dante's!" I cocked an eyebrow at him but didn't dare say anything. I didn't want to alert anyone to his presence. I had a feeling I would need him before long.

Tomas was looking at me. "I am the Consul's second choice. I can deal with Rasputin." I brightened. Anything that would get me out of facing the mad monk in that house of horrors sounded promising.

Unfortunately, Mircea did not look convinced. "Forgive me, my friend; I do not doubt your prowess, but I have seen Rasputin fight. You have not. And where my life is concerned, I prefer a sure thing."

Billy drifted a few feet away and put his hands on his hips. "All right. I'll talk; you listen. I got a glimpse into the head of that witch you helped before she ran off with the pixie. The condensed version is that Tony and the Black Circle have been selling witches to the Fey, and guess where they've been getting them? I mean, the white knights would have noticed if a bunch of magic users suddenly went missing, right?" I glared at him. It was like being caught in the dentist's chair with a chatty hygienist. It wasn't as if I could answer.

"I can defeat him." Tomas sounded certain, but Louis-César made an odd sort of sound, almost like a cat sneezing. I suppose it was French.

"You could not defeat me a century ago. You are not much stronger now."

"You were lucky! It would not happen if we dueled again!"

Louis-César looked annoyed. "I do not have to duel you. I own you."

I blinked in confusion. Had I missed something, trying to follow two conversations at once? Masters and servants usually had more of a bond than these two showed. Hell, even though Tony might try to kill Mircea, he wouldn't talk to him like that. "I thought someone named Alejandro was your master?" I asked Tomas.

"He was. One of his servants made me, but Alejandro killed him shortly thereafter and took me for himself. He was carving out an empire within the Spanish lands in the New World and he needed a warrior to help him. We succeeded, and he eventually organized a new Senate, but his tactics never changed. He acts to this day as if every question is a challenge, every plea for leniency a threat. I challenged him as soon as I grew strong enough, and I would have succeeded in ending his reign of terror, if not for outside interference."

I looked at Louis-César in surprise. "You fought him?"

The Frenchman nodded distractedly. "Tomas challenged for leadership of the Latin American Senate. Its Consul asked me to stand as his champion and I agreed. Tomas lost." He said the latter with a slight shrug, as if it almost went without saying. It seemed to me that maybe Louis-César needed to lose once in a while. Carrying around that much of an ego had to be tiring. But then, if he lost he'd probably end up dead, and in this case, so would we. All things considered, maybe a little arrogance wasn't so bad. And at least the lack of a bond was explained. Servants won through force had to be kept that way; it was never as close a relationship as through blood.

Something occurred to me. "You challenged? But you'd have to be a first-level master to do that." I'd known Tomas was powerful, but this was a shock. That Louis-César could hold a first-level master in thrall was a hell of a statement about his strength. I hadn't even known it was possible.

"Tomas is more than five hundred years old, *mademoiselle*. His mother was a high-ranking Incan noblewoman before the European invasion," Louis-César said carelessly. "She was forced by one of Pizarro's men, and Tomas was the result. He grew up in a time when a smallpox epidemic had killed many Incan nobles, leaving a vacuum of power. He organized some of the scattered tribes into a force to resist the Spanish advance, and thereby came to Alejandro's notice. Although a bastard, he—" Tomas gave a growl, and Louis-César glanced at him. "I use the term technically, Tomas. If you recall, I, too, am a bastard."

"That I am not likely to forget."

The shimmering tides of power were back, stronger than before, and this time I got caught in the middle. It felt like two showers of scalding water had been flung at me, and I yelped. "Cut it out!"

"My apologies, *mademoiselle*." Louis-César inclined his head. "You are quite right. I will chastise my servant later."

Tomas glared at him regally. "You will try."

"Tomas!" Mircea and I said it at the same time, in the same exasperated tone.

Louis-César shot him a warning look. "Be careful how you speak to me, Tomas. You do not wish me to make your punishment even more . . . thorough."

"You are a child compared to me! I was already a master vampire before you were even made!"

Louis-César smiled slightly, and his eyes flashed silver. "Not enough of one."

Billy waved a pale hand in front of my face. "Are you listening to me? Breaking news here!"

I mouthed, "Later," but he didn't go away.

"This is big, Cass! The Black Circle has kept the trade quiet by snatching witches who were fated to die young, in an accident or in the Inquisition or whatever. They could grab them at the last minute and sell them to the Fey without worrying that someone would miss them and report it. No one expected to see someone taken by the Inquisition again—they didn't acquit too many, you know? It was a neat trick to get around the treaty."

"But how did they know?" How could anyone know ahead of time when someone was fated to die? Unless . . . Mircea gave me an odd look, and I smiled innocently at him. It was a mistake. Those sharp dark eyes flitted about the room, but even a master vamp can't see Billy.

"That witch you saved was snatched by a group of dark mages that same night," Billy elaborated. "The gypsies have always stayed outside both circles, so I guess they figured they could take her without alerting the white knights." I frowned. That still didn't explain how she ended up in our century, if people from her own time took her, but there was no way for me to ask.

Mircea intervened before things could heat up any further between the vamps. "May I remind you that while you are grandstanding, time ticks away and our chances with it? Your quarrel will wait; our business will not."

"But *la mademoiselle* does not want to do it," Louis-César said, running a hand through his hair. It seemed to be a nervous habit. I noticed that his curls were darker than I remembered from my vision, or whatever it was. I wondered whether that was a trick of the light, or if hundreds of years out of the sun darkens auburn hair. "I was afraid of this. And we cannot force her."

Mircea and I looked at him, then at each other. "Is he for real?" I couldn't help asking.

Mircea sighed. "He has always been that way; it is his only real flaw." He smiled at me, and it was Tony's smile—his *let's cut the crap and get down to business* smile. It was the expression that reminded me of the job Mircea did for the Senate. He was the Consul's chief negotiator, and despite the rumors, he had not received the position because of the respect given his family name by vamps worldwide. They might be pleased to meet him for the prestige of it, something like a normal person getting to sit down with a favorite movie star, but it wouldn't cut him any slack at the bargaining table. No, Mircea had won the seat fair and square, by making the best deals of any representative the Senate had ever had. And that was with people he didn't know nearly as well as he knew me. "What will it take, *dulceață*? Security, money . . . Antonio's head on a silver charger?"

"That last one sounds tempting. But it's not enough."

Mircea and I had skipped over the whole refusal thing and gone straight to haggling. There was no point in mentioning that Mircea would kill me if I said no. He would do it because he'd have no choice—if he didn't, the Consul would give someone else the job—and because he would be quick. Quicker than Jack. I didn't like the errand they had set me, but next to an evening with the Consul's bright-eyed boy, it was a picnic. But just because I had no other options didn't mean I shouldn't get as much for my services as possible. It was, after all, a seller's market. Who else were they going to get?

Mircea was looking as if he wondered whether acting outraged because I'd demanded the life of one of his oldest retainers would work. I rolled my eyes. "Don't bother. Giving me Tony's head is no big deal and you know it. He betrayed you—you have to kill him."

He smiled slightly. "True. But it would also solve a problem for you, would it not?"

"But it won't cost you anything. Isn't your life worth a little something?"

"What else would you like then, my beautiful Cassandra?" He stepped forward, a gleam in his eye, and I put the chair between us.

"Don't try it."

He grinned at me, unrepentant. "Then name your price."

"You want my help? Tell me what happened to my father."

Rafe gave a startled squeak and looked wide-eyed at Mircea, who sighed and shook his head in disgust. I sympathized; Rafe had always had a lousy poker face—I'd started beating him at cards by age eight—and he obviously hadn't improved. He subsided under Mircea's displeasure, but the damage was done. Mircea braved it out anyway, of course; I would have thought less of him otherwise. "Your father, *dulceață*? He died in a car bomb, did he not? Is that not one reason why you are upset with our Antonio?"

"Then what did Jimmy mean? He told me not to kill him, because he knew the truth about what happened."

Mircea shrugged. "Since he was the 'hit man'—is that not the phrase?—on the job, I am sure he does know details, *dulceață*. Why did you not ask him?"

"Because Pritkin blew a hole in him before I could. But you know, don't you?"

Mircea smiled, and once again I saw where Tony got it. "Is that knowledge your price?"

I looked at Rafe, and he looked back. I thought he was about to speak when Mircea's hand descended on his shoulder. "No, no, Raphael. It would not be fair to give our Cassandra information for which she has not yet paid." He smiled, and there was more calculation than affection in it. "Do we have a deal?"

I glanced at Billy, who was floating near the ceiling with an impatient look on his face. He didn't comment, so I assumed his news didn't have any bearing on my choice. I sent him an irritated look and he disappeared, in a snit because I hadn't dropped everything for him. Typical. I'd have preferred to find out more before agreeing to Mircea's terms, but I didn't have a lot of options. It's hard to push the price too high when you're a sure thing and the buyer knows it. I literally had no choice but to help them, so technically Mircea was being generous by offering anything. Of course, he probably wanted me doing my best on the errand, so keeping me in a good mood was worth a concession or two. Or maybe he was fond of me. No, that kind of thinking was dangerous.

"Okay. We have a deal. Tell me."

"In a moment, *dulceaţă*. First, I believe we need to inform the Consul. Tomas, if you would be so good? She may have final instructions." He noticed Tomas' mulish expression. "You have my word that we will wait the attempt on your return. You will be accompanying her, will you not?"

"Yes." Tomas looked at me challengingly, but I didn't object. If Rasputin did show up, it would be nice to have someone along, especially someone who had shown he could handle himself in an emergency. Even if it was only to have company when everything went to hell. Tomas started to say something else but stopped when Mircea stepped to my side and put a hand on my shoulder.

"Now, Tomas!" Louis-César looked impatient. Tomas glared at him but he left, slamming the door behind him.

"And we need the Tears, do we not, to be on the safe side?" Louis-César nodded and left right behind Tomas.

"The Tears? Do I want to know?"

"Nothing to be concerned about, I assure you." Mircea smiled reassuringly. "The Tears of Apollo are an ancient concoction. They have been used to aid in meditative trances for centuries. They are quite safe."

"But why do we need them? I didn't have them before."

"And you quickly ran out of energy before. They will help you, Cassandra. Remember, I have a vested interest in seeing that this goes well. I would not lie to you." I believed that answer more than I would have a heartfelt declaration of concern for my welfare, and nodded. I'd use the damn Tears, whatever they were. Anything to up the odds.

Mircea glanced at Raphael. "Would you be so good as to see if clothing has been arranged for Cassie? She must be tired of wearing such a bulky robe." He gave an odd little smile. "Take your time."

Rafe looked uncertain—I could tell he didn't want to leave Mircea and me alone for some reason—but he went. Mircea locked the door behind him and leaned against it, regarding me with suddenly serious eyes. "And now for the real negotiations, my Cassandra."

Chapter 12

I looked at Mircea warily. "I'm not your Cassandra."

He began unbuttoning the remaining toggles on his shirt. "Give me a moment, *dulceaţă*, and we will see." He peeled off the shirt and tossed it over the end of the couch. He wore nothing underneath.

"What are you doing?" I sat up, my pulse leaping although he hadn't done anything really alarming. But he stood between me and the door, and that enticing face was suddenly pretty intense.

Mircea began removing his highly polished shoes. "I would prefer that we had more time, *dulceaţă*. I have long anticipated renewing our acquaintance, but did not envision quite this scenario. However"—he paused to place his shoes and socks neatly by the sofa—"I am beginning to learn that, with you, it is best to assume the unexpected."

I could have said the same about him. "Cut it out, Mircea. Just tell me what is going on."

He watched me steadily as he slowly removed the belt from the loops of his slacks. "You do not wish to be given over to the Circle, I assume?"

"What does that have to do with you getting undressed? What is this?"

Mircea prowled across the room—there was simply no other word for the way he moved—and knelt at my feet. He looked up at me soulfully. "Think of it as a rescue, *dulceaţă*.

I am your knight come to save you from all those who would do you harm."

I choked back a laugh. "That has got to be the corniest line I ever heard."

Mircea put on an exaggerated look of outrage that brought a reluctant smile to my face. "You wound me! I assure you, once upon a time, as they say, that is exactly what I was."

I thought about it and, technically, he was right. Of course, real knights in shining armor hadn't been quite the same as the legend. Most of them had spent more time harassing the peasants for taxes than rescuing ladies fair. "Okay. And what are you now?"

He didn't answer, but I noticed that his eyes had turned a glowing cinnamon amber. The only time I'd seen that before, he had been threatening Pritkin's life, but he didn't seem to be angry now. He reached behind his head to slide the platinum clasp out of his long, dark hair. "The Circle demands your return, *dulceaţă*, and by our treaty with them, we have no right to refuse. If you were a normal human, a claim by any master would be enough to hold you, but not for a powerful seer. The Pythia's court has control over all such individuals." His hair spread over his shoulders and back like a dark cape. The contrast between his midnight hair and the pale perfection of his skin was mesmerizing.

He saw me admiring it, and his voice dropped to just above a whisper. "You liked my hair once, *dulceaţă*, don't you remember? You enjoyed braiding it as a child. I went around Antonio's court with as many styles and ornaments as a doll." He lifted my hands and placed them on his shoulders, under the heavy weight of that hair. It fell like a skein of silk over my hands, and I wasn't sure which was more distracting, the feel of it or the hard muscles of his shoulders. "I did not mind you playing with me, *dulceaţă*." He moved his head to press a kiss to the back of my hand. "I do not mind it now."

I opened my shields slightly to see whether he was imitating Tomas and trying to influence me, but there was no sign that power was being exerted. The exhilarating rush I'd felt earlier was simply not there. But then, he didn't really need it. He rubbed his cheek languidly against my hand and I knew he could probably hear the pounding of my heart in my wrist. I swallowed. "What's your point, Mircea?"

His hands had moved while I was distracted, and it was a shock to feel them suddenly slide into my robe and encircle my waist. I hadn't felt him remove the belt, but it was gone. The robe didn't gape far, but it was enough to bare a line of flesh from my neck to my navel. I moved to close it, but Mircea lifted my hand away and pressed the palm to his lips. I felt a smooth hint of tongue as he swept it slowly over my skin, as if savoring the taste. A bolt of desire ran from his kiss down all my nerve endings, causing me to gasp.

"Mircea . . ."

"Do you know how you taste, my Cassandra?" he asked me softly. "I have never known anything like it. You go to my head like aged brandy." He breathed deeply of the skin above my pulse. "You cannot imagine how intoxicating I find your scent." His thumb moved slightly on my waist, up and down the center of my rib cage. It wasn't an overly sexual touch, but I caught my breath. "Or how very good you feel."

"Mircea, please."

"Anything you want," the great negotiator whispered, leaning in so that he spoke just above my mouth, his breath warm on my lips. His mouth ghosted over mine, gentle, barely there, and I shivered. He had said we were going to negotiate, but he wasn't even trying to make a deal, which alone was scary. "Anything in my power to give, it is yours." His hand moved back to the front of my robe, one finger tracing the line of exposed skin from neck to navel. Goose bumps sprung up along that path, and my breath caught.

I tried to get angry, to find any emotion that could hold back the spine-tingling flash of pleasure. "Damn it, Mircea! You know I hate games!"

"No games," he promised, pushing himself between my legs, parting them with his body. The robe gaped halfway up my thighs, but I couldn't close it with him kneeling there. I tried to shove him away, wanting some distance between us so I could think, but it was like pushing at a granite statue. "Do you want me to beg you?" he whispered, looking up at me with those glowing eyes.

"No, I . . ." I looked around for Billy, but he was off sulking. Damn it!

"I will beg," he murmured, before I could get a sentence together. He was close enough that I could tell that he smelled as good as he looked, not like expensive cologne as I'd expected, but clean and fresh, like the air after rain. "And plead"—his hands slid into the robe to caress my calves— "willingly"—they moved up to my knees, stroking the sensitive skin behind them—"gladly"—they massaged a path up my thighs—"eagerly"—his hands stopped on my hips, thumbs kneading the flesh gently. "If it pleases you."

He buried his face in my stomach, and my hands moved on their own to comb through that dusky hair. I spread it out on his shoulders, while he kissed his way up my body. I fought to clear my head, but then his lips claimed mine in a searing kiss that burned all the way down to my fingertips. Then he dropped his head and began to kiss back down the way he'd come, with slow, almost worshipful motions. The feel of cool air on my breasts as he pushed the robe completely open jogged me out of the haze slightly, but it was difficult to put thoughts together while pleasure coursed through me.

"You are beautiful, *dulceață*," he murmured, hands ghosting over me reverently. "So soft, so perfect." His touch felt so warm I expected it to leave imprints behind. His breath on the tender skin of my nipple was electrifying; his tongue, when it followed a moment later, was almost overwhelming, and when he began to suck, pulling deeply, pleasure burst inside me so large that it was almost pain.

"Mircea, please . . . tell me what is going on!"

In response, he suddenly swept me up into his arms and carried me to the bedroom. He waved a hand and the curtains over the windows snapped shut. He laid me gently on the bed and began unbuttoning his trousers. "The Silver Circle wants you very badly, Cassie. Antonio told them that you died in the car with your parents, and they only learned differently when your ward flared for the first time a few years ago. It was the Circle's own ward that your mother had transferred from herself to you, and it is unmistakable. They have been hunting you ever since. As long as you remain only a rogue sybil, they have rights over you, as they do all human magic users. There is no way to dispute their claim without risking a war. Well"—he stepped out of the trousers—"almost none."

Mircea wearing only black silk boxers was enough to confuse my brain without learning that the most powerful magical society on earth, who happened to hate me, had the right to decide my future. "I don't understand."

Mircea crawled onto the bed and I scooted back until I hit the headboard. He smiled and tugged playfully at the edge of the robe, which I'd wrapped about me protectively. "You are lovely in anything, *dulceață*, but I would prefer to dispense with this garment. Had I known this scenario would occur, I would have arranged something more appropriate." He slid his hands slowly up my calves, kneading as he went higher. "I will make sure to correct that oversight at the first opportunity."

"Mircea! I want an answer!" I drew away from him and glared. After a pause, he sat back on his heels, looking rueful.

"Why did I know it would not be so easy with you?" He sighed. "*Dulceață*, it has to be one of us. You seemed to respond to me best, and I would be honored to be your choice, but if you would prefer one of the others . . . I would not like it, but under the circumstances, I would agree."

"What are you talking about?" I was getting angry that he kept ignoring me.

"Tomas was not sent merely to guard you, Cassie. Keeping you safe was his primary function, but he was also told to ensure that the Circle's claim could be successfully disputed." Mircea quirked an eyebrow. "I am beginning to understand why he failed."

"I . . . What are you doing?" Mircea had run a hand through his waterfall of hair, and now he was sliding those beautifully shaped hands down his chest to glide over his nipples. His torso was hairless and perfectly sculpted, with toned muscles and a long waist. He followed the lines of his flat stomach to the low-slung border of his only remaining garment. His fingers lingered there, sliding along that insubstantial barrier teasingly, drawing my eyes to the line of dark hair that started below his navel and disappeared beneath the black silk. It was startling against the pale perfection of his skin and, except for the faint pink of his nipples, gave the only color to his upper body.

"Doing, *dulceață*?" he asked innocently. "I am trying my best to seduce you."

He suddenly reached over and took my hands in his, caressing the backs with his thumbs. "I will make you an offer. I will answer one of your questions for each pleasure you allow yourself; are we agreed?"

"What?" I stared at him. "I can't believe you said that!"

Mircea grinned, and suddenly, the old, teasing version was back. "You give me little choice, Cassie. You will look, and with such longing, but you will not touch. And I want your touch; I want it very much." He moved my hands to his stomach, right below the silk border. When I just sat there, dry mouthed and startled, he sighed. "But my charms do not seem sufficient, so I offer a trade. And as a token of my good faith, I will go first. The Circle can command you as a rogue sybil, but not if you become Pythia. You are beyond their reach then, Cassie; indeed, you will outrank them, so to speak. And Pritkin was not entirely honest. The chosen sybil, the heir to the Pythia's power, must remain chaste during her youth, I suspect to avoid someone gaining undue influence over her. But she cannot progress to Pythia in that state. The ancient sources all agree: at Delphi, a mature, experienced woman was selected after the early years, because it was found that the power shied away from young girls." He grinned at me again and moved my hands lower, so that I could feel the outline of him, growing firm under my touch. "No one is sure why, but the power will not pass in full to a virgin, Cassie."

I stared at him. "You have got to be kidding." Of course, it did explain why everyone except Rafe was dressed like he was on his way to a *Playgirl* photo shoot.

Mircea didn't answer, just ran those talented hands behind my knees, caressing the skin lightly. Somehow he'd already figured out what that did to me. "We tried to make it easy for you. We sent Tomas, who does not usually have difficulties—how should I put it—persuading women to enjoy his charms? But you rejected him, despite everything he did to obtain your affection." Mircea laughed shortly. "I think you have pricked his pride, *dulceață*. I am not sure that he has ever been turned down before."

I swallowed. "He could have forced me."

Mircea's face lost its amusement. "Yes," he agreed lightly, "and I would have taken his heart, as I made very plain before he left." The hands on my knees slid up to my thighs, and Mircea gripped me strongly. "You are mine, Cassie. I would have gone to you myself if I had known how strong the attraction between us would be. But I must admit that, until today, I did not truly regard you as a young woman. Not to mention that I assumed you would feel uncomfortable with your 'Uncle Mircea' suddenly acquiring such an interest."

"I never called you that." I hadn't thought of him that way, either. Eleven is young, but not too young for a crush, and I'd had it bad. It seemed things hadn't changed, at least not for me. I didn't believe for a second that Mircea felt anything. It was his turn to pretend to want me, so I could continue to be used. It hurt to know for certain that Tomas' attempts at seduction were on the Consul's orders and that Mircea's probably were, but it wasn't a surprise. Where my life was concerned, I'd learned long ago that everyone wanted to use me for something.

"What else did Pritkin lie about?"

Mircea smiled wickedly. "Is that a question, *dulceaţă*?" I swallowed nervously as his hands began to massage my lower thighs. He noted my confused look with a small sigh. "I will not hurt you, Cassie. I swear you will feel nothing but pleasure from my touch."

"You'll answer the question—in full?"

"Do I not always keep my promises?" I nodded; that much was true. At least so far. He smiled broadly and sat back on his heels. "Very well, how did Pritkin lie?" He thought for a moment. "For the most part, *dulceaţă*, he did not lie; he simply evaded. He was being honest when he said that if the sybil has gone dark or been killed, the power will pass to someone else. But he was less so when he denied—most unconvincingly—that it will choose you once you become . . . available."

"Why does the Circle hate the thought of me gaining the power?"

Mircea's rich laugh spread through the room. "They hate you because they fear you. No one can command the Pythia. The Circle is bound to protect her, even to obey her in some things, and you are the first one to potentially hold the power in centuries whom they have not indoctrinated since birth. You would not be their puppet as so many Pythias have been. You would use the power as you saw fit, and that might mean in opposition to their wishes at times." He paused for a second to slide out of his boxers, tossing them aside unself-consciously. I watched them fall to the rug with my heart in my throat and refused to look at him.

"I was told what the dark mage said to you, Cassie. He told you the truth, but, again, only in part. The mythical Cassandra was the only seer who steadfastly refused to be under the control of anyone. She ran from even Apollo himself to avoid having another dictate how her gift should be used. The Circle is afraid that you will be true to your name."

"Are you saying I have a whole army of Pritkins after me?" I was horrified. I'd been surrounded by four master vampires, one of them the reigning dueling champion, and he'd still almost killed me.

"Not necessarily. If you are malleable enough to be used, they will try to do so. Pritkin was truthful when he said that the current Pythia is dying and will not be able to control the gift much longer. They have lost their sybil and urgently need to find her or locate another. But they are caught on the horns of a dilemma: they do not wish the power to pass to you, but who is to say where it would go if they eliminated you? Possibly to one of their other adepts, but equally possibly to another rogue whose existence they missed. If they recover their lost sybil or if you are difficult, they may take the chance and kill you; if not, they will undoubtedly attempt to rule you. Either way, *dulceață*, you are far better off with us."

I thought that was debatable, but if the rest of the Circle was like Pritkin, I definitely didn't want to meet them. "What are you saying? We make love and, bam, I'm the Pythia? Is that what all this has been about?"

Mircea laughed, a joyous, faintly wicked sound. "That is another question, and you have yet to pay for the last one."

I raised my eyes to his face and resolutely kept them there. "What do you want?"

He smiled, and this time it was gentle. "Many things, Cassandra, but I will settle for simply having you look at me for now."

"I am looking at you." I received silence as his only answer. I sighed. Normally I wasn't particularly shy. Raphael often had nude male models around and I'd seen nakedness used as part of punishment too many times to count. But this wasn't some stranger I didn't know; it was Mircea, who'd suddenly gone from being an untouchable fantasy to being an all-too-available reality. I wasn't too shy to look at him, as he probably thought. I was trying hard not to jump him, at least until I got some answers, and gazing at that gorgeous body when I couldn't touch it was damn close to torture.

I licked my lips and accepted the inevitable. My eyes traveled over the fine bones of his face and perfect curve of his lips, down to the hard planes of his shoulders and chest, to his stomach and the faint line of hair that I'd found so intriguing earlier. His body was superb, like a marble statue come to life, one of those slender masterpieces by an ancient Greek genius. His sex was perfectly proportioned to the rest of him, uncircumcised and pale, but flushed with a dark pink tinge. He was already half erect, but, when my gaze lingered, he lengthened, gaining weight and width almost magically. His legs were the best I'd ever seen on a man, and his feet were as finely shaped as his elegant hands. He was exquisite.

I heard him take a ragged breath. "How can you make me feel so with only a look? Touch me, *dulceață*, or allow me to touch you or I will go mad."

Okay, maybe I'd been wrong. Mircea might be doing this at the Consul's bidding, but he wasn't exactly opposed to the idea. It made me feel a little better. "Answer the question," I said, and my voice was steady, although it came out barely louder than a whisper.

He groaned and rolled onto his stomach, giving me a

view of tight buttocks and taut shoulders. "You will have to repeat the question. My concentration is suffering."

"If we do this, will I be Pythia?"

"That I do not know, nor does anyone. The power will pass soon, almost certainly either to you or to the lost sybil. All we are attempting is to keep you in the running, so to speak. If the Pythia dies and you are still a virgin, it may result in the power passing to your rival."

"That doesn't sound so bad to me. If what I've been experiencing is only part of her power, I don't think I want the rest."

"Not even to help your father?"

I blinked. I couldn't believe I'd forgotten about that. It said something about the confused state of my head. "You promised to tell me about him, and that's not part of this deal!"

Mircea looked at me from under a curtain of dark silk. "You have no pity, *dulceață*. Nor have you paid me for your last question."

"Tell me about my father and maybe I will."

Mircea rolled off the bed and began to pace, which didn't help my pulse rate any. He stalked, like some big jungle cat, rather than merely walked. "Very well." He turned to me suddenly, his eyes flashing gold. "If you insist, then we will discuss this. I did not want to tell you, but you have forced my hand. Roger is dead, as you were told. Dead, but not gone."

"You mean he's a ghost?" I shook my head. "Not possible. I'd have known. He'd have come to me—I was right there in Tony's house for years. It's not like I'd have been hard to find."

Mircea stopped near the bed, a little too close for comfort, and continued as if I hadn't interrupted. "Roger was an employee of Antonio's, one of his favorite humans, in fact. Which made his betrayal all the more bitter. That was how Antonio viewed his refusal to give you up when ordered to do so. He could not leave Roger alive and save face, but he did not want his death to deprive him of your father's gift. You received your connection to the spirit world from him—he, too, was reportedly able to make ghosts his servants."

"That isn't what I do."

He brushed it aside. "Call it what you will. Suffice it to say that Antonio found it useful from time to time. You were clever to hide it from him, *dulceaţă*. I asked him if you had that gift as well as the Sight, and he said no."

"Eugenie told me not to tell." Only now did I understand why. Of course, ghosts could be useful, especially in dealing with other families. Since vamps can't detect them, they'd make perfect spies. Hell, he could even have sent them to let him know what the Senate was doing. A pretty big advantage, that. "What happened?"

"Your parents fled when they realized you had inherited their gifts, knowing that Tony would take you. He sent his best operatives to track them down and paid some dark mages to devise a trap for your father while he waited. It was designed to capture his spirit as it left his body after death, and it worked perfectly. When I heard what had been done to Roger, I commanded Antonio to release him, but he demurred. He preferred to keep him confined as a perpetual punishment and a warning to others, even though he had discovered that Roger could not command ghosts now that he was one."

"But he released him on your order, right?" I didn't like where this was going.

"He swore that it was impossible, and invited me to have a mage of my choosing examine the trap. I did so." He looked at me with pity. "I hired the best, Cassie, for I liked your father. But the mage, a member of the Circle itself who owed me a favor, told me that he had never seen one like it, and that all his power was not sufficient to break it. As a result, your father's ghost resides with Antonio still."

My lips felt numb. I wanted to disbelieve him, but it was exactly the sort of thing Tony would do. "There must be a way to break the spell."

"The Silver Circle should have enough power to manage it. My associate intimated as much at the time. Even if it was the Black Circle itself that wrought the trap, the Silver is stronger. But they would not willingly take on such a task. They despise your father, as they do any human working for us, and blame him for seducing your mother away from them. They would not help even were the Consul herself to petition, but if the new Pythia were to ask . . ."

"They couldn't refuse?"

Mircea sat down on the bed beside me. I resolutely kept my eyes on his. "They could, certainly, but I doubt they would. If the power goes to you, Cassandra, they will swallow their pride and try to woo you. If they thought they could buy your favor with such a task, they would likely fall over themselves to do it."

Suddenly, I was on my back and Mircea was on his hands and knees, looming over me. "And now, *dulceață*, I believe there is a little something you owe me."

I had a lot of other questions, but they temporarily fled, along with my ability to form coherent sentences. Mircea sat me up and stripped off the robe, which he threw against the wall as if it offended him. His hands returned to slide slowly down my arms, from shoulders to wrists. He lay me back carefully and let his eyes roam over me as I had done him. He surprised me by taking his time, and the weight of his gaze was enough to make my nipples contract and my whole body tense.

His hands soon followed the path his eyes had blazed. He started at my ankles, then ran them slowly up my body, stroking and teasing the flesh as he went. I was writhing by the time he was up to my knees, moaning when he paused to massage my lower stomach, and completely breathless when he captured my breasts again. He continued, however, running his fingers over my neck and face, lingering slightly on my lips, then moving up through my hair. I felt like my body was on fire by the time he stopped, and judging by the flush that stained his usual mother-of-pearl complexion, he wasn't completely unmoved, either. He swallowed several times before finding his voice. "If you have a question, Cassie, I suggest you ask it quickly."

I wasn't sure I could think of one, but I really needed something to distract him, or I was going to be an eligible candidate for the Pythia's job very soon. "How did you find me?" He parted my legs and crawled between them. I felt terribly exposed and not at all ready for this. "Mircea!"

"I swear I will answer your question, Cassie," his said, his eyes amber fire, "afterwards."

"No! That wasn't the deal."

He gave a strangled groan and collapsed onto my legs, his hair falling forward to cover my groin. He stayed that way for about a minute, his breathing harsh and unsteady, before raising his head. His face was pink and his eyes glittered darkly, but some of the fever had subsided. His voice was lower than usual, and his accent was more pronounced when he began speaking, fast and with no preamble.

"The Consul suspected what Rasputin was doing before any of us, even Marlowe. The attacks began shortly after the Circle requested MAGIC's help in finding their lost sybil, and the Consul made one of her famous, intuitive leaps. But there seemed little we could do except to aid in the search and hope they would recover her quickly. True sybils are rare, and we thought there was no other of sufficient strength to duplicate Rasputin's actions. But we made certain that those of proven ability were closely watched, in case she should die and the power pass on. I have business interests in Atlanta, Cassie. I have known where you were for some time, and of course, I put your name on the list of those to be watched."

His eyes settled between my legs and I could feel myself

blushing. I tried to wiggle out from under his touch, but it only caused him to bend and kiss the inside of my thigh over the pulse point. His lips worked gently and I felt no fangs, but that light brush of his mouth caused the trickle of liquid heat that had been building in me to suddenly become a flood. "Mircea, please . . ." I wasn't even sure what I was asking for, but he only smiled grimly.

"No, I will answer the question in full." He inhaled deeply. "And then I will pleasure you in full." I writhed under his hands, and he closed his eyes. "Cassie, please don't move. The vibrations are . . . disturbing, and my concentration is ragged as it is."

"I never agreed to sex if you answered the question! This isn't fair!"

Mircea paused and cocked an eyebrow. "Forgive me, *dulceață*, but precisely what is it you think we are doing now?"

"You know what I mean." I took a deep breath and tried to ignore the pleading my body was doing. "No intercourse."

Mircea ran his tongue along the crease of my knee and up my leg, stopping just short of where I suddenly, desperately wanted him to be. He raised his head slightly to meet my eyes, but his breath still glided over my most intimate places. My body trembled, and his fingers dug more firmly into my thighs. "You want me as badly as I want you, *dulceață*. Why deny us both?"

"You know why. It's not just about pleasure—this is setting myself up for something I'm not sure I can do." As soon as I said it, I realized I'd told the truth. The only reason I wasn't attacking Mircea was the strings that went with him. Having sex meant throwing in the towel on my independence, possibly forever. Either way I looked at it, I lost. The Senate might be a kinder, gentler alternative to the Circle, and Mircea beat the hell out of Pritkin as a jailer, but it would be a jail all the same. But if I wasn't Pythia, there would be a lot less interest in where I was and what I was doing.

"And if you do not accept your calling, how do you plan to persuade the Circle to help with your father?"

I sighed. There, as Shakespeare would have said, was the rub. I didn't want to be Pythia. The office had helped to get my mother killed and promised me only life in a gilded cage—assuming the Circle didn't kill me. Besides, Pritkin was right: I hadn't been trained. I didn't know if I could handle Seeing any more than I already did. I hadn't liked the new powers I'd obtained, and I doubted I'd enjoy the others any better, whatever they were. But, if I refused the position, I wasn't sure I could do anything to help my father. I knew Tony well enough to know how vindictive he could be. He would view my father's imprisonment as serving the double purpose of torturing both him and me, and he'd never voluntarily give him up.

"I'm not saying no," I told Mircea truthfully. "I just need some time. No intercourse yet; pick something else."

He placed a kiss on my lower stomach. "That will not be difficult, Cassie. You are a feast for the senses."

"Just answer the question."

He looked surprised, then laughed. "Do you know, I had actually entertained the notion that I would be in charge of these proceedings? I will know better next time." He grinned at me, rubbing slow, languid circles on my stomach, causing that delicious heat to build even more. I writhed under that light stroke, and it obviously pleased him. "My beautiful, fiery *dulceață*."

"I am not yours."

Mircea smirked. "On the contrary, you have always been mine. I assure you I did not stay at Antonio's court for almost a year for the pleasure of his company."

At my startled look, he laughed again, a low, touchable chuckle that tightened things low down. "I had heard of your gifts and arranged to meet you. I knew that a clairvoyant of your reputed strength would be a useful addition to my staff, but wanted to be sure what I was gaining before negotiating with Antonio. Once I met you, I suspected that I might be looking at the next Pythia, but I could not know for certain until you grew up."

He looked off into the distance and sighed. "I made a mistake in not immediately adding you to my household, but I feared that it was too prominent, and that I would not be able to keep you from coming to the Circle's attention. I left you with Antonio and ordered him to continue to hide your identity. I planned to retrieve you when you matured, but by then you had rather complicated things, had you not?"

"Wait a minute. You knew about my parents' murder?"

"I only learned after the fact, and at the time it seemed a trifling affair." He saw my frown and sighed. "Would you prefer me to lie to you? I did not know about you then, Cassie, and I could not chastise Antonio for dealing with his servant as he wished. Although I thought it a waste, it was his right. I was told that a woman had been with him in the car, but she had taken your father's name and I did not connect her with the runaway heir. Forgive me, but although your father was the most trusted of Antonio's humans, frankly that is not saying much. There was no reason to connect his wife with the Pythia's court."

"What about me? When did you learn that they had a child?" If Mircea had left a helpless baby in Tony's fat hands, my opinion of him would go down considerably.

"Not until years later," he said seriously, as if realizing how important the question was to me. "I spoke with Raphael a few months before my visit. Antonio had sent him on an errand to my court, and he took the opportunity to inform me of the truth. Of course, I immediately arranged to meet you."

I believed him, and not only because I wanted it to be true. Mircea would have protected my parents had they run to him for help. He wouldn't have permitted a valuable asset like my mother to be killed if he'd known about her. If for no other reason, it would have been bad business to annoy the Pythia and the mages when he could easily put them in his debt by returning her. "How did Tony find me?"

Mircea grinned. "How indeed, Cassie. Here I was, worried about your safety, when I should have been concerned about what dastardly plans you had for my defenseless servant. What you did to Antonio was rather well reported, even in the human press. My people immediately began searching for you, and I had a watch put on his retainers in case he stumbled over you and was foolish enough not to mention it. In that case, they were to distract him and contact me, but luck intervened. A member of a family allied with him was stranded in Atlanta overnight because of an airline delay, and saw you at a nightclub. You were telling fortunes and it jogged his memory of the young girl he had seen at court. He informed his master, who sold the information to Antonio. Fortunately I had already found you, with help from the Senate's intelligence network."

"Marlowe."

"Indeed." Mircea laughed. "The man is a marvel, although you were devilish difficult to trace, even for him. He wants to meet you, by the way. He said that you must have almost as devious a mind as he does—a rare compliment, *dulceață*. We located you less than a year ago, but it seemed safer to leave you where you were and guard you rather than to risk the Circle discovering that we had you, and invoking the treaty as they are attempting to do now." He looked sober again. "The Consul is stalling, but it will not last. We cannot fight both the Black and the White Circles at once, Cassie. You understand?"

"Yes." I thought back to the number of heart attacks I'd almost had through the years, thinking I'd sensed a vamp here or there, and it had been Mircea's people all the time. "You could have saved me a lot of trouble if you'd told me what was going on." Mircea just looked at me. He didn't bother to say what we both knew: no master vamp, much less a Senate member, would discuss anything with a mere servant. Her life would be planned out for her, and she'd be informed of it when the time was right. "Is that how you knew Tony had found me? Did your people tell you?"

Mircea gave a rueful smile. "No, you were fortunate there. Antonio ordered a gunman to put two bullets in your brain by midnight, but Raphael overheard it and called me. I gave him my protection and told him to come here. I had had concerns about Antonio for some time, but doing away with a third-level master, even if he is one's servant, requires finesse. But if he actually went against my direct orders and made an attempt on your life, I could legally kill him for disobedience. I relayed the information about you to the Senate, who had assigned Tomas to you since the sybil's disappearance. In case they had trouble reaching him, I also contacted some associates of mine in Atlanta, but they had difficulty locating you. By the time they arrived at your office, you had gone."

"You could have picked up a freaking phone, Mircea!"

"I did try to call you, *dulceață*, at your home and at your place of employment. But you did not answer. In any case, you gave us quite a scare. My associates became involved in an altercation with four vampires Rasputin had sent after you. By the time they had disposed of them, you and Tomas had already encountered the assassins Antonio dispatched. Fortunately, you dealt with them quite handily on your own."

I was back to being confused. "You mean nine vamps were after me that night?!" I couldn't believe I'd survived. Master vampires had been taken out with less. "But, if Tony and Rasputin are allies, why send two hit squads?"

Mircea smiled. "Now you are merely stalling. The short version is that Antonio sent five ninth- or tenth-level vampires to kill you as soon as he discovered where you were. When Rasputin heard what he had done, he dispatched four masters to back them up. He is wiser, I think, than Antonio. He knew that the Senate would have put guardians on you and wanted to make sure that you did not survive. You are the only power that can oppose his actions successfully, *dulceață*. He knows this."

My head was spinning. "So Tony's hit squad went to the club, and yours and Rasputin's went to the office after I left? Then who left the message on my computer?"

"What message?"

I shook my head. This was getting way too complex for me. "Never mind. What you're basically saying is that everyone is after me?"

Mircea did not answer because that dark head had gone back to work, licking a path up my inner thigh. His tongue was hot against my skin and his lips were velvet. "I do not know about everyone, *dulceață*, but I certainly am. And now, enough talk." He smiled at me wickedly. "It is time you paid in full."

Chapter 13

I tried to think of another question quickly, but it was difficult, especially when his hands clasped my buttocks and
he lifted me upward. His tongue finally reached its goal and
I gasped. He ran it over me slowly, exploring my shape,
memorizing my taste, before suddenly plunging inside as far
as it would go. I screamed and arched against him, helpless
to do anything else, and he drank me in. I felt the beginnings
of something building in me, something huge, but before it
completely tore my senses away, Mircea lifted himself
away.

I wanted to scream in frustration, but his lips sealed over
mine and I forgot. I ran my hands along that silken skin,
tracing down his spine, past his ribs to the cleft between
those beautiful buttocks. He shuddered over me, and the
feeling of him firm and hot against my stomach was almost
overpowering. I wanted him inside me more than I had ever
wanted anything, with an almost unbearable need. But when
I felt a hard, hot weight settle between my legs, I pushed at
his chest. "No, Mircea—you promised."

He laughed low in his throat, and kissed my neck. "I will
be good, *dulceață*." Before I could say that that was what
was worrying me, he dragged that heavy weight along the
full length of my sex, not penetrating, but coming teasingly
close. I was wet and aching for him, and I didn't think it was
funny. I decided that a little repayment was in order.

I slipped a hand between our bodies and grabbed him. He was thick enough that my grip could not close, but it definitely got his attention. I squeezed, marveling at how incredibly soft his skin was, and his eyes rolled back in his head. It felt odd to hold him, so hot and so velvety to the touch, and it made me feel powerful. I remembered what the woman in my vision had done to Louis-César's body and tried my best to imitate it. A few strokes and the mighty Mircea gave a small, half-strangled scream and trembled against me. I thought for a second that I had hurt him, but if anything he only grew bigger in my hand. I grinned into his startled face and, remembering what it had done to the Frenchman's body, ran a finger across the little slit on the head. He screamed for real this time and stared at me with wide eyes.

"Cassie, where"—he stopped and licked his lips—"where did you learn to do that?"

I laughed. This had possibilities. "You wouldn't believe me if I told you." I pushed at his shoulder. "Lie down."

He rolled over without question and I followed, keeping my grip but careful not to hurt him, recalling how sensitive this flesh was. I let my hand explore him as his tongue had done to me, and found his body fascinating. I'd seen many men nude, but this was my first chance to touch one so intimately, and the fact that it was Mircea was sending my blood pressure skyrocketing.

I found that the skin on his balls was the softest yet, and ran my fingers gently over it until he was groaning and thrashing beneath me. I liked doing this to him, seeing him this defenseless, his usually perfect hair tangling as sweat began to mold it to his head. It was exciting to make him spread his legs wider, exposing him to whatever I might decide to do. His helplessness was intoxicating, and it made me daring. My repertoire wasn't exactly extensive, but I have a good memory, and the Frenchwoman had been about to try something with Louis-César that sounded interesting.

I crawled between Mircea's legs, running my hands along the taut muscles. He reached for me but I pushed his hands away. "Stop it."

He subsided, but the surprise in his eyes told me that he wasn't used to being ordered around. I grabbed the length of him again as it bobbed about enticingly in front of me. He closed his eyes once more at my touch, a raw, vulnerable expression stealing over his face. I stroked him slowly, not understanding the look of pain since I knew I wasn't hurting him. "Cassie . . ." His voice broke and I shushed him. I moved closer and slowly, carefully, licked the straining shaft. It tasted good, slightly salty with an underlying smoky flavor. I liked his scent, too, which was stronger here and faintly musky. The combined sensory overload was heady. I didn't have any experience to guide me, but I decided to start at the tip and work my way down. It sounded like a good plan, but my tongue had barely touched him when Mircea bucked hard, causing me to lose my grip.

"Cassie, don't! I can't control myself if you—"

"I said be quiet," I told him crossly. I needed to focus and it would help if he stayed still and shut up. I told him as much and watched his face fill with astonishment.

"I was assured you had not done this before," he began, struggling up onto his elbows.

I gave him a warning look. "I haven't. So if you don't stay still, don't blame me if you get hurt."

He collapsed back on the bed and flung an arm over his face. He muttered something in Romanian and I ignored him. He knew I didn't speak it, and was just being difficult. If I hadn't been enjoying his body so much, I might have complained. As it was, I returned to the enthralling study of what made him moan. When I slid my lips and tongue along him this time, he stayed much quieter, except for a slight shudder that he might not have been able to help. I found that I liked licking the tip most, although the taste there was a little bitter. But it was worth it to see him struggle not to move or cry out under my touch, his hands balling into fists at his sides. I decided to see what it would take for the great Mircea to completely lose control.

I accidentally grazed his skin with my teeth when I took more of him into my mouth, and the sensation wrung a startled cry from him. After figuring out that it had been a sound of approval, I started interspersing regular nips between the licks, and he was soon whimpering faintly, as if he wasn't even aware he was doing it. A few minutes later, I found his true weakness when I moved lower to lick the downy skin over his balls. He must have been extra sensitive there, or maybe the pressure had been building for a while. Before I realized what was happening, he had grabbed my hips and positioned me above him, so that he was once more pressed against my entrance. It felt so incredibly good, so very right, that I almost let our bodies meld together. But some part of my brain spoke up, reminding me of the price, and I pulled back.

I moved too quickly and ended up falling awkwardly off the bed. A second later, Mircea's flushed face peered over the edge of the mattress, looking at me in bewilderment as I sprawled on the rug. I grabbed at my robe, and his eyes darkened. "I will personally shred that offensive garment so it will never hide your beauty again."

His voice was hoarse and the look in his eyes was wild. I didn't waste the time needed to put the robe on but wrapped it around me like a blanket. It was a poor substitute for the warmth of his skin, but it was a lot easier to think with some clothes on. My breathing wasn't too steady and I almost felt dizzy with need for him, but I backed away until the window stopped me. "We had a deal, Mircea," I told him shakily.

He sat up, which was a serious distraction considering that his arousal had not flagged in the slightest. He winced but kept his burning eyes on mine. They were more cinnamon than amber now, a blazing, beautiful reddish light. It was almost as dark as the color that had practically made

Pritkin faint; it made me want to run back and throw myself at him. I gripped the window ledge behind me for support and felt its wards sizzle. They were cool compared to the heat of my skin at the moment.

Mircea ran a hand over his face, and it was shaking. He looked up at me with desperate eyes. "Cassie, please do not do this. I have explained the situation—you know what is at stake. I want to make this pleasurable for you, not to have you hate me because of it. But this must be done. You are not like that ridiculous mage who understands nothing of us. Please do not make this complicated. It could be beautiful."

"And if I say no?" Mircea was suddenly very still. The room shimmered with barely controlled power, the way heat waves do over desert sand. "You wouldn't force me?"

Mircea swallowed and looked very intensely at the rug for a full minute. When he finally looked up, his eyes had returned to their usual rich brown. "Let there be total honesty between us, *dulceață*. I could invade your mind, use tricks to overcome your reason, and force you to give yourself to me as I know you wish to do. But if I did this, you would never trust me again. I know you too well; I know how you view disloyalty. It is the one thing you cannot forgive, and I do not want you to see me as an enemy."

"Then I can leave?" I knew the answer but needed him to explain my options.

"You know better than that." Mircea sighed and his face suddenly looked tired. "If we do not do this, the Consul will simply appoint another. I know you have feelings of some kind for Tomas, but I also know how upset you are with him. He betrayed your trust, and although it was done under orders he could not disobey, I do not think you have forgiven him for that."

I hugged myself. "No." There was a time when I'd trusted Tomas, at least as much as I did anyone, lusted after him, and maybe even loved him a little. But that had been the man in my imagination, not the real thing. I felt now like

I saw a stranger when I looked at him. I didn't want those hands on me. Besides, he had invaded my mind once on Senate orders. If commanded, I had no doubts he would do it again.

"Then Louis-César, perhaps? He is handsome. Would you prefer him?" Mircea sounded a little strangled, and I think for some reason he liked that idea even less than me being with Tomas. Perhaps because the Frenchman was a full Senate member, with equal status. Did he think I'd fall head over heels for the first guy I had sex with, and run off to Europe? If so, he didn't know me as well as he thought.

"No." I didn't want a man I barely knew, whose touch had sent me into a nightmare twice already, anywhere near me.

"Then perhaps Raphael? He looks on you as a daughter, as you know, but he would do this for you, if you prefer." I shook my head. I wouldn't put Raphael or myself through that. I wouldn't be with someone who would look on the whole thing as a chore to be endured. Mircea spread his hands. "That was my assumption as well. So you see where we are. If you turn all of us down, the Consul will appoint one of her servants to deal with the matter, and that I do not think you would enjoy. There are no other alternatives. Your abilities are too important. The power cannot be allowed to pass to someone else simply because I have not had time to court you properly."

I arched an eyebrow at him. "And what do you get out of it, Mircea? Just security? Or did the Consul agree to honor your claim if this goes well? Do you want to use me, too?"

Mircea let out a long sigh. "No one controls the Pythia, Cassie. If the power does come to you, I will not be able to hold you. I always knew that."

"Then why shield me all these years? Why do it now?" Mircea was right; I did know how vamp politics worked. He had spent a lot of time and energy protecting me, and I doubted it was simply to obtain a clairvoyant for his court.

Especially not if, once I became Pythia, he would lose control of my gift. There was more going on here than he had told me.

He did not look happy, but he answered. His usual, laughing mask had gone, replaced by a stark, pain-filled expression. "You understand what it is to lose family, *dulceaţă*. So perhaps you can appreciate what it means to me that only Radu remains of all my kin, and he . . . I told you what was done to him."

"Yes."

"What I did not tell you, for I rarely speak of it and you were only a child, is that he suffers still. Every night when he wakens, it is as if it were all being done anew. They broke him, *dulceaţă*, in mind, body and spirit. Even now, hundreds of years after his torturers are dead, he cries out in agony at their whips and brands. Every night, a thousand torments are revisited on him, again and again." Mircea's eyes were suddenly old and terribly sad; they told me that it had not been only Radu who had suffered. "I have thought of killing him many times to spare him, but I cannot. He is all I have. But I no longer believe that one night he will awaken from his nightmare."

"I'm sorry, Mircea." I resisted the impulse to go to him, to stroke his messy hair and comfort him. It was too soon for that. Years of experience had taught me to find out the whole story before offering sympathy. "But I don't see what this has to do with me."

"You are going to Carcassonne."

It took a moment for me to make the connection, and even then it didn't make sense. "You freed Radu from the Bastille."

"In 1769, yes. But a century earlier, he was not there. He was held and tortured for many years at Carcassonne." He said the name as if it was an invective, which to him it probably was. "Do you know the Pythia's alternate title, Cassie?" I numbly shook my head. "She is called the Guardian of

Time. You are my best chance, my only chance. But if the
Pythia dies and you lose your borrowed power because you
were not yet a fit vessel to hold it, I will lose the only window on time I have ever found."

Things clarified. "The Consul promised you a chance to
help Radu. That is your payment for having me solve their
little problem."

He inclined his head. "She agreed to allow me to make
up the third of our group. I will be going with you when next
you shift. While you and Tomas stop the attempt on Louis-
César, I will rescue my brother." Mircea's eyes were somber
but utterly serious. I knew in that minute that, while he
might not force me himself, he would stand aside and watch
someone else do it. He might not like it, but he would like
even less leaving Radu to his fate. I wanted to hate him for
it, but I couldn't. It was part pity—I couldn't imagine what
it had been like, caring for someone for hundreds of years
who was dangerously insane, watching him torment himself
day after day and being able to do absolutely nothing about
it. But it was more that: despite having every reason to do
so, Mircea had not lied. He was right; I could forgive almost
anything but that.

"How do you know we're even going back there again?"
If he was going to be honest with me, the least I could do
was to return the favor. "I don't have the same apprehension
or fear or whatever it was around Louis-César anymore. And
when he carried me away from Dante's, nothing happened.
For all I know the power has already passed, or it might
choose to take me somewhere else."

"We believe that Rasputin will try for him that night, the
one you have visited twice now, because it was then that
Louis-César was changed. You did not know that my brother
made him, did you?"

"I thought Tomas said he was cursed."

Mircea shook his head. "I do not know where he heard
that, Cassie. Perhaps he believes it because Louis-César did

not know what it was to have a master. Like me, he had to make his own way with little guidance. Because my brother was imprisoned, Louis-César's birth was not recorded until long after the fact. By the time any other master knew of his existence and might have tried to claim him, he was too powerful. Radu bit him for the first time the night you were there, after the jailers left them alone together in an attempt to terrorize our Frenchman. Radu called him back the two nights afterwards until he changed. Perhaps he was trying to gain a servant who could release him."

"So why didn't he?"

Mircea looked at me with some surprise. "You do not know who Louis-César was?"

I shook my head, and he smiled slightly. "I will leave him to tell you the story. Suffice it to say, he was not free to move about for a long time, and by the time he was, Radu had been moved and he could not find him. In any case, all Rasputin would have to do to eliminate our Louis-César is to stake him before the third bite; kill him when he is yet human and helpless and he will never have to fight him."

"He could kill him in his cradle even easier, or when he was a kid. You don't know it'll be then."

Mircea shook his head emphatically. "We believe that your gift has been showing you where the problem lies, where someone is attempting to alter the time line. Why else would you keep going back there? In any case, the records on Louis-César's early life are scant. The first time Rasputin can be sure where to find him is when he changed. It is on record, along with the peculiar circumstances of his master-lessness. He won't take a chance on something so important. He will try for him where he knows he will be. I know where they held Radu, Cassie. It will be a matter of a few moments to free him."

"And can you tell me the exact date his mind gave way? A city surrounds that castle, Mircea. I won't help you turn a mad killer loose on them."

Mircea spoke quickly. "I have spoken with Louis-César. Radu was quite sane when he changed him. You can help me save him, *dulceață*. Torture for others ended soon enough with death or, rarely, exoneration. But not for him. His torturers would never free him because they did not believe he could ever be redeemed, but they would not kill him, since his suffering made such a good lesson for those they wished to frighten." The emotion in his eyes was hard to witness; desperation was too mild to describe it. "There is no way out for him! You have seen that place. Can you leave him there, knowing what his fate will be? Can you trade his life for your virtue?"

It wasn't my virtue I worried about; it was my freedom. But I knew better than to try to strike a bargain over that. There was no way the Consul wouldn't at least attempt to hold on to me. If I became Pythia, perhaps I'd be able to avoid her manipulation and that of the two circles; maybe I could even help my father. It was a hell of a long shot, but it was the best one I had. I took a deep breath and pushed away from the window, letting the robe slip from my hands as I did so.

Mircea watched me walk to him, hope dawning in his eyes. I put a hand on his shoulder, in the midst of the decadent, raw silk of his hair, and ran the other lightly down the curve of his face. "You answered my question. Don't you want your reward?"

He caught me to him and began speaking softly against my lips, words of thanks and passion intermingled. Tears fell onto my neck and breasts as he kissed, licked and nibbled his way across my upper body. He lay me back carefully onto the bed and kissed his way back to the center of that building pressure that had returned with a vengeance. Soon he had me almost crying for something larger than his tongue to ease the ache. As if reading my mind, Mircea slid a finger down to my throbbing center and eased it inside. It felt wonderful, but it wasn't nearly enough.

"Mircea!" He didn't answer, but two fingers slid inside me and I bore down on them, desperate for more of him. They eased the almost-pain and increased the pleasure until I was making a high, moaning sound and riding his hand like I so badly wanted to ride his body. The pressure inside me mounted until I thought I would faint from the delicious, burning ache of it. Then it broke and all I could concentrate on was that wonderful, breathtaking sensation that swept through me over and over. I heard myself cry out his name, then the world erupted in a flash of color and a sound like a rushing wind filled my head.

A second later, I realized it hadn't been the wind. "Um, Cassie? Look, I know this isn't a real good time and all . . ." I was so drunk on the afterglow that it took me a minute to recognize Billy Joe's voice.

"Billy. You have exactly one second to *get out*." Mircea held me while I finished my orgasm, speaking softly in Romanian. I was really going to have to break him of that.

"I would, honest, but we need to talk. Something's happening. Something bad." I groaned and pushed him out of my head. He appeared, hovering over Mircea's naked shoulder.

Mircea had rolled on top of me, supporting himself with his arms, and he carefully positioned himself. "I have prepared you as well as I can, Cassie," he told me in a rough, slightly breathless voice, "but this may hurt slightly. I am considered somewhat . . . larger than usual, but I will be careful." I wanted to scream at him to get on with it—my body wanted him inside and it didn't care if it hurt.

Billy glanced at Mircea's sweat-streaked face and rolled his eyes. "Please. You shoulda seen me in my prime. The countess said I had the biggest . . ."

"Billy!"

". . . talent she'd ever seen. Anyway, he don't look that impressive to me," he said huffily.

"Shut up and get *out*!"

Billy ignored me and, before I could stop him, blew a freezing wind over Mircea. "Especially not now."

Mircea yelped and looked around in alarm, while I glared at Billy. "Have you lost your mind?"

For an answer, Billy blasted Mircea again. The cold didn't seem that bad to me, but then, I never feel ghosts the same way as everyone else. Mircea looked like he'd been hit with a blizzard; goose bumps covered his flesh, his damp hair actually had ice crystals in it and the result on our activities was the same as a cold shower.

Before I could explain to Billy exactly how much trouble he was in, Rafe's excited tones came from the doorway. "Master! I am sorry to disturb, but Rasputin is coming! He's almost here now!" Rafe had paused in the door and was staring hard at the floor, fairly vibrating in alarm. Tomas entered right behind him. I quickly pulled the quilt up, but he didn't so much as glance at me.

Mircea's eyes were blank and uncomprehending for a second, then he nodded. "How much time do we have?"

"I don't know." Rafe looked frantic. I'd never seen anyone actually wring their hands before, but he was doing it. "Louis-César has gone to meet him, but that Russian *testa di merda* has an army of weres and dark mages with him! And he has enough masters that he can try to take us in sunlight!"

Tomas nodded agreement. "The Senate is preparing a defense, but we are badly outnumbered. No one expected an attack with the duel set for tonight. I can take Cassie below. The vault should hold, for a while."

Mircea ignored Tomas' outstretched arms. He caught me up, quilt and all, and strode naked back into the living area of the suite. "Mircea." I looked up to find him grim faced and determined, and tugged on his icy hair to get his attention. "What's happening?"

Mircea glanced at me as we started towards the stairs to the Senate chamber. All around us, the iron wall sconces had turned outward, with the sharp, knifelike decorations on their bottom edges no longer pointing at the floor. I was starting to think that maybe they weren't decorations at all and hoped they knew who their friends were. "Do not worry, *dulceaţă*," Mircea was saying. "They will never breach the inner wards. And this changes little. If Rasputin does not defeat the Consul's champion before he attempts to take over, the other senates will declare him an outlaw. None of this will profit him."

"That doesn't make me feel much better, considering that we'll all be dead before the other senates can catch up with him."

"Hurry!" Tomas flung open the heavy door to the stairs as a blast came faintly from somewhere outside. "They've breached the outer defenses." Several men and a woman rushed past us, toward the sound of the explosion. They had on enough hardware to make Pritkin look underdressed. I felt their power as they passed—war mages. Well, that should buy some time.

"I assure you that will not happen, Cassie. I will protect you."

I didn't answer. Mircea would try—I didn't doubt that—but Rasputin had to be crazy to attempt something like this. And a crazy man always has a serious advantage in making mayhem.

Pritkin rounded the corner and followed us as we began our descent. I glared at him and he returned the look. "What is happening? What trickery is this?"

Everybody ignored him. The stairs shuddered under our feet and the overhead lights swung dangerously. "*Vaffan-culo!* The secondaries are down!" Rafe screamed. I didn't know what that meant, but a look at Mircea's face told me it wasn't good.

"That is impossible. They should not have been able to get through that quickly!" Mircea tucked my head into his chest, and the next second we were at the bottom of the stairs. I guess we flew, but it had happened so fast, I couldn't be sure. We moved into the Senate chamber at almost the same moment that another explosion came from above, and burning pieces of the stairway rained down behind us. A flaming splinter missed my face by a millimeter; then Mircea made a gesture and the heavy metal door into the chamber clanged shut.

Rafe stared around fearfully. "This cannot be happening!"

"You are needed to shore up the defenses," Tomas told Mircea urgently. "Give me Cassie!" He tried to take me, but Mircea jerked away and crossed the room in another lightning movement. A door opened in the rock where only flat, bare stone had existed before. It shouldn't have surprised me: this was a facility built by magic users, so there were probably more hidden doorways than visible ones. But it was still the best example of a perimeter ward I've ever seen, without a flaw even from only a few feet away. So that's how Jack had appeared out of nowhere earlier.

There was a deafening explosion behind us, and over Mircea's shoulder I saw the heavy door he had just secured blown inward like it was paper. A mage leapt through the opening, only to be speared by two pieces of iron that came out of nowhere. I glanced up to see that the chandeliers had undergone a transformation like the sconces upstairs. Those hundreds of razor-sharp points were now vibrating, sending a dull, metal throbbing echoing around the room, like the sound of thousands of feet stamping in unison at a football game. They were excitedly waiting for someone else to poke their head inside the room.

After Mircea finally convinced the wards to let us through, we swept down a long corridor. Torches burst to life left and right. Electricity tends to interfere with some types of wards and the corridor was fairly crackling with them. We went through three huge metal doors that were so heavily warded my skin felt pulled out of shape as we passed, like little hands were crawling all over me. The last one was the worst. The resistance was so strong that, for a minute, I didn't think it was going to let any of us through. But Mircea barked out a command, and finally the almost physical barrier weakened enough that we could push past.

Inside was a small room with four hallways branching off at different angles. Mircea stopped, so abruptly that Tomas almost ran into him. "Mircea! Which way?"

"How did they break through so quickly?" Mircea asked again, and for a moment I thought he was talking to me. Then I looked up and saw Tomas' face. There was nothing of the man I had known in it. It was a haughty, savage, beautiful countenance, something that would have looked right staring out from an ancient coin. I could see the Incan noble in his features; what I could not see was any sign of the gentle man I had known.

"We can talk later! Tell me the way, Mircea!"

Mircea smiled, his attention still apparently on me. "I have been a fool, it seems, Cassandra."

I glanced in confusion between the two of them. There was a building current of power in the room that worried me. The wards didn't like it either; the air was close and getting heavier by the second. "Tell me, Mircea!" Tomas demanded. "No one has to die today."

"Oh, I can assure you," Mircea replied, almost kindly, "someone will."

"What are you two talking about?!" I tried to get to my feet, but Mircea's grip didn't loosen.

Rafe answered from behind me, his voice bitter. "It seems Tomas has changed sides, *mia stella*. What was the price for your betrayal, *bastardo*?"

Tomas sneered at him, and the expression looked strange on his usually stoic face. "Did you really think I would work to keep myself in chains? I should be Consul! I would lead the Latin American Senate today if it had not been for that creature's interference. I will not let you keep me subject to the whims of a child!"

"Oh, okay." Billy Joe floated around Tomas' head.

"That's how the dark mages were able to figure out the wards so fast. Tomas told them what to expect. Guess he ain't thrilled with the idea of staying servant to that French guy." He glanced over his shoulder, back the way we came. "I'll be back in a minute."

"They will be here soon," Tomas told Mircea. "Don't be a fool. Help us, and you will be rewarded. I give you my word!"

"Why would anyone take the word of a traitor?" Rafe asked, his tone insulting. I would have told him to be quiet if I'd thought it would do any good. The expression on Tomas' face reminded me of Tony in a mood, and antagonizing him then had never been smart.

"What do you plan for Cassandra?" Mircea demanded.

Tomas' eyes flickered to me. "She has been promised to me, as part of my reward. She will not be harmed."

Mircea laughed contemptuously. "Cassandra may become Pythia. Quite a prize, Tomas. Do you really think your master will let you keep her?"

"I have no master!" Tomas shouted, and I felt a bolt of power slam against Mircea's shields, just above my head. His defenses held, but I didn't see how. I was dazed from only the near miss, and Rafe was on the floor, screaming.

"Rafe! Mircea, put me down." He ignored me. I had the impression that he and Tomas had forgotten that anybody else was in the room.

"If Rasputin kills Louis-César in anything but fair combat, your side wins nothing. You know this, Tomas. What are you planning?"

"Rasputin will be fighting Mei Ling, not Louis-César. He will win easily, and the other senates will have to acknowledge his control. The Frenchman dodged our first attempt, when Cassie and I saved the girl, but soon it won't matter."

"What?" I had the impression I'd missed something.

Mircea seemed to understand, though. "You slipped earlier, when you said he'd been cursed. But he wasn't, and you should have known that—you've been his servant for a century. I should have caught it then. Before you and Cassie interfered, Louis-César was not made; he was cursed, wasn't he? By the gypsy family whose daughter died because of him. That is the way it originally happened, is it not?"

It took a second for his words to soak in. "You have got to be kidding," I told him. He shot me a warning look, and I shut up.

Tomas apparently didn't notice. "She was their only daughter. The king ordered her death to make a lasting impression on his half brother, but her family didn't know that. They blamed the man they thought had seduced her and then had her killed when she ceased to be amusing. Her grandmother was a very powerful woman, and in her grief she cursed him with vampirism."

Rafe had managed to get back to his feet, although he didn't look good. He started to speak, but I frantically shook my head at him. The last thing I wanted was to remind Tomas that he was in the room.

Tomas was too caught up in his story to care. "When I realized Cassie had brought us to a time when Louis-César was still human, I knew it was the perfect opportunity to free myself. I thought if the girl was rescued, the curse would not be laid and he would die after a normal, human life span. I blame him for causing much suffering by his interference, but it was largely unwitting. I thought it would not be a tragedy for him to die as all men do, at his appointed time, but I should have been firmer. I do not know what went wrong, how he became vampire after all, but it does not matter." He looked at me. "You will take me back, Cassie, and this time, I will be more direct. You must help me possess a body so I will have the strength to kill him."

I stared at him. What the hell did he expect me to say: *sure thing, no problem*? I was beginning to think he was as crazy as Rasputin.

Before I could figure out what to say, Billy Joe appeared

in front of me. "Cassie! They're in the Senate chamber. If you're gonna do anything, now would be good."

"Do what? I need to touch Louis-César to shift. And he's not here!"

"Well, you better come up with something. The Senate's wards are goin' down like some first-year wardsmith crafted 'em, and the glamourie in the outer chamber ain't gonna fool anybody if they already know where it is. They'll be here any minute."

"Why should Cassandra help you?" Mircea asked, sounding as composed as if he and Tomas were having a polite conversation over tea. "What can you offer her that we cannot?"

Tomas glanced at Rafe. "The life of her old friend, for one." His eyes turned back to me. "I will guarantee Raphael's safety, Cassie, if you aid us. Otherwise, Tony has requested the right to deal with him personally for acting as Mircea's informant. You are aware what that will mean?"

"I don't get it," I told him honestly. "We lived together for months. If you were going to betray me, why not do it then? Why now?"

"I did not betray you," Tomas said intently. "Think about it. Mircea almost let you get killed; why do you trust him? Did he keep you safe? Was he there when you were attacked? I saved you; not him! And I was the one who realized that Rasputin could be the answer for both of us." He looked at me beseechingly. "Don't you see? Once Louis-César is dead, I can challenge Alejandro again, and this time I will defeat him! As it is, much of my strength has to go into resisting my master's will; it weakens me too much to do what must be done. But that burden will be lifted by the Frenchman's death, and I can then save my people. And afterwards, you will never again have to worry about anyone harming you. As Consul, I can do more than merely promise protection. I can deliver!"

"*You* contacted Rasputin? When?"

"After your first vision, when I knew for certain what you can do. I called Tony and offered to hand you over, but only to Rasputin. He promised to guarantee your life in exchange for my aid. Since his plans coincided with mine, I agreed."

"Rafe told you I'd go after Jimmy, and you told Tony." I said it, but I didn't believe it.

Tomas saw the hurt in my expression, and his softened. "I had to tell him you were going to Dante's, Cassie. If there was no deal and they found you first, you might have died."

"I almost died because they knew where I'd be, Tomas! They ambushed us."

He shook his head. "I was there to ensure your safety. You were in no danger—it was Louis-César they wanted. When he is gone, Mei Ling will not be a problem."

"Tomas!" I wanted to scream at his obtuseness. How could anyone live half a millennium and be that stupid? "Rasputin doesn't need me! Don't you get it? He already has a sybil who does whatever he wants. The only thing he wants me to do is die!"

"Very perceptive, Miss Palmer." Pritkin entered the room with guns drawn. I had forgotten about him. I guess everyone else had, too. He kept his eyes on Tomas but spoke to me. "It would seem that we are allies—for the moment. I'll keep him here, but I suggest you hurry. There are ten black knights outside. I have constructed a few surprises they do not have advance warning about, but they will not hold for long. They will be here in a matter of minutes."

"Our wards will hold!" Rafe said proudly. "The traitor could not give them the secrets of the inner wards; he did not know them."

Pritkin gave his usual sneer. "Believe what you like, vampire, but we have training exercises more difficult than your so-called defenses! If she does not act, the sybil will die and there will be nothing to stop the Senate from being replaced by one allied with the dark." He kept his eyes and his weapons steady on Tomas, but again he spoke to me. "If you can do anything, do it now."

"I don't know how!" I ran a hand through my hair, wanting to pull some of it out in frustration, and met up with something solid. My fingers curled around the hair clip Louis-César had given me when tending my cheek. It had somehow managed to hang in there all this time. I concentrated and felt a faint tingle, a distant echo of the disorientation that preceded a vision, but it wasn't enough. It had belonged to him, had been in contact with his body, so it should have worked as a focus the same way he had. But either I wasn't strong enough to make the leap with only an object, or he hadn't owned it very long and the link was weak. Either way, I needed help.

"Billy! I need something called the Tears of Apollo."

"Okay, and this would be where?"

I looked up at Mircea. "The Tears! What do they look like and where are they?"

"In the inner sanctum, in a small bottle, crystal with a blue stopper. But if we enter the chamber, Tomas will know the way. These four hallways are the last barrier. Three are false and lead only to death. Only one leads to the Consul. Once she is dead, our cause is lost."

Billy had drifted over as we spoke. "There's only one real passageway, Cass. The others are just good glamourie. I'll be right back."

"Cassie, don't do this!" Tomas looked daggers at Mircea. "He will never let you go! If you truly want freedom, help me." I shook my head and his face grew desperate. "Please, Cassie, you can't refuse! You don't understand—Alejandro is a monster! I have begged Louis-César to free me. I have told him what atrocities Alejandro has done, what he will continue to do until someone stops him, yet he refuses."

"I can't believe he won't help you. I could try—"

"Cassie! If I could not sway him in a century of pleading, why do you think he would listen to you? Alejandro has some sort of hold over him. He has something Louis-César wants and has promised it to him if he keeps me under control. I have thought about this for years and there is no other way. Alejandro must die, and therefore so must his champion."

I looked into the fervent light in Tomas' eyes and saw that he meant every word he was saying. He might want to be Consul, but he also really wanted this Alejandro dead. For all I knew, maybe the guy deserved what Tomas obviously wanted to dish out. But that wasn't up to me to decide. "I won't trade one person's life for another's, Tomas. I can't let you murder Louis-César. I'm not God, and neither are you."

Tomas gestured violently at Mircea. "Why can't you see that he only wants to use you? If you did not have your powers, you would mean nothing to him!"

"And what would I mean to you, if I couldn't help you gain the consulate?"

Tomas smiled, and it transformed his face, making him look boyish and adorable again. Like my Tomas. "You know how I feel about you, Cassie. I will give you security and peace. What can he offer?"

I was about to point out that he hadn't answered the question, when Billy came streaming back, a small bottle clutched in one insubstantial hand. "I hope you don't need nothin' else, Cass, 'cause I'm outta juice." He dropped the Tears in my palm, and the tiny bottle was surprisingly heavy.

I slid out the stopper just as Tomas lunged, not at me as I'd half expected, but at Rafe. Pritkin fired, but the shotgun blast was stopped by the heavy wards of the chamber and deflected back on him. His shields held, but his gun ended up a twisted mass of steaming metal and he was thrown back against the wall, hard.

"Give me the Tears, Cassie." Tomas held out one hand; the other had Rafe in a stranglehold. "Mircea can't protect all of you at the same time, but no one has to get hurt. Help me and I'll let him go."

I didn't have to worry about finding an answer. Tomas had, once again, underestimated the mage. I guess he thought that, with the wards rendering magical weapons and firearms useless, Pritkin couldn't be much of a threat. He found out differently when the mage jumped up, drew a cord out of his pocket and slipped it around Tomas' throat. A garrote may be crude, but it works.

Tomas let go of Rafe and Mircea didn't waste any time pushing him towards the doorway Billy had exited. Rafe had barely cleared it when the chamber's wards failed and a whole crowd of people muscled in. Pritkin yelled something and let go, pushing Tomas towards them. Mircea clutched me tight and, in the time it takes to blink, we were inside another hallway, running full out. I felt the passageway's wards slam shut behind us and got a glimpse of the scene in the outer chamber over Mircea's shoulder. Tomas was slumped on the ground, a hand to his throat, gagging. Behind him were some humans wearing enough weapons to tell me as clearly as if they'd had it tattooed on their foreheads that they were war mages. I had a glimpse of Pritkin, face distorted in a snarl as he faced them; then we rounded a corner and were in the inner sanctum.

Chapter 14

It was a small room, maybe ten by twelve, with bare stone walls, floor and ceiling. The only light came from a pair of torches, one on either side of a rather mundane-looking metal cabinet. It looked really out of place, like something that ought to be in a modern office building, not sitting in the vault of a magical stronghold. The Consul was standing before it, as still as a statue except for her living costume, holding a small silver ball in her hand. The cabinet door was open, showing rows of shelves full of black boxes.

I didn't waste time saying hello, but splashed the contents of the bottle all over Mircea and me. As soon as the liquid hit my skin, it was like a veil had been lifted. I could See everything, each image and sensation from that other time, as clearly as if I were leafing through pages in a book. Mircea put me down and I clutched him as my feet hit the floor. The images shifting through my head gave me double vision and I was afraid I'd fall.

"We have five minutes," the Consul said mildly, as if discussing the weather.

"I know." Mircea looked down at me. "Can you do it?"

I nodded. I had the scene I wanted. It was perfect—two people all alone with no one to see if they suddenly began acting strangely. It was a bonus that one of them was Louis-César. I figured he would be a lot harder to kill with Mircea in residence. "I'm going to try to jump us into a couple of bodies, since it'll give us more time. We can feed off them as Billy does me. But I don't know if this will work. I've never done it deliberately." I looked at Billy Joe, who was hovering anxiously. "Come in."

"Cassie, listen, I . . ."

"There's no time, Billy." I regarded the spirit I was trusting with my body, possibly permanently, and for a second I saw the man he might have been had he lived. "If I don't make it back, do your best to kill Tony and free my father. Promise." I didn't know if he could do it, but Billy was amazingly resourceful when he wanted to be.

He stared at me, then slowly nodded. He dissolved into a cloud of sparkling energy and flowed across my skin like an old, familiar blanket. I took him in gladly, ignored the flash of his last card game, which he should have played to lose, and felt him settle in. There was nothing left but to let go. I concentrated on the scene I'd selected, saw again that dim, candlelit room, felt the cool breeze from the window and smelled the scents of firewood, roses and sex. Then the earth gave way and we were falling.

The jolt of impact felt like I'd hit the ground after diving out a second-story window. But I barely noticed it considering the other sensations flooding through the body I had borrowed. I looked up to see Louis-César haloed in candlelight for an instant, just before he plunged into me. I cried out in surprise, but not in pain. It didn't hurt as Mircea had warned; it felt wonderful. I watched him pull out and tried to say something, but then he slammed into me again and all I wanted was for him to go faster, harder. My nails were scratching his back, but he didn't seem to mind. I looked into his eyes and saw that they had turned a beautiful liquid amber, a color Louis-César had never had in life or death.

It was difficult to think, because my thoughts were confused with those of the woman whose body I'd borrowed. I tried to focus, but all her attention was on the fine beads of sweat trailing down his face and chest, and she overrode me.

I reached up and ran a hand through his damp auburn curls to his neck, and drew him down to me. His rhythm didn't falter, but the angle changed slightly and we both groaned in response. I ran my tongue over him, tasting him, and his face grew slack with need. I wrapped my legs around his waist and pulled, driving him into me even harder. The muscles in my lower areas tightened, wrenching a strangled gasp from him. I grabbed handfuls of his hair, pulling his mouth down to mine, bending him almost double. He cried out and, finally, lost his rhythm.

I laughed into his mouth as he thrust into me in ragged bursts, as if he couldn't get enough, couldn't go fast or hard enough, to satisfy some overwhelming need. I understood it, because I was also feeling two rising tides of desire, mine and that of the woman whose body I had invaded. She didn't seem to care; at that moment, all she wanted was to be satisfied, and on that we both agreed.

I slid out from under him, causing him to clutch at me convulsively to keep our bodies together, and flipped him over. I smiled down in satisfaction. He was glorious, sprawled there among the soft, pale sheets, his hair glimmering richly in the candlelight. It should have seemed wrong, to see Louis-César's body with Mircea's knowing eyes, but it didn't.

"I want to be on top."

He didn't argue. His hands moved up my body to cup my breasts and we both sighed as I slowly settled back onto him. I liked this angle better: I liked seeing him beneath me, although I still had to fight not to have that strange, double vision. It was Louis-César's face that stared into mine, filled with longing, but it was Mircea's triumphal smile as he began moving again.

"I told you before, Cassie," he murmured, "anything you want." Then the waves of pleasure caught us both, robbing us of speech, and I didn't care. The world burst into perfect, liquid pleasure a minute later and I cried out his name, but it was not my voice and it was not the name of the body beneath me.

When the world coalesced again, I was wrapped in warm arms and soft blankets, my head pillowed on a chest that still rose and fell with slight tremors. A hand was running through my hair, soothing me, and I realized I was crying. His words were a strange mixture of French and Romanian, neither of which I understand, but somehow they warmed me anyway.

"Cassie." A murmur in my ear brought me back the rest of the way, and I left the woman to enjoy that warm, wonderful haze on her own. "You can really do this." He gazed around in wonder. "Can you choose which time to send us back as well? Can you do it before the attack, to give us time to prepare?"

His words finally helped me slam down a barrier between the woman, who was basking in the golden glow of sexual satisfaction, and myself. I glanced in panic at the door, but it remained closed, with no sign of the older woman, the guards or a crazed Russian psychopath. We seemed to be safe for the moment, but there were probably people on the way to kill him even as we lay around recovering.

"Mircea, we have to get out of here! They'll come here first!"

"Cassie, calm yourself. There is no rush. The sybil and her assistants know where this Frenchman will be. As you said, they will be along presently, expecting him to be pleasantly preoccupied and unwary. But we will be waiting for them instead." He slipped out of bed and walked over to the mirror. He touched Louis-César's cheek softly. "This is a marvel!" He examined his borrowed body in astonishment. He turned towards me as he looked over his shoulder to check out the rear view and my mouth went dry. Louis-César was simply stunning; there was no other word for it. Backlit against the fire, his hair a reddish halo around his face, he might have been a Renaissance angel come to life.

"This is the famous mask, is it?" Mircea picked up a scrap of velvet that had been flung over the mirror and held it up to his eyes. "A piece of history indeed."

"Are you going to tell me who he was now," I asked impatiently, "or do I have to guess?"

Mircea laughed and tossed the mask aside. "Not at all," he commented, unself-consciously perching on the edge of a low chest of drawers near the mirror. I wished he'd put something on. The current situation wasn't doing anything for my mental abilities.

"I will be happy to tell you the tale, if it will amuse you. His father was George Villiers, whom you may know better as the English Duke of Buckingham. He seduced Anne of Austria, Louis XIII's queen, while on a state visit to France. Louis preferred men, you see, a fact that had long left his queen frustrated and childless." He looked thoughtful for a moment. "So perhaps it was she who seduced Buckingham, hoping for an heir. In any case, she was successful. However, it seems that Louis was not pleased about the idea of having a bastard on the throne, especially not a half-English one. Anne had already named her son after the king, in the attempt, I suppose, to hint that a bastard heir was better than none at all, especially if no one knew about the substitution. The argument failed, and her firstborn was sent into hiding."

Something was starting to come together for me, some long-forgotten history lesson maybe, but I couldn't quite put my finger on it. Mircea didn't wait for me to figure it out. "Eventually, the queen had another son, whom most said was sired by her adviser, Cardinal Mazarin. Perhaps she kept quiet about the deception this time, or maybe the king was becoming afraid that he would leave no heir, because the boy came to the throne as Louis XIV. He wasn't happy to have a half-brother who looked a great deal like the Duke of Buckingham. That might call his mother's virtue into question, and cause doubts about his own parentage, and therefore his right to rule."

"The Man in the Iron Mask!" I finally made the connection. "I read that book as a kid. But that wasn't how it went."

Mircea shrugged. "Dumas was a writer of fiction. He
could say what he liked, and there were many rumors circu-
lating at the time from which to choose. But to make a long
story short, King Louis put Louis-César in prison for the rest
of his life, holding the threat of harm to his friends over his
head to keep him docile. To make the point even clearer, he
had him sent on a tour of France's most infamous house of
horrors, the leading castle in the medieval witch hunts, Carcassonne. King Louis used it as a place of incarceration for
any who disagreed with him, but the torturers and the troops
supporting them were all found dead one morning in 1661,
causing the greatest fortress of the Middle Ages to be aban-
doned. It fell into ruins and wasn't restored for two hundred
years."

"But didn't Louis-César say he was here that year, in
1661?" I looked around nervously. That was all I needed, a
homicidal maniac or a bunch of fed up townspeople to come
busting in with pitchforks, ready to slaughter everybody.

Mircea didn't look overly concerned. "Yes, he was moved
around to many prisons through the years, staying in captivity until shortly before his brother died, when the last of the
friends he was protecting passed away. Then he took off forever the velvet mask they had made him wear so no one
would notice his strong resemblance to a certain narcissistic
English duke, who had left portraits of himself all over Europe. He told me once that his jailers only forced him into
the iron mask after he was turned, and even then only when
he was transported from one prison to the other." He grinned
at me. "It was a precaution, you see, so that he didn't eat
anyone en route."

I gave him a dirty look—now was not the time for
humor—and tossed him the robe I'd used during my previous
visit. "Get dressed. We need to get out of here."

He caught the robe in midair. Nothing about the possession seemed to be bothering his reflexes, but then, I'd already found that out. "I have told you, Cassie; you are panicking for no reason. They will come to us, and after we dispose of the sybil, we will save my brother."

I blinked. I hoped I hadn't heard right. "What do you mean, dispose of her? She was kidnapped, Mircea! She may not be any happier about being part of this than I am."

He shrugged, and the casual indifference made me cold. "She aided our enemies and is indirectly responsible for the deaths of at least four Senate members." He saw my expression, and his face softened. "You have grown up as one of us, but I often forget, you are not vampyr." He gave it the Romanian pronunciation. It sounded better that way, but the implication behind his words hit me like a sledgehammer. "She is the key to all this. Once she is gone, there will be no other way for anyone to slip through time, and therefore no more threat."

I began struggling into the woman's clothes, which were scattered everywhere, and tried to come up with a response that would make sense to Mircea. I thought about the four Senate guards who had been killed. By the look of them, they had been with the Consul hundreds of years and must have served her faithfully or they wouldn't have been entrusted with protecting the Senate chamber. They may not have decided to betray her: the sybil had interfered with their transition and Rasputin was a powerful master who might have been able to force their obedience. It seemed unlikely that they would have chosen to essentially commit suicide by taking me on in front of such an audience if they had had a choice. But that fact hadn't saved them.

Vamp law was very simple, if a little on the medieval side, and intent wasn't nearly as important as in human courts. Nobody cared why you did something. If you caused problems, you were guilty, and the guilty had to pay. If you were in a quarrel with another master, your own might intervene to save you if you were useful enough to make it worthwhile, either by a duel or by offering reparations, but no one could do anything about a threat to the Senate. There was no higher power to which to appeal.

After only a minute, I gave up trying to figure out how the unbelievably complicated dress worked and threw on the lightweight slip instead. It was too thin, but at least I was covered. I crawled under the bed and retrieved the woman's shoes, then sat looking at them in annoyance. So, high heels weren't a modern invention. I couldn't believe women had been putting up with these torture devices for centuries.

"Would you like me to help, *dulceață*?" Mircea was holding out a peacock-colored dress that I assumed the woman had been wearing at some earlier time. "It has been some time since I played lady's maid, but I believe I remember how."

I narrowed my eyes at him. I bet he did. After five hundred years, Mircea probably couldn't remember all the boudoirs he'd been in. "You forget," I told him, as he helped me on with the heavy dress, "that there will still be a way into time, even if the sybil dies."

His hands were warm on my shoulders as he pulled the gown into place. He adjusted the low neckline, and his hand lingered on the exposed flesh. "The Pythia is old and sick, Cassie. She will not last much longer." I looked up into his face, and there was tenderness there, but also implacability. Mircea was willing to talk me around to his point of view, but not to really listen to mine. He had already decided how to deal with this—find the sybil, kill her, go home. It was utterly practical, if absolutely cold-blooded.

"But I will," I reminded him. "Or were you planning to kill me, too, after Radu is saved?"

Mircea widened those borrowed blue eyes, but there was none of Louis-César's innocence in them. His hands turned me around so he could reach the lacings at the back of the dress. "I have told you, *dulceață;* you are mine. You have been so since the age of eleven. You will be so forever. And no one harms what is mine. You have my word."

It sounded frighteningly like Tomas' speech. I had known, of course, that that was how he saw me. It was how any master would see a human servant, as a possession. In my case I was a useful, and therefore highly prized, possession, but that was all. But it was still hard to hear it stated so flatly. "And if I don't want to be owned? What if I want to decide for myself what I do?"

Mircea kissed the top of my head tolerantly. "I cannot keep you safe if I do not know where you are." He turned me around, the lacing completed, and lifted my hand to his lips. His eyes burned brighter than the room's candles. "You do see that, do you not?"

I saw, all right. I saw a life lived in thrall to one of the circles, to the Senate or to Mircea personally. Whatever he might say about the respect and influence my power would bring, the truth was that I would never be viewed as anything except a pawn to be used. If I became Pythia, I would never be free. Damn. I hoped metaphysical sex didn't count.

"Yes, of course." I sat down on the bed while he took my foot in his hands and drew on one of the woman's long, white stockings. I let him finish dressing me, and tried to think of some way to save the sybil, since arguing obviously wasn't going to cut it. I had to get him somewhere out of the way until I could find her and figure out whether she was in this voluntarily or not. Otherwise, the very practical vampire I was with would simply kill her. While that would solve the problem, I didn't think it was a solution I could live with.

Something occurred to me by the time he slid the last garter into place. "Mircea, you told me that your brother made Louis-César. That was why what Tomas and I did didn't change anything. Instead of being cursed with vampirism by Françoise's family, he was brought over the usual way by Radu, right?"

"Yes, it would seem our Frenchman had a destiny that would not be denied."

"Then Rasputin doesn't have to go after Louis-César directly, does he? If he destroys Radu, no one bites Louis-César and he dies at the end of a normal life, instead of living to become a master. Radu must be restrained somehow or they wouldn't have been able to keep him here. And killing someone tied down and helpless would be a lot easier for a spirit than attacking a strong, free man, wouldn't it?"

Mircea had grown pale. "I am a hundred times a fool, Cassie! Come, quickly! They may already be there!"

I resisted as he tried to draw me to my feet. "You go ahead. In case I'm wrong, I should stay here to catch them if they come."

"Rasputin is a master vampire! What could you do against him?"

"He's a master in our time, but he's only a spirit here. I have a body, so I'll be the strong one. Besides, I think Radu is a far more likely target, don't you?"

Mircea wanted to argue, but worry about his brother overcame his usual caution, and finally he went. I waited thirty seconds, then slipped out after him. I made my way to the corridor where I had encountered the swarm of ghosts and, with effort, managed to feel them even inside borrowed flesh. I couldn't see them as I had in spirit form, which was annoying, but they definitely knew I was there. I stood in the middle of that cold stone hallway and felt them crowd around me like a chill fog. A second later, the door to the torture chamber started to open and I stepped into the shadows that lined the walls. "Hide me," I whispered, "and I will help you."

The shadows wrapped around me like an invisible cloak, shielding me from the dazed eyes of the mutilated woman who appeared to be hovering in the doorway. She was suspended three feet above the ground, but although I couldn't see them, I knew who carried her. I waited until her body floated down the stairs, carried in Tomas' invisible arms, then started as a puzzled voice whispered a question in my ear.

"In English, please," I told him impatiently. In this woman's body, I could understand French if I concentrated, but it took effort and I needed my strength for other things. Slowly, Pierre appeared before me. He was nowhere near as clear as before, but I didn't feel like complaining.

"How is it that you can sense us, *madame*?"

I realized that he saw the woman I was possessing, and not myself. "It's a long story, and we don't have time for it. Bottom line is, we both want vengeance, and I think I know a way to make that happen."

A few minutes later, my ghostly army and I descended on the lower dungeons. I thought I had already seen the worst Carcassonne had to offer, but I was wrong. These chambers made the upper levels seem almost attractive by comparison, at least to me. They probably would have appeared deserted to most people, merely old, damp stone rooms too far below the waterline to be used even for storage. But to me the mossy walls and slippery floors teemed with ghostly traces, remnants of once powerful spirits who had haunted here for more centuries than I could name.

I tried to strengthen my shields, but I couldn't raise them all the way or I wouldn't be able to contact my allies. As a result, impressions crowded me from all sides, wispy pieces of lives long gone and tortures endured. I Saw Roman soldiers whipping a young boy the full number of lashes of his sentence, despite the fact that he was already dead. Right behind them, a medieval witch hunter threatened a young woman, who was heavily pregnant and pleading for the life of her unborn child. I tightened my defenses a bit more to keep the worst of the faded horrors out, but I caught an occasional one here or there. And everywhere I looked, in long, crisscrossing, glowing lines, were ghost traces. They

covered the floors and walls and wove patterns through the
air so thick it was like walking through a sickly greenish
mist. They lit the lower dungeons to the point that I aban-
doned the torch I'd lifted from an upstairs sconce. I didn't
need it.

The worst was saved for last. I followed my guides to a
tiny, inner room. I could hear sobs before I opened the door.
They abruptly cut off at my approach and the heavy latch
was wrenched out of my hand. The door flew open and
Louis-César stared out at me. For a minute, I wondered
whether something had gone horribly wrong. The robe had
parted to his navel, and beside the heavy, cherry red bro-
cade, a darker color gleamed. He was bleeding heavily from
bites on his neck and chest, and his face was ashen. When
he recognized me, he swayed, and I barely caught him before he hit the ground.

I looked behind him to see a figure kneeling in a puddle
of darkness that I identified after a moment as a hooded
cloak. Slowly, it raised its head and I saw what seemed to be
a bearded skeleton. Skin the color of moldy Swiss cheese
covered the fine bones of his face, and only the burning
amber eyes made him seem real. I took a guess. "Radu?"

A bony hand pushed the hood back. I looked at the thing
that once had had the nickname "the Handsome," and
wanted to be sick. They'd kept him under control, all right,
but they hadn't used restraints. They hadn't needed them
after they'd starved him almost to death. I hadn't heard that
blood deprivation could kill a vamp, but the thing huddled
across from me didn't look alive. I had never seen anything
like it.

"Um, we're here to help. Did Mircea tell you?" The creature huddled in the corner didn't reply. I hoped Mircea had
been right about the sanity thing, although I was beginning
to doubt it. "We, uh, should probably go. Can you walk?"

"He cannot walk, *dulceață*," Mircea said in a dull, ex-
pressionless voice. He sat on the floor beside the door and

his head flopped back against the wall as if he no longer had the strength to hold it up. "I have given him all the blood I can without risking this body's life, but it is not enough. He has been starved for years, kept conscious only by catching an occasional rat. No one visits him for weeks at a time, and when they do, it is only to bring torment."

I forced myself to look carefully at the wasted figure. It was hard to tell with the cape in place, but I could probably carry him if it came down to it. The body I inhabited was slight, but he was barely more than skin and bones. But I really preferred an alternative that didn't require me to touch him. The thought of those sticklike hands on even my borrowed body was enough to cause me to break out in chills, not to mention that I didn't like the idea of becoming dessert. Radu might not be able to feed from afar in his current state, but if he got close enough, that wouldn't be an issue. I wasn't sure if it was because his face was so emaciated that the skin had drawn back from his teeth, or if he was still hungry, but his fangs were fully extended and I didn't like it.

"What now?"

Mircea hung his head, breathing in great gasps of air as if he couldn't get enough into his lungs. "Allow me a few moments to recover, *dulceață*, and then together we will take him from this place."

I was about to agree when it became obvious that we didn't have a few minutes. Into the corridor behind us poured a dozen humans and a wind composed of too many spirits to count. I knew who they were even before they coalesced. No mere ghost, however newly dead, has that much power. A young woman, maybe in her late teens, appeared first and stepped in front of the crowd. She had a ghostly dagger in her hand that looked something like the ones that came out of my bracelet. Her eyes focused on me for a moment, and I didn't like their expression, but then they fixed

on Radu with an almost hungry look. A shadow behind her
pushed her forward.

"That one! In the cloak! Kill him quickly!"

I stood there, gaping at them for a second. It was discon-
certing to discover that my diversion had been right on target. I put myself between Radu and the girl, but she merely
walked through me. I wasn't used to a ghost being able to do
that without my permission. I had unconsciously put up a
hand to ward her off and my bracelet decided it was show-
time. I spun around, and the next second she was screaming
as two gaping holes appeared in the hazy outline of her
body. She didn't bleed, of course, but she was obviously in
pain. Great. I'd ended up hurting the person I was trying to
help.

The dark presence behind her drew back behind a wall of
humans, who surged towards me as a single entity. My daggers went back to work, but there were too many of them.
Three were dropped by those flashing knives, but most got
through. The first to reach me grabbed my shoulder, and my
ward flared, throwing him across the room to slam against
the hard stone. I stared at him in amazement. I wasn't in my
body, so how had my ward tagged along? The mage couldn't
tell me, since he'd slid down to the floor and lay still.

Another mage spoke something that sounded like the
word Pritkin had used on the were at Dante's, and a curtain
of flame leaped up all around me. I flinched back before I
realized that it wasn't touching me; the fire stopped about a
foot away, behind the golden tracery of a pentagram on the
floor. My ward had to be using a huge amount of energy to
stop a word of power, but I felt no drain. Whatever was pow-
ering it, it wasn't me.

Through the flames I saw a tall, dark shape start to ease
around the wall. He was trying to get behind me, and that
would not be good. Mircea was in no shape at the moment
to fight off a two-year-old child, much less even the spirit of

a master vamp. I glanced at the army behind me and nodded at him. "He's all yours."

A storm of shadows descended on the ghost like a swarm of bees, and he disappeared from sight with a choked scream. They might not be able to do anything to humans, but spirits were fair game. A few seconds later they reformed at my back, and the enemy specter was nowhere to be seen. "They ate him," I clarified for the tall figure who stood behind the mages, surrounded by his fellow spirits. No heroics for Rasputin. Smart, if not real brave. "Leave or I'll give them another course."

"They can't feed on humans, sybil," he said, echoing my thoughts. He moved slightly and I caught the impression of a pale face framed in greasy black hair. There was nothing handsome about it, but there was an odd, hypnotic quality to the eyes. "Even you cannot win against a dozen mages of the Black Circle. Let us have the vampire. We mean you no harm." The deep voice was heavily accented but strangely soothing. His vamp powers were weakened when he was no longer in his body, but they obviously weren't gone. He was trying to influence me, and it was working. I could suddenly see his point. Why die here, hundreds of years and thousands of miles away from anything familiar? Why give my life for someone I didn't even know and who, in any case, would be better off dying quickly than living to face centuries of torment? It seemed almost a kindness to let them past, to let Radu die. Rasputin would make it quick, and then I could—I literally slapped myself. It hurt, but the pain cleared my head. Damn! Even in spirit form, he'd almost gotten to me.

"Twelve mages?" I looked at the body of the mage by the wall, who hadn't moved a muscle; his neck was lolling at an angle that said he probably never would again. Three others had been taken out by my knives, which had returned to hover beside me, one on either side of my head. None of the three on the floor looked dead, and their buddies must have agreed because they were pulling them back towards the stairs instead of leaving them where they fell. But they also didn't look like they would be returning to the fight. "I only count eight still active, Rasputin. Ask your friends which one wants to die next."

He didn't bother. Maybe he didn't like the odds, or perhaps his friends weren't all that friendly when it came down to giving up their lives for him. Anyway, his spirit corps streamed at me in a shining cloud and got as far as the edge of my ward when my group attacked. "Don't hurt the girl!" I yelled, as thousands of spirits flashed past me in a flickering wave of color and shade. Greenish white sparks rained down everywhere as the spirits of Carcassonne began cannibalizing their enemies, draining them of every spark of life. I had a feeling there were a lot of vamp bodies that weren't going to rise after this night.

While the pyrotechnics went off over our heads, I bent to help the dazed figure of the lost sybil. She looked pale and frightened, but at least she was alive. Large gray eyes peered at me out of a small, oval face, framed by limp blond hair. "Don't worry," I told her, although it sounded pretty strange under the circumstances. "I won't let him harm you. We need to get—"

I never finished the sentence because, suddenly, everything froze. I looked around fearfully, wondering what new threat I had to deal with, and noticed that the knife was still in the sybil's hand. It was also all of about a millimeter away from my chest. I stared at it in disbelief. The bitch had been about to stab me! And, judging by the angle, it would have been a heart blow. Admittedly, it wasn't my body, but I thought it would be polite to return it without any big holes in it. Besides, I didn't know what would happen to me if the woman died. Even Billy hadn't known. Maybe I'd survive, maybe not, but I sure as hell wouldn't be much help to Radu or Louis-César. Not to mention racking up yet another death on my conscience.

"I see you received my message." A voice floated across the room, as silvery clear as chiming bells.

I looked up to see a slender, short girl with long, dark hair rippling down her back almost to her knees. She was weaving past the hovering ghosts, some of which had frozen, jaws wide, busily gulping down other phantoms. No one moved, no one breathed. It was like I'd wandered into a photograph, except that two of us continued to be active.

"What?" I eased back from the sybil and her knife, which also allowed me to back away from whoever the newcomer was.

"The one on your computer," the woman continued. "At your office. That was clever, don't you think?" She peered at Louis-César but made no move towards him. Her big blue eyes came back to me and her sweet little face took on a somewhat peevish air. "Well? Don't I at least rate a thank-you for saving your life? The obituary was real, you know. If you hadn't left your office when you did, Rasputin's men would have found you. You'd have managed to get away from them, but a couple of streets over you would have encountered the vampires sent by that Antonio person and been shot. I brought the obit forward to warn you. Clever, wasn't it?"

"Who are you?" I realized the truth the same time I asked the question, but I wanted to hear her say it.

She smiled, and her dimples were almost as big as Louis-César's. "My name is Agnes, although no one uses it anymore. Sometimes, I don't think they even remember."

"You're the Pythia."

"Right in one."

"But . . . but you look younger than me. They told me you were on your death bed, that you're really old."

She gave a small shrug. It caused me to notice what she was wearing—a long, high-necked gown much like those Eugenie used to have made for me. It looked like something out of a tea party circa 1880. "Right again, I'm afraid. In fact, it is quite possible that this little trip will do me in. My power has been fading for a while, and four hundred years is a lot to manage." She didn't sound very upset about her impending demise. "Anyway, you'll learn how to manipulate your spirit to look any way you want after a while. I prefer to remember myself as I was. In fact, in recent years, I've spent more time out of that wrinkled old hulk than in it." She flexed her fingers. "Arthritis, you know."

I stared at her. I'd somehow expected the Pythia to be more, well, regal. "What are you doing here?"

Agnes laughed. "Solving a problem, what else?" She bent over to look in the distorted face of the woman about to plunge a dagger into me. I'd moved, but the sybil hadn't; the face was still set in a scowl and the knife was caught halfway through its arc. "I spent twenty years training this one. You wouldn't think it to look at her, would you? Twenty years and look what I have to show for it." She shook her head. "I'm here because this mess is partly my fault. I chose your mother as my apprentice. I trained her for almost a decade. I loved her like a daughter. And when she took up with your father, I forbade it, telling myself that I was doing her a favor. He was a member of the vampire mafia, for God's sake! Hardly a fit match for my beautiful creation."

"I don't understand."

"I could have found her!" Crystalline tears glistened in Agnes' big blue eyes. "I told myself, if she didn't care anything about her calling, if she could throw it all away so easily, I didn't need her. I could start afresh, could choose another apprentice, make another shining star . . . only, of course, I couldn't. I was too proud to admit that it hadn't been my tutelage that made Lizzy what she was, but her own innate talent. I didn't go after her, and that vampire boss of your father's had her killed to get to you." She covered her face and wept.

I just stood there. Did she actually expect me to sympathize? I didn't feel like kicking her when she was down, especially not if she really was on her deathbed, but I also didn't feel very comforting. I settled on simply crossing my arms and waiting it out.

"You aren't the compassionate type, are you?" she asked after a minute, looking at me through her fingers. She lowered her hands and regarded me curiously. I shrugged; considering where I'd grown up, what the hell did she expect? She sighed and gave up the act. "Okay, I was wrong. My bad. But now we have to fix things. I can't train you properly because I don't have time, but quite obviously the power can't be allowed to go to Myra. She's either in this voluntarily, or she was coerced. If the former, she's evil; if the latter, she's weak. Either way, she's out of the running."

I looked at the long, sharp knife in the sybil's hand and at the expression in her eyes. I was betting on voluntary. She looked a little angry to be under some sort of mind control. I was beginning to have a certain sympathy with Mircea's point of view.

"Okay, fine. She's a bad sybil. You want to take her back with you and read her the riot act? Be my guest."

"That isn't the program."

I was in no mood to play twenty questions. "Do you have a point? Because I'm kind of busy here."

She threw up her hands. "Of course; please do forgive me for nattering on. But this is an occasion, you know. I'm merely trying to give it a hint of ceremony."

I had a bad feeling suddenly. "What occasion?"

She turned a look on me that had none of the previous playfulness. "The power has selected you. You're it; you're Pythia." She grimaced. "Congrats and all that."

I decided the woman had a few screws loose. "You can't just dump it on me like that! What if I don't want it?"

She gave a small shrug. "Your point would be?"

I stared at her. Her gall was unbelievable. "Forget it, lady. Pick another seer."

Agnes put small fists on her narrow hips and glared at

me. "The more I talk with you, the more I'm convinced that you'll either be the best of us all, or the very worst. If I had another choice, believe me, I would take it. But I don't. The power wants to come to you. Take some advice and make it an easy transition. The more you fight it, the more trouble it will give you."

"Like hell." Thank God I had an ace in the hole. "Your power can't go to a virgin. And technically, I'm still pure and untouched."

She looked at me for a second, apparently speechless. Then she collapsed into a fit of giggles. She finally got her breath back and managed to gasp out, "Says who? Don't tell me you've been listening to the mages! Please!"

"Wait a minute. The vamps believe it, too. Everyone does."

Agnes shook her head and tried to stifle a grin. It didn't work and she finally gave up. "God, you're naive. Who do you think told them that? One of the ancient Pythias got tired of the code that said a priestess had to be 'pure and un-touched,' to use your phrase. So she told the priests at Del-phi that she'd had a vision. The power would be much stronger if it came to an experienced woman. They bought it, and she got her lover. But it doesn't make a difference. Well, not about obtaining the power, at least."

"What does that mean?"

She laughed again and did a little twirl around the room, passing through a couple of mages on the way. They shud-dered slightly but didn't wake up. "It means that I suggest you complete the ritual as soon as possible if you expect to control the gift instead of vice versa." She grinned. "And I'm not exactly equipped to help you with that." She took in my crossed arms and stubborn expression and paused. I got the impression from the little frown that appeared on her forehead that she wasn't used to being questioned. "Fine, have it your way, but if you leave the ritual half done, not only will you have imperfect control, but the mages will consider you only the heir. The Pythia can't be deposed, but the heir certainly can. Your position is vulnerable until you finish this." She looked me up and down, then raised a delicate eyebrow. "I find it difficult to believe we need to have this conversation."

I was pretty damn annoyed, especially when she started dancing again. "Look, how many ways do I have to say this? No, thank you, I don't want the job."

"Perfect. Then at least I move on knowing you aren't insane." She stopped her little ballerina impression so abruptly that her skirts swirled about her legs. "I didn't want it, either, you know. I alone among the sybils of my generation would have been very happy not to have been picked. It is a great honor, but it's a heavy burden, too. Plus, you have to put up with the Silver Circle and, believe me, that's no one's idea of fun."

Her expression was suddenly somber. "For what it's worth, Cassie, I'm sorry. There hasn't been a Pythia since the first one that has had to take on the job completely untrained. But then, with your abilities, you're likely to rewrite the rule book anyway. For example, did you know that you're currently inhabiting the same time twice? Your spirit is struggling along with that girl you rescued, through the streets outside, while you're in here talking to me. I can't do that. Plus, most of our adepts take years to learn what you've managed to teach yourself in only a few days. Really, taking another spirit along with you! That's impressive."

I felt like screaming. "Will you stop talking and listen to me? I. Am. Not. The. Pythia!"

She crossed to me quickly and kissed my cheek. "You are now," she said, and disappeared. That same second, I got hit with something that felt like a Mack truck had mowed me down. There's no way to adequately describe it, so I won't even try. The closest thing I'd ever felt was when I was in Tomas' body and his heightened senses proved so distracting. Only the senses that were sharpened this time weren't smell or sight, but that awareness of other worlds, different but meshing with ours, that I'd always had a little of when I spoke with ghosts. Now I had a lot of it, and the sights and sounds around me were so distracting that I didn't even notice that time had started back up. Not, that is, until someone stabbed me in the foot.

I looked down to see that the rogue sybil had got me after all, although not in the way she'd planned. It still hurt like a bitch and blood began welling up through the satin of my little high-heeled slipper, turning the material a dark purple. I looked up at the battling forces over my head.

"Okay, I changed my mind. Eat her."

A group of ghosts broke off from the main cloud and dove for her, but Rasputin moved with vamp quickness and got there first. He grabbed her about the waist and they disappeared, along with the few of his vamps who had escaped the ghostly attack. The mages saw their ally run for it and immediately followed suit. My little knives got overly excited and chased them out the door and up the stairs and I let them go to it. Killing off a few more dark mages might alter the timeline, but at that moment I was too tired and fed up to care.

I sat down and tugged off the slipper. Damn it! The crazy bitch had almost severed a toe. Mircea handed me a handkerchief from the pocket of his robe, and I bound up the wound as best I could. I didn't think she'd lose it, unless it got infected. But considering the state of the dungeon, that seemed at least possible. Great.

I looked up to see my ghostly army hovering there, an unspoken demand in their eyes. I knew what they wanted, and there was no point trying to talk them out of it. The energy they'd stolen from Rasputin's vamps might sustain them for years, but who wanted to exist someplace like this? They had only one interest, and I had promised, but there were going to be a few conditions.

"No townspeople and no innocents," I said, and got a

creepy, collective nod in return. I sighed. "Okay, then, the rest are yours."

Immediately, a swirling maelstrom of spirits rose up, like a multihued blizzard around my head. It was so thick that it blotted out the room for an instant and so full of pent-up rage that their collective wails sounded like a freight train. Then, in the blink of an eye, they were gone. I didn't try to follow them with my senses; that was one party I preferred not to see.

I took my hands away from my ears to find Mircea watching me, a cautious look in his eyes. I sighed. I did not want to have this conversation, wanted it less, in fact, than facing Rasputin again. But there was no way out. "I think we did it," I told him. "Did you explain things to Radu?"

He nodded slowly. "Yes. He has agreed to bring Louis-César over and to leave him to develop alone as happened before. Radu will escape but avoid contact with anyone for a century, until the time I rescued him from the Bastille. And even after that, he will keep a low profile, as you would say. Will that do?"

I thought about it for a minute. It wasn't perfect, but barring locking him in a room for three and a half centuries, I didn't see an alternative. And I somehow doubted that Mircea would go along with that. "Yeah, it ought to, as long as he doesn't make any vamps until our time. Somehow Rasputin is already making unregistered vamps, and we don't need two people doing it. Oh, and tell Radu about Françoise. I get this feeling that some of the mages might try to recoup some of their losses with her tonight."

It was a measure of just how close to the edge Mircea was that he didn't question what I meant. "As you like."

I gestured around. "How much of that could you see?"

"Very little, but I received the impression from our being alive that we won."

"Not exactly." I explained the situation in brief, including my promotion. When he got back and found out Agnes was dead, he'd figure it out anyway. "You'll need to tell the Senate that Rasputin got away, and that the sybil went with him. I don't know if she'll keep the power she borrowed now, but she may." Considering that Myra had flashed out right after my talk with the Pythia, it seemed a good bet. Maybe that would fade in time, but there was no way to know for sure. Which left me with a major problem. When she recovered from my little knife attack, she could do to me what she'd been trying to do to Louis-César. The possibilities were endless, including killing me as a child or attacking my parents before I was even conceived, making sure I wasn't born at all. The only good thing for me was that, for most of my life, I was either in Tony's fortress of a house, warded like the vamp equivalent of Fort Knox, or in hiding. So I wouldn't be an easy target. But something told me that Rasputin liked a challenge.

Mircea was quiet for a long moment. When he finally spoke, he sounded as tired as I felt. "You could tell them yourself."

I smiled. "No, I don't think I can." He started to say something, but I put a finger over his lips. About one thing, at least, I was sure. "I won't go back to that, Mircea. It was bad enough before, but now everyone will be fighting over me—the Senate, the two circles, maybe Tomas . . . no. What kind of a life would that be?"

He took my hand in his and kissed the fingers carefully. His eyes were tired, but still beautiful as they met mine. The glowing, cinnamon amber completely overwrote Louis-César's blue. I had a feeling that I'd never see another pair so stunning, or so sad. "You cannot run forever, Cassie."

"I hid before. I can do it again."

"You were found before." He clutched my hand as tightly as he could and, for the moment, I let him. It might be a long time before I knew the touch of another person, much less one I cared about.

"Only by you and Marlowe," I told him gently. "Tell him

to take a vacation. He'll need one to recover from the attack. Take one yourself."

Mircea shook his head, as I'd known he would. He wouldn't lie to me even now. For a vamp, he was a hell of a catch. I reached out and ran a hand through his hair, wishing it was his own dark, straight strands under my fingers instead of the Frenchman's bronze curls. It was somehow hard to imagine never touching him again, never holding him. But the price was too high. There were simply too many strings attached.

"I will find you, Cassie. I only pray it will be before the circles do. Both of them will come after you, you can be sure of it. Do not underestimate them."

"I won't." I started to rise, but he held on to my hand.

"Cassie, stay with me! I will keep you safe; I swear it!"

I asked him the same question I had put to Tomas. This time I got an answer. "Would you want me, even if I wasn't Pythia?"

He raised my hand to his mouth. His lips were cold. "I begin to think I would prefer it."

I looked around at the body of the fallen mage, the slimy walls and the despair-filled room. I tightened my grip. "I know I would," I told him, and shifted.

ABOUT THE AUTHOR

KAREN CHANCE has lived in France, the United Kingdom and Hong Kong, but always comes back to America. She currently lives in Orlando, Florida, the home of make-believe, which may explain a lot. Visit her on the Web at www.karenchance.com.

THE VAMPIRE EARTH
series by

E.E. Knight

Louisiana, 2065. A lot has changed in the 43rd year
of the Kurian Order. Possessed of an unnatural hunger,
the bloodthirsty Reapers have come to Earth to
establish a New Order built on the harvesting of
human souls. They rule the planet. And if it is night,
as sure as darkness, they will come.

This is the Vampire Earth.

Book One:
WAY OF THE WOLF
0-451-45939-3

Book Two:
CHOICE OF THE CAT
0-451-45973-3

Book Three:
TALE OF THE THUNDERBOLT
0-451-46018-9

Book Four:
VALENTINE'S RISING
0-451-46059-6

Available wherever books are sold or at
penguin.com

J.R. Ward

DARK LOVER

THE DEBUT NOVEL IN THE
BLACK DAGGER BROTHERHOOD SERIES

In the shadows of the night in Caldwell, New York,
there's a deadly turf war going on between vampires and
their slayers. There exists a secret band of brothers like
no other—six vampire warriors, defenders of their race.
Yet none of them relishes killing more than Wrath, the leader
of The Black Dagger Brotherhood.

The only purebred vampire left on earth, Wrath has a score
to settle with the slayers who murdered his parents centuries ago.
But, when one of his most trusted fighters is killed—leaving his
half-breed daughter unaware of his existence or her fate—Wrath
must usher her into the world of the undead—a world of
sensuality beyond her wildest dreams.

0-451-21695-4

"A midnight whirlwind of dangerous characters and
mesmerizing erotic romance. The Black Dagger Brotherhood
owns me now."
—LYNN VIEHL, AUTHOR OF *THE DARKYN* NOVELS

THE ULTIMATE IN
SCIENCE FICTION AND FANTASY!

From magical tales of distant worlds to stories of
technological advances beyond the grasp of man, Penguin has
everything you need to stretch your imagination to its limits.

penguin.com

ACE

Get the latest information on favorites like
William Gibson, T.A. Barron, Brian Jacques,
Ursula K. LeGuin, Sharon Shinn, and Charlaine Harris,
as well as updates on the best new authors.

ROC

Escape with Harry Turtledove, Anne Bishop,
S.M. Stirling, Simon R. Green, Chris Bunch, Jim Butcher,
E.E. Knight, and many others—plus news on the
latest and hottest in science fiction and fantasy.

DAW

Mercedes Lackey, Kristen Britain, Tanya Huff,
Tad Williams, C.J. Cherryh, and many more—
DAW has something to satisfy the cravings of any
science fiction and fantasy lover.
Also visit dawbooks.com.

*Get the best of science fiction and fantasy
at your fingertips!*